Advance Praise for Rya

Caligula *and 7*

"Terrorism, despotism, plague, and the wrong kind of freedom: Camus's theater has never stopped speaking to us. In this long-awaited new translation, I admire Ryan Bloom's understanding of Camus's voice and moral power. 'Can this dreadful freedom really be happiness?' At last, an English-language Camus ready for the twenty-first-century stage!"
—Alice Kaplan, author of *Looking for The Stranger*

"The power of Camus's voice and ideas shines forth in this new, eminently performable translation of the plays. Bloom has achieved a difficult balance in preserving the style, tone, and rhythm of the original while rendering the dialogue contemporary and spontaneous. The result is magical, as if Camus were speaking to us today through his characters, across time and borders, about the dangerous and the beautiful, the tragic and the comic." —Anne H. Quinney, professor of French, The University of Mississippi

"Albert Camus always loved the theater and the prospects it afforded. Ryan Bloom's translations, the first for many decades, breathe new life into Camus's political dramas, which have become so relevant once more in the last, increasingly troubled decades." —Matthew Sharpe, author of *Camus, Philosophe: To Return to Our Beginnings*

Albert Camus

Caligula *and Three Other Plays*

Albert Camus was born in Algeria in 1913. He spent the early years of his life in North Africa, where he became a journalist. During World War II, he was one of the leading writers of the French Resistance and an editor of *Combat,* an underground newspaper he helped found. His fiction, including *The Stranger, The Plague, The Fall,* and *Exile and the Kingdom*; his philosophical essays, *The Myth of Sisyphus* and *The Rebel*; and his plays have assured his preeminent position in modern letters. In 1957, Camus was awarded the Nobel Prize in Literature. On January 4, 1960, he was killed in a car accident.

Ryan Bloom's translation of Camus's *Notebooks 1951–1959* was shortlisted for the French-American Foundation and Florence Gould Foundation Translation Prize. His translation of Camus's mimodrama *The Life of the Artist* appeared in *The New Yorker* in 2013 and was followed by a translation of Camus's *The First Man: The Graphic Novel* in 2018. He teaches at the University of Maryland, Baltimore County.

VINTAGE

INTERNATIONAL

ALSO BY ALBERT CAMUS

Committed Writings

Create Dangerously

Exile and the Kingdom

The Fall

The Myth of Sisyphus

Personal Writings

The Plague

The Possessed

The Rebel

Speaking Out

The Stranger

Caligula *and Three Other Plays*

ALBERT CAMUS

A New Translation by Ryan Bloom

Vintage International

VINTAGE BOOKS

A DIVISION OF PENGUIN RANDOM HOUSE LLC

NEW YORK

A VINTAGE INTERNATIONAL ORIGINAL 2023

*English-language translation
and additional notes copyright © 2023 by Ryan Bloom*

The four plays included in this volume were originally published in
France as follows: *Le Malentendu suivi de Caligula,* copyright 1944 by
Librairie Gallimard; *L'État de siège,* copyright 1948 by Librairie
Gallimard; *Les Justes,* copyright 1950 by Librairie Gallimard.

Caligula and *The Misunderstanding* were originally
published in English in 1948 in Great Britain by Hamish Hamilton
Ltd. and in the United States by New Directions under
the title *Caligula and Cross Purpose.*

The Cataloging-in-Publication Data is available
at the Library of Congress.

**Vintage International Trade Paperback ISBN: 978-0-593-31127-1
eBook ISBN: 978-0-593-31147-9**

Book design by Nicholas Alguire

vintagebooks.com

Printed in the United States of America
2nd Printing

CONTENTS

Author's Preface to the American Edition   ix

Introduction   xvii

Caligula   1
The Misunderstanding   141
State of Emergency   231
The Just   383

Appendix I
Original Prologue to *The Misunderstanding*   503

Appendix II
Original Ending to *State of Emergency*   517

Appendix III
Original Opening to *The Just*   525

Notes   539

Author's Preface to the American Edition

The plays collected here were written between 1938 and 1950.[1] The first, *Caligula,* was initially composed in 1938, after a reading of Suetonius's *The Twelve Caesars.* I'd written the play for a small theater I'd established in Algiers, intending simply to play the role of Caligula myself. Aspiring actors can be naive like that. And after all, I was twenty-five at the time, an age when you doubt everything but yourself. Well, the war forced modesty on me, and *Caligula* first premiered in 1946 at the Théâtre Hébertot in Paris.

So then, *Caligula* is an actor and director's play. But it also draws inspiration from the issues that were on my mind at the time, of course, and though French critics gave the play a very warm reception, they often spoke of it, to my great surprise, as a philosophical play. How did that happen?

As the play opens, Caligula, a relatively good-natured prince up until then, has just realized, with the passing of his sister, Drusilla, who was also his mistress, that the world as it stands is unsatisfactory. From this moment on, obsessed with the impossible, poisoned by contempt and horror, he attempts to exercise, through murder and the systematic perversion of all values, a freedom that he will eventually discover "is not the right kind." He rejects friendship and love, basic human solidarity, right and wrong. He takes those around him at their word, forces logic on them, and levels everything in sight through the power of his refusal and the destructive rage to which his lust for life leads him.

But if his truth lies in rebelling against fate, his error lies in rejecting man. You can't destroy everything without destroying yourself. That's why Caligula empties the world around him and, faithful to his logic, does what's necessary to weaponize against him the very people who will eventually kill him. *Caligula* is the story of a superior suicide. It's the story of that most human and most tragic of errors. Unfaithful to man through faithfulness to himself, Caligula accepts death after coming to see that no one can save themselves all on their own and that a person can't be free at the cost of others.

So then, it's a tragedy of the intelligence. From which it's only natural to conclude that the drama is intellectual. Personally, I think I can see the work's faults rather clearly. But philosophy is not one I find in these four acts. Or if it is there, it's in the hero's assertion: "People die and they're not happy." A rather modest ideology, you can see, and one it seems I share with Monsieur de La Palice and the rest of the world.[2] No, my ambitions lay elsewhere. For the playwright, lust for the impossible is as worthy of investigation as greed or adultery. To show it in all its fury, to illustrate its devastation, to bring forth its failures, that's what I was trying to do here, and it's on this that the work should be judged.

Just one more note. Some who found my play provocative also find it perfectly natural that Oedipus should kill his father and marry his mother and that threesomes should take place, as long as, of course, they only do so in the nice neighborhoods. For my part, I have little time for that special kind of art that chooses to shock for lack of knowing how to convince. And if, as luck would have it, I was being scandalous, it would be solely on account of that inordinate appetite for truth an artist can't abandon without giving up on his art itself.

The Misunderstanding was written in 1941, in occupied France. At the time, I was reluctantly living in the middle of the mountains of central France, a historical and geographical situation that on its own is enough to explain the sort of claustrophobia I suffered from at the time, a claustrophobia that is reflected in the play and that, true enough, leaves little room to breathe. But we were all short of breath back then. Nevertheless, the dark nature of the play bothers me as much as it bothered the public. To encourage readers to give the play a try, I'd say: (1) the play's morality isn't entirely negative; (2) think of *The Misunderstanding* as an attempt to create a modern tragedy.

The subject of the play is a son who wants to be recognized without having to say his name, and who, as a result of a misunderstanding, is killed by his mother and sister. No doubt, it's a very pessimistic view of the human condition, but it's a view that can be reconciled with a relative optimism as far as humanity is concerned, for we can ultimately see that everything would have been different if the son had said: "It's me, let me tell you my name." We can see that in an unjust or indifferent world, man can save himself, and save others, by using the most basic sincerity and trying to find the right words.

The language was also a shock. I knew it would be. But if I'd dressed my characters in peploses, maybe then everyone would have applauded.[3] Still, having contemporary characters speak the language of tragedy was the point, and to be honest, nothing could be more difficult, given you have to find a language natural enough to be spoken by contemporaries and unique enough to carry the tragic tone. To approach this ideal, I tried to add distance to the characters and ambiguity to the dialogue. As a result, the viewer should experience simultaneous feelings of familiarity and disorientation. The viewer and the reader. But I'm not sure that I've succeeded in finding the right balance.

As for the Old Servant, his character doesn't necessarily symbolize fate. When the drama's survivor calls on God, it's the Servant who answers. But maybe this is only another misunderstanding. If he says no to the one asking for his help, it's because in fact he has no intention of helping her, and because at a certain point, no one can do anything more for someone who is suffering or dealing with injustice, grief being solitary.

In any case, I'm not convinced that these explanations are very useful. I still believe *The Misunderstanding* is an easily accessible work, as long as you're willing to accept the language and the author's deep commitment to it. Theater is not a game. That's my conviction.

When *State of Emergency* premiered in Paris, the critics were unanimous. Indeed, few plays have had the pleasure of being so thoroughly savaged. A fact that's all the more regrettable given I've never stopped believing that, of all my writings, *State of Emergency* may be, with all its flaws, the one that provides the most accurate picture of me. Readers are perfectly free to decide that this image, no matter how faithful, is not to their liking. For such a judgment to have more force and freedom behind it, though, I'll first have to challenge several misconceptions. To that end, it's useful to know:

(1) that *State of Emergency* is in no way whatsoever an adaptation of my novel, *The Plague*. No doubt, I've given that symbolic name to one of my characters, but given he's a dictator, the description fits.

(2) that *State of Emergency* isn't a play designed in the classic style. Instead, it might be compared with what, in the Middle Ages, were called "morality plays" in France and "autos sacramentales" in Spain, a sort of allegorical performance featuring subjects that would have been familiar to the whole audience ahead of time. I centered my play on what, in a century of tyrants and slaves, seems to me the only living religion, by which I mean freedom. So it's completely pointless to accuse my characters of being symbolic. I plead guilty. My stated goal was to pry the theater loose from psychological speculation so as to spread over our murmuring stages those great cries that today bend or liberate the masses. I remain, from that point of view alone, convinced my attempt is worthy of attention. It's also worth noting that this play about freedom is as poorly received by right-wing dictator-

ships as by dictatorships of the left. It has run continuously in Germany for some years now but has never been performed in Spain or behind the Iron Curtain. Much more could be said about the play's underlying meaning or message, but I wish only to clarify my reader's judgment, not shape it.

The Just has had better luck. It was well received. Still, praise, like blame, can sometimes be born of a misunderstanding. So then, I'd like to further clarify:

(1) that the events recounted in *The Just* are based in history, even the surprising meeting between the Grand Duchess and her husband's murderer. What's left to be judged, then, is whether or not the way I've rendered the truth is believable.

(2) that readers shouldn't let the play's form mislead them. I've used it to try to achieve dramatic tension by classical means, which is to say by pitting characters who are equal in strength and reason against each other. But it would be wrong to conclude that everything balances out and that, with respect to the problem posed here, I'm suggesting inaction. My admiration for my heroes, Kalyayev and Dora, is deeply felt. I wanted only to show that even action has limits, that there is no good and just action that doesn't recognize these limits, and that if such limits must be surpassed, death must at least be accepted. Today, our world shows us a grotesque face

precisely because it's made by men who grant themselves the right to surpass such limits and, first and foremost, to kill others without having to die themselves. As a result, justice is employed today as an alibi, the world over, by the assassins of all justice.

Just one more note to let the reader know what won't be found in this book. Although I have the most passionate love for theater, I have the misfortune of liking only one type of play, whether tragic or comic. After a good bit of experience as a director, actor, and playwright, I feel that there's no true theater without language and style, nor any dramatic work that, following the example of our classical theater and the Greek tragedies, doesn't play with human fate, in all its simplicity and grandeur. Without claiming to be their equal, they are, at least, the models we have to set ourselves. Psychology, clever anecdotes, spicy situations, though they may amuse me as a viewer, leave me indifferent as an author. I willingly admit that this stance is dubious. But it seems better to present myself, on this point, as I am. So forewarned, readers can, if they wish, decide to read no further. As for those who aren't discouraged by this bias, I'm all the more certain of forming that strange friendship with them that, above and beyond borders, links reader and author, and which remains, when no misunderstanding is involved, the writer's royal reward.

December 1957

Introduction

Bab El Oued, Algeria. January 25, 1936. Outside the popular Padovani dance hall, black waves crash on a dark beach dotted with cafés and bathhouses. It's Saturday. The time is 9:00 P.M., and the hall, some 50 feet wide and 130 long, is filled to capacity, overflowing even, bodies crammed into corners, seats made out of windowsills open to the sea. How many people, exactly, are in the room? Two thousand, an audience member would later recall. "1,500 people of all classes," the newspaper *La Lutte Sociale* would report. Seven hundred, according to a security filing, which would note that three hundred of them were women. They've come for a performance of André Malraux's *Le Temps du mépris,* put on by the Théâtre du Travail, a newly formed troupe led by a young man barely twenty-three years old. The price of admission for the show is four francs, given to benefit the unemployed, who themselves are admitted for free. The stage, makeshift at best, has been set up atop a group of café tables gathered at the back of the room. The props are few—a couple of chairs, a cradle—the backdrop a burlap canvas painted to look like stone blocks. The show is about to begin, and with it, the career of one Albert Camus, a "student whose youthful literary talents have already," *L'Écho d'Alger* would report, "manifested themselves with great authority."

From this moment until his last, January 4, 1960, Camus would remain committed to the theater, "one of the only places in the world," he said, where he felt truly happy. In 1937, he'd establish a second troupe in Algiers, the Théâtre de l'Équipe, but then, unemployed and barely scraping by giving private French and philosophy lessons, he received word a job had opened up at a newspaper in Paris, and he packed and left the same day, March 14, 1940. By the time he reached France, he was already working on the second draft of his first solo play, *Caligula,* and by the time the German Occupation ended, he'd finished a second, *The Misunderstanding.* It was there, in post-liberation Paris, in the brief five-year period from 1944 to 1949, that all four of his full-length original plays—the two previously mentioned, as well as *State of Emergency* and *The Just*—would premiere onstage, often with the best actors, actresses, designers, and musicians Paris had to offer. After this brief period, though, Camus would write only two more original plays, both of them short, neither of them performed onstage. The first, *The Philosophers' Farce,* a Molière-esque send-up of Jean-Paul Sartre, Camus wrote under a pseudonym, Antoine Bailly, and never published; the second, a silent mimodrama titled *The Life of the Artist,* appeared in a small Algerian journal in February 1953. In these last years of his life, Camus may have spent more time in the theater than ever before, but it was time spent adapting, directing, and translating the work of other playwrights. The most well-known and well-received of these later projects were his 1956 adaptation of William Faulkner's *Requiem for a Nun* and his 1959 adaptation of Dostoyevsky's *The Possessed,* which was touring France when Camus was killed in a car accident at age forty-six.

In interviews, in prefaces, and in notes for playbills, Camus was clear about what he was trying to accomplish in the theater. He wanted, he said, to create "a modern tragedy." To create "characters drawn from the world today," but characters who were, "nevertheless, faced with the same fate that crushed Electra or Orestes." He didn't simply want to rehash those ancient Greek myths, though, as so many of his contemporaries were then doing. He wanted to create new ones. This, he was aware, would be difficult. "Modern tragedy's great problem," he wrote, "is a language problem. Characters wearing suits and ties can't speak like Cassandra or Titus. Their language has to be natural enough to be our own and, at the same time, elevated enough to carry the force of tragedy." Even *Caligula,* though grounded in ancient history, wasn't based on myth. If writing modern tragedy was his great theatrical ambition, crafting this unique language would be his great challenge.

Like many languages, French contains different registers, ranging from littéraire, the most refined, grammatically correct, and rarely spoken, to argot, the kind of slang you encounter in marketplaces and among friends. In an attempt to carry "the force of tragedy," Camus wrote his theatrical dialogue primarily in the upper, more formal registers, so that, at its most elevated, a character such as Annenkov in *The Just* can say, "*Il fallait que tout fût prévu et que personne ne pût hésiter sur ce qu'il y avait à faire,*" a line delivered in the imperfect subjunctive, one of French's five literary tenses, which are, and were in Camus's time, all but extinct in the spoken language. Similarly, as E. Freeman points out in his study of the play, Stepan, a portrait of anti-elitism, a character theatergoers might well expect not only to speak informally but even to be *against* eloquent language, nevertheless opens the play by asking his comrades three straight questions using inversion, such as "*Que dois-je faire?*" which, while commonly taught in formal education, is rarely used in day-to-day conversation. Doing so would be like walking into the office and saying, "What must I do today?" rather than "What do I have to get done?" For Camus, the tragic tone seems to have taken precedence over other considerations. He drew no dialogue-based distinction between *The Just*'s Grand Duchess, on the one hand, and *The Misunderstanding*'s backcountry peasant, Martha, on the other, so that both characters—and all his theatrical characters, for the most part, regardless of class or psychology or other distinguishing factors—speak in the same polished sentences. This, he believed, would help to create an "*always* calculated dissonance," one that would distance the characters just enough, he hoped, to make them, despite their suits and ties and modern problems, tragic.

In short, then, Camus's solution to the language problem lying at the heart of modern tragedy was to create a highly stylized, literary form of dialogue that rarely strays from the upper registers of formality. For an actor cast in one of his plays or a translator attempting to coax them into a new language, Camus's intentions are perfectly clear. When it was Camus himself who was doing the translating, though, his approach to dialogue was a little different.

"No translator," he wrote in his preface for *Le Chevalier d'Olmedo*, which he'd translated from the Spanish, "should forget that Shakespeare, for example, or the great Spanish playwrights, wrote first of all for actors, and with an eye toward performance." His goal, as he put it in the introduction to another of his translations, *La Dévotion à la croix,* was to produce "a text that, while striving to remain faithful to the letter and tone of the original, could still be spoken and recited easily. . . . In other words, it seeks to bring the show to life, to rediscover the flow of a play initially intended for popular audiences." Reflecting on these translations, he wrote: "It was then, and is now, a matter of giving a show's performers a text that, while remaining faithful to the original, can be spoken. Between free adaptation and a strict word-for-word approach, there are several different ways to conceive of the translation of a dramatic work."

If in his own plays he leaned in the direction of distance and dissonance, believing a unique language to be central to his project, in his translations of other playwrights—theatrical translation being a craft he believed should be carried out by dramatists, not by professional translators—his stated goal was to produce natural, performable dialogue.

Every translation is an explanation of sorts. An explanation not of the original text but of priorities: what gets weighted, what gets lost. In bringing Camus's plays into English, I've tried to balance both Camus's literary intentions—not only his general approach to dialogue but also his use of rhythm, repetition, thematic word choice, and other such factors—and his insistence on performability, an "ideal demand" that he said he hadn't really been able to satisfy in his own translations, though he'd "endeavored to do so."

When a word such as "nothing" plays a key role, as it does in *State of Emergency,* for example, an attempt has been made to maintain the word in translation, even if, on occasion, doing

so isn't perfectly natural. For example, when the Plague is looking for his first victim, he's about to take Nada, a character
representing nihilism, when the Secretary intervenes, saying
that Nada's "the sort of person who believes in nothing, and
that such a person could be quite useful to us," a sentence that,
from a strictly linguistic standpoint, would probably read more
naturally as "the sort of person who doesn't believe in anything." Here, preserving the larger thematic element through
the individual word choice seems to outweigh any slightly
unnatural syntax, as it does when it comes to the many jokes
and puns, such as when Nada noisily stumbles into a room
and, on noticing the Secretary sitting there, says, "Oh, excuse
me," to which the Secretary replies, "*Ce n'est rien,*" a phrase
that would smoothly translate as "It's okay" or "No big deal,"
but which literally reads "It's nothing," a play on the character's
name. This same word, on the other hand, doesn't carry the
same weight in *The Misunderstanding,* and so there performable dialogue takes precedence over "nothing." In that play, it's
a set of interlinking themes—seeing, recognizing, and speaking clearly—that play a central role, and so maintaining those
ideas, in their many forms, has been prioritized. At one point,
in a more subtle example, Martha says, "*Je ne reconnais pas vos
mots,*" which might be translated as "I don't understand the
words you're using," or, in a more natural rendering, "I don't
understand what you're saying." But both of these, which use
the natural "understand," lose the thematic "recognize." Similarly, in *Caligula* and *State of Emergency,* the idea of order and
disorder—organization and disorganization—is important,
and so, for example, I've let Caesonia say, "put the room back

in order," rather than the more colloquial "tidy the room up" or "get the room back together."

On the one hand, then, when it comes to maintaining these sorts of thematic elements, I've leaned lightly in the direction of literary intention. On the other hand, when these sorts of issues aren't of central concern, I've considered what might sound most natural on the stage today. Still, there are instances, such as Diego and Victoria's "language of love" in *State of Emergency,* where the grandiloquent dialogue appears stilted even in the original French text, and so no attempt has been made to adjust the register of such passages or make them more performable in English.

As a final note, it should also be said that every translation is also an explanation of its translator. Take the word "*grâce,*" for example, as it appears in *The Just.* The most obvious English translation is hardly a translation at all: simply remove the accent. In French, as in English, "grace" has a sense of the religious about it, as in "to say grace" ("*dire les grâces*"), but it also, in both languages, has a more legalistic sense, as in "pardon" or "mercy." In modern American usage, this second, legal sense of the word has faded somewhat, and while religion is discussed in the play, it's not, for the most part, a religious faith in God the central characters debate but a religious faith in political action. When Kalyayev, the play's hero, uses the word "*grâce,*" he doesn't primarily mean "by the grace of God," but "please forgive me." On the other hand, the police chief, Skuratov, leans on the legal sense, "pardon," and the Grand Duchess leans on the religious sense, "divine grace." Kalyayev, unwilling to act in bad faith, to escape his fate through either God or law, asks only for "forgiveness." The act he is to commit—an attempt on the Grand Duke's life—is, in his judgment, both wrong and right, good and bad, plus and minus. It has contradiction at its very core. The only way to go through with it, he believes, is by willingly sacrificing his own life, while simultaneously acknowledging the contradiction.

This is the way I, as a reader, understand the characters, and by extension, that single word, "*grâce*." It's an understanding informed by my knowledge of Camus's larger philosophy and life, certainly, but also, subconsciously and inevitably, by my own experiences and my own sense of the English language, as it's spoken where I live, among the people I've interacted with, and in the books I've read. Other readers, readers with different backgrounds and experiences, may very well, and with good reason, see things differently. The writer and translator Czesław Miłosz once said, for example, that Camus's novel *The Fall* "is nothing else but a treatise on Grace—absent Grace," and were he to translate *The Just*, perhaps he would suggest that "grace" is precisely the right word for Kalyayev to use in English and that "forgiveness" is misguided. Translation, like Kalyayev's dilemma, is full of contradiction, and there are often no definite answers to be had, only actions taken by a given person in a given time and place.

—Ryan Bloom

Caligula

————

A PLAY IN FOUR ACTS

To my friends in the THÉÂTRE DE L'ÉQUIPE[1]

Caligula was staged for the first time in 1945 at the Théâtre Hébertot, under the direction of Paul Œttly, with set design by Louis Miquel and costumes by Marie Viton.[2]

CHARACTERS

Caligula

Helicon

Cherea

Metellus

The Attendant (Patricius)

Mucius

Servants

Caesonia

Scipio

The Old Patrician (Senectus)

Lepidus

Mereia

Guards

Poets

ACT I[3]

The play opens in Caligula's palace.
Three years pass between the first act and those that
follow it.

SCENE I

A group of patricians,[4] one of them very old, stand
in a palace hallway. They appear nervous.

FIRST PATRICIAN
Still nothing?

THE OLD PATRICIAN
Nothing in the morning, nothing in the evening.

SECOND PATRICIAN
Nothing for three days now.

THE OLD PATRICIAN
The couriers go, the couriers come, they shake their heads and
say: "Nothing, no one."

SECOND PATRICIAN

The whole countryside's been searched. There's nothing more to do.

FIRST PATRICIAN

Why worry about things before they happen? Let's give it a minute. He may yet come back the same as he left.

THE OLD PATRICIAN

I saw him leaving the palace. He had a strange look about him.[5]

FIRST PATRICIAN

I was there, too. I asked him what was bothering him.

SECOND PATRICIAN

Did he answer?

FIRST PATRICIAN

A single word: "Nothing."

A pause. HELICON *enters, eating onions.*

SECOND PATRICIAN
(*still nervous*)

It's worrisome.

FIRST PATRICIAN

Oh, come on. Young people are all the same. They all act like this.

OLD PATRICIAN

Needless to say, age wipes it all away.[6]

SECOND PATRICIAN

You think so?

FIRST PATRICIAN

Let's hope he forgets.

THE OLD PATRICIAN

Oh, yes. Plenty of fish in the sea.

HELICON

What makes you think love's the issue?

FIRST PATRICIAN

What else would it be?

HELICON[7]

Indigestion, maybe. Or simply disgust at having to see all of you every day. It'd be so much easier to deal with our colleagues if only they'd try out a new look every so often. But no, the menu never changes. Always the same old gruel.

THE OLD PATRICIAN

I'd prefer to think it's love. It's more endearing that way.

HELICON

And much more reassuring. So much more reassuring. Love's the sort of sickness that spares neither the intelligent nor the dumb.

FIRST PATRICIAN

Either way, it's a good thing grief doesn't last forever. Are you able to suffer for more than a year?

SECOND PATRICIAN

Me? No.

FIRST PATRICIAN

Nobody can.

THE OLD PATRICIAN

Life would be impossible.

FIRST PATRICIAN

You see. Look here, I lost my wife last year. I cried about it a lot, and then I forgot. Every now and then, I start feeling sorry again. But really, it's nothing.[8]

THE OLD PATRICIAN

Nature handles things very well.

HELICON

Yet when I look at you, I get the feeling it occasionally drops
the ball.

CHEREA *enters.*

FIRST PATRICIAN

Well?

CHEREA

Still nothing.

HELICON

Keep calm, gentlemen, keep calm. Let's try to keep up
appearances. *We* are the Roman empire. If we get all bent out
of shape, the empire loses its head. This isn't the time for all
that. No, not at all. How about we go get some lunch? The
empire will be the better for it.

THE OLD PATRICIAN

Fair enough. We mustn't drop the substance for the shadow.

CHEREA

I don't like it. But then again, everything was going too well.
He was the perfect emperor.

SECOND PATRICIAN

He was just what we needed him to be: scrupulous and
inexperienced.

FIRST PATRICIAN

But what's the big deal, anyway? Why all the lamenting?
Nothing's stopping him from going back to how he was
before. Sure, he loved Drusilla, but she was his sister, after all,

and sleeping with her—well, that was a big enough deal on its own. But turning Rome upside down because she's dead, now that's just going too far.

CHEREA

All the same, I don't like it. This running-away business doesn't bode well.

THE OLD PATRICIAN

There's no smoke without fire.

FIRST PATRICIAN

In any case, we can't have an instance of incest appearing as some sort of tragedy. Matters of state won't permit it. Incest, okay, so be it, but be discreet about it.

HELICON[9]

You know, when it comes to incest, there's always bound to be a bit of a ruckus. The bed squeals, if I dare say so. Anyway, who told you Drusilla's even the issue here?

SECOND PATRICIAN

What else could it be?

HELICON

Guess. Keep in mind: misfortune is like marriage. You think you're choosing, then you're chosen. That's just how it is, there's nothing you can do about it. Our Caligula's unhappy, but he may not even know why. He must have felt trapped, so he ran away. We would have all done the same thing. Take me, for example. Here I am, talking to all of you, but if I'd been able to choose my own father, I would've never been born.

SCIPIO *enters.*

SCENE II

CHEREA

So?

SCIPIO

Still nothing. A couple of peasants thought they saw him running through the storm last night, not far from here.

> CHEREA *goes back over to the senators.* SCIPIO *follows him.*

CHEREA

So then, that's three full days, Scipio?

SCIPIO

Yes. I was there, following after him as usual. He walked over to Drusilla's body. Touched it with two fingers. Seemed lost in thought a moment, then spun around and left with a firm step. We've been chasing after him ever since.

CHEREA
(*shaking his head*)

That boy was too in love with books.

SECOND PATRICIAN

They all are at that age.

CHEREA

But they're not all of his rank. An artist-emperor? It's inconceivable. We've had one or two, of course—there are a few black sheep in every family—but the others all had the good sense to stay bureaucrats.

FIRST PATRICIAN

More relaxing that way.

THE OLD PATRICIAN
To each their own calling.

SCIPIO
What can we do, Cherea?

CHEREA
Nothing.

SECOND PATRICIAN
We wait. If he doesn't come back, we'll have to replace him. We're not lacking emperors among us.

FIRST PATRICIAN
No, we're only lacking character.

CHEREA
And if he comes back in a foul mood?

FIRST PATRICIAN
My god! He's only a child still. We'll make him listen to reason.

CHEREA
And if he's deaf to reason?

FIRST PATRICIAN
(laughs)
Well then, I did once write a treatise about the coup d'état, didn't I?

CHEREA
Yes, of course, if it comes to that—but really, I'd prefer to be left to my books.

SCIPIO
If you'll excuse me.

He exits.

CHEREA

He's offended.

THE OLD PATRICIAN

He's a child. Young people stand in solidarity.

HELICON

In solidarity or not, he'll get old one day, too.

A GUARD *appears.*

GUARD

Caligula's been spotted in the palace garden.

All exit.

SCENE III

For a few seconds, the stage remains empty. CALIGULA *ducks in from the left. He seems lost, he's dirty, his hair is soaked, and his legs are filthy. He brings his hand to his mouth several times. He walks toward the mirror and stops as soon as he catches sight of his own image.*[10] *He grumbles a few words that can't be made out, then goes to sit on the right side of the stage, arms hanging between his knees.* HELICON *enters from the left. Catching sight of* CALIGULA, *he stops at the far end of the stage and silently observes him.* CALIGULA *turns and sees him. A moment passes.*

SCENE IV

HELICON
(*speaking from across the stage*)

Hello, Caius.

CALIGULA
(*in a normal voice*)

Hello, Helicon.

Silence.

HELICON

You seem tired.

CALIGULA

I've done a lot of walking.

HELICON

Yes, you were away for quite a while.

Silence.

CALIGULA

It was difficult to find.

HELICON

What was?

CALIGULA

What I wanted.

HELICON

And what did you want?

CALIGULA
(*in a normal voice still*)

The moon.

HELICON

What?

CALIGULA

Yes, I wanted the moon.

HELICON

Ah!

Silence. Helicon approaches him.

HELICON

To do what with it?

CALIGULA

Well . . . it's one of those things I don't have.

HELICON

Of course. And it's all been taken care of now?

CALIGULA

No, I wasn't able to get it.

HELICON

How annoying.

CALIGULA

Yes. That's why I'm tired.

(*a moment passes*)

Helicon!

HELICON

Yes, Caius.

CALIGULA

You think I'm crazy.

HELICON

You know very well I never think. I'm too smart for that.[11]

CALIGULA

Yes. But anyway, I'm not crazy, and in fact I've never been so rational. It's just . . . I suddenly felt a need for the impossible.

(*a moment passes*)

Things don't seem satisfactory to me as they are.

HELICON

A rather widespread opinion.

CALIGULA

That's true, but I didn't know it before. Now, I know.

(*in a normal voice still*)

This world's unbearable as it is. So then, I need the moon, or happiness, or immortality—something a little mad, maybe, but not of this world.

HELICON

What you're saying makes sense, but generally speaking, there's no sense in carrying such things to their natural conclusion.

CALIGULA
(*getting to his feet, but with the same ease*)
You know nothing about it. It's because we never see any reason to carry things to their natural conclusion that nothing's ever achieved. But maybe carrying logic to its end would be enough.

(*looks at* HELICON)

I know what you're thinking. What a whole lot of fuss over the death of one woman. No, it's not that. I seem to recall that a woman I loved died a few days ago, that's true. But what is love? Not such a big deal. That death means nothing, I swear to you. It's only the sign of a truth—but it's a truth that makes the moon necessary for me. It's a very clear and simple truth, a little silly, even, but one that's hard to come by and heavy to bear.

HELICON

Well, what is this truth, Caius?

CALIGULA
(*turning away, in a neutral tone*)

People die and they are not happy.

HELICON
(*after a moment passes*)

Oh, come now, Caius, that's a truth we handle very well. Look around you. It's not the sort of thing that keeps people from going out for lunch.

CALIGULA
(*suddenly exploding*)

Well, that's because everything around me is a lie, and I . . . I want us all to live in truth! And indeed, I have the means to make them live in truth, for I know what it is they're lacking, Helicon. They've been deprived of knowledge and they lack a teacher who knows what he's talking about.

HELICON

Don't take offense at what I'm about to say to you, Caius, but first and foremost, you need some rest.

CALIGULA
(*sitting down, again gentle*)
That's not possible, Helicon. That will never again be possible.

HELICON
And why is that?

CALIGULA
If I go to sleep, who's going to give me the moon?

HELICON
(*after a moment of silence*)
True enough.

CALIGULA *stands up, the effort required obvious.*

CALIGULA
Listen, Helicon. I hear footsteps and the sound of voices.
Hush now and forget you ever saw me.

HELICON
I understand.

CALIGULA *heads for the exit. He turns around.*

CALIGULA
And please, from now on, help me out.

HELICON
I have no reason not to do so, Caius. But I know so many
things, and so few things interest me. So with what, then, may
I help you?

CALIGULA
With the impossible.

HELICON

I'll do my best.

CALIGULA *exits.* SCIPIO *and* CAESONIA
quickly enter.

SCENE V

SCIPIO

There's nobody here. Did you see him, Helicon?

HELICON

No.

CAESONIA

He really said nothing to you before making his escape,
Helicon?

HELICON

I'm not his confidant, I'm his audience. It's much wiser.

CAESONIA

Please.

HELICON

Dear Caesonia, Caius is an idealist. Everyone knows that. Or,
to put it another way, he hasn't quite figured things out yet.
Me? I have, and that's why I don't care about anything. But
Caius, on the other hand, with that good little heart of his, if
he starts putting things together, he's quite capable of taking
care of everything. And God only knows what that'll cost us.
But, if it's all right with you, it's time for my lunch.

He exits.

SCENE VI

CAESONIA *sits down, weary.*

CAESONIA

A guard says he saw him. But then again, all of Rome sees
Caligula everywhere, and all Caligula sees are his own
thoughts.[12]

SCIPIO

And which thoughts are those?

CAESONIA

How should I know, Scipio?

SCIPIO

Drusilla?

CAESONIA

Who can say? But it's true he loved her. It's truly hard to see
die today what only yesterday you held tightly in your arms.

SCIPIO
(timidly)

And you?

CAESONIA

Oh, me—I'm the old mistress.

SCIPIO

We have to save him, Caesonia.

CAESONIA

So, you do love him?

SCIPIO

I love him. He was good to me. He encouraged me. I can
remember some of the things he said to me by heart. He told me
that life isn't easy, but that there's religion, art, and love to carry

us through. He'd often say that the only mistake you could make would be to make others suffer. He wanted to be a just man.

> CAESONIA
> (*standing up*)

He was a child.

> (*goes over to the mirror and
> considers what she sees in it*)

I've never had any god other than my body, and it's to that god I'd like to pray today that Caius be returned to me.

> CALIGULA *enters. Catching sight of* CAESO-
> NIA *and* SCIPIO, *he hesitates and backs away.
> At the same moment, from the opposite side, the*
> PATRICIANS *and the* PALACE ADMINISTRATOR
> *enter. They stop, shocked, and* CAESONIA *turns
> around. She and* SCIPIO *run toward* CALIGULA.
> *He stops them with a wave of the hand.*

SCENE VII

> THE ADMINISTRATOR
> (*in a voice lacking confidence*)

We . . . we've been looking for you, Caesar.

> CALIGULA
> (*in a changed, curt voice*)

I see.

THE ADMINISTRATOR

We ... that is to say ...

CALIGULA
(*brutally*)

What do you want?

THE ADMINISTRATOR

We were worried, Caesar.

CALIGULA
(*moving toward him*)

What right do you have to worry?

THE ADMINISTRATOR

Well, uh ...

(*suddenly inspired, speaking very quickly*)

I mean, in any case, you know you have a couple of questions to attend to with regard to the treasury.

CALIGULA
(*overcome with laughter*)

The treasury? But of course, you see, the treasury is of the utmost capital concern.

THE ADMINISTRATOR

Certainly, Caesar.

CALIGULA
(*still laughing, to* CAESONIA)

It's very important, isn't it, my darling? The treasury?

CAESONIA

No, Caligula, it's a secondary concern.

CALIGULA

But that's because you know nothing about it. The treasury is a powerful interest. Everything is important: finances, public morality, foreign policy, military provisions, agrarian laws! Everything is of the utmost concern, I tell you. Everything is on equal footing: the greatness of Rome and your attacks of arthritis. Well! I'll just have to take care of all of that. Listen to me a minute, Administrator.

THE ADMINISTRATOR

We're listening to you.

The PATRICIANS *move closer.*

CALIGULA

You're loyal to me, aren't you?

THE ADMINISTRATOR
(*in a tone of reproach*)

Caesar!

CALIGULA

Well then, I have a plan to submit to you. We're going to turn the political economy upside down in two phases. I'll explain it to you, Administrator . . . as soon as the patricians have left.

The PATRICIANS *leave.*

SCENE VIII

CALIGULA *sits down close to* CAESONIA.

CALIGULA

Listen to me carefully. Phase one: All the patricians, every person in the empire who has any sort of fortune—small or large, it makes no difference—must, by mandate, disinherit their children and immediately have a will made up in favor of the state.

THE ADMINISTRATOR

But, Caesar—

CALIGULA

I didn't say you could speak. As our needs require, we will have these people put to death according to an arbitrarily established list. On occasion, we may decide to modify the order, but still in an arbitrary manner. And then we will inherit.

CAESONIA
(*pulling away*)

What's gotten into you?

CALIGULA
(*unfazed*)

In fact, the order of executions holds no importance at all. Or, rather, these executions are all of equal importance, which means they have none. Besides, they're each as guilty as the other, one as guilty as the next. You'll note, too, that it's no more immoral to steal directly from citizens than it is to slip indirect taxes into the price of commodities citizens can't do without. To govern is to steal, everybody knows that. The only difference is how you go about it. Me? I'll steal openly. It'll be a change from those small-time thieves.

(*to the* ADMINISTRATOR, *harshly*)

You'll execute these orders without delay. The wills are to be signed by every inhabitant of Rome this evening, by everyone in the provinces within a month, at the latest. Send out the messengers.

THE ADMINISTRATOR
Caesar, you're not taking into account—

CALIGULA
Listen to me very carefully, you idiot. If the treasury holds such importance, then human life does not. That much is clear. And anyone who thinks as you do has no choice but to accept such reasoning and take their life to be nothing, given they take money to be everything. As it so happens, I, for my part, have decided to be logical, and as I'm the one in power, you're going to see what logic's going to cost you. I'll exterminate all contradictors and contradictions. If necessary, I'll start with you.

THE ADMINISTRATOR
There's no question as to my willingness to act on your behalf, Caesar, I swear to you.

CALIGULA
No question about mine, either. You can trust me on that one. Though the proof is right there in my agreeing to embrace your point of view and take the treasury to be a matter of serious consideration. In short, you should thank

me, as I'm anteing up for your game and I'm playing with your cards.

(*a moment passes, and then with calm*)

In any case, my plan, in its simplicity, is brilliant, and so that's the end of discussion. You have three seconds to get out of my sight. I'm counting. One . . .

The ADMINISTRATOR *hurries off.*

SCENE IX

CAESONIA
I hardly recognize you. This is a joke, isn't it?

CALIGULA
Not exactly, Caesonia. It's an education. A method.

SCIPIO
It's not possible, Caius.

CALIGULA
Precisely.

SCIPIO
I don't understand you.

CALIGULA
Precisely. It's about what's not possible, or rather, it's about making possible what isn't.

SCIPIO
But that's a game with no limits. It's a madman's entertainment.

CALIGULA

No, Scipio. It's an emperor's virtue.

(*turns away with a wearied expression*)

I've finally come to understand the purpose of power. It's to give the impossible a chance. Starting today, and for all the days to come, my freedom will no longer know any boundaries.[13]

CAESONIA
(*with sadness*)

I don't know if that's something to be happy about, Caius.

CALIGULA

I don't know if it is either. But I guess we're going to have to live with it.

CHEREA *enters.*

SCENE X

CHEREA

I heard you'd returned. I've been praying for your health.

CALIGULA

My health thanks you.

(*a moment passes, then suddenly*)

Go away, Cherea, I don't want to see you.

CHEREA

I'm surprised, Caius.

CALIGULA

Don't be surprised. I don't like men of letters, and I can't bear their lies. They speak so as not to hear themselves, because if they heard themselves, they'd know they're nothing and wouldn't be able to go on speaking. Go on, get out of here. False witnesses horrify me.

CHEREA

If we lie, it's often without knowing it. I plead not guilty.

CALIGULA

A lie is never innocent, and yours attributes importance to people and things. That's what I can't forgive you for.

CHEREA

And yet, we have to enter a plea in favor of this world, if we wish to live in it.

CALIGULA

Don't plead—the case has already been heard. This world is of no importance, and whoever recognizes that wins their freedom.

(standing up)

That's precisely why I hate you, because you are not free. In all the Roman empire, I alone am free. But rejoice, for at last an emperor has come to teach you about freedom. Go away, Cherea, and you, too, Scipio. Friendship makes me laugh. Go and let Rome know its freedom has finally been restored and that, with it, a great trial begins.

They leave. CALIGULA *turns away.*

SCENE XI

CAESONIA

Are you crying?

CALIGULA

Yes, Caesonia.

CAESONIA

But what could have caused such a change as this? If it's true you loved Drusilla, you loved her while also loving me and many other people, too. Her death's not enough to have sent you running off through the countryside for three days and nights and to then bring you back with this cruel look on your face.

CALIGULA
(*turns around*)

Who's been saying these things to you about Drusilla, you madwoman? And is it so hard to imagine a man crying about something other than love?

CAESONIA

Forgive me, Caius. I'm only trying to understand.

CALIGULA

Men cry because things aren't what they should be.

She steps toward him.

CALIGULA

Leave it be, Caesonia.

She takes a step back.

CALIGULA

But stay by my side.

CAESONIA

I'll do as you wish.

(*sitting down*)

At my age, a person knows life's no good. But if there's evil on earth, why add to it?

CALIGULA

You can't understand. What does it matter? Maybe I'll snap out of it. But I feel these nameless beings rising up inside of me. How can I possibly fend them off?

(*turning back to her*)

Oh, Caesonia! I knew a person could lose all hope, but I didn't understand what it really meant. Like everyone else, I thought it was a sickness of the soul—but no, it's the body that suffers. My skin hurts, my chest, my limbs. My mind's a blank and my heart's sick. But worst of all, though, the most awful part, is the taste in my mouth. Not blood or death or fever but all of them at once. All it takes is a waggle of the tongue and everything goes black again, and oh how these beings disgust me. How hard it is, how bitter it is to become a man.

CAESONIA

You need to sleep, to sleep for a good long while, to let yourself go and stop thinking about everything so much. I'll watch over your slumber, and when you wake, you'll find the world's regained its flavor. Then you can put your power to loving better what can still be loved. The possible also deserves a chance.

CALIGULA[14]

But that requires slumber, that requires letting go—that is not possible.

CAESONIA

That's the sort of thing people think when they're so tired they can't see straight. A time will come when you'll have a firm grasp again.

CALIGULA

But you have to know what to hold on to. And what good does a firm grasp do me, what use is this awesome power to me, if I can't change the order of things, if I can't make it so the sun sets in the east, can't decrease suffering and make it so people don't die anymore? No, Caesonia, sleeping or staying awake, it makes no difference if I have no control over the order of the world.

CAESONIA

But that's wanting to be equal to the gods, and I can think of no greater madness than that.

CALIGULA

Even you. Even you think I'm crazy. And yet, what is a god that I should wish to be its equal? What I wish for today, with all my strength, is above and beyond the gods. I'm going to lead a kingdom where the impossible is king.

CAESONIA

You can't make the sky not be the sky, make a beautiful face ugly, a man's heart unfeeling.

CALIGULA
(*with increasing exhilaration*)

I want to stir the sky and sea together, blend beauty and ugliness, make laughter spring from suffering.

CAESONIA
(*perched in front of him and begging*)

There's good and evil, high and low, just and unjust. I swear to you that none of that is going to change.

CALIGULA
(*in the same manner*)

My will is to change it. I'll give this century the gift of equality. And then, when everything's been leveled, when the impossible is at last upon the earth and the moon is in my hands, then, maybe I myself will be transformed and the world along with me, and then, at last, people will no longer die, and they will be happy.

CAESONIA
(*crying out*)

You can't deny love.

CALIGULA
(*exploding in a voice filled with rage*)

Love, Caesonia!

(*takes her by the shoulders and shakes her*)

I've learned it's nothing. That administrator was right: it's the treasury that matters! You heard him say so, didn't you? Everything begins with that. Oh, at last, now I'm really going to live. To live, Caesonia, to live is the opposite of to love. I can promise you that, and I can invite you to a limitless celebration, to an open trial, to the finest of spectacles. We must have crowds, an audience, victims, and the guilty.

*He throws himself at the gong and begins to
strike it over and over again, on and on, his blows
growing stronger. He continues to strike it.*

CALIGULA

Bring in the guilty. We need some to be guilty. They're all guilty.

(still striking the gong)

I want the ones condemned to death brought in. The people, I
want my people. Judges, witnesses, accused, all condemned from
the start. Oh, Caesonia, I'm going to show them something
they've never seen—the only free man in this entire empire.

*At the sound of the gong, the palace slowly
begins to fill with whispers, which grow louder
and closer. Voices, weapons, footsteps, and stomp-
ing.* CALIGULA *laughs and continues to strike the
gong. Some guards enter, then exit.*

CALIGULA
(striking)

And you, Caesonia, you will obey me. You will always be there
to help me. It'll be wonderful. Swear to help me, Caesonia.

CAESONIA
(disoriented, between two strikes of the gong)

I don't need to swear, because I love you.

CALIGULA
(same manner)

You'll do everything I tell you to do.

CAESONIA
(*same manner*)

Everything, Caligula, just stop.

CALIGULA
(*still striking the gong*)

You'll be cruel.

CAESONIA
(*crying*)

Cruel.

CALIGULA
(*same manner*)

Cold and implacable.

CAESONIA

Implacable.

CALIGULA
(*same manner*)

You'll suffer, too.

CAESONIA

Yes, Caligula, but I'm losing my mind.

> *Some patricians have entered, stunned, and with them the palace attendants.* CALIGULA *strikes a last blow, lifts his mallet in the air, turns toward them, and calls out to them.*

CALIGULA
(*insane*)

Come one, come all. Step right up. I order you to step right up.

(*stamping his foot*)

This is your emperor demanding you step right up.

Everyone moves forward, filled with fright.

CALIGULA

Come quickly. And now, come closer, Caesonia.

He takes her by the hand, leads her over to the mirror, and with the mallet, maniacally shatters the image on its polished surface. He laughs.

CALIGULA

Nothing more, you see. No more memories. All faces fade away. Nothing, nothing more. And you know what's left? Come even closer. Look. Closer. Look.[15]

He plants himself in front of the mirror, an air of insanity about him.

CAESONIA
(*looking at the mirror with fright*)

Caligula!

CALIGULA *places a finger on the mirror, his appearance changed, suddenly transfixed as he says triumphantly:*

CALIGULA

Caligula.

CURTAINS

ACT II[16]

SCENE I

A group of patricians have gathered at CHEREA's *house.*

FIRST PATRICIAN

He insults our dignity.

MUCIUS

For three years now!

THE OLD PATRICIAN

He calls me his little lady. He's ridiculing me. To no end!

MUCIUS

For three years now!

FIRST PATRICIAN

And every evening, when he goes out to the countryside, he makes us run alongside his lectica.

SECOND PATRICIAN

And then he tells us the run is good for our health.

MUCIUS

For three years now!

THE OLD PATRICIAN

There's no excuse for it.

THIRD PATRICIAN

No, it can't be forgiven.

FIRST PATRICIAN

Patricius, he confiscated your property. Scipio, he killed your father. Octavius, he pulled your wife right out from under you and forced her to work in his public brothel. Lepidus, he killed your son. Are you all going to put up with this? Me? I've made my choice. Between running the necessary risk and this unbearable life of fear and powerlessness, I have no hesitation.

SCIPIO

When he killed my father, he made my decision for me.

FIRST PATRICIAN

Are the rest of you really still hesitating?

THIRD PATRICIAN

We're with you. He gave our seats at the Circus to the common people and then pushed us to fight it out with the plebes so he'd have reason to punish us afterward.

THE OLD PATRICIAN

He's a coward.

SECOND PATRICIAN

A cynic.

THIRD PATRICIAN

A phony.

THE OLD PATRICIAN

He's impotent.

FOURTH PATRICIAN

For three years now!

> *Disorderly commotion. Weapons are bran-*
> *dished. A torch falls. A table is overturned.*
> *Everyone rushes for the exit, but as they do,*
> CHEREA *enters, impassive, and halts their frenzy.*

SCENE II

CHEREA
Where's everyone running off to like this?

THIRD PATRICIAN
To the palace.

CHEREA
I see. And you think they're going to let you in?

FIRST PATRICIAN
It's not a matter of asking permission.

CHEREA
You're all so suddenly filled with energy. May I at least be
allowed to have a seat in my own home?

> *They shut the door.* CHEREA *walks toward*
> *the overturned table and sits on one of its corners,*
> *while everyone else turns toward him.*

CHEREA
It's not quite as easy as you think, my friends. The fear you're
feeling cannot take the place of courage and composure. This
is all a bit premature.

THIRD PATRICIAN
If you're not with us, get out of the way, but hold your tongue.

CHEREA

But I do think I'm with you, only not for the same reasons.

THIRD PATRICIAN

Enough chitchat!

CHEREA
(*standing up*)

Yes, enough chitchat. I want to make things perfectly clear. For even if I'm with you, I'm not among you, and that's because, as I see it, your approach seems a poor one. You've failed to recognize your true enemy, attributing petty motives to him when in fact he has only grand ones. And now you're rushing off to your own ruin. See him, first of all, for what he is, and then you'll be better able to fight him.

THIRD PATRICIAN

We see him as he is, the maddest of tyrants!

CHEREA

Don't be so sure. Insane emperors, yes, we've seen a few, but this one isn't insane enough. What I hate about him is that he knows what he wants.

FIRST PATRICIAN

He wants us all dead.

CHEREA

No, that's secondary. He puts his power in service of a higher, deadlier passion, one that threatens our very foundations. This certainly isn't the first time we've had a man among us with limitless power, but it is the first time one has used it limitlessly, going so far as to reject humanity and the rest of the world with it. Now, that's what frightens me about him. That's what I wish to fight against. Losing your life isn't such a big deal, and I'll have the courage to lose mine when the time comes, but to see the meaning of that life dissipate, our reason for living vanish, *that* is what's unbearable. A person can't live without reason.

FIRST PATRICIAN
Revenge is a reason.

CHEREA
Yes, and I'm going to share in it with you, but understand that I'm not doing so on behalf of your petty humiliations but on behalf of the struggle against a grand idea whose victory would mean the end of the world. I can accept your being ridiculed and mocked, but I cannot accept Caligula doing what he dreams of doing and all that he dreams of doing. He's turning his philosophy into corpses, and unfortunately for us, it's a philosophy that doesn't permit objections. When you can't counter, you have to strike.

THIRD PATRICIAN
So then, we have to act.

CHEREA
We have to act. But you won't destroy unjust power by coming at it head on, while it's at full strength. You can fight tyranny, sure, but impartial wickedness has to be outwitted. You have to push it along its path, and wait for its own logic to go insane. But let me remind you, having said what I've said for the sake of honesty, that I'm with you only for the time being. After that, I'll serve not a single one of your interests, eager only to be returned to the peace of a world that's once again coherent. It's not ambition that makes me act but fear, a reasonable fear of that inhuman lyricism next to which my life is nothing.

FIRST PATRICIAN
(*stepping forward*)
I think I understand, for the most part. What's essential is that you judge, as we do, that the foundations of our society have

been shaken. For us, isn't it, wouldn't you agree, a question of morals above all else? Family values are shaking, the respect for work has been lost, the whole country is given over to blasphemy. Virtue is calling us to come to its aid. Are we going to refuse to hear it? At the end of the day, conspirators, are you just going to sit there and accept that patricians are being forced to run alongside Caesar's lectica every night?

THE OLD PATRICIAN
Are we going to let him call them "my darling"?

THIRD PATRICIAN
Let him pull their wives right out from under them?

SECOND PATRICIAN
And take their children?

MUCIUS
And their money?

FIFTH PATRICIAN
No!

FIRST PATRICIAN
Very well said, Cherea. Very good, too, that you calmed us down. It's too soon to act: the people, even today, they would be against us. Will you lie in wait with us until the moment is right?

CHEREA
Yes, we'll let Caligula carry on. Push him along, even. Systematize his madness. A day will come when he'll stand alone before an empire filled with the dead and the parents of the dead.

> *General clamoring. Trumpets outside. Silence. Then, whispered from one set of lips to the next, a name: Caligula.*

SCENE III

CALIGULA *and* CAESONIA *enter, followed by* HELICON *and some soldiers. The scene takes place in silence.* CALIGULA *stops and gazes at the conspirators. He goes from one to the next, straightens one person's buckle, steps back to have a look at another, gazes at them all again, passes his hand over his eyes, and exits without saying a word.*

SCENE IV

CAESONIA
(*sarcastic, gesturing at the disorder*)
Were you fighting among yourselves?

CHEREA
We were fighting among ourselves.

CAESONIA
(*same manner*)
And why were you fighting among yourselves?

CHEREA
We were fighting about nothing.

CAESONIA
So then, it isn't true?

CHEREA
What isn't true?

CAESONIA
You weren't fighting among yourselves.

CHEREA

So then, we weren't fighting among ourselves.

CAESONIA
(*smiling*)

Perhaps it would be best to put the room back in order.
Caligula is horrified by disorder.

HELICON
(*to the* OLD PATRICIAN)

You'll end up making the man do something out of character.

THE OLD PATRICIAN

But what have we ever done to him?

HELICON

Nothing, and that's just it. It's unheard of to be so dull
and ordinary. It's the sort of thing that ends up becoming
unbearable. Put yourselves in Caligula's place.

(*a moment passes*)

Of course, you were doing a little conspiring, weren't you?

THE OLD PATRICIAN

But that's not true, you see. How could he think such a thing?

HELICON

He doesn't think it, he knows it. But I guess in some way,
deep down, he kind of wants it to be so. All right, let's get this
disorder cleaned up.

They get to it. CALIGULA *enters and observes.*

SCENE V

CALIGULA
(*to the* OLD PATRICIAN)

Hello, my darling.

(*to the others*)

Cherea, I've decided to have a bite to eat at your place. Mucius, I've gone ahead and invited your wife.

The ADMINISTRATOR *claps his hands. A slave enters, but* CALIGULA *stops him.*

CALIGULA

Just a moment! Gentleman, you're aware state finances have held up only because people have gotten accustomed to them. Well, yesterday custom ceased to be enough, and so I find myself now in desperate need of doing a little downsizing. In the spirit of sacrifice, which you'll appreciate, I'm sure, I've decided to scale back my standard of living, to free a few slaves, and to assign all of you as my staff. Now if you will, kindly prepare the table and serve us.

The senators look at each other and hesitate.

HELICON

Go on, gentlemen, a little can-do attitude. You'll find, by the way, that it's easier to slide down the social ladder than to climb back up it.

The senators hesitantly begin to move about.

CALIGULA
(*to* CAESONIA)

What's the punishment reserved for lazy slaves?

CAESONIA

The whip, I believe.

> *The senators pick up the pace and begin clumsily setting the table.*

CALIGULA

Go on, give it a little effort. You need a system. Above all else, a system.

(*to* HELICON)

They seem to be a little out of practice.

HELICON

To be honest, they've never had to use their hands before, except when lashing out or giving orders. We'll just have to be a little patient, that's all. It takes only a day to make a senator, but a worker, that takes ten years.

CALIGULA

I'm afraid we may need more like twenty to make workers out of these senators.

HELICON

All the same, they'll get there. In my opinion, they've got a knack for it. Servitude agrees with them.

> *A senator mops his brow.*

HELICON

Look, they're even beginning to break a sweat. It's a step in the right direction.

CALIGULA

Good. Let's not ask too much of them. It's not so bad. And besides, even a brief moment of justice is nothing to be sniffed at. And speaking of justice, we'll have to get a move on: an execution awaits me. Ah, Rufius sure is lucky I'm always getting hungry.

(confidentially)

Rufius, he's the knight who's going to have to die.

(a moment passes)

No one's going to ask me why he has to die?

Absolute silence. By this point, the slaves are bringing food to the table.

CALIGULA
(in a good mood)
Go on, then, I see you've all gotten smarter.

(nibbling on an olive)

You've finally realized you don't have to have done something in order to die. Soldiers, I'm pleased with you. Aren't you pleased, Helicon?

> *He stops nibbling and, with a prankster's grin,*
> *looks out at the guests.*

HELICON

Certainly! What an army! But if you want my opinion, they're
a little too smart now, and they're not going to want to fight
anymore. If they keep this up, the empire will crumble.

CALIGULA

Perfect. Let's relax a little. Sit wherever you'd like. No
special protocol. All the same, this Rufius of ours sure is
lucky—though I'm sure he doesn't even appreciate this little
respite he's been given. Still, a few hours won out against
death—well, that's priceless.

> *He eats, as do the others. It quickly becomes*
> *clear that* CALIGULA *lacks table manners.*
> *There's no reason for him to toss his olive pits on*
> *his neighbors' plates or spit bits of gristle on the*
> *serving dish, no reason to pick his teeth with his*
> *nails or wildly scratch his head, yet these are the*
> *things he does during the meal, as if they were*
> *perfectly natural. But then suddenly* CALIGULA
> *stops eating and stares insistently at one of the*
> *guests,* LEPIDUS.

CALIGULA
(brutally)

You seem to be in a foul mood. Would that be because I had
your son put to death?

LEPIDUS
(*with a lump in his throat*)

Of course not, Caius, on the contrary.

CALIGULA
(*glowing*)

On the contrary! Oh, how I love a face that contradicts the heart's concerns. Your face is sad, but your heart . . . ? On the contrary, right, Lepidus?

LEPIDUS
(*resolutely*)

On the contrary, Caesar.

CALIGULA
(*happier and happier*)

Oh, Lepidus, no one's dearer to me than you. Let's have a laugh together, shall we? Tell me a good story.

LEPIDUS
(*overstepping*)

Caius!

CALIGULA

Okay, okay. Then I'll tell one. But you'll laugh, won't you, Lepidus?

(*an evil glint in his eye*)

If only for your second son.

(*laughing once again*)

Anyway, you're not in a foul mood.

(*drinking, then pushing for the desired response*)

On the . . . On the . . . Come on, Lepidus.

LEPIDUS
(*wearied*)

On the contrary, Caius.

CALIGULA

Good times!

(*drinking*)

Now, listen to this.

(*dreamily*)

Once upon a time, there was a poor emperor whom nobody loved. He, who loved Lepidus, had Lepidus's youngest son killed so as to remove that love from his heart.

(*changing his tone*)

Naturally, it's not true. Funny, though, right? You're not laughing. Nobody's laughing. Listen to me.

(*with violent anger*)

I want everybody to laugh. You, Lepidus, and everyone else. Stand up, laugh.

(*banging on the table*)

I want—you hear me—I want to see you laugh.

> *Everybody stands up. Throughout the rest of*
> *the scene, the actors, except* CALIGULA *and* CAE-
> SONIA, *play their parts as if they were marionettes.*

CALIGULA
(*spilling himself onto his bed, glowing, laughing uncontrollably*)
No, but just look at them, Caesonia. It's all breaking down.
Honesty, respectability, concern for what others might think,
conventional wisdom—nothing means anything anymore. All
vanish in the face of fear. Fear, eh, Caesonia, that beautiful,
undiluted feeling, pure and impartial, one of the few that
draws its nobility from the gut.

> (*touching his forehead, taking a drink,*
> *then speaking in a friendly tone*)

Now, let's talk about something else. Look at you, Cherea, so
very quiet.

CHEREA
I'm ready to speak, Caius, as soon as you permit me to do so.

CALIGULA
Perfect. So then, shut up. I'd like to hear from our friend Mucius.

MUCIUS
(*reluctantly*)
At your command, Caius.

CALIGULA
Well, tell us about your wife. You can start by sending her over
here to sit on my left.

MUCIUS's wife goes to CALIGULA.

CALIGULA
Well, Mucius? We're waiting.

MUCIUS
(*a little lost*)
But . . . my wife . . . I love her.

Laughter all around.

CALIGULA
Of course, my friend, of course. What could be more ordinary!¹⁷

> *He pulls* MUCIUS's *wife close to him and
> absent-mindedly licks her left shoulder, more and
> more at ease.*

CALIGULA
By the way, when I came in earlier, you were conspiring, weren't
you? You were carrying on with a little conspiracy, huh?

THE OLD PATRICIAN
Caius, how could you—

CALIGULA
That's of no importance at all, my sweetheart. Everyone has
to get old. No importance at all, really. You're all incapable of
acting courageously. It's just occurred to me that I have some
matters of state to handle, but first, we have to take care of
those imperious desires nature stirs in us.

> *He stands and leads* MUCIUS's *wife into a
> neighboring room.*

SCENE VI

<small>MUCIUS</small> looks as if he's about to stand up.

<small>CAESONIA</small>
(amiably)

Oh, Mucius, I could certainly go for some more of that
excellent wine.

<small>MUCIUS</small>, subdued, serves her in silence. A
moment of awkwardness. The seats creak. The
dialogue that follows is a little stiff and affected.

<small>CAESONIA</small>

Well then, Cherea. Why don't you go ahead and tell me what
you were fighting about a little while ago?

<small>CHEREA</small>
(coldly)

It all stemmed from our discussion, dear Caesonia, about
whether or not poetry has to be murderous.

<small>CAESONIA</small>

That's very interesting. But it's beyond my womanly
comprehension. Still, it's a wonder your passion for art should
lead you to trade blows.

<small>CHEREA</small>
(same manner)

Indeed. But Caligula used to tell me that there's no deep
passion without a bit of cruelty.

<small>HELICON</small>

No love without a touch of violation.

CAESONIA
(*eating*)

There's some truth in those words. Don't you think?

THE OLD PATRICIAN

He's a dynamic psychologist.

FIRST PATRICIAN

He spoke to us so eloquently about courage.

SECOND PATRICIAN

He really must write down all his ideas. It would be invaluable.

CHEREA

Not to mention it would give him something to do. And it's clear he could use a few distractions.

CAESONIA
(*still eating*)

Well, you'll be delighted to hear he's already thought of doing that, and he's currently in the process of writing a rather large treatise.

SCENE VII
—————

CALIGULA *enters with* MUCIUS's *wife.*

CALIGULA

I'm returning your wife to you, Mucius. She's all yours. Now, if you'll excuse me, I have some orders to give.

He quickly exits. MUCIUS, *pale, stands up.*

SCENE VIII

CAESONIA
(*to* MUCIUS, *still standing*)

This rather large treatise will be the equal of even the most famous works, Mucius, you can be sure of that.

MUCIUS
(*still gazing at the door* CALIGULA *went through*)

And what's it about, Caesonia?

CAESONIA
(*indifferent*)

Oh, that's beyond me.

CHEREA

So then, we have to assume it'll be about the murderous power of poetry.

CAESONIA

Dead-on, I believe.

THE OLD PATRICIAN
(*cheerfully*)

Well, that will give him something to do, as Cherea said.

CAESONIA

Yes, sweetheart. Though you might be a bit disturbed by the book's title.

CHEREA

What is it?

CAESONIA

The Centurion's Sword.[18]

SCENE IX

CALIGULA *enters in a rush.*

CALIGULA

Forgive me, but these matters of state are just as pressing.
You're to close the public granaries, Administrator. I've just
signed the decree. You'll find it in the bedroom.

THE ADMINISTRATOR

But—

CALIGULA

Tomorrow, there'll be a famine.

THE ADMINISTRATOR

But the people will get restless.

CALIGULA
(*with force and precision*)

I said that there will be a famine tomorrow. Everyone knows
what a famine is. It's a plague. Tomorrow, there will be a
plague—and I will stop the plague when it pleases me.

(*explaining to the others*)

After all, I have only so many ways of proving I'm free. A
person is always free at someone else's expense. It's bothersome,
but that's how it is.[19]

(*glancing over at* MUCIUS)

Apply that thought to jealousy, and you'll see what I mean.

(*dreaming*)

All the same, how ugly it is to be jealous. To suffer due to vanity and imagination. To picture his wife . . .

MUCIUS *squeezes his fists and opens his mouth.*

CALIGULA
(*very quickly*)

Eat, gentlemen. Did you know we've been hard at work, Helicon and I? We've been developing a little treatise about executions. You'll let us know what you think.

HELICON

That is, if we ask your opinion.

CALIGULA

Let's be generous, Helicon. Let's let them in on our little secrets. Go on, section three, first paragraph.

HELICON
(*stands and recites mechanically*)

"Execution relieves and delivers. It is universal, fortifying, and as just in its application as in its intention. A person dies because he is guilty. A person is guilty because he is subject to Caligula. Now, everyone is subject to Caligula. Thus, everyone is guilty. From which it is derived that everyone dies. It is just a matter of time and patience."

CALIGULA
(*laughing*)

What do you think of that? Patience! That's a real gem. And I have to say, that's what I admire most in all of you.

Now, gentlemen, you may go. Cherea has no further
need of you here. You stay, though, Caesonia. And Lepidus
and Octavius, too. Mereia, as well. I'd like to discuss the
organization of my brothel with you. It's been worrying me
quite a bit.

> *The others slowly exit.* CALIGULA *follows*
> MUCIUS *with his eyes.*

SCENE X

CHEREA

At your command, Caius. What seems to be the trouble? Are
the personnel of poor quality?

CALIGULA

No, but the earnings aren't so good.

MEREIA

We'll have to increase the rates.

CALIGULA

Mereia, you've just missed a perfect opportunity to keep your
mouth shut. Given your age, these questions don't concern
you, and so I'm not asking your opinion.

MEREIA

Then why'd you have me stay?

CALIGULA

Because, in just a moment, I'm going to need a dispassionate
opinion.

> MEREIA *steps aside.*

CHEREA

If I may, Caius, I would say, speaking from a place of passion, that we shouldn't fiddle with the rates.

CALIGULA

Of course not. But that means we're going to have to increase turnover. I've already explained my plan to Caesonia. She'll fill you in on the details. Me? I've had a little too much wine, and I'm starting to get sleepy.

He stretches out and shuts his eyes.

CAESONIA

It's very simple. Caligula's creating a new badge of honor.

CHEREA

I don't see the connection.

CAESONIA

And yet, there it is. The distinction will be founded as the Order of Civic Heroes. It will be awarded to those citizens who frequent Caligula's brothel the most.

CHEREA

That's brilliant!

CAESONIA

I think so. I forgot to tell you—the award will be given out each month after the entrance tickets have been certified, and any citizen who hasn't earned the honor by the end of a twelve-month period will be exiled or executed.

THIRD PATRICIAN

Why "or executed"?

CAESONIA

Because Caligula says it doesn't matter which. What's essential is that he be able to choose.

CHEREA

Bravo. Today the treasury's been bailed out.

HELICON

And in such a moral fashion, you'll note. After all, it's better to tax vice than ransom virtue, as they do in republican societies.

> CALIGULA *half opens his eyes and looks over at old man* MEREIA, *who, standing to one side, pulls out a small vial and takes a gulp from it.*

CALIGULA
(*still lying down*)

What're you drinking, Mereia?

MEREIA

It's for my asthma, Caius.

CALIGULA
(*going over to him, pushing the others aside, and sniffing his mouth*)

No, it's an antidote.

MEREIA

Of course not, Caius. That's a good one. I have difficulty breathing at night, and I've been using this to help me for a long time now.

CALIGULA

So then, are you afraid of being poisoned?

MEREIA

My asthma—

CALIGULA

No. Let's call things as they are: you're afraid I'm going to
poison you. You're suspicious of me. You're watching me.

MEREIA

Goodness gracious, no!

CALIGULA

You suspect me. In a way, you don't trust me.

MEREIA

Caius!

CALIGULA
(*harshly*)

Answer me!

(*calculating*)

If you're taking an antidote, you're ascribing to me the
intention of poisoning you.

MEREIA

Yes, I mean, no.

CALIGULA

And the moment you thought I'd decided to poison you, you
took the necessary steps to counteract my will.

> *Silence. At the beginning of the above back-
> and-forth,* CAESONIA *and* CHEREA *begin to creep
> away.* LEPIDUS *is left alone to anxiously follow
> the conversation.*

CALIGULA
(*more and more to the point*)

That makes two crimes, then, and one inescapable alternative.
Either I didn't want you put to death and you unjustly
suspected me—me, your emperor—or I did want it, and
you—an insect—you are counteracting my plans.

> *A moment passes.* CALIGULA *looks the old
> man over with satisfaction.*

CALIGULA

Well, Mereia? What do you say to that logic?

MEREIA

It's . . . it's thorough, Caius . . . but doesn't apply to the case at hand.

CALIGULA

And a third crime—you take me for a fool. Listen to me
carefully. Of these three crimes, only one does you any honor,
and that's the second one, because the moment you assume
I've ruled against you and you try to thwart my decision, that
implies a rebellion on your part. You're a leader of men now, a
revolutionary. That's a fine thing.

(*sadly*)

I like you a lot, Mereia. That's why you'll be convicted of your
second crime and not the others. You'll die a man's death, for
having rebelled.

> *Throughout this speech,* MEREIA *has been
> slowly shrinking into his seat.*

CALIGULA

Don't thank me. It's only natural. Here.

(*holding a vial out to him, then in a friendly tone*)

Drink this poison.

MEREIA, *racked with sobs, shakes his head no.*

CALIGULA
(*impatient*)

Come on, come on.

MEREIA *tries to escape, but* CALIGULA, *with a wild leap, catches him at the center of the stage, throws him onto a low seat, and after several seconds of struggle, forces the vial between his teeth, breaking it open with his fist. After a few convulsions,* MEREIA *dies, his face covered in water and blood.*

CALIGULA *stands up and mechanically wipes his hands.*

He gives a fragment of MEREIA'*s vial to* CAESONIA.

CALIGULA

What is it? An antidote?

CAESONIA
(*calmly*)

No, Caligula. It's asthma medication.

CALIGULA
(*looking at* MEREIA, *then, after a silence*)

It doesn't matter. It's all the same. A little sooner, a little later . . .

> *He abruptly exits, a busy look about him, still wiping his hands.*

SCENE XI

LEPIDUS
(*appalled*)

What do we do?

CAESONIA
(*simple and straightforward*)

First, get rid of the body, I think. It's awfully unpleasant.

> CHEREA *and* LEPIDUS *take hold of the body and drag it backstage.*

LEPIDUS
(*to* CHEREA)

We'll have to act quickly.

CHEREA

We have to be two hundred strong.

YOUNG SCIPIO *enters. Noticing* CAESONIA,
he makes a move as if to leave.

SCENE XII

CAESONIA

Come here.

YOUNG SCIPIO

What do you want?

CAESONIA

Come closer.

*She lifts his chin and looks him in the eyes. A
moment passes.*

CAESONIA
(*coldly*)

He killed your father?

YOUNG SCIPIO

Yes.

CAESONIA

You hate him?

YOUNG SCIPIO

Yes.

CAESONIA

You want to kill him?

YOUNG SCIPIO

Yes.

CAESONIA
(*letting go of his chin*)

But why tell me?

YOUNG SCIPIO

Because I'm not afraid of anyone. Kill him or be killed, either way it'll be over. And anyway, you won't betray me.

CAESONIA

You're right. I won't betray you. But I want to tell you something. Or rather, I'd like to speak to what's best in you.

YOUNG SCIPIO

My hatred. That's what's best in me.

CAESONIA

Just hear me out. What I want to tell you is both difficult and obvious, but it's something that, if truly heard, would bring about the only definitive revolution that exists in this world.

YOUNG SCIPIO

So say it, then.

CAESONIA

Not yet. Think, first, of your father's contorted face as they tore his tongue from him. Think of his mouth filling with blood and of those howls he let out, like a tortured animal.

YOUNG SCIPIO

Yes.

CAESONIA

Now think of Caligula.

YOUNG SCIPIO
(*his voice filled with hatred*)

Yes.

CAESONIA

Now listen—try to understand him.

She exits, leaving YOUNG SCIPIO *confused and disoriented.* HELICON *enters.*

SCENE XIII

HELICON

Caligula's on his way back. Maybe you should go get something to eat, Poet?

YOUNG SCIPIO

Help me, Helicon.

HELICON

That would be dangerous, my dove. And poetry doesn't speak to me.

YOUNG SCIPIO

You could help me. You know so many things.

HELICON

I know that time flies, and we have to hurry up and eat. I also know you could kill Caligula—and that he wouldn't look unfavorably on such an event.

CALIGULA *enters.* HELICON *exits.*

SCENE XIV

CALIGULA

Ah, it's you.

(*stops, almost as if unsure how to act*)

It's been a long time since I last saw you.

(*moving slowly toward him*)

What have you been up to? Still writing? Will you show me your latest work?

YOUNG SCIPIO
(*also uncertain, torn between his hatred
and something he can't identify*)

I've been writing poems, Caesar.

CALIGULA

About what?

YOUNG SCIPIO

I don't know, Caesar. About nature, I guess.

CALIGULA
(*more comfortable*)

A beautiful subject. And vast. What's it done for you? Nature, I mean?

YOUNG SCIPIO
(*pulling himself together, ironic and wry*)

It consoles me for not being Caesar.

CALIGULA

Ah! And do you think it could console me for being him?

YOUNG SCIPIO
(*same manner*)

Well, I think it's healed graver wounds than that.

CALIGULA
(*oddly humble*)

Wounds? You say it with such spite. Is it because I killed your father? Ah, but if you only knew how appropriate the word is. Wound!

(*his tone of voice changes*)

There's nothing like a little hatred to awaken the intellect.

YOUNG SCIPIO
(*stiff*)

I answered your question about nature.

CALIGULA *sits down, looks at* SCIPIO, *then suddenly grabs his hands and forcefully pulls him to his feet.* CALIGULA *takes* SCIPIO's *face between his hands.*

CALIGULA

Recite your poem for me.

YOUNG SCIPIO

Please, Caesar, I'd rather not.

CALIGULA

Why?

YOUNG SCIPIO

I don't have it on me.

CALIGULA

You don't know it by memory?

YOUNG SCIPIO

No.

CALIGULA

Then at least tell me what it's about.

YOUNG SCIPIO
(*still stiff and as if with regret*)

In the poem, I spoke of . . .

CALIGULA

Well?

YOUNG SCIPIO

No, I don't know.

CALIGULA

Try.

YOUNG SCIPIO

In the poem, I spoke of a certain harmony of earth—

CALIGULA
(*interrupting him but engrossed*)

Of earth and foot.

YOUNG SCIPIO
(*surprised, hesitates, then continues*)

Yes, it's something like that.

CALIGULA

Continue.

YOUNG SCIPIO

And also of Roman mountain ranges and the fleeting,
overwhelming calm evening sets upon them—

CALIGULA

Of the swifts' cries in the green sky.

YOUNG SCIPIO
(*letting himself relax a little*)

Yes, again.

CALIGULA

Well?

YOUNG SCIPIO

And of that subtle moment when a sky still full of gold
suddenly shifts and shows us its other face, spangled with
shining stars.

CALIGULA

Of the smell of smoke, of trees, and of waters climbing from
earth to night.

YOUNG SCIPIO
(*with everything he's got*)

Cicadas calling and the falling heat, dogs and chariots on a last
rotation, farmers' voices—

CALIGULA

And the city streets sunk in the shadows of mastic shrubs and
olive groves—

YOUNG SCIPIO

Yes, yes! That's what it's about. But how did you know?

CALIGULA
(*pulling* SCIPIO *against him*)

I don't know. Maybe because we hold the same truths dear.

YOUNG SCIPIO
(*trembling, burying his head against* CALIGULA's *chest*)

Oh, what does it matter? Everything inside me wears love's face.

CALIGULA
(*still soothing him*)

That's the virtue of an open heart, Scipio. If only I could be as transparent as you. But my lust for life, I know all too well how strong it is—and it won't be satisfied with nature. You can't understand. You come from another world. You're as pure in good as I'm pure in evil.

YOUNG SCIPIO

I *can* understand.

CALIGULA

No. This thing inside me, this lake of silence, these rotting weeds.

(*sudden change in tone*)

Your poem sounds beautiful, but if you want my opinion—

YOUNG SCIPIO
(*same manner*)

Yes.

CALIGULA

The whole thing lacks blood.

SCIPIO *suddenly pushes away and looks at* CALIGULA *in horror.*[20] *Still backing away, he speaks in a hushed voice, his eyes fixed on* CALIGULA.

YOUNG SCIPIO

Oh, you monster, you disgusting monster. You were playing again. You were just playing, weren't you? And you're pleased with yourself.

CALIGULA
(*with a little sadness*)

There's some truth in what you say. I was playing.

YOUNG SCIPIO
(*same manner*)

What a vile, bloodstained heart you must have. How tortured with wickedness and hatred you must be.

CALIGULA
(*gently*)

Hush, now.

YOUNG SCIPIO

Oh, how I pity you. How I hate you.

CALIGULA
(*angry*)

Be quiet.

YOUNG SCIPIO

And what dreadful solitude you must feel.

CALIGULA *explodes, throws himself on* SCIPIO, *and takes him by the collar, shaking him.*

CALIGULA

Solitude! You think you know it—you—solitude? The kind known to poets and the powerless. That solitude? Or which one? Oh, you can't know how alone you never are. How everywhere you go, the weight of the future and past follow you. The people we've killed are with us. And if it were only them, things would still be easy. But those we've loved, those we haven't loved who loved us, the regrets, the desire, the bitter and the sweet, the whores and gangs of gods.

(letting go of SCIPIO *and backing toward his seat)*

Alone! Oh, if only! If in place of this poisonous solitude
of presences I've created, if only I could taste the truth, the
silence, and the rustling of a tree.

(sitting down, suddenly weary)

Solitude! That it is not, Scipio. It's peopled with gnashing
teeth, filled to the brim with lost clamors and noises. And
then, lying next to those women, caressing them, when night
closes in on us and, far from my finally contented flesh, I
believe, there between life and death, I've got something of a
hold on myself, it's then my solitude fills with the sour stink
of pleasure pooling in the armpits of the woman sunk deep in
sleep beside me.

He seems exhausted. A long silence.

> YOUNG SCIPIO *crosses behind* CALIGULA
> *and then approaches him, hesitant. He reaches
> out to* CALIGULA *and places his hand on his
> shoulder.* CALIGULA, *without turning, places
> one of his hands atop* SCIPIO*'s.*

YOUNG SCIPIO

All men have something to comfort them in life. It's what
helps them keep going. It's what they turn to when they feel
completely worn out.

CALIGULA

That's true, Scipio.

YOUNG SCIPIO

So then, is there nothing in your life like that, nothing that
brings you to the point of tears, no silent refuge?

CALIGULA

Yes, maybe there is.

YOUNG SCIPIO

What is it, then?

CALIGULA
(*slowly*)

Contempt.

CURTAINS

ACT III[21]

SCENE I

Before the curtains rise, the sound of cymbals and drums. The curtains open on a sort of village fair. At the center, a backdrop hangs in front of a small stage, on which we find HELICON *and* CAESONIA, *cymbal players on either side of them.* YOUNG SCIPIO *and several of the* PATRICIANS *sit with their backs to the audience.*

HELICON
(*calling out like a barker*)
Step right up, step right up!

Cymbals.

HELICON
The gods have descended on the earth once more. Caius, Caesar, and god, otherwise known as Caligula, has lent them his human form. Step right up, mere mortals, the sacred miracle is about to begin right before your very eyes, a special

favor bestowed on the blessed reign of Caligula, the divine
secrets on display for all to see.

Cymbals.

CAESONIA

Step right up, gentlemen! Worship and give your obols. The
celestial mysteries are available today at a price fit for every
budget.

Cymbals.

HELICON

Get a behind-the-scenes glimpse of Olympus, its intrigues,
its intimacies and tears. Step right up, step right up! See the
whole truth about your gods.

Cymbals.

CAESONIA

Worship and give your obols. Step right up, gentlemen. The
show is about to begin.

*Cymbals. Slaves move about, placing a vari-
ety of objects on the stage.*

HELICON

An awesome reconstruction of truth, an unprecedented
performance, the majestic settings of divine power brought down
to earth. A sensational, immoderate attraction, with lightning

Slaves light the Greek fires.

and thunder

Slaves roll a barrel filled with stones.

and fate itself taking its triumphal march. Step right up and behold!

> *He pulls the backdrop aside, revealing* CALIG-
> ULA, *grotesquely dressed as Venus, sitting on a
> pedestal.*

CALIGULA
(*amiably*)

Today, I am Venus.

CAESONIA

The time to worship begins. Bow—

All except SCIPIO *bow down.*

CAESONIA

—and repeat after me the sacred prayer of Caligula-Venus:
"Goddess of sorrows and dance . . ."

THE PATRICIANS

"Goddess of sorrows and dance . . ."

CAESONIA

"Born of the waves, bitter and sticky with salt and seafoam . . ."

THE PATRICIANS
"Born of the waves, bitter and sticky with salt and seafoam . . ."

CAESONIA
"You, who are like laughter and regret . . ."

THE PATRICIANS
"You, who are like laughter and regret . . ."

CAESONIA
"Resentment and desire . . ."

THE PATRICIANS
"Resentment and desire . . ."

CAESONIA
"Teach us the indifference that rebirths love . . ."

THE PATRICIANS
"Teach us the indifference that rebirths love . . ."

CAESONIA
"Educate us to the truth of this world, which is that it has
none . . ."

THE PATRICIANS
"Educate us to the truth of this world, which is that it has
none . . ."

CAESONIA
"And grant us the strength to live up to this unparalleled
truth . . ."

THE PATRICIANS
"And grant us the strength to live up to this unparalleled truth . . ."

CAESONIA
Break!

THE PATRICIANS
Break!

CAESONIA
(*beginning again*)

"Fill us with your gifts, spread your impartial cruelty on our faces, your wholly objective hatred, open above our eyes your hands filled with flowers and murders."

THE PATRICIANS
". . . your hands filled with flowers and murders."

CAESONIA

"Welcome your lost children. Receive them in the stripped asylum of your indifferent and woeful love. Give us your purposeless passions, your woes deprived of reason, and your joys without future . . ."

THE PATRICIANS
". . . and your joys without future."

CAESONIA
(*very loudly*)

"You, so empty and burning, so inhuman yet so earthly, intoxicate us with the wine of your equivalence and forever satiate us in your black and dirty heart."

THE PATRICIANS
"Intoxicate us with the wine of your equivalence and forever satiate us in your black and dirty heart."

When this last sentence has been spoken, CALIGULA, *motionless until now, snorts and speaks in a stentorian voice.*

CALIGULA

Granted, my children, your wishes will be fulfilled.

He sits on the pedestal cross-legged. One by one, the PATRICIANS *bow down before him, give their obol, and line up on the right side to wait. The last of them, in his bewilderment, forgets to give his obol before backing away.* CALIGULA *leaps to his feet.*

CALIGULA

Hey! Hey! Come here, my boy. To worship is good but to enrich is better. Thank you. That's better. If the gods' only riches were the love of mortals, they'd be as poor as poor Caligula. And now, gentlemen, you can go spread throughout the city the astonishing miracle you've been permitted to witness: you've seen Venus, or what's called seeing by your eyes of flesh,[22] and Venus has spoken to you. Go now, gentlemen.

The PATRICIANS *begin to move.*

CALIGULA

Wait a second! When you leave, take the hallway on the left. I've posted guards in the one on the right. They're waiting there to assassinate you.

The PATRICIANS *exit in a disorderly fashion, eager to get away. The slaves and musicians disperse.*

SCENE II

HELICON *points a threatening finger at*
SCIPIO.

HELICON

Still playing the little anarchist, aren't you, Scipio.

SCIPIO
(*to Caligula*)

You blasphemed, Caius.

HELICON

What can that possibly mean?

SCIPIO

You're besmirching the heavens after having bloodied the
earth.

HELICON

This young man sure likes big words.

He goes to lie down on a divan.

CAESONIA
(*very calmly*)

Don't get carried away, my boy. As we speak, there are people
in Rome dying for speeches far less eloquent than yours.

SCIPIO

I've decided to speak the truth, Caius.

CAESONIA

Well, Caligula, this is what your reign's been lacking. A fine
moralist figure.

CALIGULA
(*interested*)

So then, you believe in the gods, Scipio?

SCIPIO

No.

CALIGULA

Then I don't understand—why are you so quick to see blasphemy?

SCIPIO

I can reject something without feeling obligated to besmirch it or deprive others of the right to believe in it.

CALIGULA

What modesty! Here we have true modesty. Oh dear, Scipio, how happy I am for you. And envious, too, you know, for that's the one feeling I may never experience myself.

SCIPIO

It's not me you're jealous of, it's the gods themselves.

CALIGULA

If it's all right with you, that will remain my reign's great secret. The only thing I can be blamed for today is having pushed the path of power and freedom one small step forward. For a man who loves power, being rivaled by the gods is something of an annoyance. I've rid of all that. I've proved to those illusory gods that a man, if he has the will, can exercise, with no formal training, their ridiculous vocation.

SCIPIO

That's the blasphemy I'm talking about, Caius.

CALIGULA

No, Scipio, that's seeing things clearly. It's just that I've come to understand there's only one way to be the gods' equal—be as cruel as they are.

SCIPIO

Be a tyrant.

CALIGULA

What is a tyrant?

SCIPIO

A blind soul.[23]

CALIGULA

Don't be so sure of it, Scipio. A tyrant is someone who sacrifices
his people to his ideas or ambitions. Me? Well, I have no ideas
and there's nothing left for me to aspire to as far as accolades
and powers go. If I exercise this power, I do so as compensation.

SCIPIO

For what?

CALIGULA

For the gods' stupidity and hatred.

SCIPIO

Hatred doesn't make up for hatred, and power isn't a solution.
I only know of one way of balancing out the world's hostility.

CALIGULA

And what way is that?

SCIPIO

Poverty.

CALIGULA
(*grooming his feet*)

I'll have to give it a try sometime.

SCIPIO

And in the meantime, so many people are dying all around you.

CALIGULA

So few, really, Scipio. Do you have any idea how many wars
I've refused to take part in?

SCIPIO

No.

CALIGULA

Three. And do you know why I've refused to take part in them?

SCIPIO

Because you laugh in the face of Rome's greatness.

CALIGULA

No. Because I respect human life.

SCIPIO

You've got to be kidding me, Caius.

CALIGULA

Or, at least, I respect it more than I respect some ideal of conquest. But it's true I don't respect it any more than I respect my own life. And if it's easy for me to kill, it's because it's not difficult for me to die. No, the more I think about it, the more I'm persuaded I'm not a tyrant.

SCIPIO

What does it matter if it costs us as much as if you were one?

CALIGULA
(*a little impatient*)

If you knew how to tally things up, you'd know that even the most modest war, undertaken by the most reasonable tyrant, would cost you a thousand times more dearly than all the whims of my fancy.

SCIPIO

But at least it would be reasonable. And being able to understand something is what's most important.

CALIGULA

Nobody understands fate, and that's why I took the role of fate on myself. I assumed the gods' stupid and incomprehensible face, and that's the face your compatriots were worshipping only a moment ago.

SCIPIO

And that's the blasphemy I'm talking about, Caius.

CALIGULA

No, Scipio, that's drama! Acting! The mistake these people make is in not having a strong enough belief in theater, because if they believed, they'd know anyone can become god and play a part in heaven's tragedies. All you have to do is harden your heart.

SCIPIO

That may, in fact, be true, Caius. But if it is, then I believe you've set the stage for a day when legions of human gods will rise up all around you, remorseless as you, and drown your ephemeral divinity in blood.

CAESONIA

Scipio!

CALIGULA
(*in a clear, firm voice*)

Let him be, Caesonia. You wouldn't believe how well you put it, Scipio—I've set the stage. It's hard to imagine the day you speak of, but I do dream about it sometimes. And on all those faces rising from the depths of that bitter night, in those features twisted by hatred and anguish, it's with rapture that I recognize the only god I've ever worshipped in this world—miserable and cowardly as the human heart.

(*irritated*)

Now, go away. You've already said far too much.

(*changing his tone*)

I still have my toenails to paint. There's a pressing matter for you.

> *All exit, except* HELICON, *who walks around* CALIGULA, *who is absorbed in grooming his feet.*

SCENE III

CALIGULA

Helicon!

HELICON

Yes?

CALIGULA

Your work's going well?

HELICON

Which work is that?

CALIGULA

Well, the moon, of course!

HELICON

It's coming along. It's only a matter of patience now. But I'd like to have a word with you.

CALIGULA

I may have patience, but I don't have a lot of time. Make it quick, Helicon.

HELICON

As I've said, I'll do the best I can. But first, I have some serious things to tell you about.

CALIGULA
(*as if he didn't hear what was said*)
Of course, I've already had her, you know.

HELICON
Whom?

CALIGULA
The moon.

HELICON
Yes, of course. But did you know there's a plot against your life?

CALIGULA
I had her good, all right. Only two or three times, it's true, but still, all the same, I had her.

HELICON
I've been trying to tell you about it for some time now.

CALIGULA
It was last summer. For as long as I'd been staring at her, caressing her there against the garden's columns, well, I guess she eventually figured it out.

HELICON
Stop this game, Caius. Even if you don't want to listen to me, my role is to speak to you all the same. Too bad if you don't hear it.

CALIGULA
(*still busy painting his toenails*)
This polish is worthless. To get back to the moon, though, it happened one beautiful August evening.

> HELICON *turns away, frustrated, no longer moving or speaking.*

CALIGULA

She liked to play coy. I'd already gone to bed. At first, she was all bloody, down there by the horizon, but then she began to rise, lighter and lighter, her speed increasing. The higher she climbed, the brighter she became. She'd become like a lake of milky water amid a night filled with pulsating stars. She arrived in the warmth, gentle, weightless, and naked. She crossed the bedroom's threshold and, with that slow certainty of hers, crept to the edge of my bed, cast herself into it, and flooded me with her smiles and brilliance.

Truly, this polish is worthless. But you see, Helicon, how I can say, without bragging, that I had her.

HELICON

Are you ready to listen to me, to understand the threat being posed to you?

CALIGULA

(*stopping and staring intently at* HELICON)

I want only the moon, Helicon. I already know how I'm going to die, but I've yet to exhaust the list of things that can keep me living. That's why I want the moon. And you're not to return here until you've procured her for me.

HELICON

Then I'll do my duty, and I'll say what I have to say. A conspiracy has formed around you. Cherea is the leader. I intercepted this tablet, which tells you all you need to know. I'll leave it here for you.

HELICON *leaves the tablet on one of the seats and heads for the exit.*

CALIGULA

Where are you going, Helicon?

HELICON
(*on the threshold*)

To find you the moon.

SCENE IV[24]
_____

A scratching noise at the opposite door. CALIG-
ULA *whips around and sees the* OLD PATRICIAN.

THE OLD PATRICIAN
(*hesitant*)

If you'll allow me, Caius?

CALIGULA
(*impatient*)

Well, come on, then.

(*looking him over*)

Well, sweetheart, you've come to have another look at Venus.

THE OLD PATRICIAN

No, it's not that. Shhh! Oh, my! Forgive me, Caius, I meant
only to say . . . well . . . you know I love you very much . . . and I
ask for nothing more than to be able to spend my golden years
in peace—

CALIGULA

Speak! Speak!

THE OLD PATRICIAN

Yes, okay, good. Well . . .

(*very quickly*)

It's very serious, that's all.

CALIGULA

No, it's not serious.

THE OLD PATRICIAN

What isn't?

CALIGULA

What are we talking about, my love?

THE OLD PATRICIAN
(*looking around him*)

We're talking about . . .

(*squirming a little and then bursting out*)

A conspiracy against you.

CALIGULA

You see, it's as I said. It's not at all serious.

THE OLD PATRICIAN

They mean to kill you, Caius.

CALIGULA
(*going to him and taking him by the shoulders*)

Do you know why I can't believe you?

THE OLD PATRICIAN
(*gesturing as if swearing to the truth*)

On the gods' honor, Caius.

CALIGULA
(*in a gentle tone, slowly pushing him toward the door*)
Don't swear. Above all else, don't swear. Just listen. If what
you said is true, then I'd have to assume you've betrayed your
friends, wouldn't I?

THE OLD PATRICIAN
(*a little bit confused*)
We're talking about my love for you, Caius.

CALIGULA
(*in the same tone*)
And I can't take that to be the case. I've always detested
cowardice, so much so I'd never be able to keep myself from
having a traitor put to death. But I'm well aware of your worth,
oh yes I am, and I'm sure that you wouldn't want to betray
anyone or die.

THE OLD PATRICIAN
Surely, Caius, surely!

CALIGULA
So then, you see I was right not to believe you. You're not
a coward, are you?

THE OLD PATRICIAN
No, not at all.

CALIGULA
Or a traitor?

THE OLD PATRICIAN
That goes without saying, Caius.

CALIGULA
And thus there is no conspiracy. Tell me, was it just a
joke?

THE OLD PATRICIAN
(*breaking down*)

A joke, a simple joke . . .

CALIGULA

Nobody wants to kill me, that's obvious, isn't it?

THE OLD PATRICIAN

Nobody, of course not, nobody.

CALIGULA
(*breathing deeply, then slowly*)

Then be gone, sweetheart. A man of honor is such a rare creature in this world of ours that I couldn't bear the sight of one for too long. I'll have to be alone for a while to savor this great moment.

SCENE V

Without getting up from his seat, CALIGULA *considers the tablet for a moment. He grabs it and reads it. He takes a deep breath and calls for one of the guards.*

CALIGULA

Bring Cherea.

The GUARD *goes to leave.*

CALIGULA

Wait a second.

The GUARD *stops.*

CALIGULA

Be polite.

The GUARD *exits.*

CALIGULA *paces back and forth a minute, then heads for the mirror.*

CALIGULA

You've decided to be logical, you imbecile. It's just a question of how far it'll go.

(*with irony*)

If they were to bring you the moon, everything would be different then, wouldn't it? The impossible would become possible, and just like that, all at once, everything would be transfigured. Why not, Caligula? Who knows?

(*looks around him*)

There are fewer and fewer people around me. Curious, isn't it?

(*to the mirror, in a hushed voice*)

Too many dead, too many dead. They're thinning out. Even if they brought me the moon, there's no going back for me now.

Even if the dead again bathed beneath the sun's caress, still the murders wouldn't stay buried.

(his voice furious)

Logic, Caligula. You have to follow logic. Power to its natural conclusion, desertion to its natural conclusion. No, we can't go back now. Now we have to go to the very end!

CHEREA *enters.*

SCENE VI

> CALIGULA *is slouched in his seat, his cloak riding up so it looks as if he has no neck. He appears exhausted.*

CHEREA

You asked to see me, Caius?

CALIGULA
(his voice weak)

Yes, Cherea. Guards! Some torches.

Silence.

CHEREA

Was there something specific you wanted to tell me?

CALIGULA

No, Cherea.

Silence.

CHEREA
(*a little annoyed*)

You're sure my presence is needed?

CALIGULA

Absolutely sure, Cherea.

(*another moment of silence, then suddenly attentive*)

Forgive me. I'm distracted, and I'm doing a very bad job of welcoming you. Take a seat, and let's have a chat, as friends. I could really use a talk with someone intelligent.

CHEREA *sits down.*

For the first time since the start of the play,
CALIGULA *seems to be his normal self.*

CALIGULA

Do you think two men, Cherea, equals in pride and character, can at least once in their life speak to each other with all their heart, as if standing before each other naked, stripped of all prejudices, of their own particular interests, of the lies by which they live?

CHEREA

I think it's possible, Caius—but I think you're incapable of it.

CALIGULA

You're right. I just wanted to know if we were thinking along the same lines. Okay then, let's put our masks back on. Let's get out our lies. Let's speak as if in battle, covered to the hilt. Why don't you like me, Cherea?

CHEREA

Because there's nothing likable in you, Caius. Because such things can't be had by command. And also, because I understand you all too well and a person can't like in someone else the very face they're trying to mask in themselves.

CALIGULA

Why hate me?

CHEREA

There you are mistaken, Caius. I don't hate you. I judge you to be harmful and cruel, selfish and vain, but I can't hate you, because I don't think you're happy. And I can't look down on you, because I know you're not a coward.

CALIGULA

So then, why do you want to kill me?

CHEREA

I already told you—I judge you harmful. I have a taste, a need for security. Most people are like me. They're unable to live in a universe where the most bizarre thought imaginable can suddenly, just like that, become reality—where, most of the time, it does come, like a knife into the heart. I don't want to live in a universe like that, either. I prefer to keep things under control.

CALIGULA

Security and logic don't go together.

CHEREA

That's true. It's not logical, but it is sane.

CALIGULA

Go on.

CHEREA

I have nothing more to say. I don't want to take part in your logic. I have a different idea of my duties as a man, and I know most of your subjects think as I do. You're a worrisome inconvenience for everyone. It's only natural that you should go.

CALIGULA

That's all quite clear and legitimate. To most people, it would even seem obvious. Not to you, though, because you're intelligent, and a person either pays dearly for intelligence or denies it. Me? I pay. But you? Why are you unwilling to deny it or pay the price?

CHEREA

Because I'd like to live and be happy, and I don't think a person can be either of the two while pushing the absurd to all its logical conclusions. I'm like everybody else. To feel free of those I love, I sometimes wish them dead; I covet women whom laws of family or friendship forbid me from coveting. If I were being logical, then that would mean I'd either have to kill or possess them. But I judge such abstract ideas[25] to be of little importance. If everyone acted on such notions, we could neither live nor be happy. And that, again, is what I find most important.

CALIGULA

So then, you must believe in some higher ideal.

CHEREA

I believe some actions are more beautiful than others.

CALIGULA

I believe they're all equivalent.

CHEREA

I know, Caius, and that's why I don't hate you. But you're a worrisome inconvenience, and you have to go.

CALIGULA

Fair enough. But why announce it to me and risk your life?

CHEREA

Because others will take my place and because I don't like to lie.

Silence.

CALIGULA

Cherea!

CHEREA

Yes, Caius.

CALIGULA

Do you think two men, equals in pride and character, can at least once in their life speak to each other with all their heart?

CHEREA

I think that's what we've just done.

CALIGULA

Yes, Cherea. But you thought I was incapable of doing so.

CHEREA

I was wrong, Caius. I recognize that and thank you. And now I await your sentence.

CALIGULA
(*distracted*)

My sentence? Oh! You mean . . .

(*pulling the tablet from his cloak*)

You recognize this, Cherea?

CHEREA

I knew you had it.

CALIGULA
(*in a passionate manner*)

Yes, Cherea, and your candor was all a show. The two men weren't speaking with all their heart. Not that it really matters anyway. Now we can stop this game of sincerity and go back to living as in the past. Still, you're going to have to try to understand what I'm about to tell you. You're going to have to submit to my insults and moods. Listen, Cherea. This tablet is the only proof.

CHEREA

I'm leaving, Caius. I'm tired of this contortionist game. I know it all too well, and I no longer wish to play it.

CALIGULA
(*in the same passionate and attentive voice*)

Hold on a minute. This *is* the only proof, isn't it?

CHEREA

I don't think you need proof to put a man to death.

CALIGULA

That's true, but for once I'd like to contradict myself. It won't hurt anyone, and it feels so good to contradict yourself from time to time. It helps you get a little rest. I need some rest, Cherea.

CHEREA

I don't understand, and I have no appetite for such complications.

CALIGULA

Of course not, Cherea. You're a sane man, you are. You have no extraordinary desires.

(*bursting out in laughter*)

You want to live and be happy. That's all!

CHEREA

I think it would be best to leave it at that.

CALIGULA

Not yet. Have a little patience, will you? I have the proof right here, just look. I'd like to think I can't have you sentenced to death without it. That's what I'm thinking, anyway, and that's what will help put me at rest. Well! Just look at what happens to proof in the hands of an emperor.

> *He holds a torch to the tablet.* CHEREA *goes over to him. The torch is between them. The tablet begins to melt.*

CALIGULA

You see, conspirator. It's melting, and as the proof disappears, a morning of innocence rises over you. Over that admirable brow of yours, Cherea. How handsome, an innocent man, how handsome. Behold my power. The gods themselves can't grant innocence without first having punished. But your emperor needs only a torch to absolve and encourage you. Go on, Cherea. Follow that magnificent reasoning you just told me about to the very end. Your emperor awaits his rest. This is his way of living and being happy.

CHEREA *stares at* CALIGULA *in amazement. He barely begins to lift his arm, seems to understand, opens his mouth, then leaves suddenly.* CALIGULA *continues to hold the flame to the tablet and, smiling, follows* CHEREA *with his eyes.*

CURTAINS

ACT IV

SCENE I[26]

The stage is in semidarkness. CHEREA *and*
SCIPIO *enter.* CHEREA *goes to the right, then to
the left, then comes back over to* SCIPIO.[27]

SCIPIO
(*drawn in on himself*)

What do you want from me?

CHEREA

Time's running out. We have to be certain about what we're
going to do.

SCIPIO

Who's saying I'm not certain?

CHEREA

You didn't come to our meeting yesterday.

SCIPIO
(*turning away*)

That's true, Cherea.

CHEREA

I'm older than you, Scipio, and I'm not in the habit of asking
for help—but it's true that I need you. This murder requires
reputable people to vouch for it, and amid all these wounded
vanities and ignoble fears, you and I are the only ones whose
reasons are pure. I know if you were to leave us, you wouldn't
betray us. But that's not the point. What I really want is for
you to stay with us.

SCIPIO

I understand. But I can't do it, I swear to you.

CHEREA

So you're on his side, then?

SCIPIO

No, but I can't be against him, either.

(*a pause, then in a hushed voice*)

Even if I were to kill him, my heart would still be with him.

CHEREA

Yet he killed your father.

SCIPIO

Yes, that's how it all started, but that's also how it'll all end.

CHEREA

He disavows what you avow. He ridicules what you cherish.

SCIPIO

That's true, Cherea. But I see something of myself in him. The
same flame burns through both our hearts.

CHEREA

There are times when a person has to choose. Me? I've silenced
any part of myself that I could see in him.

SCIPIO

I can't choose, because on top of what I suffer, I suffer what he suffers. I'm unfortunate enough to understand it all.

CHEREA

So you've chosen to see it his way, then.

SCIPIO
(*crying out*)

Oh, please, Cherea. I'll never be able to see it anyone—not anyone—else's way ever again.

A moment passes, the two looking at each other.

CHEREA
(*with emotion, moving toward* SCIPIO)

You know, I hate him even more for what he's done to you.

SCIPIO

Yes, he's taught me to see things through.

CHEREA

No, Scipio. He's taken your hope away, and to deprive such a young soul of hope is a crime worse than any other he's so far committed. I swear to you, that alone would be enough for me to rage and kill him.

He heads for the exit. HELICON *enters.*

SCENE II

HELICON

I've been looking for you, Cherea. Caligula's planning a
friendly little get-together. You'll have to wait for him here.

(*turning to* SCIPIO)

But you, my little lamb. We have no need of you. You can go.

SCIPIO
(*Exiting, he turns toward* CHEREA.)

Cherea!

CHEREA
(*very gently*)

Yes, Scipio.

SCIPIO

Try to understand.

CHEREA
(*very gently*)

No, Scipio.

SCENE III

*The sound of weapons backstage. Two guards
enter from the right, driving the* OLD PATRI-
CIAN *and* FIRST PATRICIAN *forward, both of
them looking terribly frightened.*

FIRST PATRICIAN
(*to the* GUARD, *trying to speak in a firm tone*)
Oh, come on, what could a person possibly want with us at
this hour of night?

THE GUARD
Sit there.

He points at some seats to the right.

FIRST PATRICIAN
If he means to put us to death like the others, there's no need
for all this messing around.

THE GUARD
Sit there, you old mule.

THE OLD PATRICIAN
Let's have a seat. This man knows nothing. That much is
obvious.

THE GUARD
Yes, sweetheart. That much is obvious.

He exits.

FIRST PATRICIAN
Oh, we needed to act quicker, I just knew it. Now we're going
to be tortured.

SCENE IV

CHEREA
(*calm, sitting down*)

What's this all about?

FIRST PATRICIAN/THE OLD PATRICIAN
(*at the same time*)

The plot's been discovered.

CHEREA

And?

THE OLD PATRICIAN
(*trembling*)

It'll be torture.

CHEREA
(*unshaken*)

I remember this one time Caligula gave eighty-one thousand sesterces to a slave, a thief, who didn't confess when tortured.

FIRST PATRICIAN

That won't make it any easier.

CHEREA

No, but it proves he likes courage, and you should bear that in mind.

(*to the* OLD PATRICIAN)

Would it be asking too much of you not to chatter your teeth like that? I can't stand the sound.

THE OLD PATRICIAN

It's just that—

FIRST PATRICIAN

Enough messing around. We're playing for our lives here.

CHEREA
(*without reacting*)

Do you know Caligula's favorite remark?

THE OLD PATRICIAN
(*on the verge of tears*)

Yes. He says it to the executioner: "Kill him slowly so he can feel himself dying."

CHEREA

No, it's better than that. After an execution, he yawns and says, in all seriousness: "What I really admire most is my insensitivity."

FIRST PATRICIAN

You hear that?

The sound of weapons is heard.

CHEREA

Such words reveal a weakness.

THE OLD PATRICIAN

Would it be asking too much of you not to philosophize? I can't stand the sound.

In the background, a slave enters carrying weapons, which he then lays out on a seat.

CHEREA
(*who hasn't seen him*)

We should at least acknowledge that the man exerts an undeniable influence. He forces us to think. He forces everyone to think. Insecurity—well, that certainly gets you thinking. That's why he's so hated.

THE OLD PATRICIAN
(*trembling*)

Look.

CHEREA
(*noticing the weapons, his voice changing a little bit*)

Perhaps you were right.

FIRST PATRICIAN

We needed to act quicker. We waited too long.

CHEREA

Yes. That's a lesson that's come a little too late.

THE OLD PATRICIAN

But this is madness. I don't want to die.

> *He gets up and tries to escape. Two guards spring forward, smack him, and forcefully grab hold of him. The* FIRST PATRICIAN *huddles down in his seat.* CHEREA *speaks a few inaudible words. Suddenly a strange, shrill, bouncy music made up of sistrums and cymbals bursts from the background. The patricians fall silent and watch.* CALIGULA, *in a short dancer's dress, with flowers on his head, appears as a silhouette against the back curtain, mimes a couple of ridiculous-looking dance steps, and disappears. As soon as he does, a* GUARD *says, in a solemn voice: "The show is over." While all of this is going on,* CAESONIA *silently slips in behind the audience. She speaks*

*in a neutral voice that, nevertheless, causes them
to jump.*

SCENE V

CAESONIA

Caligula has asked me to inform you that though in the past
he's always called on you for matters of state, today he's invited
you to commune with him in artistic feelings.

(*a pause, then in the same voice*)

He added, by the way, that those who refuse this communion
will have their heads cut off.

They're silent.

CAESONIA

Forgive me for insisting, but I have to ask—did you find the
dance beautiful?

FIRST PATRICIAN
(*after hesitating a moment*)

It was beautiful, Caesonia.

THE OLD PATRICIAN
(*overflowing with gratitude*)

Oh, yes, Caesonia!

CAESONIA

And you, Cherea?

CHEREA
(*coldly*)

It was high art.

CAESONIA

Perfect. Then I'll go and let Caligula know.

SCENE VI
———

HELICON *enters.*

HELICON

Tell me, Cherea, was it really high art?

CHEREA

In a certain sense, yes.

HELICON

I understand. You're very good, Cherea. Fake as any other upstanding citizen.[28] But very good at it, really. Me? I'm not very good at it. And yet, that won't keep *me* from preventing *you* from laying a finger on Caius, even if that's what he himself wishes.

CHEREA

I'm sorry, did you say something? I must have missed it. I do want to commend you on your devotion, though. I like good servants.

HELICON

Oh, you're proud of yourself, aren't you? Yes, I serve a madman, but you—whom do you serve? Virtue? I'll tell you what I think of virtue. I was born a slave. Your airs of virtue,

Mr. Upstanding Citizen—well, I first learned to dance them under the crack of a whip. But, Caius, he never lectured me. He freed me and took me into his palace. That's how I was able to observe all of you, the virtuous. And what I saw was that you look like crap and smell of it, too, that spoiled stench of those who've never suffered or risked a thing. I've seen the noble drapery of our statues hung over atrophied hearts, over greedy faces and fickle hands. You, judges? You who make a show of virtue, who dream of security as little girls dream of love, you who will die in terror all the same, never even knowing you've been lying your whole life, standing in judgment of those who've suffered immeasurably, who bleed a thousand new wounds every day. You will be the first to slap me down, no question about it! Look down on the slave, Cherea! He's above your virtue, because he can still love that miserable master of his, the one he'll defend from your noble lies and perjurious lips.

CHEREA
Dear Helicon. You're letting yourself go to eloquence. Frankly, you used to have better taste.

HELICON
My apologies, really. That's what happens when a person spends too much time with you. Old married couples end up looking like each other, down to the number of hairs in their ears. But I'm pulling myself together, don't you worry, I'm pulling myself together. Let me put it this way—you see this face? Good. Give it a good look. Perfect. Now you've seen your enemy.

He exits.

SCENE VII

CHEREA

And now we have to act quickly. You two stay here. We'll be a hundred strong by evening.

He exits.

THE OLD PATRICIAN

Stay here, stay here! Me? Well I'd really like to go.

(*sniffing*)

It smells of death here.

FIRST PATRICIAN

Or lies.

(*sadly*)

I said his dance was beautiful.

THE OLD PATRICIAN
(*conciliatory*)

It was, in a sense. It was.

Several patricians and knights enter in a whirlwind.

SCENE VIII

SECOND PATRICIAN

What's going on? Do you know? The emperor called for us.

THE OLD PATRICIAN
(*distracted*)

Perhaps for the dance.

SECOND PATRICIAN

What dance?

THE OLD PATRICIAN

Or, the artistic feeling, I suppose.

THIRD PATRICIAN

I was told Caligula's very sick.

FIRST PATRICIAN

That he is.

THIRD PATRICIAN

What's wrong with him?

(*with delight*)

By all the gods, is he going to die?

FIRST PATRICIAN

I don't think so. His sickness is fatal only to others.

THE OLD PATRICIAN

If we dare say so.

SECOND PATRICIAN

I see. But doesn't he have some sickness less serious and more advantageous to us?

FIRST PATRICIAN

No, his sickness suffers no competition. If you'll excuse me, I have to go see Cherea.

He exits. CAESONIA *enters. A brief silence.*

SCENE IX
———

CAESONIA
(*seemingly indifferent*)

Caligula's suffering stomach pains. He's vomiting blood.

The patricians gather around her. Unbeknownst to them, CALIGULA *has slipped in at the back of the room to listen.*

SECOND PATRICIAN

O all-powerful gods, I vow, if he recovers, to deposit two hundred thousand sesterces in the state treasury.

THIRD PATRICIAN
(*over-the-top*)

O Jupiter, take my life in place of his.

CALIGULA
(*moving toward the* SECOND PATRICIAN)

I accept your offer, Lucius. I appreciate it. My treasurer will be at your place tomorrow.

(*going to the* THIRD PATRICIAN *and hugging him*)

You can't possibly know how moved I am.

(*a pause, then tenderly*)

So, then, you do love me?

THIRD PATRICIAN
(*earnest*)
Oh, Caesar! There's nothing I wouldn't give for you.

CALIGULA
(*hugging him again*)
That's going a little too far, Cassius. Really, I don't deserve such love.

CASSIUS *is about to protest.*

CALIGULA
No, no, I'm telling you, I'm not worthy of it.

He calls for two guards.

CALIGULA
Take him.

(*to* CASSIUS, *gently*)

Go on, my friend. And remember, Caligula's given his heart to you.

THIRD PATRICIAN
(*vaguely unsettled*)
But where are they taking me?

CALIGULA

To death, of course. You've given your life for mine and now I'm feeling much better. I don't even have that awful taste of blood in my mouth anymore. You've healed me. Aren't you happy, Cassius, to be able to give your life for another when that other's name is Caligula? Here I am, refreshed and ready for all the festivities to come.

They drag the THIRD PATRICIAN *away kicking and screaming.*

THIRD PATRICIAN

I don't want to go. This has to be a joke.

CALIGULA
(*dreamily, between screams*)

Soon, Cassius, all paths to the sea will be covered in mimosas. Women will wear light dresses. The sky will be wide and beating, all of life smiling down on us.

CASSIUS *is almost at the exit.* CAESONIA *gently pushes him toward it.*

CALIGULA
(*turning around, suddenly serious*)

Life, my friend. If you'd loved it enough, you wouldn't have played with it so recklessly.

They drag CASSIUS *away.*

CALIGULA
(*coming back to the table*)

And when you lose, you have to pay up.

(*a moment passes*)

Come, Caesonia.

(*turns to the others*)

By the way, I've just had a lovely thought I'd like to share with you. So far, my reign's been too happy. No widespread plague, no cruel religion, not even a coup d'état. Nothing, really, that would pass a person on to posterity. You see, that's kind of why I'm trying to compensate for fate's caution. I mean . . . I don't know if you're following me, but—

(*with a little laugh*)

—well, I'm here to take the plague's place.

(*changing his tone*)

But hush now. Cherea's coming. They're all yours, Caesonia.

>   *He exits.* CHEREA *and the* FIRST PATRI-
>   CIAN *enter.*

SCENE X

CAESONIA

Caligula is dead.

> *She turns, as if she were crying, and gives a
> sharp look at the others, who keep their mouths
> shut. Everyone seems appalled, but for different
> reasons.*

FIRST PATRICIAN

You're . . . you're sure of this misfortune? It seems impossible.
He was just here a minute ago, dancing.

CAESONIA

That's just it. The effort did him in.

> CHEREA *moves quickly from one to the next,
> then turns back to* CAESONIA. *Everyone remains
> quiet.*

CAESONIA
(*slowly*)

You're not saying anything, Cherea.

CHEREA
(*also slowly*)

It's a great misfortune, Caesonia.

> *Caligula makes a sudden, dramatic entrance.
> He goes to Cherea.*

CALIGULA

Well played, Cherea.

(*spinning around and looking at the others, then, cheerfully*)

Oh, well, that didn't work.

(*to* CAESONIA)

Don't forget what I told you.

He exits.

SCENE XI
———

CAESONIA *silently watches as he goes.*

THE OLD PATRICIAN
(*buoyed by unflagging hope*)

Might he really be sick, Caesonia?

CAESONIA
(*looking at him with hatred*)

No, sweetheart, but what you don't know is that the man sleeps only two hours a night, and the rest of the time he wanders the palace galleries, unable to rest. What you don't know, what you've never bothered to ask yourself, is what this human being thinks about during those deadly hours that begin in the middle of the night and run to the sun's return. Sick? No, that he is not. Unless, of course, you'd like to invent a name and some prescriptions for the ulcers that cover his soul.

CHEREA
(*seemingly moved*)

You're right, Caesonia. We do know that Caius—

CAESONIA
(*quickly cutting in*)

Oh, you know it all too well. But like anyone else who doesn't have a soul, you can't stand anyone who has too much.[29] Too much soul! Well now, that's inconvenient, isn't it? So then we'll just call it a sickness and all the pedants will be pleased and justified.

(*in a different tone of voice*)

Have you ever known what it's like to love, Cherea?

CHEREA
(*back to his usual self*)

We're too old to learn now, Caesonia. And anyway, it's not clear Caligula will leave us the time.

CAESONIA
(*having pulled herself together*)

That's true.

(*sitting down*)

And here I almost forgot Caligula's instructions. You know today's a day set aside for art.

THE OLD PATRICIAN

According to the calendar?

CAESONIA

No, according to Caligula. He's summoned several poets. He'll ask them to improvise on a given subject. He specifically asked that the poets among you compete. He even called for young Scipio and Metellus by name.

METELLUS

But we're not prepared.

CAESONIA
(*as if she didn't hear him, in a neutral voice*)
Naturally, there'll be rewards. There will also be punishments.

The others take a small step back.

CAESONIA

I can tell you, between us, that they aren't so bad.

CALIGULA *enters. He's in a darker mood than ever before.*

SCENE XII
——

CALIGULA

Is everything ready?

CAESONIA

Everything.

(*to a* GUARD)

Bring in the poets.

A dozen poets enter, two by two, descending from the right in unison.

CALIGULA

And the others?

CAESONIA

Scipio, Metellus!

The two of them join the poets. CALIGULA *sits in the back, on the left, with* CAESONIA *and the other patricians. A brief silence.*

CALIGULA

Subject: death. Time limit: one minute.

The poets write on their tablets as quickly as they can.

THE OLD PATRICIAN

Who will be the jury?

CALIGULA

I will. Is that not enough?

THE OLD PATRICIAN

Oh, yes! Absolutely enough.

CHEREA

Will you take part in the competition, Caius?

CALIGULA

No need for that. I did a piece on the subject long ago.

THE OLD PATRICIAN
(*overdoing it*)

Where might one find a copy of it?

CALIGULA

I recite it all the time, in my own way.

CAESONIA *looks at him, anguished.*

CALIGULA
(*dramatically*)

Does my face displease you?

CAESONIA
(*gently*)

Forgive me.

CALIGULA

Oh, please, stop with the humility! Above all else, stop with the humility. You're already hard enough to take as it is, but your humility . . .

CAESONIA *slowly gathers herself up.*

CALIGULA
(*to* CHEREA)

As I was saying. It's the only piece I've ever composed. But that, in itself, proves that I'm the only artist Rome has ever known, the only one, you hear me, Cherea, to practice what he preaches.

CHEREA

Only because you have the power to do so.

CALIGULA

Indeed. Others create to make up for their lack of power. Me?
I don't need to compile a body of work: I live it.

(*harshly*)

Now, then—are the rest of you ready?

METELLUS

I think we're ready.

EVERYONE

Yes.

CALIGULA

Good. Listen to me carefully, then. You're going to step
forward, I'm going to blow a whistle, and the first person will
begin reading. At my next whistle, the first reader will stop and
the second will begin. And so on. The winner, of course, will
be the one who hasn't been interrupted by a whistle. Get ready.

(*turning toward* CHEREA, *then, confidentially*)

Organization is needed in everything, even art.

The whistle blows.

FIRST POET

Death, when beyond the black banks—

> *Whistle. The* POET *steps down to the left. The
> others will all do the same after their turn. The
> scene is mechanical.*

SECOND POET

The three Fates in their lair—

Whistle.

THIRD POET

I call out to you, O death—

Forceful whistling.

The FOURTH POET *steps forward and takes a dramatic pause. The whistle blows before he's spoken.*

FIFTH POET

When I was but a small child—

CALIGULA
(*yelling out*)

No! What could some fool's childhood have to do with the subject? You want to tell me what it has to do with it?

FIFTH POET

But, Caius, I haven't finished—

Forceful whistling.

SIXTH POET
(*stepping forward, clearing his throat*)

Inexorable, she advances—

Whistle.

SEVENTH POET
(*mysterious*)
Oration, abstruse and diffuse—

Spasmodic whistling.

SCIPIO *steps forward without a tablet.*

CALIGULA
Your turn, Scipio. You don't have a tablet?

SCIPIO
I don't need one.

CALIGULA
We'll see about that.

He chews on his whistle.

SCIPIO, *very close to* CALIGULA, *without looking at him, recites in a sort of weary tone.*

SCIPIO
Pursuit of the happiness that purifies,
Sky from which the sun trickles out,
Festivities, singular and savage,
Such hopeless delusions of mine.

CALIGULA
(*gently*)
Stop, please.

(*to* SCIPIO)

You're too young to understand death's true lessons.

SCIPIO
(*staring at* CALIGULA)

I was too young to lose my father.

CALIGULA
(*suddenly turning away*)

The rest of you get in your rows. Go on. A false poet is too harsh a punishment for my taste. Until now, I'd been turning over the idea of keeping you on as allies. Sometimes, I even imagined you'd form my last line of defense. But that was all for naught, and now I'm going to have to cast you out among my enemies. The poets are against me, so I can say this really is the end. Exit in an orderly fashion! You're to file out in front of me, licking your tablets clean to erase the traces of your infamies. Attention! Forward, march!

> *Rhythmic blowing of the whistle. The poets, marching in unison, file out to the right, licking their immortal tablets.*

CALIGULA
(*very low*)

All of you, out.

> *At the door,* CHEREA *takes the* FIRST PATRICIAN *by the shoulder.*

CHEREA

The time has come.

> *Young* SCIPIO, *who hears what's said, hesitates*
> *at the foot of the door, then goes to* CALIGULA.

CALIGULA
(*cruelly*)

Can't you leave me in peace, like your father now does?

SCENE XIII

SCIPIO

Come on, Caius, there's no need for that now. I know you've
already chosen.

CALIGULA

Leave me.

SCIPIO

Indeed, I am going to leave you, for I believe I understand
you now. Neither for you, nor for me, who is so much like
you, is there any way out. I'll have to get far away from here to
discover the reason for all this.

> *A moment passes. He gazes at* CALIGULA,
> *then speaks with great emphasis.*

SCIPIO

Goodbye, dear Caius. When it's all over, don't forget that I
loved you.

He exits. CALIGULA *watches him. Motions toward him. Then suddenly shakes himself and goes back over to* CAESONIA.

CAESONIA

What did he say?

CALIGULA

It's beyond your comprehension.

CAESONIA

What are you thinking about?

CALIGULA

About him. And about you, too. But it's all the same thing.

CAESONIA

What's the matter?

CALIGULA
(*gazing at her*)

Scipio's gone. And with him, my last friendship. But you, I wonder why you're still here?

CAESONIA

Because you like me.

CALIIGULA

No. If I had you killed, maybe then I'd understand.

CAESONIA

That would be one solution. Do it, if you will. But can't you, even for just a moment, let yourself go, let yourself live freely?

CALIGULA

I've been practicing living freely for some time already.

CAESONIA

That's not what I mean. Try to understand me. It can be so good to live and love with a pureness of heart.

CALIGULA

We each earn our purity as best we can. Me? I do it by
following things to their logical conclusion. Which doesn't
prevent me, by the way, from having you killed.

(*laughing*)

That would be my crowning achievement.

> CALIGULA *gets up and turns the mirror
> toward himself. He walks in circles, barely mov-
> ing, letting his arms dangle down like an animal.*

CALIGULA

It's funny. When I'm not killing, I feel so alone. The living
aren't enough to people the universe and to keep the worries
at bay. When all of you are around, you make me feel this
limitless emptiness I dare not look into. I'm only at ease when
I'm with my dead.

> *He plants himself in front of the audience,
> leaning forward a little. He's forgotten about*
> CAESONIA.

CALIGULA

Them? They are real. They are like me. They're waiting for me,
pressing in on me.

(*nodding his head*)

I have long talks with this one or that one, one who cried
out to me begging to be pardoned and whose tongue I had
cut out.

CAESONIA
Come. Lie down next to me. Put your head in my lap.

CALIGULA *obeys.*

CAESONIA
You're all right. It's all gone quiet now.

CALIGULA
It's all gone quiet! You exaggerate just a little. Don't you hear
those rattling chains?

They're heard.

CALIGULA
Can't you make out those thousand little whispers that betray
the hatred lying in wait?

Whispers.

CAESONIA
Nobody would dare—

CALIGULA
Oh yes, stupidity would.

CAESONIA
Stupidity doesn't kill. It keeps people in line.

CALIGULA

Stupidity is murderous, Caesonia. It's murderous as soon as it feels offended. Oh, it's not the people whose sons or fathers I've killed who will strike me down. Them? They've come to understand. They're with me now. They have that same taste in their mouth. But the others, the ones I've mocked and ridiculed, oh, against their vanity, I am defenseless.

CAESONIA
(*emphatically*)

We'll defend you. There are a lot of us here who still love you.

CALIGULA

There are fewer and fewer of you. I've done everything in my power to make it so. And anyway, let's be fair—stupidity isn't the only thing against me. There's also the loyalty and courage of those who wish to be happy.

CAESONIA
(*same manner*)

No, they won't kill you. If they tried, something would descend from heaven and consume them before they ever touched you.

CALIGULA

From heaven! There is no heaven, you poor woman.

(*sitting down*)

But why so much love all of a sudden? That's not part of our arrangement, is it?

CAESONIA
(*standing up and walking around*)

So, it's not enough to see you killing other people. No, I have to know you'll be killed, too. It's not enough to receive you, cruel and wrecked, to smell the stink of murder on you when you climb atop me? Every day, I watch as your face becomes less and less human.

(*turning to him*)

I'm old and getting ugly, I know, but my concern for you is what matters now. My soul no longer cares that you don't love me. I want only to see you get better, you who are but a child still. An entire life ahead of you. And what more could you really ask for than an entire life?

CALIGULA
(*standing and looking at her*)
You've stuck around for quite a while now.

CAESONIA
That's true. You are going to keep me, though, aren't you?

CALIGULA
I don't know. All I know is why you're still around. It's for all those nights of sharp and joyless pleasure, for all the things you know about me.

He takes her in his arms and, with one of his hands, pulls her head back a little.

CALIGULA
I'm twenty-nine years old. That's not old. But still, my life seems so long to me now, so filled with spoils and corpses, so very complete, and here you are, the final witness. And I can't help but feel a sort of shameful affection for the old woman you'll one day be.

CAESONIA

Tell me you want to keep me!

CALIGULA

I don't know. All I can say, and it's the most awful thing, is that this shameful affection is the only pure feeling life has so far given me.

> CAESONIA *pulls away from him.* CALIGULA *follows her. She places her back against him and he hugs his arms around her.*

CALIGULA

Wouldn't it be better if the final witness were to disappear?

CAESONIA

It doesn't matter. I'm only happy to have heard what you just said. But why can't I share this happiness with you?

CALIGULA

Who says I'm not happy?

CAESONIA

Happiness is generous. It doesn't live on destruction.

CALIGULA

Well then, there are two kinds of happiness, and I chose the murderous one. For I am happy. There was a time I believed I'd reached the outer limits of grief. But no! There was further still to go. At the far end of that land lay a barren and magnificent happiness. Look at me.

> *She turns toward him.*

CALIGULA

I laugh, Caesonia, when I think that all of Rome has spent the last four years avoiding saying the name Drusilla. Rome has spent the last four years fooling itself. Love isn't enough for me. That's what I understood then. That's what I understand still, today, looking at you. To love a person is to accept growing old with them. I'm not capable of that kind of love. Old Drusilla would have been much worse than dead Drusilla. People think a man suffers because the person he loves will one day die. But his true suffering isn't so trivial. His true suffering is noticing that not even sorrow lasts. That even grief loses its meaning.[30]

You see, I had no excuses, not even the shadow of love or the bitterness of melancholy. I have no alibi.[31] And yet, I'm freer today than I've been in years, freed as I am from memory and illusion.

(*giving an enthusiastic laugh*)

I know nothing lasts. Imagine knowing that! In all of history, only two or three of us have ever truly experienced it, have ever achieved this demented happiness. You've watched a rather curious tragedy play out to the end, Caesonia. Now it's time for the curtains to come down on you.

He walks behind her and wraps his forearm around her neck.

CAESONIA
(*terrified*)

Can this dreadful freedom really be happiness?

CALIGULA
(*slowly crushing* CAESONIA'*s throat with his arm*)

You can be sure of that, Caesonia. Without it, I would have
been a self-righteous man. Thanks to it, I've acquired the
divine wisdom of the solitary.

> *His excitement grows more and more as, little
> by little, he strangles* CAESONIA, *who lets him do
> so without resisting, her hands held out in front of
> her. He leans in close to her ear and speaks.*

CALIGULA

I live, I kill, I exercise destruction's delirious power, a power
next to which the creator's seems but a pale imitation. That's
what it means to be happy. That's what happiness is, this
unbearable deliverance, this all-embracing contempt, the
blood, the hatred surrounding me, the unparalleled isolation
of the man who holds his entire life before his eyes, the
boundless joy of the unpunished murderer, this ruthless logic
that crushes human life—

(*laughing*)

—that's crushing you, Caesonia, in order to finally perfect that
eternal solitude I desire.

CAESONIA
(*struggling weakly*)

Caius!

CALIGULA
(*more and more excited*)

No, no affection now. Now there's only time to get it over
with, because time is running out. Oh, my dear Caesonia, time
is running out!

> CAESONIA *lets out the death rattle.* CALIG-
> ULA *drags her to the bed and drops her on it. He
> looks at her as if a little lost.*

CALIGULA
(*his voice hoarse*)

And you, too. You were guilty. But killing is no answer.[32]

SCENE XIV

> *He spins around, haggard, and moves toward
> the mirror.*

CALIGULA

Caligula! You, too, you, too, you are guilty. A little more, a
little less, isn't that right? But who would dare condemn me in
this world without a judge, where no one is innocent?

> (*pressing himself against the mirror,
> voice completely distressed*)

You can clearly see Helicon hasn't come. I will not be getting
the moon. Oh, but how bitter it is to be right and to have to

follow things through to their logical conclusion. For I'm afraid of conclusions. There, the sound of weapons! Innocence prepares its triumph! How am I not in their place? I'm afraid. How disgusting, after having looked down on all those others, to now feel the same cowardice in my soul. But it doesn't matter. Not even fear will last. I'm going back to that great emptiness where the heart is at rest.

He takes a couple of steps backward, then returns to the mirror. He seems calmer. He begins to speak again, but in a lower, more focused voice.

CALIGULA

Everything seems so complicated, and yet it's all so very simple. If I'd had the moon, if love was enough, everything would be different. But where to quench this thirst? For me, what heart, what god could hold the depth of a lake?

(kneeling and weeping)

Nothing in this world, or the other, is worthy of me. But I know, and you know, too—

(reaching his hands toward the mirror and crying)

—that it would have been enough for the impossible to be. The impossible! I've searched the ends of the earth for it, the very limits of myself. I've reached out my hands—

(crying out)

—I reach out my hands, and it's you I find, always you
standing there in front of me, and for you, I'm full of hatred.
I didn't take the right path. I've gotten nowhere, achieved
nothing. My freedom isn't the right kind.[33] Helicon! Helicon!
Nothing! Nothing still. Oh, this is a heavy night! Helicon isn't
coming—we will be forever guilty! This is a night as heavy as
human suffering.

*The sounds of weapons and whispers can be
heard coming from backstage.*

HELICON
(*surging out from the back*)
Look out, Caius! Look out!

An unseen hand stabs HELICON.[34]

CALIGULA *stands up, takes a stool in hand,
and approaches the mirror, his breath coming
heavy. He fakes a leap forward, then backward,
observing the symmetrical movement of his double in the mirror, then throws the stool at it as
hard as he can, screaming out.*

CALIGULA
To history, Caligula, to history.

*The mirror shatters, and at that very moment,
armed conspirators enter from every exit.* CALIG-

ULA *faces them with an insane laugh. The* OLD
PATRICIAN *strikes him in the back,* CHEREA
square in his face. CALIGULA's *laughter turns to*
hiccupped gasps. All of the conspirators are strik-
ing at him now, and with one last gasp, laughing
and wheezing, he shouts:

CALIGULA

I am still alive!

CURTAINS[35]

The Misunderstanding

A PLAY IN THREE ACTS

To my friends in the THÉÂTRE DE L'ÉQUIPE

Foreword[1]

After twenty years of absence and silence, a man returns to the small Bohemian village where his mother and sister run an inn. In doing so, he hopes to recover his homeland. But he doesn't want to identify himself. He wants to be identified without having to say, "It's me!" So then, the only question is if this is possible, if a homeland of the heart exists, and if ultimately, "yes or no," as he himself says, having such "dreams make sense." It is precisely as a yes or no that he will receive his answer.

This play, aspiring only to tragedy, is resistant to theory. However, if the author absolutely had to have one, it would be this: man carries his share of illusions and misunderstandings within him, and they are what have to be killed off. In sacrificing them, man frees another part of himself, the best part, the one that rebels and seeks freedom.

That, as you will surely see, could be the subject of another play.

The Misunderstanding was staged for the first time in 1944, at the Théâtre des Mathurins, under the direction of Marcel Herrand.[2]

Martha   The Mother

Maria   Jan

The Old Servant[3]

ACT I

SCENE I

Afternoon. The waiting area of an inn. It's clean and bright. Everything inside is neat and tidy.

THE MOTHER

He'll come back.

MARTHA

He said so?

THE MOTHER

Yes. While you were out.

MARTHA

He'll come back alone?

THE MOTHER

I don't know.

MARTHA

Is he rich?

THE MOTHER

He isn't worried about the price.

MARTHA

All the better if he's rich, but he also has to be alone.

THE MOTHER
(*wearied*)

Alone and rich. Yes. And then we'll do it all over again.

MARTHA

That's right, we'll do it all over again. But we'll be compensated for our trouble.

Silence. MARTHA *looks at her mother.*

MARTHA

You're acting strange, Mother. You haven't quite seemed yourself for some time now. I hardly recognize you.

THE MOTHER

I'm tired, my dear, nothing more. I'd like to have a rest.

MARTHA

I can take care of whatever you have to do around the house. That way you'll have your days free.

THE MOTHER

That's not exactly the kind of rest I was talking about. No, it's just an old woman's dream. I only wish for a little peace, a quiet letting go.

(*giving a weak laugh*)

It's a stupid thing to say, Martha, but there are nights I almost feel drawn to religion.

MARTHA

You're not so old as all that, Mother. You have better things to do.

THE MOTHER

Oh, you know I'm only kidding. It's nothing, really. At the end of a life, you can indulge in a little letting go. You can't always be as tense and tough as you are, Martha. It's not right for someone your age. A lot of girls I know, born the same time you were, dream of nothing but fun and games.

MARTHA

Their fun and games are nothing compared to ours, you know that.

THE MOTHER

Let's not go there.

MARTHA
(*slowly*)

It seems certain words burn your mouth these days.

THE MOTHER

What does it matter to you, so long as I don't back out of certain acts? Never mind, who cares. All I meant to say is that it would make me happy to see you smile sometimes.

MARTHA

I do, I swear.

THE MOTHER

I've never seen you do it.

MARTHA

That's because I smile in my bedroom, when I'm alone.

THE MOTHER
(*looking at her closely*)

What a tough face you have, Martha.

MARTHA
(*walking toward her, speaking calmly*)

A face you don't love?

THE MOTHER
(*still looking at her, after a silence*)

I guess I do.

MARTHA
(*agitated*)

Oh, Mother! Once we've put away enough money to get out
of this place, this place with no horizon, once we leave this
inn and this rainy town behind us and forget all about this
shadow-filled land, the day we're finally standing out there in
front of that sea I've so long dreamed of, that's the day you'll
see me smile. But it takes a lot of money to live in freedom by
the sea. That's why we mustn't let ourselves be afraid of words.
That's why we must take care of this man who's come to us. If
he's rich enough, maybe my freedom will begin with him. Did
he say much to you, Mother?

THE MOTHER
No. Two sentences is all.

MARTHA
How did he seem when he asked for the room?

THE MOTHER
I don't know. I can't see well, and I didn't give him a good
look. I know from experience that it's better not to look at
them. It's easier to kill what you don't recognize.[4]

(*a moment passes*)

You should be happy. I'm not afraid of words anymore.

MARTHA
It's better that way. I don't like insinuations. Crime is crime,
and you have to know what you're after—and it seems you did
know, because you thought of it a moment ago when you were
talking with the visitor.

THE MOTHER

I didn't think of it. I responded out of habit.

MARTHA

Habit? These opportunities have been few, and you know it.

THE MOTHER

I guess so, but a second crime is all that's needed for a habit
to form. With the first, nothing begins. No, it's more that
something ends. And then, though our opportunities have
been few, they've been stretched out over the course of many
years, and memory has a way of reinforcing habits. Yes, it really
was habit that led me to respond, that warned me not to look
at him, that assured me he wore a victim's face.

MARTHA

We're going to have to kill him, Mother.

THE MOTHER
(*voice lowered*)

I guess so. We're going to have to kill him.

MARTHA

You say it so strangely.

THE MOTHER

It's just that I'm tired, and I'd like this one to be the last.
Killing is awfully exhausting. It doesn't matter to me if I die
out in front of the sea or in the middle of these plains of
ours—I just want us to leave together afterward.

MARTHA

We will leave, and what an amazing moment it'll be. Pull
yourself together, Mother, there's only a little work left to be
done. You know very well it's not even a matter of the killing.
He'll drink his tea, he'll go to sleep, and while he's still very
much alive, we'll carry him out to the river. It'll be a long time

before they find him washed up against the dam,[5] washed up with others who weren't as lucky as he was, who threw themselves into the water with their eyes open. That day we saw them clearing out the dam, you said to me, Mother, that ours were the ones who suffered the least, that life is crueler than we are. Pull yourself together now. Soon you'll have your rest, and we'll finally escape this place.[6]

THE MOTHER

Yes, I'll pull myself together. Sometimes, I really am content with the thought that ours have never suffered. It's hardly a crime at all, more like an intervention, a little helping hand stretched out to unknown lives. It does seem true that life is crueler than we are. Maybe that's why I find it hard to feel guilty.[7]

The OLD SERVANT *enters. He goes and sits behind the counter without saying a word. He'll stay there throughout the rest of the scene without moving.*

MARTHA

Which room should we put him in?

THE MOTHER

It doesn't matter which, as long as it's on the first floor.

MARTHA

Yes, those two flights of stairs gave us a little too much trouble last time.

(*sitting down for the first time*)

Is it true, Mother, that out there the beach sand burns your feet?

THE MOTHER

I've never been out there, you know that. But I've heard the sun devours everything.

MARTHA

I read in a book that it eats straight to the soul, leaving the body radiant but empty on the inside.

THE MOTHER

Is that what you dream of, Martha?

MARTHA

Yes. I've had enough of always having to carry my soul around with me. I can't wait to find a country where the sun kills all questions. This place here is not my home.

THE MOTHER

Well, we've got a lot to do before we get there. If all goes well, I'll go with you, of course. But it won't feel like going home for me. At a certain age, there is no home where rest is possible, and if you've been able to build yourself a simple brick house furnished with memories, a place where you can occasionally drift off to sleep—well, that's quite a lot already. Of course, it would also be something to be able to find both sleep and forgetting together.

(*standing and going over to the door*)

Get everything ready, Martha.

(*a moment*)

If it's really worth the trouble.

> MARTHA *watches her go. Then she, too, exits,
> but through a different door.*

SCENE II[8]

> *The* OLD SERVANT *goes to the window, sees*
> JAN *and* MARIA, *then hides. The* OLD SERVANT
> *remains onstage alone for a couple of seconds.*
> JAN *enters. He stops, looks around the room, and
> catches sight of the* OLD SERVANT *by the window.*

JAN

Nobody's here?

> *The* OLD SERVANT *looks at him, crosses the
> stage, and leaves.*

SCENE III

> MARIA *enters.* JAN *whips around to face her.*

JAN

You followed me.

MARIA

I'm sorry, I just couldn't. I'll go in a minute, but before I do, let
me have a look at where I'll be leaving you.

JAN

Someone could come, and then what I want to do would no longer be possible.

MARIA

We should be so lucky to have someone come. Then I could reveal you to them, despite your plans.

He turns away from her. A moment passes.

MARIA *looks around.*

MARIA

So, this is it, huh?

JAN

Yes, this is it. It was twenty years ago I walked out that door. My sister was a little girl then. She was playing over there in that corner. My mother didn't come to hug me. I didn't really think much of it at the time.

MARIA

I can't believe they didn't recognize you right away, Jan. A mother always recognizes her son.

JAN

She hasn't seen me in twenty years now. I was a teenager then, practically a little boy still. My mother's gotten old and her eyesight's not so good anymore. I barely recognized her myself.

MARIA
(*impatiently*)

I see. So, you came in, you said, "Hello," you sat down. You didn't recognize anything.

JAN

My memory wasn't accurate. They welcomed me without a word. They served me the beer I asked for. They looked at me but couldn't see me. It was all more difficult than I thought it would be.

MARIA

You know very well it wasn't difficult, and all you had to do was say something. In a situation like this, you just say, "It's me," and everything else falls in place.

JAN

Yes, but I'd been imagining all sorts of possibilities. I was even kind of expecting the prodigal's feast.[9] And then when they gave me the beer on credit, I was so moved I couldn't speak.

MARIA

A single word would have been enough.

JAN

I couldn't find one. It's nothing, really. I'm in no rush. I came out here to bring good fortune and, if I can, some happiness, too. When I heard my father had died, I realized I had certain responsibilities to these two women, and once I'd realized that, I did what had to be done. I guess it's not as easy as they say, though, to come back home again. It takes a little time to make a son out of a stranger.

MARIA

But why didn't you let them know you were coming? There are times you have to do what any other person would do. When you want to be recognized, you give your name—that's obvious. You end up getting everything all confused by pretending to be something you're not. How could you not be treated as a stranger in a house where you present yourself as a stranger? No, no, this is all wrong. It's not healthy.

JAN

Come on, Maria, it's not so serious as all that. And anyway, it fits with my plan. It'll give me a chance to get a look at them from the outside. I'll get a better idea of what'll make them happy. Then I'll figure out a way for them to recognize me. It's only a matter of finding the right words.

MARIA

There's only one way. It's to do the first thing anyone else would do, which is to say, "It's me," and then let your heart speak.

JAN

The heart isn't so simple.

MARIA

But it uses only simple words.[10] It really wouldn't have been so difficult to say, "I'm your son. This is my wife. We've been living together in a country we love, living out in front of the sea and sun, but it wasn't enough to make me happy, and now I need to be with you."

JAN

That's not fair, Maria. I don't need them, but I've come to realize they may need me, and that a man's never really alone.

A moment passes. MARIA *turns away from him.*

MARIA

Maybe you're right. Forgive me. It's just that I've been feeling so suspicious about everything since we arrived in this country, a place I search in vain for a single happy face. This Europe of yours is so sad. I haven't heard you laugh once since we arrived, and me, I've become this suspicious person. Oh, why did you make me leave my country? Let's get out of here, Jan. We're not going to find happiness here.

JAN

It's not happiness we came here to find. We have happiness.

MARIA
(*emphatically*)

Then why not be happy with it?

JAN

Happiness isn't everything. Men have their duties, and mine is to get to know my mother again, a homeland—

> MARIA *waves her hand.* JAN *signals for her not to move—footsteps can be heard. The* OLD SERVANT *passes by the window.*

JAN

Someone's coming. Go, Maria, please.

MARIA

Not like this—I can't go like this.

JAN
(*as the footsteps get closer*)

Over there.

> *He pushes her behind the door at the back of the room.*

SCENE IV

> *The back door opens. The* OLD SERVANT *crosses the room without seeing* MARIA *and exits out the opposite door.*

JAN

Go, quickly now. You see, luck is on my side.

MARIA

I want to stay. I'll be quiet. I'll just wait with you until you're recognized.

JAN

No, you'd give me away.

> *She turns away from him, then comes back to him and looks him in the face.*

MARIA

We've been married for five years, Jan.

JAN

Almost five years.

MARIA
(*lowering her head*)

This is the first night we'll have been apart.

> *He doesn't say anything. She looks back up at him.*

MARIA

I've always loved everything about you, even the things I didn't understand. I can see that, deep down, I wouldn't want you to be any other way. I'm not a very difficult wife. But here, that empty bed you're sending me back to scares me and so does the thought that you're leaving me behind.

JAN

You mustn't doubt my love.

MARIA

Oh, I don't doubt it. But there's your love, and then there are your dreams, or your duties—it's all the same thing. You run away from me so often it's almost as if you need a break from me, but I . . . I can't take a break from you, and tonight—

(*throws herself against him*)

—tonight I won't be able to bear it.

JAN
(*hugging her tight against him*)

This is a little childish, isn't it?

MARIA

Of course it's a little childish, but we were so happy back there and it's not my fault if nights in this country scare me. I don't want you to leave me alone here.

JAN

I won't leave you for long. Understand, Maria, that I have my word to keep.

MARIA

Which word is that?

JAN

The one I gave myself the day I realized my mother needed me.

MARIA

You have another word to keep.

JAN

Which other one?

MARIA

The one you gave me the day you promised to live beside me.

JAN

I think I should be able to balance the two. What I'm asking of you isn't much. It's not just some whim. Give me one evening, one night to get my bearings, to get to know these people I love just a little better, to figure out how to make them happy.

MARIA
(*shaking her head*)

Being apart is always too much to ask of those who really love each other.

JAN

Oh, you know I really love you, you animal.

MARIA

No, men never know how to really love. Nothing satisfies them. All they know how to do is dream, how to conjure up new duties, how to look for new lands and new homes. While we, we know you have to dive headfirst into love, share the same bed, join hands, fear absence. When we love, we dream of nothing else.

JAN

What are you trying to say? There's nothing more to this than getting to know my mother again, trying to help her and make her happy. As for my dreams or my duties, you have to take them as they are. I'd be nothing without them, and you'd love me less if I didn't have them.

MARIA
(*suddenly turning her back to him*)

I know you're always able to come up with good reasons,
convincing reasons, but I'm not going to listen to you anymore.
I'm going to cover my ears whenever you use that voice I know
so well. It's the voice of your solitude, not of your love.

JAN
(*coming up behind her*)

Let's not go there, Maria. I'm only asking you to leave me here,
alone, so that I can see things a little clearer. It's not such a terrible
thing to ask and it's not such a big deal to sleep under the same
roof as one's mother. God will take care of the rest. Though God
also knows I'm not forgetting you in all this. It's just that a person
can't be happy in exile or oblivion. A person can't remain a
stranger forever. I want to get to know my country again, to make
everyone I love happy. I'm not looking any further than that.

MARIA

You could do all that with a few simple words, but the way
you're going about it, it's just not right.

JAN

It is right, because, yes or no, it's the way I'll figure out if these
dreams make sense.

MARIA

I hope it'll be a yes, that they do make sense. But me, the only
thing I dream of is that country where we were happy. The
only duty I feel is to you.

JAN
(*taking her against him*)

Let me go do this. I'll end up finding the words that'll make it
all right.

MARIA
(*defeated*)

Oh, go on dreaming then. What does it matter, as long as I have your love? Usually, when I'm pressed against you, I don't want to be unhappy. I hold on tight and wait for you to come down from the clouds, and then my time comes around. If I'm unhappy today, it's because I'm so sure of your love and still so certain you're going to send me away. That's why the love men give is heartbreaking. They can't help but leave what they love best.

JAN
(*taking her face in his hands and smiling*)

That's true, Maria, but look at me, I'm in no great danger. Really. I'm doing it the way I want, and I'm at peace with that. All you have to do is entrust me to my mother and sister for just one night. It's not such a dreadful thing.

MARIA
(*pulling herself away from him*)

Goodbye, then, and may my love protect you.

(*walking to the door, stopping, holding
her empty hands out to him*)

But see how bereft I am. You go off to make discoveries, and you leave me behind to wait.

She hesitates, then goes.

SCENE V

> JAN *sits down. The* OLD SERVANT *enters,*
> *holds the door open for* MARTHA, *and then leaves.*

JAN

Good afternoon. I've come for the room.

MARTHA

I know. We're getting it ready. We have to get you registered in
our guest book.

> *She goes to find the guest book, then comes back.*

JAN

You have a rather odd servant.

MARTHA

That's the first time anyone's ever complained about him. He
always does exactly what he needs to do.

JAN

Oh, it's not a complaint. He's just not like most other people,
that's all. Is he mute?[11]

MARTHA

It's not that.

JAN

So then, he does speak?

MARTHA

As little as possible and only when necessary.

JAN

Well, in any case, he doesn't act as if he's heard what's said
to him.

MARTHA

It's not that he doesn't hear, it's just that he doesn't hear well.
Can you give me your full name, please?

JAN

Hasek, Karl.

MARTHA

Just Karl?

JAN

That's all.

MARTHA

Birthplace and date of birth?

JAN

I'm thirty-eight.[12]

MARTHA

Where were you born?

JAN
(*hesitating*)

In Bohemia.[13]

MARTHA

Occupation?

JAN

No occupation.

MARTHA

A person has to be very rich or very poor to live with no
profession.

JAN
(*smiling*)

I'm not very poor, and for a variety of reasons, I'm happy
about that.

MARTHA
(*in a different tone*)

Then you must be Czech, of course?

JAN

Of course.

MARTHA

Permanent address?

JAN

Bohemia.

MARTHA

You came from there?

JAN

No, I come from Africa.[14]

She looks as if she doesn't understand.

JAN

From the other side of the sea.

MARTHA

I know.

(*pausing*)

You go there often?

JAN

Fairly often.

MARTHA
(*dreaming for a moment, then returning to her questioning*)

Where are you headed?

JAN

I don't know. That depends on a lot of different things.

MARTHA

You plan to settle down here?

JAN

I don't know. That depends on what I find here.

MARTHA

Regardless—no one's waiting for you?

JAN

No, theoretically speaking. No one.

MARTHA

I suppose you have some form of identification.

JAN

Yes, I can show it to you.

MARTHA

Don't trouble yourself. I just need to note if it's a passport or an identity card.

JAN
(*hesitating*)

A passport. Here. You want to see it?

> She takes it in her hands and is about to read it
> when the OLD SERVANT appears in the doorway.

MARTHA

No, I didn't call for you.

> He leaves. MARTHA, *seeming distracted, re-*
> *turns the passport to* JAN *without having read it.*

MARTHA

Back home, do you live close to the sea?[15]

JAN

Yes.

> *She stands up, makes as if to put the notebook away, then changes her mind and holds it open in front of her.*

MARTHA
(*with a sudden hardness*)

Ah, I almost forgot—do you have a family?

JAN

I had one, but I left them a long time ago.

MARTHA

No, I meant, "Are you married?"

JAN

Why are you asking me that? I've never been asked that sort of question in any other hotel.

MARTHA

It's right here on the questionnaire we have to give the regional administration.

JAN

That's strange. Yes, I'm married. In any case, you must have seen my wedding ring?

MARTHA

I didn't see it. Can you give me your wife's address?[16]

JAN

She stayed back in her country.

MARTHA

Ah! Perfect.

(*shutting the guest book*)

Can I get you something to drink while you wait for the room
to be ready?

JAN

No, I'll just wait here. I hope I won't be bothering you.

MARTHA

Why would you be bothering me? This room is here to receive
customers.

JAN

Yes, but a single customer can sometimes be more of a bother
than a big crowd.

MARTHA
(*tidying the room*)

Why's that? I don't suppose you plan on telling me tall tales.
I don't have time for people who come around here looking
for fun and games. The locals have known that for a long time
now. What you'll find here is that you've chosen a nice, quiet
inn. Almost nobody comes here.

JAN

That can't be good for business.

MARTHA

We've lost a few sales, but we've gained our peace and quiet.
And you can't put a price on peace and quiet. Besides, a single
good customer is better than a bustling operation. What we're
looking for is just the right customer.

JAN

But ...

(*hesitating*)

Shouldn't you enjoy life sometimes? Don't the two of you feel all alone out here?

MARTHA
(*suddenly whirling around to face him*)

Listen, I can see I'm going to have to give you a warning. Here goes. On entering this establishment, you have all the rights of a customer, but nothing more. That said, you'll be very well taken care of, and I don't think you'll ever feel the need to complain about how you were received. You have no need to worry about our solitude, just as you mustn't worry about disturbing us, about being welcome or not being welcome. Take advantage of all the benefits of being a customer, but take no more than that.

JAN

I apologize. I was only trying to be sympathetic. I didn't mean to upset you. It just seemed to me that maybe we weren't such strangers after all, you and I.

MARTHA

I can see I'm going to have to repeat to you that it's not a question of upsetting me or not upsetting me. Rather, you seem determined to speak in a way that doesn't suit the situation, and I'm only trying to point that out to you. I assure you I'm not doing it out of anger. Wouldn't it be best, for both of us, to keep our distance? In any case, if you continue to speak in a way not befitting a customer, we'll simply refuse you service. But if you try to understand, as I think you will, that the two women renting you a room aren't also obligated to invite you into their personal lives, then all will go well.

JAN

That makes sense. There's no excuse for having let you believe I thought otherwise.

MARTHA

There's no harm done. You're not the first to try to speak to us that way. But I've always spoken clearly enough for there to be no possibility of confusion.

JAN

You do indeed speak clearly, and I realize I don't really have anything else to say . . . at the moment.

MARTHA

Why's that? Nothing's preventing you from speaking as any other customer would.

JAN

And what way of speaking is that?

MARTHA

Most people talk a little bit about everything, about their travels or politics, about anything, really, except us. That's all we ask. On occasion, some have even spoken of their personal life, and that's okay, too. After all, listening is included as one of the services for which we're paid. But it goes without saying, the price of room and board doesn't obligate the innkeeper to answer questions. My mother sometimes does, out of indifference, but me, I refuse on principle. If this all makes sense to you, not only will we be in agreement but you'll also find you still have a lot of things left to tell us, and you'll discover that it can sometimes be a pleasure to have someone listen to you when you talk about yourself.

JAN

Unfortunately, I'm not so good at talking about myself. But then again, it wouldn't even be useful to do so. If I'm going to be staying for only a little while, you won't need to get to know me. And if I end up staying longer, you'll have plenty of time to get to know who I am without my having to say a thing.

MARTHA

I just hope you won't hold some pointless grudge against me for what I've said. I've always found it beneficial to tell things as they are, and I couldn't let you go on speaking in a way that would have ended up ruining our relationship. What I'm saying only makes sense. Seeing as, before today, we shared nothing in common, there's really no reason we should suddenly find ourselves sharing intimacies.

JAN

I've already forgiven you. I certainly understand that intimacy doesn't just come out of nowhere. It takes time. Now, if it seems everything's been cleared up between us, I'll be all the happier for it.

The MOTHER *enters.*

SCENE VI

THE MOTHER

Good afternoon, sir. Your room is ready.

JAN

Thank you very much, madame.

The MOTHER *sits down.*

THE MOTHER
(*to* MARTHA)

You've filled out the form?

MARTHA

Yes.

THE MOTHER

Can I have a look at it? You'll forgive me, sir, but the police are very strict. So then, hold on, it looks as if my daughter forgot to note if you're here on business, as a tourist, or for your health.

JAN

As a tourist, I suppose.

THE MOTHER

To see the monastery, no doubt? People speak very highly of our monastery.

JAN

I've certainly heard about it. I also just wanted to have a look around again. I used to know the area well. Some of my fondest memories are from here.

MARTHA

You lived in the area?

JAN

No, but I had the chance to pass through here a long time ago. I've never forgotten it.

THE MOTHER

It's a small little village, but it is our own.

JAN

It is, but I like it quite a bit here. Since I've been back, I've
almost had the feeling of being home.

THE MOTHER

Will you be staying long?

JAN

I don't know. That probably seems strange to you, but
really, I don't know. A person has to have reasons to stay
somewhere—some friendships, a couple of people who care
about you. Otherwise, there's no real reason to stay in one
place rather than someplace else. And, given you never know
how you're going to be received, it's only natural I don't know
what I'm going to do.

MARTHA

That's not really saying much.

JAN

True, but I don't know how to express myself any better.

THE MOTHER

Well, you'll tire soon enough.

JAN

No, I have a faithful heart, and I'm quick to make memories,
when given the chance.

MARTHA
(*impatiently*)

The heart has no business here.

JAN
(*appearing not to have heard, speaking to the* MOTHER)

You seem awfully disillusioned. Has it been that long you've
lived here in this hotel?

THE MOTHER

It's been years and years like this. So many years I no longer
know when it began. So many years I've forgotten who I was
then. This one here's my daughter.[17]

MARTHA

You have no reason to tell him these things, Mother.

THE MOTHER

That's true, Martha.

JAN
(*very quickly*)

We'll leave it there, then. I really do understand how you feel,
madame. That's what happens at the end of a life filled with
work. But maybe everything would've been different if you'd
had a man's arm to support you and give you the help every
woman should receive.

THE MOTHER

Oh, I had one once, but there was too much to do. My
husband and I barely got by. We didn't even have time to
think of each other. Even before he died, I think I'd already
forgotten him.

JAN

Yes, I understand, but . . .

(*hesitating a moment*)

. . . a son who could have leant you his arm, maybe you
wouldn't have forgotten him?

MARTHA

You know we have a lot to do, Mother.

THE MOTHER

A son! Oh, I'm too old a woman for all that. Old women unlearn even to love their sons. The heart wears out, sir.

JAN

That's true, But I know he'd never forget.[18]

MARTHA
(*placing herself between them and speaking with determination*)
A son who came here would find what any other customer is sure to find: benevolent indifference. All the men we've received here have made do with that. They've paid for their room and received a key. They haven't spoken from their heart.

(*a moment passes*)

That's made our work easier.

THE MOTHER

Don't go there.

JAN
(*reflecting*)

So, they've stayed a long time, then?

MARTHA

Some a very long time. We did what we had to do to keep them here. Others, who were less well off, left the next day. We could do nothing for them.

JAN

I have a lot of money, and I'd like to stay here a while, if you'll have me. I forgot to say I can pay in advance.

THE MOTHER

Oh, we're not asking you to do that.

MARTHA

If you're well-off, all will be well. Just don't talk about your heart anymore. We can do nothing for it. The way you were speaking was so exhausting I almost asked you to leave. Take your key and get settled in your room, but know that you're in a house without resources for the heart. Too many gray years have passed over this little village, and over us, too. Little by little, they've chilled this house. They've carried away any feelings of sympathy we may have had. So let me say once again—you'll find nothing resembling intimacy here. You'll find what we always have in store for our few visitors, and what we have in store for them has nothing to do with the heart's passion. Take your key—

(*holding it out to him*)

—and don't forget: we welcome you here out of our own interest, and in peace and quiet, and if we keep you here, it will be out of our own interest, and in peace and quiet.

He takes the key. She leaves. He watches her go.

THE MOTHER

Don't pay too much attention to all that, sir. Though it's true there are some subjects she's never been able to bear.

She gets up, and he goes to help her.

THE MOTHER

No need, my son, I'm not an invalid. You see these hands? They're still strong. They could lift a man up by the legs.[19]

A moment passes. He looks down at his key.

THE MOTHER

Did I say something wrong?

JAN

No, I'm sorry, I hardly heard what you said. But why'd you call me "my son"?

THE MOTHER

Oh, I do get confused. It wasn't out of familiarity,[20] believe me. It was only a manner of speaking.

JAN

I understand.

(*pausing*)

May I go to my room?

THE MOTHER

Go on, sir. The old servant is waiting for you in the hallway.

He gazes at her. He wants to speak.

THE MOTHER

Do you need something?

JAN
(*hesitating*)

No, madame. But . . . thank you for your welcome.

SCENE VII

The MOTHER *is alone. She sits back down, places her hands on the table, and contemplates them.*

THE MOTHER

Why did I mention my hands to him? But if he'd only looked at them, maybe then he would have understood what Martha was saying to him.

He would have understood, he would have left. But he doesn't understand. But he wants to die. And all I want is for him to go away so that I can lie back down and sleep. Too old! I'm too old to again close my hands around his ankles, to keep his body balanced all the way down the path to the river. I'm too old for that last bit of effort it'll take to throw him into the water, that effort that'll leave my arms dangling limp, that'll leave me short of breath, muscles knotted, not even enough strength left to wipe the water from my face, the water that'll gush up under the weight of that sleeping body. I'm too old! Come on, come on—he's the perfect victim. I'll just have to give him the sleep I'd hoped to have for myself tonight. And it's—

MARTHA *suddenly enters.*

SCENE VIII

MARTHA

What are you dreaming about now? You know we still have a
lot to do.

THE MOTHER

I was thinking about that man. Or, rather, about myself.

MARTHA

It'd be better to think about tomorrow.[21] Be positive.

THE MOTHER

That's the phrase your father used, Martha. I recognize it very
well. But I just want to be sure this is the last time we're going
to have to be positive. It's strange, you know. He said it to
chase off the fear of the gendarmes, and you—you use it only
to dispel that small desire for honesty I just felt.

MARTHA

What you call a desire for honesty is only a desire for sleep.
Set your weariness aside until tomorrow, and then, when
everything's finished, then you can let yourself go.

THE MOTHER

You're right, I know. But admit it—this visitor doesn't appear
to be like the others.

MARTHA

Yes, he's a little too preoccupied and his look of innocence is a
bit much. What would become of the world if the condemned
began entrusting their heartaches to the executioner? That
would set a bad example. And in any case, his indiscretion
irritates me. I want to be done with it.

THE MOTHER

Now there's a bad example. In the past, we didn't bring anger
or compassion to our work. We carried only the necessary
indifference. Today, me, I'm exhausted, and here you are,
irritated. So, do we really have to be so stubborn, then, to press
on when things appear to be going poorly, to cast all that aside
for the sake of a little more money?

MARTHA

No, not for money, but to be able to forget this country and
have a house in front of the sea. You may be tired of your life,
but me, I'm sick to death of these closed-off horizons, and
I don't think I can live with them for even another month.
We've both outlived this inn, and you, being old, you want
nothing other than to close your eyes and forget. But I, still
faintly able to feel the beatings of my twenty-year-old heart,
all I want is to leave that feeling behind forever, even if, to do
so, we have to plunge a little deeper into the life we wish to
escape. And anyway, you have to help me, you who brought
me into the world in a country of clouds instead of a land of
sunshine.

THE MOTHER

I don't know if, in some way, Martha, it wouldn't be
better for me to be forgotten—as I've been forgotten by
your brother—rather than hear you speak to me like
this.

MARTHA

You know very well that I don't mean to hurt you.

(*pausing a moment, then ferociously*)

What would I do without you by my side, what would I
become apart from you? I, at least, wouldn't be able to forget
you, and if the weight of this life sometimes causes me to lose
sight of the respect I owe you, for that I ask your forgiveness.

THE MOTHER

You're a good daughter, and I suspect it must be difficult to
understand an old woman like me sometimes. But I'd like
to take the moment to tell you what I tried to tell you a few
minutes ago: not tonight . . .

MARTHA

Why not? Why wait until tomorrow? You know very well
we've never done it like that before. You know we shouldn't
give him time to see other people, that we should act while we
have him in hand.

THE MOTHER

I don't know why. Just not tonight. Let him have the night.
Give us this reprieve. Maybe, through him, we'll save ourselves.

MARTHA

We don't need to be saved. That sort of talk is ridiculous. You
can only hope that by working tonight you'll have earned the
right to drift off to sleep afterward.

THE MOTHER

That's what I meant by being saved: sleep.

MARTHA

Well, then, that salvation, I swear to you, is within our grasp.
We have to decide, Mother. It will be tonight or it won't be
at all.

CURTAINS

ACT II

SCENE I

The bedroom. Night begins to creep into the room. JAN *is looking out the window.*

JAN

Maria was right. This time of night isn't so easy.

(*pausing a moment*)

What's she doing now, what's she thinking over there in her hotel room, heart closed up tight, eyes dry, all curled up in the hollow of an armchair? Over there, evenings are promises of happiness. But here . . .

(*looking around the room*)

Come on, there's no reason for such anxiety. A person has to know what he wants. It's here in this room that everything will be settled.

A sudden knock at the door. MARTHA *enters.*

MARTHA

I hope I'm not disturbing you, sir. I wanted to bring you some
fresh towels and water.

JAN

I thought they'd already been brought.

MARTHA

No, the old servant can be a bit forgetful sometimes.

JAN

That's okay. But I hardly dare to tell you that you're not
disturbing me.

MARTHA

Why's that?

JAN

I'm not sure it would be within our arrangement.

MARTHA

You see, you're clearly incapable of answering like anyone else
would.

JAN
(*smiling*)

Give me a little time. I'll get used to it.

MARTHA
(*working*)

You're leaving soon. You won't have time for anything.

*He turns away and looks out the window. She
studies him. His back remains turned, and she
talks to him as she works.*

MARTHA

I'm sorry, sir, if this room isn't as comfortable as you might like it to be.

JAN

It's particularly clean, which is the most important thing. And besides, you've recently remodeled it, haven't you?

MARTHA

Yes. How can you tell?

JAN

A couple of details.

MARTHA

In any case, more than a few customers have complained about the lack of running water, and you can't really blame them. For some time now, we've also been meaning to install an electric bulb above the bed. If you read in bed, it's a pain to have to get up to turn off the switch.

JAN
(*turning back toward her*)

Actually, I hadn't noticed. But it doesn't seem like such a big inconvenience.

MARTHA

You're very forgiving. I'm glad our inn's many imperfections make no difference to you. I know they'd be enough to drive some people away.

JAN

Despite our arrangement, let me just say that you are quite unusual. It seems to me, for example, that the role of the innkeeper isn't to highlight the establishment's defects. Really, it almost seems as if you were trying to get rid of me.

MARTHA

That's not exactly what I had in mind.

(*making a decision*)

Though it's true my mother and I were rather hesitant about having you here.

JAN

I noticed you weren't doing much to keep me. But I don't understand why. My credit's good, I assure you, and I don't give the impression, I don't think, of a man running away from some crime.

MARTHA

No, that's not it. You don't seem like a criminal at all. We have other reasons. We've been planning to leave the hotel for some time now, and every day we tell ourselves this is the day we're going to close the place up and start packing. It would be easy enough to do, we rarely have any customers. But we didn't realize how little interest we have in our old line of work until you arrived.

JAN

So then, you'd prefer to see me go?

MARTHA

I told you, we're hesitating, and I, especially, am hesitating. In fact, the decision is mine to make, and I still don't know what I'm going to do.

JAN

Well, I don't want to be a burden on you. Please keep that in mind. I'll do whatever you'd like. But I have to say that it

would suit me to stay another day or two. I have some business
to take care of before continuing on my travels, and I was
hoping to find the peace and quiet I need here.

MARTHA

Believe me, I understand your request, and if you'd like, I'll
give it another thought.

*A moment passes. She takes an indecisive step
toward the door.*

MARTHA

You'll be going back to the country you come from, then?

JAN

Maybe.

MARTHA

It's a beautiful country, isn't it?

JAN
(*looking out the window*)

Yes, it's a beautiful country.

MARTHA

They say there are beaches over there that are completely
empty.

JAN

It's true. No trace of man at all. In the early morning, you find
seagull tracks in the sand, but that's the only sign of life. As for
the evenings—

He stops himself.

MARTHA
(*gently*)

As for the evenings, sir?

JAN

They're enough to shatter you. Yes, it's a beautiful country.

MARTHA
(*with a new sense of focus*)

I've often thought of those evenings. Visitors have told me about them, and I've read what I could. Often, on days like today, in the middle of this country's bitter spring, I think of the sea and the flowers out there.

(*pausing, then almost inaudibly*)

And what I imagine blinds me to everything else around me.

He studies her carefully, then calmly sits down
in front of her.

JAN

I understand. Spring grabs you by the throat out there, the flowers above the white walls blooming by the thousands. If you go for a walk in the hills around my city, even for just an hour, you'll come back wearing the honey scent of yellow roses on your clothes.

She sits down, too.

MARTHA

That must be marvelous. Here, what we call spring, well, it's a rose and two freshly sprouted buds in the cloister garden.

(*contemptuously*)

That's all it takes to stir the men of my country. Their hearts are like that stingy rose. A single gust of wind would shrivel them. They get the spring they deserve.

JAN

You're not being completely fair. You also get fall.

MARTHA

What's fall?

JAN

A second spring, where all the leaves are like flowers.

(*looking at her intently*)

Maybe you'd see people around here bloom in a similar way, if only you'd have a little patience with them.

MARTHA

I have no patience left for this Europe where autumn wears the face of spring and spring the scent of poverty. But I relish the thought of that other country where summer crushes everything, where winter rains drown the cities, and where, at long last, things are what they are.

> *A silence. He looks at her with greater and greater curiosity. She notices and suddenly stands up.*

MARTHA

Why are you looking at me like that?

JAN

Forgive me, but, well, seeing as we've set aside our agreement, I just want to say that it seems as if, for the first time, you just spoke to me like a human being.

MARTHA
(*violently*)

You probably misheard. And even if it were true, you'd have no reason to get all excited. The human part of me isn't the best part of me. The human part of me is the part that desires, and to get what I desire, I think I'd crush anything that stood in my way.

JAN
(*smiling*)

That's the sort of violence I can understand. But there's no reason for me to be afraid of it, seeing as I'm not an obstacle in your path. I have no reason to oppose your desires.

MARTHA

You certainly have no reason to oppose them. But you don't have any reason to fulfill them, either, and in some cases, that's enough to set things in motion.

JAN

What makes you think I have no reason to fulfill them?

MARTHA

Common sense, and a desire to keep you out of my plans.

JAN

So then, we're returning to our arrangement now.

MARTHA

Yes, and as you can clearly see, we were wrong to set it aside. But I'd like to thank you for telling me about those lands you've known, and I'd also like to apologize for having perhaps wasted your time.

(*already at the door*)

Still, I have to say that for my part, the time wasn't entirely wasted. It's awoken desires in me that had perhaps drifted off to sleep. If it's true you wished to stay here, you have, without knowing it, won your case. I'd just about decided to ask you to leave, but as you can see, you've appealed to the human part of me, and now I'd like you to stay. My taste for the sea and those countries filled with sun will win out in the end.

He looks at her for a moment without speaking.

JAN
(*slowly*)

You really have a strange way of speaking. But I'll stay, if you'll allow me to, and if it's also no inconvenience to your mother.

MARTHA

My mother's desires aren't as strong as mine. That's only natural. But it means she doesn't have the same reasons I do for wanting you here. She doesn't think about the sea and untrammeled beaches enough to admit we need you to stay. Those reasons matter only to me. But, at the same time, she doesn't really have any strong reasons to oppose me, and that's enough to settle the matter.

JAN

So then, if I've understood, one of you accepts me out of self-interest, the other out of indifference?

MARTHA

What more can a visitor ask for?

She opens the door.

JAN

Well, then, I'm happy to hear it. But surely you understand that everything seems a little strange here, the manner of speaking, the people. This house really is quite unusual.

MARTHA

Maybe the only unusual thing here is the way you're acting.

She exits.

SCENE II[22]

————

JAN
(*gazing at the door*)

Maybe that's all it is . . .

(*walking over to the bed and sitting down*)

But the only thing that girl makes me want to do is leave, find Maria, and be happy again. This whole thing is stupid. What am I doing here? But no, I'm responsible for my mother and sister. I've gone on forgetting them for too long.[23]

(*standing up*)

Yes, everything will be settled here in this room.
    But how cold it is! I don't recognize a thing. The whole

place has been redone. It looks like any other hotel room now, in any of those other foreign cities where lonely men show up each night. I've been there. At the time, it seemed there was an answer to be found. Maybe I'll find it here.

(*gazing outside*)

It's getting cloudy out.[24] And now my old anxieties are coming back to me, here in the pit of my stomach, here like a raw wound irritated by every move I make. I know its name. It's fear of eternal solitude, terror that there is no answer. And who would answer in a hotel room?

> *He walks over to the bell. He hesitates a moment, then rings it. Nothing. A moment passes in silence, then footsteps and a knock. The door opens. The* OLD SERVANT *is standing in the doorway. He remains still and silent.*

JAN

It's nothing. I apologize. I just wanted to know if someone would respond, if the bell worked.

> *The* OLD SERVANT *looks at him, then closes the door. His footsteps fade into the distance.*

SCENE III

JAN

The bell works, but he doesn't speak. That's not an answer.

(*looking to the heavens*)

What to do?

> Two knocks at the door. The SISTER enters with a tray.

SCENE IV

JAN

What's this?

MARTHA

The tea you asked for.

JAN

I didn't ask for anything.

MARTHA

Oh? The old man must have misheard.[25] Half the time he misunderstands things.[26]

> She sets the tray on the table. JAN waves at it.

MARTHA

Should I take it away?

JAN

No, no, I appreciate it all the same.

She looks at him. She exits.

SCENE V
———

JAN
(*picking up the cup, looking at it, then setting it back down*)
A glass of beer on credit, a cup of tea by mistake.

(*picking up the cup, silently holding
it a moment, then barely audible*)

O God, help me find my words or make me give up this futile
business so I can go back to Maria's love again. Give me the
strength to choose what I really want and to stick with it.

(*laughing*)

Well then, here's to the prodigal's feast!

He drinks. There's a sharp knock at the door.

JAN

Yes?

The door opens. The MOTHER *enters.*

SCENE VI

THE MOTHER

Excuse me, sir, but my daughter told me she brought you
some tea.

JAN

It's right there.

THE MOTHER

You already drank it?

JAN

Yes, why?

THE MOTHER

If you'll excuse me, I'll come take the tray.

JAN
(*smiling*)

I'm sorry for having disturbed you.

THE MOTHER

Oh, it's nothing. It's just the tea wasn't meant for you.

JAN

Ah, so that's what happened. Your daughter brought it, but I
hadn't ordered anything.

THE MOTHER
(*with a sort of weariness*)

Yes, that's what happened. It would have been better if—

JAN
(*surprised*)

I'm really very sorry, but your daughter said she wanted to
leave it and I didn't think—

THE MOTHER

I'm sorry, too. But there's no need for you to apologize. It was only a mix-up.[27]

She clears the tray and goes to leave.

JAN

Madame!

THE MOTHER

Yes.

JAN

I've just made a decision. I think I'm going to be leaving tonight, after dinner. I'll still pay you for the room, of course.

She looks at him in silence.

JAN

I can see I've caught you by surprise. Please don't think it has anything to do with anything you've done. I feel nothing but sympathy for you, great sympathy, even. But to be honest, I feel a little ill at ease here, and I'd prefer not to prolong my stay.

THE MOTHER
(*slowly*)

Oh, it's nothing to worry about, sir. In theory, you're free to do whatever you'd like. But maybe you'll change your mind between now and dinner. Sometimes you go with a gut feeling, and then things start to work out and you get used to it all.

JAN

I don't think I will, madame. But still, I wouldn't want you to
think I'm leaving unhappy. Quite the opposite, really. I'm very
grateful to you for having welcomed me as you did.

(*hesitating*)

I sensed in you a sort of goodwill toward me.

THE MOTHER

That's only natural, sir. I've no personal reason to feel hostility
toward you.

JAN
(*holding back his emotion*)

Be that as it may, if I'm telling you all of this now, it's only
because I want us to part on good terms. Maybe I'll come
back again some other time. In fact, I'm sure I will. But for the
moment, I feel I've made a mistake and have no business being
here. To be completely honest with you, I have the painful
feeling that this house is not my home.

She continues to look at him.

THE MOTHER

Yes, of course. But that's usually the sort of thing a person feels
at first.

JAN

You're right. You can see I'm a little preoccupied. And then,
it's also never easy coming back to a country you've been away
from for so long. You must understand that.

THE MOTHER

I understand what you're saying, sir, and I wish things had worked out better for you. But I don't think, on our end, there's anything more we can do.

JAN

No, certainly not, and I'm not blaming you for anything.[28] It's just that you're the first people I've encountered since being back here, so it's only natural that some of these difficulties would be first felt with you. There are more to come, I'm sure. It goes without saying, of course, that it's all on my end. I'm still a little out of sorts.

THE MOTHER

When things aren't working out, there's nothing anyone can do about it. In a way, your deciding to leave troubles me, too. But then I tell myself that, after all, I don't really have any reason to attach any importance to it.

JAN

It's quite enough that you share my troubles and that you've made an effort to understand me. I don't think I can really express how touched I am by what you just said and how happy it makes me.

(*reaching out to her*)

You see—

THE MOTHER

It's our job to make all our customers feel comfortable.

JAN
(*disheartened*)

Right. Of course.

(*pausing a moment*)

Well then, I owe you an apology and, if you think it appropriate, a little compensation.

He wipes his hand across his brow. He seems more tired. He has more trouble expressing himself.

JAN

You've probably prepared things for me and incurred some expense, so it's only natural that—

THE MOTHER

We certainly have no reason to ask for compensation. It's not for us that I regret your uncertainty, but for you.

JAN

(*leaning against the table*)

Oh, well, that's nothing to worry about. The most important thing is that we be on good terms and that you don't think too poorly of me. I'll never forget this place of yours, believe me, and I hope that, when I come back, I'll be in a better frame of mind.

She walks to the door without a word.

JAN

Madame!

She turns around. He speaks with some difficulty but finishes with more ease than he began.

JAN

I would like . . .

(*trailing off*)

I'm sorry. All this traveling has tired me out.

(*sitting down on the bed*)

I'd at least like to thank you . . . I also want you to know that, as a guest, I won't be leaving this house indifferent.

THE MOTHER

Thank you for the kind words, sir.

She exits.

SCENE VII

He watches her go. He makes a move, but in doing so, shows signs of fatigue. He seems to give in to his weariness, leaning over onto a pillow.

JAN

I'll come back with Maria tomorrow, and I'll say, "It's me." I'll make them happy. It's all so clear now. Maria was right.

(*sighing, his body half stretched out over the bed*)

Oh, I don't like how everything feels so far away tonight.

He lies down completely, speaking words that can't be heard, in a voice that's barely perceptible.

JAN

Yes or no?

He stirs. He sleeps. The stage is almost completely dark. A long silence. The door opens. The two women enter with a lamp. The OLD SERVANT *follows behind them.*

SCENE VIII

MARTHA
(after shining a light on the body, in a hushed voice)
He's asleep.

THE MOTHER
(using the same voice, but raising it little by little)
No, Martha! I don't like the way you're forcing my hand. You're dragging me into this, starting it so I'll have to finish it. I don't like the way you're walking over my doubts.

MARTHA
It's a way of making things easier. In the state you were in, I had to take action to help you.

THE MOTHER
I know it had to end like this. All the same . . . I don't like it.

MARTHA
Come on, focus on tomorrow, and let's get moving.

*She searches through his coat, pulls a wal-
let from it, and counts the bills. She empties all
of the sleeping man's pockets. While she's doing
this, his passport falls out and slips behind the
bed. The women don't see it fall out, and the
OLD SERVANT goes to pick it up, and then
he withdraws.*

MARTHA

There. Everything's ready. In just a few minutes, the river waters
will flood. Let's go down. We'll come back to get him when we
hear the water flowing over the dam. Come on, let's go.

THE MOTHER
(*calmly*)

No, we're fine here.

She sits down.

MARTHA

But . . .

(*looking at her mother, then with defiance*)

Don't think this is going to scare me. Wait here.

THE MOTHER

We'll wait, of course. Waiting is good, waiting is restful. In
a little while, we'll have to carry him along the path, all the
way out to the river, and before we've even begun, already
I'm exhausted, an exhaustion so old my blood can no longer
bear it.

(swaying back and forth as if half-asleep)

And all the while, he has no idea. He sleeps. He's through with
this world. Everything will be easy for him from now on. He'll
just slip from a slumber peopled with images to a slumber
without dreams, and what comes as a terrible wrenching for
everyone else will be nothing but a long sleep for him.

MARTHA
(defiantly)

Then let's be happy about it! I have no reason to hate him, and
I'm glad at least he'll be spared the suffering. But now . . . it
seems the waters are rising.

(listening, then smiling)

Oh, Mother, Mother, it will all be over soon.

THE MOTHER
(same manner)

Yes, it'll all be over soon. The waters are rising. And all the
while, he has no idea. He sleeps. He no longer knows the
exhausting feeling of working to make a decision, of working
to be finished. He sleeps, no longer having to steel himself, to
force himself, to demand of himself what he cannot do. The
cross of that inner life that forbids rest, diversion, or weakness
is no longer his to bear . . . He sleeps and thinks no more, no
longer has any tasks or duties, oh no, no, and I, exhausted and
old, oh, how I envy him his sleeping now and dying soon.

(silence)

You have nothing to say, Martha?

THE MOTHER

MARTHA

No. I'm listening. I'm waiting to hear the water.

THE MOTHER

In a moment. In only a moment. Yes, another moment still. And all the while happiness is, at least, still possible.

MARTHA

Happiness will be possible afterward. Not before.

THE MOTHER

Did you know, Martha, that he'd planned to leave tonight?

MARTHA

No, I didn't know that. But if I had, I'd have done the same thing. I'd already decided.

THE MOTHER

He told me that a few minutes ago and I didn't know what to say.

MARTHA

So, you saw him then?

THE MOTHER

I came up to stop him from taking a sip. But it was too late.

MARTHA

Yes, it was too late. And I have to tell you, he's the one who made up my mind for me. I was hesitating. But then he started telling me about those lands I'd been dreaming of, and by doing that, by touching me, he weaponized me against him. That's the way innocence is rewarded.

THE MOTHER

And yet, Martha, he ended up understanding. He told me he felt this house was not his home.

MARTHA
(*forceful and impatient*)

Of course this house is not his home, but that's because it's
nobody's, and nobody will ever find rest or warmth in it. If
he'd understood that a little quicker, he would have saved
himself, and we'd have avoided having to teach him that this
room of ours is made for sleeping, and this world of ours for
dying. Enough now, we—

The sound of water can be heard in the distance.

MARTHA

Listen, the water's flowing over the dam. Come, Mother, and
for the love of that God you sometimes call on, let's get this
over with.

The MOTHER *takes a step toward the bed.*

THE MOTHER

Let's go, then. Even though it seems to me that dawn will
never come.

CURTAINS

ACT III

SCENE I

The MOTHER, MARTHA, *and the* OLD SER-
VANT *are onstage. The* OLD SERVANT *is sweeping and tidying the room. The* SISTER *is behind
the counter, pulling her hair back. The* MOTHER
is crossing the set, heading for the door.

MARTHA

You can clearly see that dawn has come.

THE MOTHER

Yes, and tomorrow I'm sure I'll be glad to have gotten it over
with, but right now the only thing I feel is how exhausted
I am.

MARTHA

This is the first morning in years I've been able to breathe.[29] It's
as if I can already hear the sea. I feel so happy I could scream.

THE MOTHER

All the better, Martha, all the better. But now I feel so old I
can't really share in any of this with you. Tomorrow, everything
will be better.

> MARTHA

Yes, everything will be better, I hope. But just, please, don't go on complaining. Let me sit back and be happy for a minute. I can feel myself turning back into the girl I once was. My body burns once more, and, oh, how I feel like running. Oh, just tell me—

She stops.

> THE MOTHER

What is it, Martha? I no longer recognize you.

> MARTHA

Mother . . .

(hesitating, then fiery)

Am I still beautiful?

> THE MOTHER

You are, this morning. Crime is beautiful.[30]

> MARTHA

What does crime matter now? I'm being born for a second time. I'm going to a land where I'll be happy.

> THE MOTHER

That's nice. I'm going to have a rest. But I'm happy to know life is finally about to begin for you.

> *The* OLD SERVANT *appears at the top of the stairs and descends toward* MARTHA, *hands her the passport, then exits without saying a word.*

MARTHA *opens the passport and reads it without reaction.*

THE MOTHER

What's that?

MARTHA
(*in a calm voice*)

His passport. Read it.

THE MOTHER

You know very well my eyes are tired.

MARTHA

Read it! You'll recognize his name.

The MOTHER *takes the passport, goes to sit at a table, spreads out the booklet, and reads. For a long time, she stares at the page in front of her.*

THE MOTHER
(*in a neutral voice*)

Well, I always knew it would turn out like this, and then I'd have to go and end it.

MARTHA
(*coming out in front of the counter*)

Mother!

THE MOTHER
(*same manner*)

Let me be, Martha. I've lived long enough. I've lived a lot longer than my son did.[31] I didn't recognize him, and I killed him. Now I can go off and join him at the bottom of the river, there where the grass already covers his face.

MARTHA

Mother! You're not going to leave me all alone, are you?

THE MOTHER

You've been a great help to me, Martha, and I'm sorry to leave you. If it still means anything, I have to say that you have, in your own way, been a good daughter. You've always shown me the respect you owed me. But my strength's all gone now, and this old heart of mine, which thought it had turned away from the world, has once again learned to feel grief. I'm no longer young enough to deal with it. And anyway, when a mother is no longer able to recognize her own son, her role on this earth is over.

MARTHA

Not if her daughter's happiness is yet to be achieved. I don't understand what you're saying to me. I don't recognize the words coming out of your mouth. Didn't you teach me to respect nothing?

THE MOTHER
(*in the same indifferent voice*)

Yes, but I—I've just learned I was wrong, and that on this earth where nothing's guaranteed, we have our certainties.

(*with bitterness*)

A mother's love for her son is my certainty today.

MARTHA

Aren't you certain a mother can love her daughter?

THE MOTHER

I wouldn't want to hurt you now, Martha, but it's true that it's not the same thing. It's not as strong.[32] How could I live without my son's love?

MARTHA
(*blistering*)

A love so fine it forgot you for twenty years!

THE MOTHER

Yes, a love so fine it survived twenty years of silence. But what does it matter? It's a love fine enough for me, given I can't live without it.

She stands up.

MARTHA

You couldn't possibly say that without some shadow of rebellion, without a thought for your daughter.

THE MOTHER

No, I have thoughts of nothing now, much less rebellion. It's punishment, Martha, and I suppose the time comes when all murderers feel as I do, empty on the inside, barren, with no possible future. That's why we lock them away. They're good for nothing.

MARTHA

You're speaking that language I despise. I can't bear to hear you talk of crime and punishment.

THE MOTHER

I say what comes to my lips, nothing more. Oh, I've lost my freedom, and hell is on the way.[33]

MARTHA
(*coming at her, violently*)

You never said any of that before. All these years, you've stood right there by my side, and with a firm hand, you've lifted the legs of those who had to die. You weren't thinking of freedom

and hell then. You kept right on doing what you'd been doing.
What can your son possibly change about that?

THE MOTHER

I kept on doing what I'd been doing. That's true. But out of
habit, like a dead person. All it took was a little grief to bring
me around. That's what my son came to change.

MARTHA *makes a move as if to speak.*

THE MOTHER

I know, Martha. It's not rational. What can grief possibly
mean to a criminal? But you can see it's not the sort of pain
a real mother would feel. I haven't even cried out yet. No,
it's nothing more than the suffering of love reborn, and yet,
it's more than I can bear. I know this suffering has no reason
either.

(*with a new tone*)

But I, who've tasted it all, from creation to destruction, I have
to say, the world itself isn't rational.

With conviction, she heads for the door, but
MARTHA *steps in front of her and blocks the*
doorway.

MARTHA

No, Mother, you're not going to leave me. Don't forget that
I'm the one who stayed and he's the one who left, that you've
had me by your side your whole life while he left you in silence.

A price has to be paid for that. It has to be taken into account.
You have to come back to me.

THE MOTHER
(*gently*)
What you say is true, Martha, but him . . . I killed him.

MARTHA *half turns away, head tilted back,*
seeming to look at the door.

MARTHA
(*after a silence, with growing passion*)
Everything life can give to a man has been given to him. He
left this country. He's known other places, the sea, people who
are free. Me? I stayed here. I stayed, small and dark, bored,
sunk in the heart of the continent, growing up in the thick
of the land. My lips have never been kissed, and not even
you have ever seen me without my clothes on. I swear to you,
Mother, a price has to be paid for that, and you cannot rob me
right as I was about to receive what I'm owed, not on the vain
pretext that a man has died. What you have to understand is
that for a man who has lived, death is but a small concern. We
can forget about my brother, your son. What happened to
him is of no importance: he had nothing left to learn. But I,
you deprive me of everything and strip me of everything he's
enjoyed. Must he also take my mother's love from me, take it
down to that icy river of his forever?

They look at each other in silence. The SISTER
lowers her eyes. Very low.

MARTHA

I'd settle for so little. There are some words I've never known
how to say, Mother, but it seems to me there would be such
sweetness in going back to our normal, everyday life.

The MOTHER *takes a step toward her.*

THE MOTHER

You recognized him?

MARTHA
(*suddenly lifting her head*)

No! I didn't recognize him. Not a single image of him remained
in my head. What happened was meant to happen. You said it
yourself—this world of ours isn't rational. But you're not entirely
wrong to ask the question. If I had recognized him, I know now
it wouldn't have changed a thing.[34]

THE MOTHER

There are moments even the most hardened murderers lay
down their arms.

MARTHA

I've known such moments, too. But if I were going to bow my
head, it wouldn't have been to an unknown and indifferent
brother.

THE MOTHER

To whom, then?

MARTHA *bows her head.*

MARTHA

To you.

Silence.

THE MOTHER
(*slowly*)

Too late, Martha. There's nothing more I can do for you.

(*turning to her daughter*)

Are you crying, Martha? No, you wouldn't know how. Do you remember when I used to hold you tight?

MARTHA

No, Mother.

THE MOTHER

That makes sense. It was a long time ago and I so quickly forgot how to open my arms to you. But I've never stopped loving you.

> *She gently nudges* MARTHA *aside, who lets herself be moved, little by little, from the passage.*

THE MOTHER

I know that now, now that my heart has started speaking, now that I'm alive again, right as I can no longer bear to go on living.

> *The passage is clear.*

MARTHA
(*putting her face in her hands*)

But then what could be stronger than your daughter's desperation?

THE MOTHER

Exhaustion, maybe, and a thirst for rest.

> *She exits without her daughter trying to stop her.*

SCENE II

> MARTHA *runs to the door, slams it shut, presses herself against it. She bursts into feral screams.*

MARTHA

No! It wasn't for me to be my brother's keeper, yet here I am, exiled in my own country, rejected by my own mother. But it wasn't for me to be my brother's keeper. This is the injustice done to innocence. Look how he's got what he wanted, while I am still alone, far from the sea for which I thirst. Oh, how I hate him! My entire life's been spent waiting for the wave that would carry me away, and now I know it'll never come. Now I'm left to live with, on my right and on my left, in front of me and behind, crowds of peoples and nations, of plains and mountains that block out the sea breeze, smothering its repeated calls with their chattering and murmuring.

(*lower*)

Others are much luckier. There are some places, places as far from the sea as this, where the evening wind occasionally carries the scent of seaweed, where it speaks of humid beaches, alive with the cries of seagulls, or of strands of golden shore stretching off into nights without end. But the wind dies long before it ever reaches here, and I know I'll never get what I'm owed. Even if I were to press my ear to the ground, I still wouldn't hear the icy waves crashing or the measured breathing of a happy sea. I'm too far from what I love, and my distance has no remedy. I hate him. I hate him for having got what he wanted. Me? My homeland is this crude, landlocked place where the sky has no horizon.[35] My hunger knows only this country's[36] sour plum trees, and my thirst has nothing but the blood I've spilled. That's the price a person pays for a mother's affection.

Well then, let her die! She doesn't love me. Let all the doors be slammed shut around me. Let her leave me to my righteous indignation. Before I die, I will not lift my eyes and pray to heaven. Out there, where you can escape, can be delivered, can roll in the waves and press your body against another's, out on that land defended by the sea, the gods dare not set foot. But here where your gaze is blocked off on all sides, all the land is designed to draw the face upward and make the gaze pray. Oh, I hate this world that reduces us to God. Nobody's ever set me on my feet, not I who suffers such injustice. I will not kneel. Deprived of my place on this earth,[37] rejected by my mother, alone with my crimes, I'll leave this world unreconciled.

There's a knock at the door.

SCENE III

MARTHA

Who's there?

MARIA

A visitor.

MARTHA

We're not accepting any more guests.

MARIA

I've come to meet my husband.

She enters.

MARTHA
(*looking at her*)

Who's your husband?

MARIA

He arrived yesterday and was supposed to meet me this morning. I'm surprised he hasn't done so yet.

MARTHA

He said his wife was abroad.

MARIA

He has his reasons for that. But we're supposed to meet now.

MARTHA
(*who hasn't stopped staring at her*)

That will be difficult for you. Your husband's not here anymore.

MARIA

What do you mean? Didn't he rent a room here?

MARTHA

He rented a room, but he left during the night.

MARIA

I have a hard time believing that, given all the reasons I know he has for staying here. But the way you're speaking worries me. Say whatever it is you have to say.

MARTHA

I have nothing to say, other than that your husband is no longer with us.

MARIA

I don't understand. He couldn't have left without me. Did he go for good or did he say he'd be back later?

MARTHA

He's gone for good.

MARIA

Listen to me. All I've been doing since yesterday is waiting, waiting here in this foreign land, and now my patience has run out. Worry drove me here to find my husband, and I will not leave until I see him or find out where he is.

MARTHA

That's none of my business.

MARIA

You're wrong about that. It is your business. I don't know if my husband would approve of what I'm about to tell you, but I'm tired of all this carrying on. The man who arrived here yesterday morning is your brother, the one you haven't heard from in years.

MARTHA

You're not telling me anything I don't already know.

MARIA
(*blistering*)

Then what's going on? Why isn't your brother here, at home?
Didn't you recognize him, and weren't you and your mother
happy to have him back?

MARTHA

Your husband isn't here because he's dead.[38]

> MARIA *gives a start, remaining silent for a
> moment, staring intently at* MARTHA. *Then she
> smiles and makes a move as if to approach her.*

MARIA

You're pulling my leg, aren't you? Jan often said that, even as a
little girl, even then you already took pleasure in making other
people squirm. We're practically sisters and—

MARTHA

Don't touch me. Stay right where you are. We share nothing in
common.[39]

(*pausing a moment*)

Your husband died last night, and I can assure you I'm not
pulling your leg. There's nothing left for you here.

MARIA

You're crazy! Stark raving mad! No, it's too sudden. I can't
believe you. Where is he? Let me see his dead body. That's the
only way I'll believe what I can't even begin to imagine.

MARTHA

That's impossible. Where he is now, no one can see him.

MARIA *makes a move toward her.*

MARTHA

Don't touch me, stay right where you are. He's at the bottom
of the river where my mother and I carried him last night, after
we put him to sleep. He didn't suffer, but he did die, and it was
us, his mother and I, who killed him.

MARIA
(*recoiling*)

No, no . . . It's me, I'm the one who's gone crazy, hearing
words no one on earth's ever heard before. I knew no good
would come of this place, not for me, but I'm not prepared
to give into such madness. I don't understand. I don't
understand you . . .

MARTHA

It's not my job to convince you, only to inform you. You'll
come around to the truth in your own time.

MARIA
(*as if lost in her head*)

Why—why did you do this?

MARTHA

What gives you the right to question me?

MARIA
(*crying out*)

My love gives me the right!

MARTHA

What does that word even mean?

MARIA

It means everything that's now tearing me up inside, gnawing
away at my bones, this delirium that's opening my hands to

murder. If it weren't for this stubborn disbelief stuck in my heart, oh, you lunatic, you'd learn what the word means when you felt your face being torn apart beneath my fingernails.

MARTHA

Clearly you speak a language I don't understand. I have a hard time with words like love and joy and grief.

MARIA
(*with a great effort*)

Listen to me. Let's stop this game, if that's what it is. Let's not get lost in a maze of empty words. Tell me, very clearly, what I very clearly want to know, before I lose control.

MARTHA

It's hard to be any clearer than I've already been. Last night, we killed your husband to take his money, as we've done with several other visitors before him.

MARIA

So then, his mother and sister are criminals?

MARTHA

Yes.

MARIA
(*still with the same effort*)

Had you already figured out he was your brother?

MARTHA

If you must know, there was a misunderstanding. And if you understand anything at all about the world, you won't be surprised.

MARIA
(*returning to the table, wrists against her chest, in a dull voice*)

Oh, God,[40] I knew this little game could end only in blood.

That we both, he and I both, would be punished for taking
part in it. Misfortune was written in the stars.

(*stopping in front of the table and speaking
without looking at* MARTHA)

He wanted you to recognize him, wanted to come back home
again, to bring you happiness, but he couldn't find the right
words. And while he was looking for his words, you killed him.

(*beginning to cry*)

And there you were, like two lunatics, blind to the wonderful
son who'd come back to you . . . and he was wonderful . . .
and you've no idea what a proud heart, what a discerning soul
you've just killed. He could have been your pride and joy, just
as he's been mine. But alas, you were his enemy—you are his
enemy—you who can speak so coldly about something that
should send you running out into the streets, kicking and
screaming like a wild animal.

MARTHA

Judge nothing, for you don't know everything. By now my
mother has rejoined her son and the currents have begun to eat
away at them. Soon enough, they'll be found, and then they'll
be placed in the same soil together. I see no reason why any of
this should make me run out kicking and screaming. I have a
different idea of the human heart, and, to be perfectly honest,
your tears disgust me.

MARIA
(*turning back to her with hatred*)

These are the tears of a joy forever lost. Trust me, for you, they're better than the dried-out grief that will soon come, that could kill you without a second thought.

MARTHA

Nothing you've said has had the least effect on me. Really, it's all rather insignificant. I, too, have seen and heard enough, and I've decided it's time to go, only I don't want to get all mixed up with them. What do I want with their company? I'll leave them to their newfound affection, to their dark embrace. Neither you nor I have any part in it anymore. To us, they'll be forever unfaithful. Fortunately, I still have my room, and it'll be a good place to die alone.

MARIA

Oh, you can go and die, and the whole world with you. I've lost the one I love. Now I have to live with that terrible solitude and the torture it makes of every memory.

> MARTHA *comes up behind her and speaks over her head.*

MARTHA

Don't exaggerate. You've lost your husband and I've lost my mother, and now we're even, after all. But you've lost him only once, after years of happiness together, having never been rejected by him. Me? My mother rejected me, and now she's dead, and I've lost her twice.

MARIA

He wanted to share his wealth, to make you both happy. That's what he was thinking about, alone, in his room, while you were preparing his death.

MARTHA
(*voice suddenly filled with hopelessness*)

Your husband and I are also even. I felt the same desperation he did. Like him, I believed I had a home. I imagined crime was the hearth around which my mother and I were forever united. Who in this world could I turn to if not to the one who'd killed beside me? But I was wrong. Crime is its own form of solitude, even if a thousand people commit it together. So it's only right I should die alone, after having lived and killed alone.

MARIA *turns toward her in tears.*

MARTHA
(*recoiling and returning to her hardened voice*)

Don't touch me! I already told you not to touch me. The thought of a human hand being able to impose its warmth on me before I die, the thought that anything resembling such hideous human affection could still hunt me down, it makes the blood rushing to my temples boil.

They turn to face each other, standing very close together.

MARIA

Don't worry. I'll let you die as you wish. I'm blind now. I can't even see you. And neither you nor your mother will ever be but fugitive faces met and lost amid a tragedy that never ends. I feel neither hatred nor compassion for you. I can no longer love or loathe anyone.

(*suddenly hiding her face in her hands*)

In truth, I've hardly had time to suffer or rebel. The misfortune is greater than I am.

> MARTHA, *who'd turned away and taken a couple of steps toward the door, comes back toward* MARIA.

MARTHA

But not great enough, if you can still cry about it. And so I see I still have something left to do before I leave you forever. I still have to render you hopeless.

MARIA
(*looking at her in horror*)

Oh, leave me alone! Just go away and leave me alone!

MARTHA

Indeed, I am going to leave you, and it'll be a relief for me, too. I can hardly bear all your love and tears. But I can't die leaving you with the idea that you're right, that love isn't in vain, that this has all been some sort of accident, for it's now that everything's in order, and it's of that you must be convinced.

MARIA

And what order is that?

MARTHA

The one where no one's ever recognized.

MARIA
(*lost*)

Oh, what do I care, I can barely hear you. My heart's been ripped out and torn to shreds. All that matters to it is the man you killed.

MARTHA
(*violently*)

Shut up! I don't want to hear any more talk of him. I loathe him! He's nothing to you anymore. He's gone to that bitter house now, the one we're exiled to forever. The fool! He got what he wanted, he found who he was looking for, and now here we all are, everything in order. Understand, then, that neither for him nor for us, neither in life nor in death, is there ever any peace or homeland.

(*with a contemptuous laugh*)

Because you can't really call that a homeland, can you? Down deep there in that soil deprived of light, that place you go to feed blind creatures.

MARIA
(*in tears*)

Oh, God! I can't . . . I can't bear the way you're speaking, and he wouldn't have been able to bear it, either. The whole reason he set out on this journey was to find another homeland.

MARTHA
(*reaching the door and turning suddenly*)

That madness got what it had coming. Soon, you'll get what's
coming to you.

(*with the same laugh*)

We're being robbed, I tell you. What's the point of this great
call, this emergency of the soul? Why cry out for the sea or
love? It's pathetic. Well, your husband knows the answer now:
it's that dreadful house where we'll all eventually be packed
nice and tight together.

(*with hatred*)

One day you too will know the answer, and on that day, if
you could, you'd look back on this moment with delight, this
moment when you believed you'd received the most heart-
wrenching of exiles. Understand, then, that your grief will
never equal the injustice done to man, and let me wrap things
up with a little advice. I certainly owe you some advice, don't I,
seeing as I killed your husband.

Pray to your god and ask that he make you like stone. That's
the sort of happiness he saves for himself, and it's the only true
happiness there is. Do as he does, then, and deafen yourself
to all the world's cries, become stone while you still can. But
if you feel too cowardly to take part in such speechless peace,
then come on and join us in that home we all share. Goodbye,
sister! It's all very easy, you see. All you have to do is choose

between the dumb happiness of stones and that slimy bed where we'll be awaiting you.[41]

> *She exits.* MARIA, *having grown more disoriented as she listened, wobbles and puts her hands out in front of her.*

MARIA
(*crying out*)

Oh, God, I can't live in this desert. Hear me calling on you, and I'll find my words.

> (*falling to her knees*)

Yes, hear me calling, I place myself in your hands. Have mercy on me, turn yourself toward me! Hear me, give me your hand! Have mercy, Lord, on those who love each other and who have now been parted!

> *The door opens and the* OLD SERVANT *appears.*

SCENE IV
———

THE OLD SERVANT
(*in a crisp, clear voice*)

You called me?

MARIA
(*turning toward him*)

Oh, I don't know. But please help me. I need someone to help
me. Have mercy and say that you'll help me.

THE OLD SERVANT
(*in the same voice*)

No.

CURTAINS

State of Emergency

───────

A PLAY IN THREE PARTS

For Jean-Louis Barrault

Foreword

In 1941, Barrault had the idea of putting together a play based on the plague myth, a topic that had also tempted Antonin Artaud. Over the next couple of years, it began to seem that the simplest thing, for his given purpose, would be to adapt Daniel Defoe's essential book, *A Journal of the Plague Year*, as a framework for the stage production.

When he heard I was going to publish a novel on the subject, he asked if I'd like to write dialogue for the framework he'd created. I had other ideas. In particular, I thought it would be better to set Daniel Defoe aside and return to Barrault's original concept.

In short, our task was to imagine a myth that would make sense to a contemporary audience, one situated here in 1948. *State of Emergency* is the manifestation of that attempt, and it's one I have the weakness of believing is worthy of some attention. But:

(1) It should be absolutely clear that no matter what anyone says, *State of Emergency* is no way an adaptation of my novel.

(2) It's not a play with a traditional structure, but one whose stated ambition is to combine many different forms of dramatic expression, from lyrical monologues to collective theater, on through mime, straightforward dialogue, farce, and the use of a chorus.

(3) If it's true I wrote all the text, the fact nevertheless remains that Barrault's name should be listed right next to mine. We weren't able to do so, for reasons that seem respectable enough, but it should be absolutely clear that I remain in Jean-Louis Barrault's debt.

November 20, 1948
A.C.

State of Emergency was staged for the first time on October 27, 1948, by the Compagnie Madeleine Renaud–Jean-Louis Barrault at the Théâtre Marigny (directed by Simonne Volterra).[1]

Score by Arthur Honegger.

Set design and costumes by Balthus.

Directed by Jean-Louis Barrault.

CHARACTERS[2]

The Plague	The Secretary
Nada	Victoria
The Judge	The Judge's Wife
Diego	The Governor
The Alcalde	The Men of the City
The Women of the City	The Guards

PART ONE

PROLOGUE

—————

A musical overture built around what sounds like an air-raid siren.

The curtain rises. The stage is completely dark.

The overture fades out, giving way to the sound of the air-raid siren, which continues to drone in the distance.

Suddenly a comet appears in the background, moving from stage left to stage right.

The light from the comet reveals, in silhouette, the walls of a fortified Spanish city, as well as several people standing with their backs to the audience. The figures are motionless, their heads turned up toward the comet.

The clock strikes four. The dialogue is hard to make out, as if murmured.

—It's the end of the world!

—Come on, man!

—If the world dies . . .

—Come on, man. The world, maybe, but not Spain.

—Spain can die, too, you know.

—On your knees!
—The comet's evil! It's trouble!
—Not Spain, man, not Spain.

> *Two or three heads turn. One or two people
> begin to cautiously move about, then everything
> falls still again. The droning gets more intense,
> grows earsplitting, and develops into an ominous
> musical accompaniment, almost clear enough to
> be a voice. While this is happening, the comet
> is growing larger than ever before.[3] Suddenly a
> woman cries out, the dreadful sound instantly
> silencing the music and returning the comet to its
> normal size. The woman runs offstage, breathless.
> The town square begins to buzz with activity. The
> dialogue, a little clearer and more sibilant, is still
> not fully comprehensible.[4]*

—It's a sign of war!
—It certainly is!
—It's a sign of nothing.
—That depends.
—That's enough. It's the heat.
—The Cádiz heat.
—Enough.
—The whistling's too loud.
—It's really deafening.
—It's a curse on the city!
—Oh, no! A curse on you, Cádiz!
—Silence! Silence!

*Everyone is again staring up at the comet
when the voice of a civil guard* OFFICER *is heard,
clear and comprehensible this time.*

THE OFFICER

Go home. You've seen what you've seen, and all that you've
seen is a whole lot of sound and fury. Sound and fury,
signifying nothing. In the end, Cádiz is still Cádiz.

A VOICE

Still, it's a sign, and signs don't appear for nothing.

A VOICE

O great and dreadful God![5]

A VOICE

War's coming, that's what the sign's about.

A VOICE

No one believes in signs these days, you dog! Fortunately, we're
far too smart for all that.

A VOICE

Yeah, and talking about that kind of stuff will get your face
smashed in, you filthy pig. That's what you are. And you know
what we do to pigs around here? We bleed 'em!

THE OFFICER

Go home. War is our business, not yours.

NADA

Oh, dear! If only that were true! No, what's true is that officers
get to die tucked comfortably in bed, while the gun blasts and
sword blows, those are set aside for the rest of us!

A VOICE

Nada, here comes Nada. Here he is, the fool himself!

A VOICE

What's the meaning of all this, Nada? You must know.

NADA
(*he's disabled*)

What I have to say, you don't want to hear. You'll only laugh. Why don't you ask the student over there? He'll be a doctor soon. Me? I'm gonna have a little talk with my bottle.

He lifts a bottle to his lips.

A VOICE

What's he talking about, Diego?

DIEGO

What's it to you? Keep your heart strong. That's the only thing you have to worry about.[6]

A VOICE

Ask the civil guard officer.

THE OFFICER

The civil guard thinks you're disturbing the peace.

NADA

The civil guard is lucky. It has such simple ideas.

DIEGO

Look, it's coming back—

A VOICE

O great and dreadful God.

The droning begins again. The comet passes for the second time.

—Enough!
—That's enough!

—Cádiz!

—It's whistling!

—It's a curse . . .

—On the city . . .

—Silence! Silence!

> *The clock strikes five. The comet disappears.*
> *Daybreak.*

NADA
(*perched atop a boundary stone, snickering*)

There you have it! I, Nada, light of this city by dint of my
erudition and understanding, drunkard by dint of my disdain
for all things and my disgust for honorifics, mocked by
men for having held fast the freedom born of contempt, I,
following this little light show we've just witnessed, I'd like to
give you a warning, free of charge. I wish to inform you that
we are where we are now, and that, more and more, we're going
to be where we are now.

Mind you, we were already here, but it took a drunkard like
me to see it. Where is it? Where are we? That's for you, men of
reason, to figure out. Me? My opinion's always been the same,
and I'm resolute in my principles: life is worth death, man is
the wood out of which pyres are built. Oh, believe me, you're
in for it now. That comet's a bad sign. A warning bell tolling
just for you!

Oh, you think that's farfetched, do you? Well, I'm
not surprised. So long as you're able to have your three meals
a day, work your eight hours, and keep your two women,
you're able to go on imagining everything's in order and all's

well with the world. No, all's not well and everything's
not in order—it's in a line. You're all lined up nice and
neat, a calm look about you, perfectly ripe for the picking.
Go on, good people, the warning's been given, and I'm at
peace with my conscience. As for the rest, don't you worry
about a thing—they'll look after you up there. And
you know what that means: they're not always the most
accommodating.

JUDGE CASADO

Don't be blasphemous, Nada. You've been running around
taking potshots at heaven for a long time now.

NADA

Did I mention heaven, Judge? Well, in any case, I approve
of what they do up there. I'm a judge, too, in my own way.
And besides, I've read in books that it's better to be heaven's
accomplice than its victim. And just so you know, I've got a
feeling heaven's not to blame for all this. So long as men go on
smashing windows and breaking faces, you'll notice that the
good Lord, who knows what's what, will seem like nothing but
a choirboy.

JUDGE CASADO

It's libertines like you who bring celestial warnings down upon
us. For it is a warning indeed. One sounded for all whose
hearts are corrupt. Be afraid, for the worst is yet to come, and
pray God that he pardon your sins. On your knees, then! On
your knees, I tell you!

Everyone begins to kneel, except NADA.

JUDGE CASADO

Be afraid, Nada, be afraid and get down on your knees.

NADA

I can't kneel, not with this paralyzed, unbending knee. As for fear, I'm prepared for anything, even the worst thing, by which I mean, of course, your morals.

JUDGE CASADO

So, you believe in nothing, then, you wretch?

NADA

Nothing in this world, aside from wine, and nothing in heaven, either.

JUDGE CASADO

Forgive him, O God of mine, for he knows not what he says. Spare this city of your children.

NADA

Ite, missa est.[7] Diego, come treat me to a bottle over at the Sign of the Comet. You can tell me how things are going with your lovers.

DIEGO

I'm about to marry the judge's daughter, Nada, and I'd rather you not go on offending her father. It offends me, too.

Trumpets. A HERALD *surrounded by guards.*

THE HERALD

By order of the governor, each of you are to return to your regularly scheduled tasks. Good governments are governments in which nothing happens. Such is the will of the governor, that nothing should happen in his government, so that it may remain as good as it's always been. Rest assured, then, inhabitants of Cádiz, that nothing that's happened here today is worth the trouble of getting alarmed or upset about. For this reason, each of you, from this six o'clock hour onward, must take it as a given that no comet whatsoever has ever appeared on the horizon of this city. Anyone who contravenes this decision, any resident who speaks of comets as anything other than past or future astral phenomena, will be punished with the full weight of the law.

Trumpets. He leaves.

NADA

Well, Diego, what'd you say? That's a new twist!

DIEGO

It's a bunch of nonsense! Lying is always a bunch of nonsense.

NADA

No, it's a policy, and one I approve of, given it's designed to suppress everything. Oh, what a good governor we have here. If his budget's in the red, if he's fooling around outside the home, he simply cancels the deficit and denies the affair. Cuck, your wife *is* faithful, and you, cripple, you *can* walk, and you blind people, *look*: the moment of truth is upon us!

DIEGO

Speak no evil, you old windbag. The moment of truth is the moment the death march begins.

NADA

Precisely. Death to the world! If I could have it all right here in front of me, like a bull trembling on its hooves, its little eyes burning with hatred, drool lining its pink muzzle like dirty lace, oh boy, what a time we'd have! This old hand of mine wouldn't hesitate to swiftly sever the spine of that blasted beast and strike it down for all eternity!

DIEGO

You despise too many things, Nada. Conserve your contempt—you'll need it later.

NADA

I need nothing. I'll hold my contempt tight till the day I die, and nothing of this earth, neither king nor comet nor moral, nothing will ever rise above me.

DIEGO

Relax. Don't raise yourself up so high. We'll like you a lot less way up there.

NADA

I am above all things, and desire nothing more.

DIEGO

No one's above honor.

NADA

What is honor, my son?

DIEGO

It's what keeps me going.

NADA

Honor is a past or future astral phenomenon. Suppress it.

DIEGO

All right, Nada, I have to go. She's expecting me, and really, that's the reason I don't believe in this catastrophe you claim is coming. I have to focus on being happy, which is a big enough job on its own, one that requires peace in both town and country.

NADA

I already told you, my son: we're already there. Hope for nothing. The show's about to begin, and I've barely enough time to run over to the market to raise a glass, at last, to the indiscriminate killing that's about to get under way.

The stage goes dark.

END OF PROLOGUE

Lights. The stage is astir, the gestures livelier, the movements more rushed. Music. The shopkeepers raise their shutters, clearing the front of the set. The marketplace is now visible. Little by little, the people's CHORUS *fills the marketplace, rejoicing. They are led by the fishermen.*

THE CHORUS

Nothing is happening, nothing will happen. Fresh and ripe, fresh and ripe! We're not about to be picked clean, not with the summer's abundance having just arrived.

(cry of joy)

Spring has barely ended, and already that golden orange of summer hurtles across the sky, rising as it does at the peak of the season, and drizzling down over Spain in a stream of honey, while all the fruits of all the summers of the world—gooey grapes, butter-colored melons, figs plump with blood, apricots ablaze—all come rolling into the stalls of our market at the same time.

(cry of joy)

O fruits! Here, tucked in wicker baskets, they complete
the long and precipitous race that brought them from the
countryside, there where they began to weigh heavy with
water and sugar, where they hung above warm blue meadows,
amid the fresh gushing of a thousand sun-drenched springs,
the springs gradually gathering into a single youthful stream,
the stream sucked up by the roots and trunks and led to the
heart of the fruit, fattening it, making it heavier and heavier,
and eventually flowing out of it as an inexhaustible fountain of
slow-moving honey.

Plumper, plumper, and plumper still! So plump the
rains from the heavens above eventually cause them to sink
to the opulent grasses below, and it's from there they roll
off and embark on the rivers, travel the long lengths of all
the world's roads, and are greeted at all four corners of the
horizon by the people's joyful whispering, by the clarion calls
of summer (*brief trumpet blast*) coming from the human
cities in droves, testifying that the earth is sweet and that the
nourishing heavens remain faithful in their role of gathering
abundance.

(*collective cries of joy*)

No, nothing is happening. Summer has arrived, bearing
offerings, not the catastrophe of vines picked clean. Winter
will come later, so leave the stale bread for tomorrow. Today,
sea bream, sardines, langoustines, fish, fresh fish from calm
seas, cheese, rosemary cheese, goat milk as frothy as soapsuds,
and on marble platters, meat done up in a white paper crown,
meat scented with clover, providing blood, sap, and sunshine

for man's rumination. Have a bite! Raise a toast! Let's drink
to the riches of the season. Let's drink until oblivion. Nothing
will happen!

*Hurrahs. Cries of joy. Trumpets. Music. In all
four corners of the market, brief scenes unfold.*

FIRST BEGGAR

Spare some change, my man, some change, Grandma.

SECOND BEGGAR

Better late than never!

THIRD BEGGAR

You hear what we're saying?

FIRST BEGGAR

Nothing's happened, that much is obvious.

SECOND BEGGAR

But maybe something will happen.

He steals a watch off a passerby.

THIRD BEGGAR

Always give charity. Better to be safe than sorry!

Over at the fish stalls:

THE FISHERMAN

Sea bream as fresh and pink as a carnation, the flower of the
seas right here, and you come to complain?

OLD WOMAN

Your sea bream is dogfish.

THE FISHERMAN

Dogfish! Never been a dogfish in my shop until you got here, you old witch.

OLD WOMAN

Oh, my. You are your mother's son. Can't you see this white hair of mine?

THE FISHERMAN

Fly away, you old comet!

Everyone stops, fingers held to lips.

Over at VICTORIA'*s window,* VICTORIA *is on the inside of the bars and* DIEGO *is on the outside:*

DIEGO

It's been so long!

VICTORIA

You loon, we've only been apart since eleven this morning.

DIEGO

Yes, but your father!

VICTORIA

My father said yes. We were sure he'd say no.

DIEGO

I was right to walk straight up to him and look him in the eye.

VICTORIA

You were right. But while he was thinking about it, I closed my eyes and listened to that distant gallop growing inside me, getting closer and closer, the beats quicker and quicker, and more and more of them, too, until my whole body was trembling—and then father said yes, and so I opened my eyes, and the world's first morning was there before me. In the corner of the room where we'd been, I saw the black horses of love still quivering, only now they were calm and at peace. It was for us they were waiting.

DIEGO

As for me, I was neither deaf nor blind. All I could hear was my blood gently champing at the bit. My joy was suddenly without impatience. Behold, O city of light, you've been delivered to me for life, from now until the hour the earth comes calling. Tomorrow, we'll set out together, the two of us riding on the same saddle.

VICTORIA

Yes, and speaking our own language, too, even if others think it crazy. Tomorrow, you'll kiss my lips. Just looking at yours, I can feel my cheeks burning. Say, is that the stormy southern wind?

DIEGO

It is the stormy southern wind, and it's burning me, too. Where do I find the fountain that will cure me of all this?

He approaches the window, and she puts her arms through the bars and squeezes his shoulders.

VICTORIA

Oh, it hurts to love you so much! Come closer.

DIEGO

How beautiful you are!

VICTORIA

How strong you are!

DIEGO

What is it you wash this face of yours with to make it as white as almonds?

VICTORIA

I wash it with pure water. It's love that makes it graceful.

DIEGO

Your hair is as fresh as night.

VICTORIA

Because every night I wait for you by my window.

DIEGO

Is it pure water and night that's left the scent of lemon trees on you?

VICTORIA

No, that blew in on the wind of your love, a wind that, in only a single day, has covered me in flowers.

DIEGO

The flowers will fall.

VICTORIA

The fruits await you.

DIEGO

Winter will come.

VICTORIA

But it will come with you. Do you remember what you sang to me that first time? It's still true, isn't it?

DIEGO

A hundred years after I shall die
The earth will ask me
If I've finally forgotten thee
And I shall reply, No, not I![8]

She's silent.

DIEGO
You're not saying anything.

VICTORIA
The happiness has me all choked up.

Over at the ASTROLOGER'S *tent:*

THE ASTROLOGER
(*speaking to a woman*)
My beautiful child, the sun crossed through Libra at the
moment of your birth, which means you may consider yourself
under the rulership of Venus, your ascendant sign being Taurus,
which, as everyone knows, is governed by Venus. Thus, your
nature is to be affectionate, loving, and easygoing. Delight in
this knowledge, but beware, for Taurus makes you susceptible
to celibacy, which risks leaving all these precious qualities of
yours unemployed. In fact, I can see Venus and Saturn coming
together, a combination unfavorable to marriage and children.
Moreover, this coming together is a harbinger of odd appetites
that make one fearful of future ills affecting the belly. But don't
dwell on this. Rather, seek out the sun, which strengthens
the mind and morale, and which rules over the stomach's
movements. Choose Tauruses as friends, my dear, and don't
forget that your position is well oriented, easy, and favorable,
and that it may keep you bathed in joy. That'll be six francs.

The ASTROLOGER *takes the money.*

THE WOMAN

Thank you. You're sure about what you've told me, aren't you?

THE ASTROLOGER

Always, my dear child, always. But beware! Nothing's happened this morning, that much is obvious, and what hasn't happened can turn my reading upside down. I'm not responsible for what hasn't happened.

The woman leaves.

THE ASTROLOGER

Horoscopes here, get your horoscope read! The past, the present, the future, all of it guaranteed and fixed in the stars! Fixed, I say!

(*spoken as an aside*)

If comets start getting all mixed up in things, this job's gonna be impossible. I'll have to become a governor or something.

GYPSIES
(*in unison*)

A friend who wishes you well . . .

A brunette who smells of orange . . .

A wondrous trip to Madrid . . .

The Americas' heritage . . .

INDIVIDUAL GYPSY

After your blond friend dies, you'll receive a dark letter.

On a makeshift stage set up in the background, drum roll.

ACTORS

Open your beautiful eyes, graceful ladies, and you, gentlemen, lend your ears! These actors here, the greatest and most famous in the kingdom of Spain, have been persuaded—and it was no easy task, mind you—to step away from the court and out into this market to perform, for your pleasure, *The Spirits,* a sacred act by the immortal Pedro de Laribala. A play that'll leave you breathless, that's been swiftly lifted on the wings of genius, up to the heights of universal acclaim. A prodigious production so beloved by our king that he had it performed twice a day, a production he'd still be glued to at this very moment if I hadn't convinced this unparalleled troupe of actors of the urgency and the benefit in bringing it here to this market for the edification of the citizens of Cádiz, the most discerning in all of Spain! So step right up, the show is about to begin.

> *The play begins, but the actors can't be heard, their voices smothered by the hustle and bustle of the market.*

—Fresh and ripe, fresh and ripe!
—See the lobster woman, half woman, half fish!
—Fried sardines! Fried sardines!
—The greatest of all escape artists here, no prison capable of constraining him!
—Try some tomatoes, my lovely. They're as smooth and pure as your heart.
—Lace and wedding linens!
—No pain and no spiel, Pedro will pull your teeth, no big deal!

NADA
(*coming out of the tavern, drunk*)

Smash it all up! Puree the tomatoes and heart. Imprison the great escape artist and bust in Pedro's teeth. Death to the astrologer, who won't have seen that one coming. Let's have a bite of this lobster woman and abolish everything that can't be drunk!

> *A lavishly dressed foreigner, a* MERCHANT, *enters the market surrounded by a large gathering of girls.*

THE MERCHANT
Come get your comet ribbons, comet ribbons here!

EVERYONE
Shh! Shh!

> *They go over to him and explain the foolishness of his words.*

THE MERCHANT
Come get your astral ribbons, astral ribbons here!

> *Everybody buys a ribbon.*

> *Cries of joy. Music. The* GOVERNOR *and his entourage arrive in the market, and everyone settles in to listen.*

THE GOVERNOR

Your governor has come to greet you, and he is delighted to see you assembled here as usual, carrying out these little tasks that create such peace and prosperity for Cádiz. No, certainly nothing's changed, and that's a good thing. Change irritates me—I love my habits!

A MAN OF THE PEOPLE

No, Governor, nothing's really changed. The rest of us, we poor people, we can assure you of that. We just scrape by each month. We survive on onions, olives, and bread, and as for chicken stew,[9] we're happy knowing other people are able to eat it every Sunday night.[10] This morning, there was a buzz in the city, and above the city, too. In truth, we were scared. We were scared something was about to change and all us poor wretches would suddenly be forced to eat chocolate.[11] But thanks to you, gracious governor, with your help, we now understand that nothing's happened and that our ears have simply deceived us. We are most reassured by you.

THE GOVERNOR

The governor is delighted to hear this. Nothing good can come of something new.

THE ALCALDES[12]

Well said, Governor! Nothing good can come of something new. The rest of us, we alcaldes, appointed for our wisdom and years of experience, we would like to believe that our gracious poor people over there weren't putting on airs of irony just now. Irony is a virtue that tears things down. A gracious governor prefers the type of vices that build up.

THE GOVERNOR

Until then, may nothing move! I am the king of immobility!

THE TAVERN DRUNKS
(*surrounding* NADA)

Yes, yes, yes! No, no, no! Let nothing move, gracious governor.
Everything's spinning around us, and how much suffering it
all brings. We want immobility! Let all movement cease. Let
everything be suppressed, except for wine and folly.

THE CHORUS

Nothing's changed! Nothing is happening and nothing has
happened! The seasons spin on their axis, and in the smooth
sky circulate sage celestial bodies whose calm geometry
condemns those crazy and subversive stars setting fire to
the sky's prairies with their flaming tresses, disturbing the
planets' sweet music with their screaming air-raid sirens,
throwing off gravity's eternal laws with their wake, causing the
constellations to grind, paving the way for fatal collisions of
stars at all the sky's crossroads. In truth, everything is in order,
the world is in balance. This is the prime of the year, the height
of the still season. Happiness, happiness! Summer's arrived!
Whatever else may be, here we take pride in our happiness.

THE ALCALDES

If heaven has its habits, you can thank the governor, for he is
the king of habits—and he doesn't like crazy hair, either. No,
his whole kingdom is well combed.

THE CHORUS

Well behaved! Well behaved we will remain, given nothing's
ever going to change. What would we do, hair blowing in the
wind, eyes inflamed, mouths screeching? We'll take pride in
others' happiness.

THE TAVERN DRUNKS
(*surrounding* NADA)

Suppress movement, suppress it, suppress! Don't move, let's not move a muscle! Let the hours flow by, and this reign will remain uneventful. The still season is the season closest to our hearts, because it's the hottest one, and it leads us to drink.

> *The air-raid siren, which has been buzzing in the background for a while now, suddenly reaches a fever pitch, while two muted but immense blows reverberate in the background. On the makeshift stage, an actor continues his pantomime, advancing toward the audience, then staggering and falling. The other actors immediately surround him. Not a word, not a movement: absolute silence.*

> *A couple of seconds of stillness, and then a general hurrying about.*

> DIEGO *cuts his way through the crowd, which is slow to part, and comes upon the man.*[13]

> *Two doctors arrive and examine the body, then step to one side and have a heated discussion.*

> *A young man asks one of the doctors what's going on, but the doctor shoos him away. The young man presses him for information, and, encouraged by the crowd, pushes for an answer, shakes him, makes appeals, and eventually finds*

himself so close to the doctor that their lips are practically touching. A sharp inhalation, as if the young man had sucked a word from the doctor's mouth. He steps to one side and, with great difficulty, as if the word were too big for his mouth and the effort to get it out too great, announces:

—The Plague.

Everyone goes weak-kneed, each repeating the word louder and louder, faster and faster as they all begin to flee, crisscrossing around the GOVERNOR, *who has climbed back up onto his platform. The movement accelerates, grows more frenzied, and turns to panic. When the voice of an old* PARISH PRIEST *is heard, the people stop where they are, standing in groups.*

THE PARISH PRIEST

To the church, to the church! The punishment has now arrived. That old evil sickness is upon the city! It is he whom the heavens have always sent to cities overrun with corruption, sent to smite them for their mortal sin. Your cries will be crushed in your lying mouths and a mark will be blazed upon your heart. Pray, now, for our god of justice to forgive and forget. Get thee to church! Get thee to church!

Some of them rush to the church, while others robotically turn left and right, the death knell ringing out. On the third platform, the ASTROLOGER,

as if making a report to the GOVERNOR, *speaks in
a completely neutral voice.*

THE ASTROLOGER

A malignant coming together of hostile planets has just been
written in the stars. It serves as an announcement of drought,
famine, and plague for all comers—

A group of gossiping women blanket his voice.

—He had this enormous thing stuck to his throat, sucking
his blood out with so much force it sounded like it was using
a straw!
—It was a spider, a big, black spider!
—Green, it was green!
—No, it was a sea lizard!
—Are you blind? It was an octopus, as big as a human cub.
—Diego, where's Diego?
—So many people are going to die that there won't be anyone
left alive to bury them.
—Oh! If only I could get out of here.
—Get out! Get out!

VICTORIA

Diego, where's Diego?

*Throughout this scene, the sky fills with signs,
and the air-raid siren grows louder and louder,
accentuating the general sense of terror. A
man, face in the spotlight, steps out of a house and
yells, "The world ends forty days from now!"*[14]

*and panic again sets in, people crisscrossing the
stage, repeating, "Forty days from now, the end
of the world." Guards come and arrest the man in
the spotlight, while on the other side of the stage a
SORCERESS appears, handing out remedies.*

THE SORCERESS

Lemon balm, mint, sage, rosemary, thyme, saffron, lemon
peel, almond paste . . . Hear ye, hear ye, these remedies are
infallible!

*A cool wind rises as the sun begins to set, caus-
ing people to raise their heads.*

THE SORCERESS

The wind! Here comes the wind! Pestilence abhors the wind.
Everything will get better now, you'll see.

*As she's speaking, the wind dies down, the
air-raid siren once again grows louder, the two
muted but immense blows reverberate, a little
more deafening this time, a little bit closer.
Two men in the middle of the crowd fall to the
ground. All go weak-kneed, then back away, trying to distance themselves from the bodies. Only
the SORCERESS stays where she is, the two men
lying at her feet, their groins and throats bearing
the markings. The sick men writhe, reaching out
two or three times, and then die as night slowly*

descends over the crowd, which continues to back farther and farther away, out toward the sides of the stage, the corpses left alone in the center.

Darkness.

A light goes on in the church. A spotlight illuminates the king's palace. A light goes on in the JUDGE's *house. The action alternates between these locations.*[15]

AT THE PALACE

THE FIRST ALCALDE

Your honor, the epidemic has taken off with a rapidity exceeding our resources. The neighborhoods are more contaminated than we'd initially thought, which leads me to believe it would be best for us not to say a word, to hide the truth from the people at all costs. And anyway, the sickness is mostly attacking the poor and overpopulated outskirts at the moment, and though our situation is unfortunate, at least that's something we can be happy about.

Murmurs of approval.

AT THE CHURCH

THE PARISH PRIEST

Come forth and let each publicly confess the worst sin he's
committed. Open your hearts, ye who are damned! Tell
each other the evils you've done and those you've thought of
doing, lest sin's poison suffocate you and lead you as surely
straight to hell as this many-tentacled plague will . . . I, for
my part, confess that I'm often guilty of not giving enough
charity.

> *Three mimed confessions will play out during
> the following dialogue.*

AT THE PALACE

THE GOVERNOR

Everything's settled then. The annoying thing is that I was
supposed to go hunting today. These things always seem to
crop up when one has important business to take care of.
Whatever is one to do?

THE FIRST ALCALDE

You don't want to miss the hunt, even if you go only to set an
example. The city needs to see that you're able to show calm in
the face of such adversity.

AT THE CHURCH

EVERYONE

Forgive us, O Father, for what we've done and for what we've yet to do.

AT THE JUDGE'S HOUSE

The JUDGE, *surrounded by his family, reads psalms.*

THE JUDGE

"The Lord is my refuge and my fortress.
He will deliver me from the fowler's trap
And from the murderous plague."[16]

THE WIFE

Can't we go out and do something, Casado?

THE JUDGE

You've already gone out and done enough for one lifetime, woman. And it hasn't made us any happier.

THE WIFE

Victoria hasn't come back yet, and I'm worried something bad has happened to her.

THE JUDGE

You never took the time to think of what bad things might happen to you—and that's how you lost your honor. Stay inside. This house is a respite amid the pestilence. I've planned everything out so that we can stay barricaded here for the duration of the plague and wait for it to end. God willing, we will suffer nothing.

THE WIFE
You're right, Casado, but we're not the only ones around. Other people are suffering. Victoria may be in danger.

THE JUDGE
Forget other people. Think of this house. Think of your son, for example. Hoard all the supplies you can, price be damned. Reap them, woman, reap them! The time has come to reap them!

(reading)

"The Lord is my refuge and my fortress ..."

AT THE CHURCH

The following is taken up.

THE CHORUS
You need have no fear
Neither from the terrors of the night
Nor the arrows that fly through the day
Neither from the plague that creeps through the shadows
Nor the epidemic that shows up in midafternoon.

A VOICE
O great and dreadful God!

> *The town square is illuminated. People mean-*
> *der to the rhythm of a copla.*

THE CHORUS

You've signed your name in the sand.
You've written it on the sea.
All that's left is pain and suffering.

> VICTORIA *enters. Spotlight on the town square.*

VICTORIA

Diego? Where's Diego?

A WOMAN

He's with the sick. He's taking care of the ones who call out
to him.

> *She runs to the end of the stage and collides*
> *with* DIEGO, *who's wearing the same type of*
> *mask the plague doctors wear. She backs away,*
> *screaming.*

DIEGO
(*gently*)

Are you that scared of me, Victoria?

VICTORIA
(*with a small cry*)

Oh, Diego! At last, it's you. Take off that mask and hold me
tight. Hold me, hold me, and I'll be saved from this evil sickness.

> *He doesn't move.*

VICTORIA

What's changed between us, Diego? I've been looking for you
for hours, tearing through the city, terrified by the thought
that this evil sickness may have come for you, too, and here
you are, wearing that awful mask of suffering and disease. Get
rid of it, please get rid of it, and take me in your arms!

He takes off the mask.

VICTORIA

When I see your hands, my mouth runs dry. Kiss me!

He doesn't move.

VICTORIA

Kiss me, Diego, I'm dying of thirst. Have you forgotten we
were engaged only yesterday, you to me and me to you? I
waited all night for day to come, the day you'd kiss me with
everything you've got. Now! Quickly!

DIEGO

I feel such pity, Victoria!

VICTORIA

And I do, too, but I pity us. And that's why I've been looking
for you, running through the streets calling your name, my
arms outstretched to entwine with yours.

She takes a step toward him.

DIEGO

Don't touch me! Keep your distance!

VICTORIA

Why?

DIEGO

I don't even recognize myself anymore. I've never been afraid
of another human being, but this, this is something else.
Honor's no use to me now. I can feel myself giving in.

She takes a step toward him.

DIEGO

Don't touch me. The sickness may already be inside me, and
if it is, I'd pass it on to you. Wait a minute. Let me catch my
breath. This exhaustion's suffocating. I can't even remember
how to turn these people over in their beds anymore. My
hands are shaking from the horror of it all, my eyes are clogged
with pity.

(*cries and moans*)

But still they call out to me. Can you hear? I have no choice
but to go to them. Take care of yourself. Take care of us. This,
too, shall pass, that much is certain!

VICTORIA

Don't leave me.

DIEGO

This, too, shall pass. I'm too young and I love you too much
for it to be otherwise. Death gives me the chills.[17]

VICTORIA
(*rushing toward him*)

I'm alive. Me!

DIEGO
(*recoiling*)
How shameful, Victoria, how shameful.

VICTORIA
Shameful? Why shameful?

DIEGO
I think I must be scared.

Moans are heard. He rushes off toward them.

People meander to the rhythm of a copla.

THE CHORUS
Who is right and who is wrong?
Belies that
everything on earth is lies.
That the only truth is death.[18]

Spotlight on the church and on the GOVER-
NOR's *palace.*

Psalms and prayers at the church.

The FIRST ALCALDE *addresses the people
from the palace.*

THE FIRST ALCALDE
Order of the Governor: From this day forward, as a sign of
penitence with regard to our common misfortune, and to avoid

the risk of further contagion, all forms of public gathering are prohibited, and all forms of entertainment, too. Furthermore—

A WOMAN
(*yelling out from amid the crowd*)

There! There! They're hiding one of the dead ones over there. We can't allow it. We'll all be tainted! Shame on you! It must be buried.

> *Chaos and confusion. Two men go and drag the woman away.*

THE ALCALDE

Furthermore, the governor is now in a position to reassure city dwellers regarding changes to the unexpected pestilence that has befallen our city. In the opinion of all doctors, the wind rising from the sea will be enough to drive the plague out. God willing—

> *Two immense blows interrupt the* ALCALDE, *followed by two more, while the death knell wildly tolls and prayers surge from the church in waves. Then a terrified silence settles over everything, during which two strangers appear onstage, a* MAN *and a woman. All eyes follow them. The man is corpulent, his head bare. He wears a sort of uniform with a medal on it. The woman is also wearing a uniform, but with a collar and white cuffs. In her hand, she carries a notepad. They move toward the governor's palace and salute him.*

THE GOVERNOR

What do you strangers want from me?

THE MAN
(*in a courteous tone*)

Your position.

ALL

What? What did he say?

THE GOVERNOR

I have to say, your timing is rather poor, and such insolence could end up costing you dearly. But no doubt we've simply misunderstood each other. Who are you?

THE MAN

You'll never guess!

THE FIRST ALCALDE

I don't know who you are, stranger, but I know where you're going to end up!

THE MAN
(*calm and composed*)

Very impressive, you are. What do you think, my dear? Do we really need to tell them who I am?

THE SECRETARY

Usually, we're a little more graceful about it.

THE MAN

Perhaps these gentlemen are pressed for time.

THE SECRETARY

No doubt they have their reasons. After all, we're only visitors here, and we have to respect the customs of the places we visit.

THE MAN

I hear you, but don't you think it might create a bit of chaos among these sensible folks?

THE SECRETARY
A bit of chaos is better than rudeness.

THE MAN
You're quite convincing, but I do still have a few concerns ...

THE SECRETARY
There are two possibilities ...

THE MAN
I'm listening ...

THE SECRETARY
Either you say it or you don't say it. If you say it, then they'll know. If you don't say it, then they'll find out.

THE MAN
It's perfectly clear to me now.

THE GOVERNOR
Enough of this! Before I proceed to take the appropriate measures, I'll ask you one last time: Who are you and what do you want?

THE MAN
(as calm as ever)
I am the plague. And you?

THE GOVERNOR
The plague?

THE MAN
Yes, and I need to take your position. I'm sorry to have to do so, believe me, but I've got a lot of work ahead of me. If I were to give you, oh, two hours, let's say, would that be enough time for you to hand over power to me?

THE GOVERNOR
Okay, now you've gone too far, and you're going to have to be punished for this little charade of yours. Guards!

THE MAN

Wait! I don't want to force anyone. My policy is always to do things the right way. I understand that my conduct may seem surprising, and that, really, you don't know me, but I'd like it very much if you would cede your position to me without forcing me to prove myself. Won't you take my word for it?

THE GOVERNOR

I don't have time to waste on this nonsense. This joke's already gone on long enough. Arrest this man!

THE MAN

Then we're going to have to resign ourselves to what has to be done, but this is all so tedious and annoying. My dear friend, would you like to go ahead and strike someone from the list?

> *He points an arm toward one of the guards.*
> *The* SECRETARY *appears to cross something out*
> *on her notepad. A dull thud sounds. The* GUARD
> *falls. The* SECRETARY *examines the body.*

THE SECRETARY

Everything's in order, as it should be, Your Honor. The three marks are in place.

(to the others, in a friendly tone)

One mark, and you're suspect. Two, and you've been infected. Three, and you're struck from the list. Nothing could be simpler.

THE MAN

Ah, I forgot to introduce you to my secretary. Of course you already know her, but one meets so many people these days . . .

THE SECRETARY

They're forgiven! Besides, they always recognize me in the end.

THE MAN

You can see how good-natured she is! Cheerful, content, comfortable in her own skin.

THE SECRETARY

I can't take credit for any of that. It's so much easier to work when you're surrounded by fresh flowers and smiles.

THE MAN

An excellent policy. But let's get back to the topic at hand!

(*to the* GOVERNOR)

Have I given you sufficient proof of my seriousness? You've nothing to say? Well then, of course, I must have frightened you. But this whole thing goes completely against my wishes, believe me. I would have preferred an amicable arrangement, a deal based on mutual trust, guaranteed by your word and mine, a gentleman's agreement, if you will. After all, it's not too late to do it the right way. Does the two-hour time frame seem sufficient to you now?

The GOVERNOR *shakes his head no.*

THE MAN
(*turning toward the* SECRETARY)

How unpleasant this is!

THE SECRETARY
(*shaking her head*)

So stubborn, this one! All these delays!

THE MAN
(*to the* GOVERNOR)

Yet, I'd still like to obtain your consent. I'd rather not take any action without your agreeing to it. Doing so would go against my policies. My colleague will therefore proceed with striking as many names from the list as is necessary to obtain your freely given approval of the small reform I've suggested. Are you ready, my dear friend?

THE SECRETARY

A moment to sharpen my pencil—its tip gets a bit blunt—and then all will be for the best in this best of all possible worlds.[19]

THE MAN
(*sighing*)

This job really would be quite unbearable without your optimism.

THE SECRETARY
(*sharpening her pencil*)

The perfect secretary is certain that everything can always be fixed, that there are no irreparable accounting errors, no missed appointments that can't be rescheduled. No cloud without a silver lining. War itself has its virtues, and even cemeteries can be good business propositions, so long as leases on land in perpetuity are revoked every ten years or so.

THE MAN

A golden tongue, you have. Has your pencil found its point?

THE SECRETARY

It has, and we may begin.

THE MAN

Here we go!

> *The man points at* NADA, *who steps forward*
> *and bursts out in a drunken laugh.*

THE SECRETARY

Might I point out to you that this one's the sort of person who believes in nothing, and that such a person could be quite useful to us?

THE MAN

Good point. Let's take one of the alcaldes, then.

> *Panic among the* ALCALDES.

THE GOVERNOR

Stop!

THE SECRETARY

A good sign, Your Honor!

THE MAN
(*attentive and eager to please*)

Is there something I can do for you, Governor?

THE GOVERNOR

If I turn things over to you, will my life, the lives of my loved ones, and those of the alcaldes be saved?

THE MAN

But of course. That is how it works, you know.

The GOVERNOR *confers with the* ALCALDES,
then turns to the people.

THE GOVERNOR

People of Cádiz, you understand, I'm sure, that everything
has changed now, and that it's only with your best interests in
mind that I'm handing the city over to this new power that's
come before us. The deal I've negotiated will undoubtedly
save us from the worst occurring, and it will give you peace of
mind knowing that a working government will continue to
function outside your walls, a government that may one day
be of use to you. I need not tell you that my submission, er, so
to speak, has nothing to do with my own personal safety, but
instead—

THE MAN

Forgive me for interrupting, but it would please me to see you
publicly clarify that you're voluntarily agreeing to these rather
useful arrangements and that this is of course a deal made of
your own free will.

The GOVERNOR *looks to the side. The* SECRE-
TARY *raises the pencil to her mouth.*

THE GOVERNOR

Right. Of course. I've negotiated this new deal of my own
free will.

*He stammers, backs away, and makes his
escape. The crowd begins to disperse.*

THE MAN
(*to the* FIRST ALCALDE)

Come now, don't be off so quickly! I could use a man who has
the people's trust, a man through whom I can make my wishes
known.

The FIRST ALCALDE *hesitates.*

You will, of course, accept . . .

(*to the* SECRETARY)

My dear . . .

THE FIRST ALCALDE

But of course. It's a great honor.

THE MAN

Perfect. So then, with that agreed upon, my dear, you're to
inform the alcalde of our bylaws, which he's then to make
known to these fine people so that they can begin living within
regulations.

THE SECRETARY

Ordinance drawn up and issued by the first alcalde and his
advisors.

THE FIRST ALCALDE

But I haven't drawn anything up yet.

THE SECRETARY

We've spared you the trouble, and anyway, it seems to me you
should be flattered that our team has gone to the trouble of
drafting a document you'll have the honor of signing.

THE FIRST ALCALDE
Certainly, but—

THE SECRETARY
Ordinance acting as an official promulgation in full compliance with the wishes of our beloved sovereign[20] to announce regulations and charitable assistance for those of our citizens touched by infection, and to set forth all other rules, and to appoint all other persons, such as supervisors, guards, executors, and gravediggers, whose solemn oath shall be to strictly enforce orders given to them.

THE FIRST ALCALDE
What kind of language is this, pray tell?

THE SECRETARY
It's to get them used to a bit of obfuscation. The less they understand, the more obediently they act. With that in mind, here are the ordinances you're to have cried out in the town square, one after the next, so that even the slowest of minds will find them easy to swallow. Here come our messengers. Their friendly faces will help fix in place the memory of their words.

The messengers introduce themselves.

THE PEOPLE
The governor's running away, the governor's running away!

NADA
As is his right, people, as is his right. He is the state, and the state must be protected.

THE PEOPLE

He was the state, and now he's nothing. With him running
away, it's the plague that's the state now.

NADA

What's it matter to you? The plague or the governor, it's still
the state.

> *The people wander around, seeming to look*
> *for the exits. A messenger steps out of the crowd.*

THE FIRST MESSENGER

All infected homes must now be marked with a black star
in the middle of the door, at least a foot wide, adorned with
the following inscription: "We are all brothers." The star is
required to remain in place, under full penalty of the law, until
the house is cleared to reopen.

> *He steps aside.*

A VOICE

What kind of law's that?

ANOTHER VOICE

The new kind, of course.

THE CHORUS

Our masters said they'd protect us, yet here we are, left all
alone. Terrible mists are beginning to thicken all throughout
the city, slowly smothering the scent of fruits and flowers,
staining the season's glory, stifling the summer jubilation.
O Cádiz, city of the sea! Only yesterday, the desert wind grew

thick as it passed over Africa's gardens, as it traveled across
the strait, arriving here, reaching out to make our daughters
swoon, but now the wind, the only thing that could purify the
city, has died. Our masters said nothing would ever happen,
and now we see that the others were right, that something
is happening, that we are in the midst of it, that we have to
escape, and escape without delay, before the doors are shut,
sealing us up with our misfortune.

THE SECOND MESSENGER

All primary foodstuffs shall from this day forth be at the
disposal of the community, which is to say that they will be
distributed in equal minuscule portions to all those who can
prove their loyal allegiance to the new society.

The first door closes.

THE THIRD MESSENGER

All lights shall be extinguished by 9:00 P.M., after which no
private citizen may remain in any public place or move about
in the city streets without an authorized pass, which will only
be issued in the rarest of cases and always arbitrarily. Any
attempt to circumvent these regulations will be punished by
the full weight of the law.

VOICES
(*crescendoing*)

—They're going to close the doors.
—The doors are closed.
—No, they're not all closed yet.

THE CHORUS

Run! Run for the ones that are still open. We are the sons of
the sea, and it's there, it's there we must reach, there, a country
without walls or doors, there where virgin beaches lie with sand
cool and fresh as lips, there where the horizon runs so far into
the distance it's exhausting. Run to the wind. To the sea! At last,
the sea, the open sea, the waters that cleanse, the wind that frees!

VOICES

To the sea! To the sea!

The exodus begins in earnest.

THE FOURTH MESSENGER

It is strictly forbidden to provide assistance to any person
struck with illness, unless that assistance is delivered as a
denunciation of the individual, who will then be taken care
of by the authorities. Denouncing members of one's own
family is highly recommended and will be rewarded with the
allocation of a double share of food rations, otherwise known
as the patriot's share.

The second door closes.

THE CHORUS

To the sea! To the sea! The sea will save us. What can sickness
and war do to the sea? It has seen and covered so many
governments! It offers nothing more than red mornings and
green evenings, and from evening to morning, waters endlessly
lapping through nights overflowing with stars!

O solitude, desert, baptism by salt! To be alone before the
sea, in the wind, facing the sun, finally freed from these cities
sealed up like tombs, from these human faces locked away by
fear. Quick! Quick! Who will deliver me from man and his
terrors? I was happy at the peak of the season, abandoned
amid the fruit, with nature's balance and the benevolent
summer. I've loved the world, Spain and I together, but I can
no longer hear the sound of the waves, only the clamor, the
panic, the insults and cowardice, only my brothers heavy with
sweat and anguish, now too heavy to bear. Who will return me
to the seas of forgetfulness, the calm waters of the open sea, its
liquid roads and covered wakes? To the sea! To the sea, before
the doors are closed!

A VOICE

Quick! Don't touch that guy. He was near the dead!

A VOICE

He's got the markings!

A VOICE

Get away! Get away!

They hit him. The third door closes.

A VOICE

O great and dreadful God!

A VOICE

Quick! Grab the essentials, the mattress and the birdcage.
Don't forget the dog's collar. The pot of fresh mint, too. We'll
chew our way to the sea.

A VOICE

Thief! Thief! He took the embroidered tablecloth from my wedding.

They give chase. They catch him. They knock him around. The fourth door closes.

A VOICE

Hide that, would you! Hide our provisions.

A VOICE

I have nothing for the road. Won't you give me some bread, brother? I'll give you my guitar. It's inlaid with mother-of-pearl.

A VOICE

This bread's for my children, not for people who go around calling themselves my brother. Relatives come in degrees.

A VOICE

Bread! All my riches for a single loaf of bread!

The fifth door closes.

THE CHORUS

Quick! There's only a single door left open! The pestilence is moving faster than we are. It hates the sea and doesn't want us to reach it. There where nights are calm and the stars spin above the masts. What will the plague make of this place? It wants to keep us beneath it. It loves us in its own special way. It wants us to be happy in the way it wants us to be happy, not in the way we want to be happy. Forced pleasures, a cold life,

happiness in perpetuity. Everything is settling in place, and
we can no longer feel that ancient wind blowing fresh against
our lips.

A VOICE

Don't leave me, Father! I'm one of your poor children.

The priest flees.

THE POOR MAN

He's running away! He's running away! Hold me close.
It's your job to take care of me. If I lose you, then I've lost
everything.

The priest escapes. The POOR MAN *falls to the
ground and cries out:*

THE POOR MAN

Christians of Spain, you've been forsaken!

THE FIFTH MESSENGER
(*enunciating each word clearly*)

Finally, and in summary . . .

The PLAGUE *and his* SECRETARY *stand in
front of the* FIRST ALCALDE, *smiling and con-
gratulating one another.*

THE FIFTH MESSENGER

In order to avoid airborne communication of the contagion,
given that words themselves can spread infection, every
inhabitant is now ordered to hold a vinegar-soaked swab in

their mouth at all times, which will protect the individual
from sickness, while also encouraging discretion and silence.

> *From this point forward, all of the characters
> will have a handkerchief in their mouth, and as a
> result, fewer voices will be heard, and the orches-
> tra will grow softer and softer. The* CHORUS,
> *which began with multiple voices, will end up
> with only a single voice, and the final pantomime
> will unfold in complete silence, the characters'
> cheeks puffed out, lips sealed.*

> *The last door slams shut.*

THE CHORUS

Misfortune! Misfortune! We're alone now, we and the plague.
The last door has closed, and we'll no longer hear a single thing.
The sea is too far off in the distance. Now we're left to suffer, to
walk circles around this narrow city, this city without trees or
waters, this city padlocked behind tall, slick doors crowned with
screaming crowds. Cádiz has become a bullring, black and red,
and ready for the ritualized murders to commence. Brothers,
this misery is beyond any fault of our own. We don't deserve this
prison.[21] Our hearts weren't innocent, but we loved the world
and its summers: that should have been enough to save us. The
winds are dying down and the sky is emptying. We're about to
be silenced for a good long while, so one last time, before our
lips are sealed by terror's gag, let us cry out in the desert.

> *Moans and silence.*

*All that remains of the orchestra are the
bells. The buzz of the comet slowly resumes. The
PLAGUE and his SECRETARY appear in the governor's palace. The SECRETARY moves forward,
scratching a name out with each step she takes,
the beating of a drum punctuating each flick of
her wrist. NADA sniggers as the first death cart
creaks past.*

*The PLAGUE stands at the top of the set and
flicks his wrist. Everything stops, movements and
sounds.*

The PLAGUE speaks.

THE PLAGUE

I am in charge now. Me! That's a fact, and therefore a right.
But it's the type of right that's not open for discussion: you just
have to get used to it.

Indeed, make no mistake about it—if I'm in charge, then
we're going to do things my way, in which case it would be
more accurate to say that I make things operate. All of you,
you Spaniards, you tend to be a little romantic and all too
ready to see me as a black king, some sort of sumptuous insect.
Everyone knows you need your fill of pathos! Well, guess
what? I don't carry a scepter—no, not me. I carry the look of
something more like a noncommissioned officer. That's one
of the reasons you're so vexed by me, and it's good for you to
be vexed: you've got a whole lot left to learn still. Your king

has black nails and a pressed uniform. He presides not from
a throne but from a chair. The barracks are his palace, the
courthouse his hunting lodge. The state of emergency has been
declared.

That's why, you'll note, when I arrive, pathos exits. It's
forbidden, pathos is, along with a few other mood swings, such
as those ridiculous agonies of happiness, the stupid faces of
lovers, the selfish contemplation of nature, and the culpability
of irony. Instead of all that, I bring you organization.[22] It'll be
a little upsetting at first, but eventually you'll understand that
clear organization is much better than cloudy pathos. In order
to illustrate this beautiful thought, I'll begin by separating the
men from the women, this action backed by the force of law.

The guards take action.

THE PLAGUE

Your days of monkeying around are over. Now, it's time to get
serious.

I think you know what I mean. Starting today, you'll
learn to die according to schedule. In the past, you died in
the Spanish way, more or less at random, anyone's guess as to
when, if you will. You died because it got cold after having
been hot, because your mule stumbled, because the horizon
of the Pyrenees was blue, because in spring the Guadalquivir
River attracts the lonely, or because there exist foul-mouthed
fools who kill for profit or honor, even though it's far more
distinguished to kill for the pleasures of logic. Yes, you died
poorly. A dead person here, a dead person there, this one

in bed, that one in the bullring: pure libertinism. Happily, though, a little administration can clean up such disorder. The same death will be administered to everyone, according to a well-ordered list. You'll have your file, and you'll no longer die on a whim. Fate will be so much the wiser moving forward, stationed behind its office desk. You'll all be statistics now, which means you'll finally have some use, because, oh, yes, I forgot to tell you: you're going to die, that much is obvious, but after you die, you'll be cremated, too . . . or even before . . . it's more sanitary that way, and sanitary is part of the plan. Spain first!

So, get yourselves all lined up in rows, because to die well, that's the most important thing! At that price, you'll gain my favor. But beware of unreasonable ideas, the passions of the soul, as you say, those little fevers that lead to such great rebellions. I've suppressed such indulgences and put logic in their place. I abhor difference and unreason. Starting today, you'll be reasonable, which is to say you'll wear your badges. A bubonic star marked on your groin, yes, but also one worn beneath the armpit, there for all to see, the designation that you've been infected. The others, those who are convinced these things are of no concern to them, those who continue to line up outside the bullrings on Sundays, they'll keep their distance from those of you who are suspect. But don't be bitter: it *does* concern them. They are on the list, and I never forget a name. Everyone is suspect, and that's a good place to begin.

Indeed, none of this prevents me from being sentimental. I love birds, the first violets, the fresh mouths of young girls. Such things can be refreshing from time to time, and it's true that I am an idealist. My heart . . . But now I'm getting a little soft, and I don't want to take things too far. So then, let me sum it all up. I'm here to bring you silence, order, and absolute justice. I'm not asking you to thank me—it's only natural that I do these things for you—but I do demand your active collaboration. My government is now in session.

CURTAINS

PART TWO

*A square in Cádiz. On the left side of the stage, the
cemetery caretaker's lodge. On the right side, a quay.
Near the quay, the* JUDGE's *house.*

*As the curtain rises, gravediggers outfitted in prison
uniforms are sifting through the dead. A cart squeaks
from somewhere in the wings, then rolls into view and
stops at the center of the stage. The prisoners load it. The
cart continues on its way toward the caretaker's lodge.
As it reaches the entrance to the cemetery, military
music begins to play, and the front-facing wall of the
caretaker's lodge slides open so that the audience can
see inside. It looks like a schoolyard. The* SECRETARY
*is sitting above ground level, as if on a throne. A little
below her are a couple of tables, the kind from which
ration cards are distributed. The* FIRST ALCALDE *sits
behind one of the tables, his mustache white, his func-
tionaries surrounding him. The music grows louder.
On the other side of the stage, guards round up various people in the vicinity and lead them to the front
of the caretaker's lodge, and also inside of it, men and
women in separate groups.*

The center of the stage is illuminated. From the top

> *of his palace, the* PLAGUE *directs an army of invis-*
> *ible workers who can be seen only in a slight stirring*
> *around the edges of the set.*

THE PLAGUE

Come on, people, hurry it up. Things move rather slowly in
this city, that much is clear. Not the hardest workers, these
people. No, they're more the leisurely sort. Me? I can conceive
of such inactivity only in barracks or waiting lines.[23] That's
the right sort of leisure, the kind that drains both heart and
legs. The sort of leisure that serves no purpose. Hurry it up!
Finish putting up my tower, so surveillance can get under
way. Surround the city in barbed hedges. To each their own
spring—mine bears roses made of iron. Light the ovens, they'll
be our bonfires. Guards! Mark our star on the houses I plan to
take good care of. You, my dear friend, start drawing up our
lists and preparing our certificates of existence.[24]

The PLAGUE *exits.*

THE FISHERMAN
(*serving as the coryphaeus*[25])

A certificate of existence? What's that for?

THE SECRETARY

What's that for? How would you be able to live without a
certificate of existence?

THE FISHERMAN

We've lived very well so far without one.

THE SECRETARY

That's because you weren't governed back then, whereas now
you are, and the central premise of our government is precisely

that one always requires a certificate for everything. One can do without bread and women, but a certification of good standing, no matter what it is that's standing well—well now there's something you can't do without.

THE FISHERMAN
My family's been casting our nets into these waters for three generations now, all very clean and proper, and never with any written papers, that much I can assure you.

A VOICE
We're butchers, down the generations, from father to son, and we've never needed a certificate for slaughtering sheep before.

THE SECRETARY
You were in a state of anarchy then, that's all! You'll note, of course, we have nothing against slaughterhouses—quite the opposite! We've simply introduced a few improvements in accounting. That's where our superiority lies. As for casting wide nets and reeling them in, you'll see we're pretty strong in that department, too.

Mister First Alcalde, do you have the forms?

THE FIRST ALCALDE
Right here.

THE SECRETARY
Guards, will you please help the gentleman step forward.

They force the FISHERMAN *to step forward.*

THE FIRST ALCALDE
(*reading*)
Name, first and last, and occupation.

THE SECRETARY

Skip the obvious parts. The gentleman will fill in the blanks on his own time.

THE FIRST ALCALDE

Curriculum vitae.

THE FISHERMAN

I don't understand.

THE SECRETARY

This is the part where you list the important events in your life. It's a way for us to get to know you.

THE FISHERMAN

My life is my own. It's a private matter. It's nobody else's business.

THE SECRETARY

Private! That sort of word means nothing to us. Naturally, we're asking only about your public life. The only life you're allowed to have. Let's move on to the specifics, Mister Alcalde.

THE FIRST ALCALDE

Married?

THE FISHERMAN

In '31.

THE FIRST ALCALDE

Motives for getting married?

THE FISHERMAN

Motives! I think my brain's gonna explode!

THE SECRETARY

That's what the question says. It's right here. And it's a good way to start making public some of these things that have to stop being personal.

THE FISHERMAN

I got married because that's what you do when you're a man.

THE FIRST ALCALDE

Divorced?

THE FISHERMAN

No, widowed.

THE FIRST ALCALDE

Remarried?

THE FISHERMAN

No.

THE SECRETARY

Why?

THE FISHERMAN
(*shouting*)

I loved my wife.

THE SECRETARY

Bizarre! Why?

THE FISHERMAN

Can everything be explained?

THE SECRETARY

Yes, in a well-organized society.

THE FIRST ALCALDE

Personal records?

THE FISHERMAN

What's that even mean?

THE SECRETARY

Have you ever been convicted of plunder, perjury, or rape?

THE FISHERMAN

Never!

THE SECRETARY

An upstanding citizen. I suspected as much. Mister First Alcalde, add to the file the words: to be watched.

THE FIRST ALCALDE

Patriotic feelings?

THE FISHERMAN

I've always served my fellow citizens well. I've never let a poor man go without a decent helping of fish.

THE SECRETARY

That sort of response is not permissible.

THE FIRST ALCALDE

Oh, I can explain this one! Patriotic feelings are, as you're aware, my line of work. It's a matter of knowing, my good man, if you're the type of person who respects the existing order for the sole reason that it exists.

THE FISHERMAN

Yes, when it's fair and reasonable.

THE SECRETARY

Dubious! Write down that his patriotic feelings are dubious. And then read the last question.

THE FIRST ALCALDE
(*having trouble deciphering the words*)

Reasons for being?

THE FISHERMAN

On my mother's grave, I swear I don't understand a word of whatever language it is you're speaking.

THE SECRETARY

The form's asking you to give your reasons for being alive.

THE FISHERMAN

Reasons! What sorts of reasons would you have me give?

THE SECRETARY

You see! Note that down clearly, Mister First Alcalde—the undersigned acknowledges that his existence is unjustifiable. That'll give us more leeway when the time comes. And you, the undersigned, you understand better now that the certificate of existence issued to you will be provisional and of limited duration.

THE FISHERMAN

Provisional or not, give it to me so I can get back home already. They're expecting me there.

THE SECRETARY

Certainly. But before we do, you'll need to provide a health certificate, which will be issued to you, after a few formalities, on the first floor, Division of Current Affairs, Office of Unsettled Cases, Ancillary Ward.

> *He exits. During the course of the scene, the cart carrying the dead will arrive at the cemetery door and begin to unload. As it does, a drunken* NADA *will jump from the cart screaming:*

NADA[26]

But I'm not dead, I tell you!

> *They try to put him back on the cart. He escapes into the caretaker's lodge.*

NADA

Jeez! If I were dead, I think we'd know it!
Oh, excuse me.

THE SECRETARY

It's nothing. Step forward.

NADA

They loaded me up on the cart, but it's just that I had too
much to drink, that's all. A life of suppression.

THE SECRETARY

Of suppressing what?

NADA

Everything, my lovely. The more we suppress, the better things
go. If we could suppress everything—well, that would be
paradise! Take lovers, for example. Oh, how they disgust me.
When I find a pair walking in front of me, I spit on them. On
their backs, of course, because some of them can be spiteful.
And children! What filthy beasts. And flowers, with their
stupid smell, and rivers, incapable of changing course. Agh!
Suppress it all! Let's suppress it all! That's my philosophy. God
rejects the world, and I . . . I reject God. Long live nothing,
since nothing's the only thing that exists.

THE SECRETARY

And how do we suppress all that?

NADA

Drink. Drink yourself to death and it all goes away.

THE SECRETARY

Inefficient. Our method is better. What's your name?

NADA

Nothing.[27]

THE SECRETARY

What?

NADA

Nothing.

THE SECRETARY

I'm asking you for your name.

NADA

That is my name.

THE SECRETARY

Well, that's fantastic! With a name like that, we'll make magic together. Come on over to this side. You'll make a fine bureaucrat here in our kingdom.

DIEGO *and* VICTORIA *enter.*[28]

THE SECRETARY

Mister First Alcalde, will you get our new friend Nothing up to speed. While they're doing that, you, guards, you go out and sell our badges.

(*taking a step toward* DIEGO)

Hello. Would you like to buy a badge?

DIEGO

What type of badge?

THE SECRETARY

You know, the Plague's badge.

(*a beat*)

You're free to refuse, by the way. It's not required.

DIEGO

Well then, I refuse.

THE SECRETARY

Very well.

(*moving toward* VICTORIA)

And you?

VICTORIA

I don't know you.

THE SECRETARY

Very well. Let me just point out to you, though, that those who refuse to wear this badge are required to wear another one.

DIEGO

Which other one?

THE SECRETARY

Oh, well, the badge of those who refuse to wear the badge. That way, we can tell right away who we're dealing with.

The FISHERMAN *enters.*

THE FISHERMAN

I apologize for interrupting, but—

THE SECRETARY
(*turning toward* DIEGO *and* VICTORIA)

See you soon!

(*to the* FISHERMAN)

What is it now?

THE FISHERMAN
(*his anger building*)

I was just on the first floor, and I was told I had to come back
over here to get a certificate of existence, because without
a certificate of existence, they won't give me a certificate of
health.

THE SECRETARY

Classic!

THE FISHERMAN

Excuse me? Classic?

THE SECRETARY

Yes, because it proves this city of ours is beginning to be well
administered. It's our belief that you're guilty—guilty of being
naturally governed—but that's the sort of thing you have to
feel for yourself—that you're guilty—and you won't come to
that verdict—guilty—until you're good and tired, and so we're
tiring you out, that's all. When you're really good and tired,
then the rest will take care of itself.

THE FISHERMAN

May I at least have this damn certificate of existence?

THE SECRETARY

Theoretically, no, because before being able to get a certificate
of existence you first need to have a certificate of health. It
seems there's no way around it.

THE FISHERMAN

Well then . . . ?

THE SECRETARY

Well then, it's left to our discretion, our pleasure, if you will,
and like all good pleasures, this one won't last very long. So

okay, we'll grant you a certificate, a special favor, but it'll be valid for only a week. In a week, we'll reevaluate.

THE FISHERMAN

Reevaluate what?

THE SECRETARY

Reevaluate if there's reason for us to renew it for you.

THE FISHERMAN

And if it's not renewed?

THE SECRETARY

Well then, your continued existence will no longer be guaranteed, and we'll probably have to proceed with striking your name from the list.

Mister Alcalde, have thirteen copies of this certificate drawn up.

THE FIRST ALCALDE

Thirteen?

THE SECRETARY

Yes! One for the interested party and twelve for administrative use.

The center of the stage is illuminated.

THE PLAGUE

Get our great and pointless works projects under way. You, dear friend, prepare to balance the scales of deportation and concentration. Speed up the processing of innocents. Get them in the guilty column, so our workforce will remain well stocked. Deport the important! We're running out of men, all right. Where are we with the census?

THE SECRETARY

It's in progress. Everything's for the best, and it seems these
fine people have understood me.

THE PLAGUE

My dear friend, you really are too warm and fuzzy. You feel
the need to be understood. That's a strike against you in our
profession. These fine people—as you call them—naturally,
they've understood nothing, but that's of little importance.
The essential thing is not that they understand but that they
execute. Ha! That's an appropriate term, don't you think?

THE SECRETARY

Which term is that?

THE PLAGUE

Execute. Go on, people, execute yourselves, execute! Ha! What
a brilliant expression!

THE SECRETARY

Magnificent!

THE PLAGUE

Magnificent! It's all there in that one word. The first thing
you think of is an execution, such a tender and moving scene,
but then there's also the idea that the person being executed
is collaborating in their own execution, and isn't that the very
goal and foundation of all good government?

Noises in the distance.

THE PLAGUE

What's that?

The CHORUS OF WOMEN *grows louder.*

THE SECRETARY

The women are getting restless.

THE CHORUS

And this one has something to say.[29]

THE PLAGUE

Step forward.

A WOMAN
(*stepping forward*)

Where's my husband?

THE PLAGUE

How lovely! The human heart, as they say. What's happened to this husband of yours?

THE WIFE

He didn't come home.

THE PLAGUE

Seems normal enough. Nothing to be worried about. He's found another bed, that's all.

THE WIFE

He's a real man. He has some respect.

THE PLAGUE

Now, there's genius for you. Would you look into it, my dear friend?

THE SECRETARY

First and last name.

THE WIFE

Galvez, Antonio.

The SECRETARY *looks through her notebook and then whispers into the* PLAGUE'*s ear.*

THE SECRETARY

Well! You'll be happy to hear he's living the saved life.

THE WIFE

The saved life?

THE SECRETARY

A life of luxury!

THE PLAGUE

That's right. I had him deported along with a few others who were making too much noise. I wanted to spare them.

THE WIFE
(*backing away*)

What've you done?

THE PLAGUE
(*with rabid glee*)

I've concentrated them. Until now, they've lived willy-nilly, frivolously, diluted, if you will, a little soft, so to speak. They're much firmer now that I've concentrated them!

THE WIFE
(*fleeing to the* CHORUS, *which parts to welcome her*)

O misery! Misery befall me!

THE CHORUS

Misery! Misery befall us all!

THE PLAGUE

Silence! Don't just stand around! Do something! Busy yourselves!

(*with stars in his eyes*)

They're executing, they're occupying, they're concentrating. Grammar is a good thing. It can be made to serve any purpose.

The stage light flashes to the caretaker's lodge, where NADA *is seated next to the* ALCALDE. *Constituents are lined up in front of him.*

A MAN

The cost of living's gone up, and our wages are no longer enough to get by on.

NADA

We know. There's a new pay scale in effect now. We've just established it.

THE MAN

What kind of raise will we be getting?

NADA

Oh, it's very straightforward! Pay Scale 108. "The bylaw, covering reevaluation of salaries, interprofessional and subsequent, carries suppression of base salary and unconditional freedom of sliding scales, thus encouraging earnings of a maximum salary yet to be determined. The sliding scale, deducting the fictitious increases granted by Pay Scale 107, will continue, however, to be calculated, regardless of the conditions of reclassification, based on the base salary previously suppressed."

THE MAN

But what sort of raise are we talking about with all that?

NADA

Raises are for later, pay scales are for today. We're raising wages with a pay scale, that's all there is to it.

THE MAN

But what are they supposed to do with a pay scale?

NADA
(*screaming*)

They can eat it!
Next.

Another man steps forward.

NADA

You want to open a business. Oh my, what a lovely idea. Well, okay, you can start by filling out this form. Place your fingers in the ink. Okay, good. And now press them here. Perfect.

THE MAN

Where can I wipe them off?

NADA

Where can I wipe them off?

(*flipping through a file*)

Nope, nowhere. That's not part of the rules and regulations.

THE MAN

But I can't leave them like this.

NADA

Why not? What harm's it doing you, given you're not allowed to touch your wife anyway? It even seems a good thing, in your case.

THE MAN

What? A good thing?

NADA

Yes. It humbles you, so it's good. But let's get back to your business. Would you prefer the benefits of Article 208,

Chapter 62, Circular 16, the spot rate for the fifth general
set of rules and regulations, or Paragraph 27, Article 207,
Circular 15, the spot rate for special regulations?

A MAN
But I don't know how either of those work.

NADA
Of course not, man! You don't know how they work and
neither do I. But since we have to make a decision, let's set it
up so you'll benefit from both.

THE MAN
That's very generous of you, Nada. I appreciate it.

NADA
Don't thank me. It looks like one of these articles grants you
the right to have your shop, while the other strips you of the
right to sell anything.

THE MAN
What's the point, then?

NADA
Order![30]

A woman arrives, distraught.

NADA
What is it, woman?

THE WOMAN
They've requisitioned my house.

NADA
Okay.

THE WOMAN
They're using it for administrative services.

NADA

That seems perfectly logical.

THE WOMAN

But now I'm out on the street, and they'd promised to find me housing.

NADA

You see, they've thought of everything.

THE WOMAN

Yes, but now I have to file a request, which will then have to be processed, and in the meantime, my kids are out on the street.

NADA

All the more reason to file the request, then. Here, fill out this form.

THE WOMAN
(*taking the form*)

But will they get to it right away?

NADA

It can be gotten to right away provided you provide a justification of urgency.

THE WOMAN

What's that?

NADA

A paper attesting to the urgency of your getting off the streets.

THE WOMAN

My children don't have a roof over their head. What could be more urgent than giving them one?

NADA

We don't hand out housing simply because children are in the street. We hand out housing when you provide a certificate of authenticity. It's not the same thing.

THE WOMAN

I've never heard anything so twisted. That's devil speak—
a language no one understands.

NADA

No coincidence there, woman. That's the whole point. To
make sure nobody understands one another, even when they're
speaking the same language—and let me tell you, we're fast
approaching that perfect moment when everyone will be
able to speak and no one will hear a word spoken, when the
two types of language will face off here in this city with such
stubborn obstinacy that they'll tear each other apart, leading,
by necessity, to that final solution: silence and death.

> *The* WOMAN *and* NADA *speak the following
> passages over each other.*

THE WOMAN

Justice is children with full bellies and not a spot of cold in
their bones. Justice is my little ones birthed and living on an
earth filled with joy. The sea having provided their baptismal
waters, they require no other riches, and I ask nothing more
for them than their share of bread and a poor man's sleep. It's
nothing, what I ask, and yet it's something you refuse. And
if you refuse the needy their bread, there is no luxury, no fine
use of language, no cryptic promise that will ever grant you
absolution.

NADA

Choose to live on your knees rather than die standing, so the
universe can find its balance, its order hanging from a gallows' T,
shared between the tranquil dead and the ants now well fed

and fattened, a puritanical paradise deprived of prairies and bread, a place where police angels with capitalized wings float among the blessed, filled and satiated with papers and forms, prostrate before the honored God, destroyer of all things, decidedly devoted to dispelling the old delusions of a world far too delicious to persist.

> *The two stop speaking over each other.* NADA
> *now speaks alone.*

NADA

Long live nothing! Nobody understands anyone else anymore: the perfect moment has arrived!

> *The center of the stage is illuminated. Shacks*
> *and barbed wire, as well as watchtowers and a*
> *couple of other hostile-looking structures, can be*
> *seen in silhouette.* DIEGO *enters, wearing a mask,*
> *a hunted look about him. He notices the build-*
> *ings, the people, and the* PLAGUE.

DIEGO
(*addressing the* CHORUS)

Where's Spain? Where's Cádiz? These buildings, these fences, they aren't part of any country I know. We're in another world now, a world in which human beings can't live. Why are you all silent?

THE CHORUS

We're scared! O if only the wind would pick up . . .

DIEGO

I'm scared, too. It's good to let it out, to shout out that you're
scared! Shout it out! The wind will answer.

THE CHORUS

We were once a people, and now we're a mass. We were once
invited; now we're summoned. We once traded in bread and
milk; now we're given provisions. We shuffle forward.

(shuffling forward)

We shuffle forward and get nowhere, saying nobody can do
anything for anybody and that we've no choice but to stay in
line and wait, stay in the spot we were assigned. What's the
point of shouting? Our women's faces no longer have that
rosy shade that once made us swell with desire. O Spain is
gone! Shuffle forward! Shuffle forward! O sorrow! It's we who
shuffle and stagnate. We who suffocate in this walled city.[31] O
if only the wind would pick up!

THE PLAGUE

Now there's some wisdom for you. Come closer, Diego, now
that you understand.

> *The scratching sound of names being crossed
> out reverberates in the sky.*

DIEGO

We're innocent!

> *The* PLAGUE *bursts out laughing.*

DIEGO
(*shouting*)

Innocence. Can an executioner like you understand what that means? Innocence!

THE PLAGUE

Innocence? Never heard of it.

DIEGO

Then come a little closer. Let whichever one of us is stronger kill the other one.

THE PLAGUE

The strongest is me, Innocent. Look.

> *He gestures to the guards, who make a move toward* DIEGO, *who flees.*

THE PLAGUE

Run after him! Don't let him escape! He who flees belongs to us! Mark him.

> *The guards run after* DIEGO. *The chase is mimed on the risers. Whistles. Air-raid siren.*

THE CHORUS

He's running away! He's scared, and he said so. He's not in control, he's out of it, he's crazed! We, we've become wise and well behaved. We've let ourselves be administered. But alone in our silent offices, we hear that long-repressed cry, the cry of separated[32] hearts, which speaks to us of the sea beneath a midday sun, of the scent of reeds in the evening, of the cool arms of our women. Our faces are shut up, our steps counted, our hours ordered, but our hearts refuse the silence. They refuse lists and reference numbers, walls that never end, barred windows, daybreak broken with shotgun blasts. They refuse like the one running off toward the houses, fleeing this setting of shadows and numbers, trying finally to find a place of refuge. But the only refuge is the sea, the sea from which these walls separate us. Only let the wind pick up, and we'll once again be able to breathe.

> DIEGO *hurries inside a house. The guards stop in front of the door and post their sentries there.*

THE PLAGUE
(*screaming*)

Mark him! Mark them all! They can still hear what hasn't been said! They can no longer protest, and yet their silence is still grating. Smash their mouths in! Gag them and teach them nothing but buzzwords, then repeat them over and over until they repeat them back to us, until they've finally become the good little citizens we need them to be.

> *From up in the theater rigging, swarms of slogans descend on the stage, a static quality to them, as if amplified through loudspeakers, the slogans growing louder and louder as they're repeated, blanketing the closed-mouthed* CHORUS *until total silence reigns supreme.*

THE PLAGUE

One plague, one people!

Concentrate yourselves, execute yourselves, occupy yourselves!

One good plague is better than two helpings of freedom!

Deport them, torture them, there will always be something left!

The JUDGE's *house is illuminated.*

VICTORIA

No, Father. You can't possibly turn in our old maid under the pretext that she's contaminated. Have you forgotten that she raised me, that she's served you all these years without a single word of complaint?

THE JUDGE

Who would dare take back a decision they've already made?

VICTORIA

You don't get to decide everything. Sorrow also has its place—its rights.

THE JUDGE

My job is to protect this house and to keep evil from entering it. I—

Diego bursts into the room.

THE JUDGE

Who gave you permission to enter?

DIEGO

Fear drove me into your home. I'm running from the Plague.

THE JUDGE

You're not running from it, you're carrying it.

> *He points to the mark on* DIEGO's *armpit.*
> *Silence. Two or three whistles are heard in the*
> *distance.*

THE JUDGE

Get out of this house.

DIEGO

Save me! If you kick me out, they'll toss me in with all the others, and then I'll just be another body on the pile.

THE JUDGE

I am a servant of the law. I cannot welcome you here.

DIEGO

You served the previous law. You have nothing to do with the new one.

THE JUDGE

I don't serve the law[33] for what it says, I serve the law because it's the law.

DIEGO

And if the law's the crime?

THE JUDGE

If crime becomes the law, it ceases to be crime.

DIEGO

And then it's virtue that has to be punished.

THE JUDGE

If it has the arrogance to dispute the law, then, yes, it must be punished.

VICTORIA
You're not acting on the law, Casado, you're acting on fear.

THE JUDGE
Your friend here is also afraid.

VICTORIA
But he hasn't betrayed anyone yet.

THE JUDGE
He will. Everyone betrays because everyone's afraid, and everyone's afraid because no one is pure.

VICTORIA
I belong to this man, Father. You gave your blessing. You can't take him from me today after having given him to me yesterday.

THE JUDGE
I haven't said yes to your marriage. I said yes to your departure.

VICTORIA
I knew you didn't love me.

THE JUDGE
(*looking at her*)
All you women horrify me.

A violent knock shakes the door.

THE JUDGE
What's that?

A GUARD
(*from outside*)
This house has been condemned for having harbored a suspect. All residents have been placed under surveillance.

DIEGO
(*bursting out in laughter*)

The law's always right, as you well know, but this one's a little
bit new and you didn't know it quite that well. Judge, jury, and
witness, we're all brothers now!

> *The* JUDGE's *wife, young son, and daughter*
> *enter.*

THE WIFE

They've barricaded the door.

VICTORIA

The house has been condemned.

THE JUDGE

Thanks to him. I'm going to denounce him. Then they'll
open the door back up.

VICTORIA

Honor forbids you from doing it, Father.

THE JUDGE

Honor is the business of men and there are no men left in
this city.

> *Whistles are heard. The sound of running.*
> DIEGO *listens, his eyes frantically scanning the*
> *room, seizing suddenly on the child.*

DIEGO

Look here, Jurist. You move a muscle, and I'll smash your son's
mouth against the plague mark.

VICTORIA

That's cowardly, Diego.

DIEGO

Nothing's cowardly in a city of cowards.

THE WIFE
(*running toward the* JUDGE)

Promise, Casado! Promise this crazy man whatever he wants.

THE JUDGE'S DAUGHTER

No, Father, don't do it. This is none of our business.

THE WIFE

Don't listen to her. You know very well she hates her brother.

THE JUDGE

She's right. This is none of our business.

THE WIFE

You, too, then? You hate my son, too.

THE JUDGE

Your son, indeed.

THE WIFE

Oh! You're no man at all, daring to bring up what's already
been forgiven.

THE JUDGE

I haven't forgiven, I've followed the law. As far as the public's
concerned, that makes me the child's father.

VICTORIA

Is it true, Mother?

THE WIFE

You, too? Now you're going to look down on me, too?

VICTORIA

No, but at the same time, it feels like everything's collapsing.
My mind's reeling.

The JUDGE *makes a move for the door.*

DIEGO

The mind reels, but the law supports us, isn't that right, Judge? We're all brothers!

(*holding the child in front of him*)

You're my brother, too, and I'm going to give you a nice brotherly kiss.

THE WIFE

Wait, Diego, I beg you! Don't be like that man whose heart has hardened. He'll soften yet.

(*running to the door to block the* JUDGE's *path*)

You'll give in, won't you?

THE JUDGE'S DAUGHTER

Why would he give in? What good is this bastard to him? He's only taking up space.

THE WIFE

Shut up! Envy's eaten away at your soul and left you all black inside.

(*to the* JUDGE)

But you, you who are nearing death, you know there's nothing on this earth to envy, aside from sleep and quiet. You know the sleep of your solitary bed will be restless if you allow this to happen.

THE JUDGE

I have the law on my side. That's what will allow me to rest.

THE WIFE

I spit on your law. I have my own set of rights, the right of
lovers not to be separated, the right of the guilty to be forgiven
and the repentant to be recognized as such. Yes, I spit on your
law. Did you have the law on your side when you made those
cowardly excuses to that captain who'd challenged you to a
duel, when you cheated your way out of conscription? Did you
have the law with you when you suggested your bed to that
young girl filing a case against a dishonorable master?

THE JUDGE

Shut up, woman.

VICTORIA

Mother!

THE WIFE

No, Victoria, I won't shut up. I've kept nice and quiet all these
years. I did it for my honor and for God's love, but there's no
more honor now, and a single strand of this child's hair is more
precious to me than heaven itself. No, I won't shut up. At the
very least, I'm going to tell this man here that he's never had
righteousness on his side, because righteousness—you hear
me, Casado—righteousness is on the side of those who suffer,
howl, and hope. It is not—no, it cannot be—with those who
kick away ladders and count their riches.

DIEGO *releases the child.*

THE JUDGE'S DAUGHTER

The righteousness of adultery, you mean?

THE WIFE
(*shouting*)

I don't deny my faults, and I'll shout them out for the whole world to hear. But I know, in my want and misery, that the flesh has its faults, whereas the heart has its crimes. What a person does in the heat of passion must be shown mercy.[34]

THE JUDGE'S DAUGHTER

Have mercy on the bitches!

THE WIFE

Yes! For they've a belly to enjoy and beget.

THE JUDGE

Woman! You plead your case poorly. I'm going to denounce the man who has caused all this trouble, and I'll be doubly content in doing so, given it'll be done in the name of the law and hatred.

VICTORIA

Woe unto thee who has at last told the truth. The only way you've ever judged is through your hatred, a hatred you drape with the law, sure enough, but even the best of laws takes on a bad taste in your mouth, the sour mouth shared by those who've never loved anything. Agh! The disgust is choking me. Go on, then, Diego. Gather us up in your arms and we can all rot away together. Only let this man, the one for whom life is a punishment, let him live.

DIEGO

Leave me. I'm ashamed to see what we've become.

VICTORIA

I'm ashamed, too. I'm so ashamed I could die.

> DIEGO *sprints to the window and jumps out.*
> *The* JUDGE *runs after him.* VICTORIA *escapes*
> *out the back door.*

THE WIFE

The time's come for the buboes to burst. We're not the only ones. The whole city's caught the same fever.

THE JUDGE

Bitch!

THE WIFE

Judge!

Darkness. Light on the caretaker's lodge. NADA *and the* ALCALDE *are getting ready to leave.*

NADA

The order's been given for all district leaders to have their constituents vote in favor of the new government.[35]

THE FIRST ALCALDE

It's not that simple. Some may still vote against it.

NADA

Not if you implement the proper policies.

THE FIRST ALCALDE

The proper policies?

NADA

The proper policies call for free elections. That is to say, all votes in favor of the government will be considered as having been freely cast. As for the rest, in order to eliminate any unseen biases that may have impeded true freedom of choice, they will be tabulated following the preferential method, aligning the split ticket to the ratio of uncast ballots as related to the one-third of votes eliminated. Make sense?

THE FIRST ALCALDE

Perfect sense, sir. Or, I think I understand, at least.

NADA

I admire you, Alcalde. Whether you've understood or not, don't forget that the foolproof result of this method should always be to count as invalid any votes cast against the government.

THE FIRST ALCALDE

But you said these were free elections?

NADA

They are, indeed. Only we're setting out from the premise that a vote against is not a free vote. It's an emotional vote, and so a vote shackled by the passions.

THE FIRST ALCALDE

I never thought about it like that!

NADA

Well, that's because you didn't have a fair idea of what freedom is.

> *The center of the stage is illuminated.* DIEGO *and* VICTORIA *arrive, running to the front of the stage.*

DIEGO

I want to run away, Victoria. I don't know what I'm supposed to do anymore. I don't know where my duty lies. I just don't understand.

VICTORIA

Don't leave me. A person's duty is to those they love. Stand firm.

DIEGO

But how can I love you if I've no respect for myself? I'm too proud for all that.

VICTORIA

Who's keeping you from respecting yourself?

DIEGO

You, the one in whom I see no failings.

VICTORIA

Oh, for our sake, for the sake of our love, don't say such things or I'll fall to the ground before you and let all my cowardice spill out. For what you say, it's not true. I'm not so strong. I fail. I fail when I think of all the time I could have given myself over to you. Where did the time go when waters welled up in my heart at the mere mention of your name? Where did the time go when I heard a voice inside me yell, "Land ho!" whenever you appeared. Yes, I fail. The cowardly regret is killing me. And if I'm still standing, it's only because the rush of love propels me forward. But if you were to go away, my race would be run, and I would collapse to the ground.

DIEGO

Oh, if only I could tie myself to you and, with my limbs bound to yours, sink to the bottom of a sleep with no end.

VICTORIA

I'm waiting for you.

> *He moves slowly toward her, and she moves slowly toward him, their eyes never leaving each other. Just as they're about to come together, the* SECRETARY *suddenly appears between them.*

THE SECRETARY

What is this?

> VICTORIA
> (*shouting*)

It's love!

> *An awful noise in the sky.*

> THE SECRETARY

Shh! There are certain words that mustn't be spoken. You should have known that one was forbidden. Look.

> *She smacks* DIEGO *near his armpit, marking him for the second time.*

> THE SECRETARY

Before you were suspect. Now you're infected.

> (*looking at* DIEGO)

Too bad. Such a cute boy.

> (*to* VICTORIA)

You'll forgive me, but I prefer men to women. I have a better connection with them. Have a nice evening.

> DIEGO *looks at the new mark on his body, horrified. His eyes wildly scan his surroundings. He runs to* VICTORIA, *pulling her body against his.*

DIEGO

Oh, how I hate that your beauty will outlive me. It's a curse
that it will serve somebody else.

He presses her against him.

DIEGO

There! Now, I won't have to be alone. What good is your love
if it doesn't rot alongside me?

VICTORIA
(*struggling*)

You're hurting me! Let go of me!

DIEGO

Oh? You're scared.

(*shaking her and laughing like a madman*)

Where have love's black stallions gone? You're in love when
everything's going well, but the moment misfortune strikes,
the stallions go galloping away. The least you can do is die
with me.

VICTORIA

With you, yes, but never against you. I despise this look of fear
and hatred that's come over you. Let go of me! Leave me free
to find the affection I used to know in you. Then my heart will
speak again.

DIEGO
(*half letting go*)

I don't want to die alone! And now the most precious part of
my life is turning away from me, refusing to follow me.

VICTORIA
(*throwing herself against him*)

Oh, Diego, all the way to hell. If that's what it takes, then I'll see you there . . . My legs trembling against yours. Kiss me! Kiss me so this cry welling up inside of me doesn't escape, oh, don't let it escape, it's escaping, oh—

> *He kisses her passionately, then pulls away and leaves her trembling at the center of the stage.*

DIEGO

Look at me! No, no, there's nothing! No mark! I haven't infected you with my madness.

VICTORIA[36]

Come back. Now it's the cold that's making me tremble. Only a moment ago, your chest was burning my hand and my blood was coursing through me like a flame, but now—

DIEGO

No! Leave me. I can't get all this pain and suffering out of my head.

VICTORIA

Come back! All I'm asking is to be consumed by the same fever, to suffer the same plague, our voices united in a single scream.

DIEGO

No! From now on, I belong with the others, with those who've been marked. The way they suffer horrifies me. It fills me with the sort of disgust that used to cut me off from the world, but now, at the end of the day, I'm right there beside them, sharing in the same misery. They need me.

VICTORIA

If you were to die, I'd envy the earth that marries your body.

DIEGO

You're on the other side, with the living.

VICTORIA

I can be with you, though, if you'll just give me a good, long kiss.

DIEGO

They've forbidden love. Oh, how everything in me yearns for you! How I'll miss you!

VICTORIA

No! No! I'm begging you. I know what they want. They've set it all up to make love impossible, but I'll be the strongest woman they've ever seen.

DIEGO

I'm not the strongest man. And that's not a defeat I wanted to share with you.

VICTORIA

I'm complete now! All I know is my love. Nothing frightens me anymore. When the heavens crash down upon us, I'll go down shouting out how happy I am, if only I'm holding your hand.

Voices shouting in the distance.

DIEGO

Others are shouting out, too.

VICTORIA

I'm deaf to death.

DIEGO

Look!

The cart passes.

VICTORIA

My eyes can no longer see. Love has dazzled them.

DIEGO

But the sky pressing down on us is filled with sorrow.

VICTORIA

It's hard enough to carry my own love. I'm not going to add
the weight of the world's pain on top of it. That's a man's
quest, one of those vain, stubborn, sterile quests you set out
on to distract yourself from the only battle that would truly be
difficult, the only victory of which you could truly be proud.

DIEGO

What else in this world am I to overcome if not the injustice
that's done to us?

VICTORIA

The misery inside of you. The rest will follow.

DIEGO

I'm alone. The misery is too much for me.

VICTORIA

I'm right here beside you, arms at the ready.

DIEGO

You're so beautiful, and I'd love you so much if only I weren't
so afraid.

VICTORIA

You'd have so little to fear if only you'd love me.

DIEGO

I do love you. I just don't know which one of us is right.

VICTORIA

The one who isn't afraid—and my heart isn't afraid. It burns
with a single flame, clear and tall, like those fires our mountain
dwellers light to call out to each other. It's calling out to you,
too . . . You see, it's our Midsummer's Day, our Day of Saint John.

DIEGO

Here amid the mass graves.

VICTORIA

Mass graves or meadows, what do they have to do with my
love? At least it doesn't hurt anyone. It is kind and giving.
Your madness, your sterile devotion, for whom do they do any
good? Not for me. Certainly not for me, the one you stab with
every word.

DIEGO

Don't cry, my fierce one! O hopelessness! Why has this evil
come upon us? I would have drunk those tears and then, my
mouth burned by their bitterness, I would have placed as many
kisses on your cheeks as an olive tree has leaves.

VICTORIA

Ah! There you are. You're speaking our language again, the one
you'd forgotten.

(*holding her hands out*)

Let me have a look at you.

DIEGO *backs away, pointing to the markings.*
She reaches her hand out, hesitates.

DIEGO

You, too. You're afraid, too.

> *She presses her hand flat against the markings. He backs away, disoriented. She reaches her arms out.*

VICTORIA

Come quickly! There's nothing to be afraid of anymore.

> *But the groans and curses redouble. His eyes dart around the room like a madman's, and then he runs off.*

VICTORIA

Ah! Solitude.

WOMEN'S CHORUS

We are the caretakers. This whole affair is beyond our control, and all we can do is wait for it to end. We'll keep our secret until winter, when freedom will arrive, when men's howls will fall silent and they'll return to us to claim what they can't live without: the memory of open waters, summer's empty sky, love's eternal scent. Until then, we wait here like dead leaves in a September shower, aloft one minute, flattened to the ground the next, the water's weight too heavy to bear. We, too, are on the ground now. With our backs bent, we wait for the battle cries to run out of breath, we listen to the soft moans of slow surf on the happy seas somewhere deep down inside of us. When the almond trees are covered in ice-crusted blossoms, it's then we'll begin to stir, sensitive to the first winds of hope that are soon to pick up again in that second spring. It's then those we love will walk toward us, and as they draw near, we'll be like those heavy barques lifted little by little by the rising tide, sticky with salt and water, filled with rich scents, until finally we float on thick seas. O let the wind pick up, let the wind pick up . . .

> *Darkness.*

> *Light on the quay.* DIEGO *enters and hails someone he can just make out in the distance, out near the sea. In the background, the* MEN'S CHORUS.

DIEGO

Ahoy! Ahoy!

A VOICE

Ahoy! Ahoy!

> *A boatman appears, his head the only part of him visible above the quay.*[37]

DIEGO

What're you doing?

THE BOATMAN

I'm stocking up on supplies.

DIEGO

For the city?

THE BOATMAN

No. In theory, the city's stocked by the administration.
Stocked in ration tickets, of course. Me? I bring supplies of
bread and milk. There are a couple of ships anchored offshore.
Some families have quarantined out there to escape infection.
I bring their letters in and their provisions out.

DIEGO

But that's forbidden.

THE BOATMAN

Forbidden by the administration, yes, but I don't know how to
read, and I was out at sea when the town criers announced the
new law.

DIEGO

Take me.

THE BOATMAN

Where?

DIEGO

Out to sea. Onto the boats.

THE BOATMAN

That sort of thing's forbidden.

DIEGO

You haven't read or heard the law.

THE BOATMAN

Ah, no. Not forbidden by the administration, but by the
people out on the boats. You're not a safe bet.

DIEGO?

Not a safe bet?

THE BOATMAN

After all, you could be carrying them with you.

DIEGO

Carrying what?

THE BOATMAN

Shh!

(*looking around them*)

Germs, of course. You could carry the germs out to them.

DIEGO

Name your price. I'll pay it.

THE BOATMAN

Don't push so hard. My character is weak.

DIEGO

As much money as it takes.

THE BOATMAN

You'll take it on your conscience, then?

DIEGO

Very well.

THE BOATMAN

Embark. The sea is beautiful.

DIEGO *goes to step down, but the* SECRETARY
appears behind him.

THE SECRETARY

No! You may not embark.

DIEGO

What?

THE SECRETARY

That's not part of the plan. And besides, I know you, you won't desert us.

DIEGO

Nothing's going to stop me from going.

THE SECRETARY

If I want to stop you, that's all it takes. And I do want to stop you, because I have business with you. You know who I am.

> *She begins to back away, and he follows, as if pulled by a magnet.*

DIEGO

To die is nothing, but to die so defiled—

THE SECRETARY

I can understand. You see, I'm simply an executant, an underling. But, at the same time, I've been given authority over you. The authority of the veto, if you like.

> *She flips through her notebook.*

DIEGO

Men of my blood belong only to the earth!

THE SECRETARY

Well, that's what I meant. You're mine, in a certain way. Only in a certain way. And maybe not in the way I'd prefer . . . When I look at you . . .

> *(modest and down-to-earth)*

I like you, you know. But I have my orders.

> *She toys with the corner of her notebook.*

DIEGO
I prefer your hatred to your smiles. You disgust me.

THE SECRETARY
As you wish. Anyway, this conversation we're having doesn't
really fall within regulations. Exhaustion tends to make me
sentimental. On nights like tonight, with all this bookkeeping
to do, I sometimes let myself go.

> *She flips the notebook over in her fingers.*

DIEGO *tries to snatch it from her.*

THE SECRETARY
No, really, my darling, don't be so pushy. What would you see
in it anyway? It's a notebook, that's all, a planner, half agenda,
half filing system. With pages that can be torn out.

(*giving a laugh*)

It's my little cheat sheet, if you will. A few reminders.

> *She reaches a hand toward him, as if to caress
> him.*

DIEGO *makes for the boat.*

DIEGO

Agh! He left!

THE SECRETARY

Well, look at that! Yet another man who thinks he's free, and who is nevertheless inscribed like all the rest.

DIEGO

You and your doublespeak. You know very well that's the sort of thing a man can't bear. Get it over with already, would you?

THE SECRETARY

But it's all very simple and straightforward. I'm telling the truth. Every city has a section in the planner. Here's the one for Cádiz. I assure you it's very well organized and no one is ever forgotten.

DIEGO

No one's ever forgotten, and yet they all escape you.

THE SECRETARY
(*indignant*)

Not at all! Or . . .

(*thinking about it*)

Maybe there are a few exceptions, I suppose. It's possible we forget one or two every now and again, but they always end up betraying themselves. As soon as they pass a hundred, they have to boast and brag and announce it to the world on the front page of the newspaper, the morons. All we have to do is wait, and then, in the morning, as I comb through the papers, I jot down their names. I collate them, as we say. None slip by us, of course.

DIEGO

But for a hundred years they will have refused your will, just as this entire city refuses you today.

THE SECRETARY

A hundred years is nothing! It seems like a lot to you only because your vision is so limited. So zoomed in and close-up. I, on the other hand, see the bigger picture. You understand that, don't you? In a file with 372,000 names, what's one person, even if that one is a hundred years old? Just a small question for your consideration. And in any case, we make up the difference by taking a few who are no older than twenty. It's all about the average. We do the crossing-out a little quicker, and voilà! Like this . . .

> *She crosses out a name in her notebook. A cry comes from the sea and then the sound of a body falling into the water.*

THE SECRETARY

Whoops! I did it without thinking, and look, there went the Boatman. What a coincidence!

> DIEGO *stands tall, looking at her with horror and disgust.*

DIEGO

You make me want to vomit.

THE SECRETARY

The work I do is thankless, I know. It's exhausting, and you really have to apply yourself to it. At first, I was kind of groping around in the dark. Now my hand is steady.

She takes a step closer to DIEGO.

DIEGO

Don't come near me.

THE SECRETRAY

Soon there'll be no more mistakes. A little secret. A well-oiled machine, perfected. You'll see.

She moves closer and closer to him, sentence after sentence, until they're touching. Suddenly he grabs her by the collar, trembling with anger.

DIEGO

Finish it! Finish this filthy joke of yours! What are you waiting for? Do your job! Quit messing around with me, amusing yourself with me, someone who stands head and shoulders above you. Oh, you better kill me now, because that's the only way you're going to save this beautiful system of yours, this system that leaves nothing to chance. Oh, but you worry only about the big picture. A hundred thousand men, now that's when things get interesting, but a hundred thousand is only a statistic, and statistics are incapable of speaking. Oh, we'll plot out some curves and graphs, huh? We'll work at the level of generations—it's so much easier! And that way the work can be done in silence, with the peaceful scent of ink. But I warn you, a single individual taken on their own, oh, that's a far more troublesome and uncomfortable fact, crying out as individuals do, in agony and joy. As long as I'm alive, I'll continue to disturb your beautiful order with all the cries of chance. I reject you. I reject you with all my being!

THE SECRETARY

My darling!

DIEGO

Shut up! I come from a tribe that used to honor death as much as life, but then your masters came along, and now living and dying are both dishonorable.

THE SECRETARY

It's true.

DIEGO
(*shaking her*)

It's true that you lie and that you'll go on lying from now until the end of time. Oh yes, I understand your system very well. You hit these people with hunger pangs and the suffering of being separated from those they love, and you do it to distract them from rebelling. You drain them, you devour their time and energy, so that they have neither the leisure nor the burning desire to express their fury. Be happy! They're barely treading water. They're alone, despite their numbers, and I'm alone, too. Each of us is alone because of the cowardice of the others. But I—enslaved as they are, humiliated as they are— I'm here to tell you you're nothing, that this blanket of power you've rolled out across the sky, this blanket you've used to obscure the sky, it's nothing but a shadow cast upon the earth, and any second now a furious wind is going to dispel it. You thought everything could be accounted for in facts and figures, but in that lovely nomenclature of yours, you forgot wild roses, shapes and signs in the sky, summer faces, the great voice of the sea, those human instants of heartbreak and anger.

She laughs.

DIEGO

Don't laugh. Don't laugh, you fool. You've lost, I tell you. In the midst of what appear to be your greatest victories, you've already lost, because in human beings—look at me—in human beings there's a strength you can't diminish, a burning madness swirled with fear and courage, deeply ingrained and forever victorious. It's this force that's going to rise up, and when it does, then you'll know your glory was nothing but smoke.

She laughs.

DIEGO

Don't laugh! Don't be so quick to laugh.

> *She laughs. He slaps her, and as he does, the* CHORUS OF MEN *tear off their gags and sing out a long cry of joy. In the heat of passion,* DIEGO's *mark has begun to fade. He places his hand where it was and gazes at it.*

THE SECRETARY

Magnificent!

DIEGO

What?

THE SECRETARY

You're magnificent when you're angry! I like you even more.

DIEGO

What's going on?

THE SECRETARY

You can see very well. The mark's disappearing. Keep it up,
you're on the right track.[38]

DIEGO

I'm cured?

THE SECRETARY

I'll let you in on a little secret . . . Their system is excellent,
you're quite right about that, but there's one little defect in
their machine.

DIEGO

I don't understand.

THE SECRETARY

There's a defect, my darling. For as long as I can remember,
all it's ever taken for their machine to start grinding is for a
person to overcome their fear and rebel. Now, I'm not saying
the thing stops completely, far from it, but it does at least
begin to grind a little, and sometimes it ends up getting really
jammed.

Silence.

DIEGO

Why are you telling me this?

THE SECRETARY

You know, try as I may, I still have my weaknesses. And anyway, you'd already figured it out on your own.

DIEGO

Would you have spared me if I hadn't slapped you?

THE SECRETARY

No. I came here to conclude our business, according to the rules.

DIEGO

So then, I am the strongest.

THE SECRETARY

Are you still afraid?

DIEGO

No.

THE SECRETARY

Then there's nothing I can do to you. That, too, is in the rules—though I can tell you this is certainly the first time that particular rule has met with my approval.

> *She slowly withdraws from the stage.* DIEGO *pats his hands over his body, then gazes at them a moment before suddenly turning toward a moaning sound that's now audible. He walks in silence toward a sick man who is gagged. Pantomime.* DIEGO *reaches out for the gag and unties it. It's the* FISHERMAN. *They look at each other in silence, then:*

THE FISHERMAN
(*with effort*)

Good evening, brother. It's been a long time since last I spoke.

DIEGO *smiles at him.*

THE FISHERMAN
(*raising his eyes to the sky*)

What's that?

> *It is, in fact, the sky brightening. A light wind is picking up, shaking a door and causing some drapes to flutter. The people, gags undone, eyes raised to the sky, now surround* DIEGO *and the* FISHERMAN.

DIEGO

The wind from the sea . . .

CURTAINS

PART THREE

The residents of Cádiz bustle about in the town square. DIEGO, *stationed just above them, is helping to guide the work. The lighting is bright and vivid, making the* PLAGUE's *sets less impressive and more clearly cutout facades.*

DIEGO

Scrub off the stars!

They're scrubbed off.

DIEGO

Open the windows!

The windows are opened.

DIEGO

Fresh air! Fresh air! Gather up the sick!

General moving about.

DIEGO

Don't be afraid anymore! That's the most important thing. Stand up tall if you're able! Why are you shrinking away?[39] Keep your chin up, the time for pride has come. Throw off your gags and shout out with me that you're no longer afraid.

(*raising his arms*)

O blessed rebellion, living refusal, honor of the people, give those who are gagged the strength of your scream.

THE CHORUS

We hear you, brother, and we, the impoverished who live on olives and bread, for whom a single mule is a fortune, we who taste wine but twice a year, on our birthday and anniversary, we have begun to hope. But the old fears haven't left our hearts yet. Olives and bread create a taste for life, and as little as we may have, we're afraid of losing even that, along with our life.

DIEGO

You'll lose olives, bread, and life if you let things keep going as they're going! Today, you must overcome your fear, even if all you want is to hold on to your bread. Wake up, Spain!

THE CHORUS

We're poor and ignorant, but we've been told the plague follows the year's paths, that it has its spring where it sprouts and blooms, its summer where it bears fruit. We've been told when winter comes, there perhaps it withers. But is it winter, brother? Is it really winter? Does this wind that's picked up really come from the sea? We've always been forced to pay for everything with misery as our currency. Must we now pay with a currency of blood?

THE WOMEN'S CHORUS

Another affair for men! We, we're here to remind you of the moment now opening before us, the morning's first carnations, the sheep's black wool, the scent of Spain at last! We are weak in body, and we can do nothing against you and your big bones, but whatever you do amid your melee of shadows, don't forget our flowers of flesh.

DIEGO

It's the plague that makes us wither away, the plague that separates lovers and blights the morning's first flowers. It's the plague, above all else, that we must fight.

THE CHORUS

Is it really winter? In our forests, the oaks are still covered in lustrous acorns, wasps swarming their trunks. No! It isn't winter yet.

DIEGO

Then use your anger to make it winter!

THE CHORUS

But will we find hope at the end of our road? Or will we die hopeless?

DIEGO

Who's talking about being hopeless? Hopelessness is a gag. What rips the silence from this besieged city is the thundering of hope, the flashing bolts of happiness. Stand tall, I say! If you want to hold on to your bread and hope, destroy your certificates, smash the office windows, step out of fear's waiting

lines, and shout it out—*freedom*—so that the whole of the
heavens can hear you.

THE CHORUS

We are the most impoverished. Hope is our only wealth. So
how, then, could we allow ourselves to be deprived of it? We're
ready to throw off our gags, brother!

(*great cry of deliverance*)

O over this dry land, cracked by heat and sun, here now,
the first rains come! Here now, fall appears, a time when
everything grows green again, when the fresh wind blows in
from the sea. Hope lifts us like a wave.

DIEGO *exits.*

> *The* PLAGUE *enters on the same level where*
> DIEGO *was but from the opposite side. The* SEC-
> RETARY *and* NADA *follow him.*

THE SECRETARY

What's the meaning of all this? We're awfully chatty now,
aren't we? I'd appreciate it if you'd put your gags back in place.

> *A couple of people in the middle of the square
> put their gags back in place, but many of them,
> roused by* DIEGO'*s words, continue to carry out
> their work in an orderly fashion.*

THE PLAGUE

Things are starting to shift.

THE SECRETARY

Yes. As usual.

THE PLAGUE

Well, we're just going to have to tighten restrictions.[40]

THE SECRETARY

Let's get the tightening started, then.

> *Wearily, she opens her notebook and flips through it.*

NADA

Let's get to it! We're on the right track! To comply with regulations or not to comply with regulations, that is the whole question of morality and philosophy![41] But in my opinion, Your Honor, we haven't gone far enough.

THE PLAGUE

You talk too much.

NADA

It's just that I'm excited, that's all. I've learned so much from you. I mean, suppression, that's always been my gospel truth, but before you came along, I didn't have good reason for it. Now, I've found reason in rules and regulations.

THE PLAGUE

Rules and regulations don't suppress everything. Be careful—you're out of line!

NADA[42]

Don't forget there were rules and regulations before you came along. What had yet to be put in place was an overall system,

a final solution, the human race indexed, all of life replaced
with a table of contents, the universe laid off, heaven and earth
finally demoted.

THE PLAGUE
Get back to work, you lush. And you, get on with it!

THE SECRETARY
Where do we start?

THE PLAGUE
Where but at random? That's the most shocking approach.

> *The* SECRETARY *crosses out two names. Warn-
> ing shots. Two men fall.*

> *Ebb. Those who were working stop, stunned
> and terrified. The* PLAGUE*'s henchmen rush out
> and put crosses on all the doors, close the win-
> dows, toss the corpses around, etc.*

DIEGO
(*in the background, in a calm voice*)
Long live death. It doesn't scare us.

> *Flow. The people begin to work again. The
> guards retreat. The same pantomime as before,
> only in reverse. The wind picks up as the people
> move forward and dies down when the hench-
> men return.*

THE PLAGUE

Strike that one from the list!

THE SECRETARY

Impossible!

THE PLAGUE

Why?

THE SECRETARY

He's not afraid anymore.

THE PLAGUE

How about that? Does he know?

THE SECRETARY

He has his suspicions.

> *She crosses a name out. Dull thuds. Ebb.*
> *Same scene.*

NADA

Excellent! They're dropping like flies! O if only the earth could
tilt on its axis.

DIEGO
(*calmly*)

Help up anyone who falls.

> *Ebb. Same pantomime in reverse.*

THE PLAGUE

This guy's going too far!

THE SECRETARY

Indeed, he's going too far.

THE PLAGUE

Why do you say it with such sadness in your voice? You haven't given him any information, have you?

THE SECRETARY

No. He must have figured it out on his own. He has the gift, I guess.

THE PLAGUE

He has the gift, but I have the means. We'll have to try another way. Now get to it.

He exits.

THE CHORUS
(*removing their gags*)

Ahh!

(*sigh of relief*)

Here we see the first sign of retreat, the tourniquet loosening, the sky unwinding, and the fresh air blowing in. Now we hear returning the sound of those springs evaporated by the plague's black sun. Summer is on its way out. We'll no longer have vines filled with grapes, no longer have melons, green beans, and salads fresh from the ground. But hope's waters have tenderized the tough soil and promised us winter's refuge, roasted chestnuts, the first stalks of corn with kernels still green, walnuts fresh as soap, milk by the fire—

THE WOMEN

We are ignorant, yet able to say these riches shouldn't come at too steep a price. The world over, and under all masters, there

will always be fresh fruit within reach, wine for the poor, and
a fire made of twigs and vines, the place we wait for all this to
pass . . .

> Over at the JUDGE's house, the JUDGE's
> DAUGHTER *climbs out of one of the windows
> and runs to hide among the women.*

THE SECRETARY
(*descending toward the people*)

My word! It's as if a revolution were taking place—though
that's not the case, of course, as you well know. And anyway,
starting a revolution is no longer left up to the people. That
way of doing things is really quite outdated. Revolutions no
longer need insurgents. Today, the police can take care of it all
on their own; they can even overthrow the government. And
isn't that so much the better, after all? Like this, the people
can kick back and relax while a few of our best and brightest
minds do the work for them, figuring out just what amount of
happiness will be in their best interest.

THE FISHERMAN
That's it, I'm gutting this treacherous eel right now.

THE SECRETARY
Come now, my good friends. Wouldn't it be better to just leave
things as they are? When a system of order has already been
established, the cost of changing it is always too high. And
even if the current system seems unbearable, perhaps a few
arrangements could be made.

A WOMAN
What sorts of arrangements?

THE SECRETARY

Oh, I don't know! That's not for me to say. But you women
are well aware that every upheaval has its price and that a
properly negotiated settlement is sometimes worth more than
a ruinous victory.

>*The women approach. A few men step away
>from the group surrounding* DIEGO.

DIEGO

Don't listen to a word she says. It's all part of her plan.

THE SECRETARY

What plan? I speak reason and have nothing else in mind.

A MAN

What type of arrangements were you talking about a
minute ago?

THE SECRETARY

Naturally, it would be necessary to give it some thought,
but, for example, we could set up a committee with you,
a committee to decide, by majority vote, who gets crossed
off. The committee would hold full ownership over
this notebook in which the crossing-off is done. You'll
note, of course, that this is only an example of a possible
arrangement . . .

>*She flaps the notebook in front of her. A man
>snatches it.*

THE SECRETARY
(*feigning indignation*)

Want to give the notebook back now? You know very well
how valuable it is. All it takes is a striking through of one of
your fellow citizen's names, and voilà, dead.

> *Men and women surround the man with the
> notebook, an excited buzz running through them.*

—We've got it!
—No more deaths!
—We're saved!

> *The* JUDGE'S DAUGHTER *emerges from the
> crowd and violently snatches the notebook from
> the man, runs off to a corner, rapidly flips through
> the pages, and crosses something out. A loud cry
> comes from the* JUDGE'*s house, followed by the
> sound of a body falling. Men and women rush the
> girl.*

A VOICE

Damn you! You're the one who needs to be eliminated.

> *A hand reaches out and snatches the note-
> book, flipping through it until the girl's name
> appears. A hand crosses it out. The girl falls with-
> out a sound.*

NADA
(*screaming*)

Forward, march, all those united in suppression! It's no longer a matter of suppressing other people, it's a matter of self-suppression now! In this, we're all together, oppressors and oppressed, hand in hand! Let's go, Tauruses! It's time to clean house.

He exits.

A MAN
(*enormous, holding the notebook*)

It's true we've got a bit of cleaning up to do. And this opportunity to wizen a few of those sons of bitches who got all nice and fat while we were starving to death is too good to pass up.

> *The* PLAGUE, *who's just reappeared, bursts out in a tremendous laugh, while the* SECRETARY *demurely returns to her place beside him. Everyone onstage stands motionless, their eyes raised, waiting while the* PLAGUE's *henchmen spread out and begin to put back in place the signs and sets associated with the* PLAGUE.

THE PLAGUE
(*to* DIEGO)

And there you have it! I don't have to do a thing. They do the work all on their own. Are they really worth all this trouble you're going to?

DIEGO *and the* FISHERMAN *leap onto the stage, rush the man with the notebook, throw a few punches, and push him to the ground.* DIEGO *takes the notebook and tears it up.*

THE SECRETARY
Pointless. I have a backup.

DIEGO *pushes the men back to the other side.*

DIEGO
Quick, get to work! You've been played!

THE PLAGUE
When they're afraid, they're afraid for themselves. But when they hate, they hate other people.

DIEGO
(*coming up right in front of him*)
Neither fear nor hatred, that's our victory!

Faced with DIEGO*'s men, the henchmen slowly retreat.*

THE PLAGUE
Silence! I'm the one who sours the wine and dries up the fruit. I kill the vine if it's about to give grapes, and I turn it green if you need to feed the fire. Your simple pleasures disgust me. This country where people claim to be free without being rich disgusts me.[43] I bring prisons and executioners and strength and blood! This city will be razed to the ground, and history, buried in the rubble, will finally die out in that beautiful

silence of all perfect societies. So then, give me silence or I'll crush it all.

> *Pantomimed struggle amid a frightful racket: the groaning of garrotes, a buzzing noise, the sound of names being crossed out, tides of slogans. As the struggle turns to the advantage of* DIEGO*'s men, the tumult subsides and the* CHORUS, *indistinct still, drowns out the sounds of the* PLAGUE.

THE PLAGUE
(*with a gesture of rage*)

We still have hostages!

> *He waves his hand. The* PLAGUE*'s henchmen exit the stage while the others regroup.*

NADA
(*from the top of the palace*)

There'll always be something. Everything carries on so as not to carry on, and my offices carry on, too. The city could crumble, the sky could explode, humans could desert the earth, and the office buildings would still open for their regularly scheduled hours to administer the nothingness. *L'éternité, c'est moi*,[44] and my paradise has its archives and record books.

> *He exits.*

THE CHORUS

They're fleeing. Summer comes to a victorious end, and so it
is that humans sometimes win. So it is that victory looks like
our ladies' bodies beneath love's rain, there where the flesh is
happy, lustrous, and warm, there where hornets buzz as around
bunches of September grapes, the harvest of the vine spilling
over the stomach's surface, aflame at the tips of drunken
breasts. O my love, desire explodes like a ripened fruit, the
body's glory finally spurting out. From all over the heavens,
mysterious hands extend their flowers, setting vin jaune aflow
from forever running fountains. Such are the celebrations of
victory. Off we go to find our women!

> *In silence,* VICTORIA *is brought out on a
> stretcher.*

DIEGO
(rushing over)

Agh! I don't know if I want to kill someone else or die myself.

(arriving at the seemingly inanimate body)

Oh, my wonderful, victorious woman, as wild as love itself,
turn your face a little toward me. Come back, Victoria. Don't
let yourself go to that other side of the world where I can no
longer be with you. Don't leave me here on this cold earth.
My love, my love! Hold tight, hold on tight to the edge of this
earth where we're still together. Don't let yourself slip away. If
you die, for all the days I have left to live, the afternoons will be
black as night.

WOMEN'S CHORUS

Now the truth is before us.[45] Things weren't serious until we had a body all twisted up and suffering. So much shouting, such beautiful language—long live death—and then death itself comes and rips the throat from the one you love. That's when love returns, right when it's too late. When there's no time left.

VICTORIA *groans.*

DIEGO

There's still time. She's trying to sit up. You're going to stand before me again, aren't you? Stand there tall and shining like a torch, with your flaming black hair and that face blazed with love, that face whose dazzling radiance carried me through those nights of combat, nights during which, because I carried you with me, my heart was able to bear it all.

VICTORIA

I'm sure you'll forget about me, Diego. Your heart won't be able to bear the absence. It wasn't able to bear a little misfortune. Oh, it's an awful torment to die knowing you'll be forgotten.

She turns away.

DIEGO

I won't forget you. My memory will be longer than my life.

THE CHORUS OF WOMEN

O suffering body, once so desirable, O royal beauty, the sparkle of day. Man cries out for the impossible, woman suffers all that is possible. Kneel down, Diego. Shout out your sentence, accuse yourself, the time for repentance has come, Deserter!

This body was your homeland. Without it, you're nothing.
Your memory won't redeem a thing.

> *The* PLAGUE *quietly approaches* DIEGO. *Only*
> VICTORIA's *body stands between them.*

THE PLAGUE

Ready to give up?

> DIEGO *looks at* VICTORIA's *body, his hope*
> *having drained away.*

THE PLAGUE

You don't have the strength to keep going. You can't even see
straight, whereas I—I have my sight set on power.

DIEGO
(*after a silence*)

Let her live. Kill me.

THE PLAGUE

What?

DIEGO

I'm offering you a trade.

THE PLAGUE

What trade?

DIEGO

I want to die in her place.

THE PLAGUE

That's the kind of thing a person thinks when they're tired.
Look, dying isn't the most pleasant experience, and she's already
through the worst of it. Let's just leave things as they are.

                              DIEGO

It's the kind of thing a person thinks when they're the
strongest one around.

                          THE PLAGUE

Look at me. I am power itself!

                              DIEGO

Take off your uniform.

                          THE PLAGUE

You've lost your mind.

                              DIEGO

Go on, undress. When powerful men take off their uniforms,
it's not a pretty sight to see.

                          THE PLAGUE

Be that as it may, their power lies in having invented the
uniform in the first place.

                              DIEGO

And mine lies in rejecting it. My offer stands.

                          THE PLAGUE

Think about what you're saying. Life is good.

                              DIEGO

My life is nothing. What matters is what I live for. I'm not
a dog.

                          THE PLAGUE

So, a first cigarette? That's nothing? The scent of afternoon
dust stirring out on La Rambla?[46] The evening rains? A
woman yet to be known? A second glass of wine? All of it,
nothing?

                              DIEGO

It's something, but she'll live a better life than I will.

THE PLAGUE

Not if you stop trying to take care of other people.

DIEGO

On the path I walk, there is no stopping, not even if I wanted to. I will not spare you!

THE PLAGUE
(*changing his tone*)

Listen. If you offer me your life in exchange for hers, I'm required to accept it, and so, yes, this woman will live, but let me offer you a different deal. I'll give you this woman's life, and I'll let you both run away together, too—provided you leave me to do as I wish with this city.

DIEGO

No. I know where my strength lies.

THE PLAGUE

Well then, I'll be frank with you. Either I'm master of everything or I'm master of nothing. That's the rule. If you slip away from me, the city slips away from me. The rule's been in place so long I don't even know where it comes from.

DIEGO

You may not know, but I do. It comes from the depths of time, and it's so much bigger than you, so much higher than your gallows. It's the rule of nature. We've won.

THE PLAGUE

Not yet! I've still got this body here. My hostage. My trump card. My final asset. Look at her. If ever a woman bore the face of life, it's this one here. She deserves to live, and you want to make sure that she does. Me? Well, I'm obligated to return her to you, but it can be in exchange for your own life or in exchange for the city's freedom. Choose.

> DIEGO *looks at* VICTORIA. *In the back-*
> *ground, the murmuring of gagged voices.* DIEGO
> *turns to the* CHORUS.

DIEGO

Dying is hard.

THE PLAGUE

It's hard.

DIEGO

But it's hard for everyone.

THE PLAGUE

Fool! Ten years of this woman's love is worth far more than an
entire century of freedom for these men.

DIEGO

This woman's love is my kingdom, meant for me alone. That
gives me the right to decide what to do with it. The freedom of
these men, though, it belongs to them. I have no right to make
decisions about it.

THE PLAGUE

A person can't be happy without hurting other people. That's
the justice of this world.

DIEGO

I wasn't made for that kind of justice, and I don't accept it.

THE PLAGUE

Who's asking you to accept it? The world order isn't going to
change simply to suit your desires. If you want to change it,
drop these fantasies of yours and have a look at reality.

DIEGO

No, I know how those prescriptions work. To eliminate
murder, you have to kill; to heal injustice, you need a little

violence. That kind of thing's been going on for centuries. For centuries, the lords and masters of your universe have encouraged the world's wounds to fester and rot—under the pretext of healing them, of course—and yet here you are, continuing to extol your old prescriptions, and why not, right? No one's laughed them out of the room yet.

THE PLAGUE

No one laughs because I get things done. I am effective.

DIEGO

That's for sure. Effective and practical. Like an ax.

THE PLAGUE

It takes only one look at these men to know that any old justice is good enough for them.

DIEGO

Ever since the doors of the city were sealed, I've had all the time in the world to look at them.

THE PLAGUE

Well then, now you know they'll always abandon you, and a man so abandoned must perish.

DIEGO

No, you're wrong. If I'd been abandoned, the whole thing would be easy. But whether by choice or by force, they are with me.

THE PLAGUE

What a lovely flock of sheep, they are, and such a strong stench, too!

DIEGO

I know they're not purebreds, perfect and clean, but neither am I, seeing as I was born among them. I live for my city, and I live for my time.

THE PLAGUE

The time of slaves!

DIEGO

The time of free men!

THE PLAGUE

You amaze me. No matter how hard I look, I can't seem to find these free men of yours? Where are they?

DIEGO

In your prison camps and pits filled with dead bodies. It's the slaves who are on the thrones.

THE PLAGUE

Put your free men in my police uniforms, and you'll see what they become.

DIEGO

It's true they can sometimes be cowardly and cruel. They have no more right to power than you do. No man is virtuous enough to be granted absolute power. But that's also why they have a right to compassion, which is something you'll be denied.

THE PLAGUE

What's cowardly is to live as they do, small and needy and always half bent over.

DIEGO

It's half bent over that I stand beside them. If I'm not faithful to a poor man's truth, a truth I share with them, how could I be faithful to that greater and more solitary truth inside of me?

THE PLAGUE

The only thing I have faith in is contempt.

(*gesturing toward the* CHORUS *slumped behind them*)

Look—doesn't that just say it all!

DIEGO

The only thing I have contempt for is executioners. No
matter what you do, these men will be greater than you are.
If one of them happens to kill someone, it happens in the
heat of the moment. You, though, you massacre according
to law and logic. Don't mock their lowered heads, lowered
by centuries of fearful comets passing above them. Don't
laugh at their look of dread, born of centuries of death and
of watching their love ripped to shreds. The greatest of their
crimes has always had an excuse, but I can find no excuse
for the crimes so long committed against them, crimes you
finally had the idea of codifying into this dirty systematic
order of yours.

The PLAGUE *takes a step toward him.*

DIEGO

I will not lower my eyes!

THE PLAGUE

I can see you won't lower them. Well then, let me be the one
to tell you—you've just passed the last test. If you'd left the city
to me, you'd have lost this woman, and you'd have lost yourself
along with her. Now, it's likely the city will go free. You see,
all it takes is a madman like you . . . Of course, it's obvious the
madman's going to die, but in the end, sooner or later, the rest
will be saved.

(*somberly*)

And the rest don't deserve to be saved.

DIEGO
The madman's going to die . . .

THE PLAGUE
Oh? Is something wrong? No, really, this is just classic—the moment of hesitation arrives. Pride will carry the day.

DIEGO
I've always had a thirst for honor, and the only place I'll find it today is among the dead.

THE PLAGUE
As I said, it's pride that kills them. It's all very tiring for someone who's getting to be an old man like I am.

(*in a hardened voice*)

Prepare yourself.

DIEGO
I'm ready.

THE PLAGUE
Here come the markings—they're going to hurt.

DIEGO *stares, horrified, as the markings once again appear on his body.*

THE PLAGUE
There! Suffer a little before dying. That's a rule I live by. When hate burns me up inside, other people's suffering is

like a cool morning dew. Moan and groan a little. Yes, that's good. Let me watch you suffer a little more before I leave this city.

(looking at the SECRETARY*)*

Come on, you, get to work!

THE SECRETARY
Yes, if I must.

THE PLAGUE
Tired already?

> The SECRETARY *nods her head yes, and as she does, her appearance suddenly morphs into that of an old woman in a death mask.*

THE PLAGUE
You know, I've always thought you didn't hate enough. Me? My hatred requires a constant supply of fresh victims. Well, hurry up and take care of this for me, and then we'll get started again somewhere else.

THE SECRETARY
It's true hate's not enough to keep me going, because it's not in my job description. But then, it's also kind of your fault, too. When all a person does is work with files and folders, they forget how to really care about anything.

THE PLAGUE
Those are some fine words you've got there. If you're looking for something to keep you going—

> *He gestures toward* DIEGO, *who falls to his knees.*

THE PLAGUE
—you can find it in the joy of destroying. *That* is your function.

THE SECRETARY
Destruction it is, then. But I'm not really comfortable with it.

THE PLAGUE
What in the world makes you think my orders are up for discussion?

THE SECRETARY
My memory of the world. I still have some old memories. I was free before you came along, a partner in the business of chance. Back then, no one hated me, because I was the one who brought things full circle, who made love eternal, who gave destinies their shape. I was steady and sure. But then you came along and enlisted me in the service of logic and order, of rules and regulations, and now I've lost the ability to be helpful every now and again.

THE PLAGUE
Who's asking for your help?

THE SECRETARY
Those overwhelmed by their misfortunes—which is to say almost everyone. I was often able to work side by side with them. I was able to exist in my own special way. Today, I have to force them, and still they refuse me to their dying breath. Maybe that's why I liked this one here, this guy you're ordering me to kill. He chose me of his own free will. In his own special way, he took pity on me. He was willing to schedule a time for us to meet.

THE PLAGUE

Careful. You don't want to irritate me. We have no need for pity.

THE SECRETARY

Who could need pity more than those who feel compassion for no one? When I say I like this guy, what I mean is I envy him. That's the pitiful form love takes in conquistadors like us. You know it very well, and you know it makes us worthy of a little pity.

THE PLAGUE

I order you to shut up!

THE SECRETARY

You know it very well and you also know that, in killing, a person begins to envy the innocence of those one kills. Oh, if for just one second I could set aside this endless stream of logic and let myself believe I rely on a body of flesh and blood. I'm so sick of shadows. I envy all these miserable people, yes, even this woman—

(*gesturing at* VICTORIA)

—who'll come back to life only to scream and cry like an animal. She at least will have her suffering to rely on.

DIEGO *begins to fall over. The* PLAGUE *picks him up.*

THE PLAGUE

Stand up, man! The end can't come for you until this lady does what she has to do—and as you can see, she's getting a little emotional at the moment. But fear not! She'll do what she has

to do. It's in her job description and it's in the rules. The wheels
of the machine are grinding a little, that's all. But be happy, you
fool. I'm returning the city to you now, before the whole thing
seizes up completely.

Cries of joy from the CHORUS. *The* PLAGUE
turns toward them.

THE PLAGUE

Yes, I'll be getting on my way now, but don't feel too
triumphant. I'm happy with what I've accomplished. We've
got some good work done here, as we have in other places.
I like all the noise that's been made in my name, and now I
know you won't forget me. Look at me! Look one last time at
the only power that exists in this world. Gaze upon the face of
your one true ruler and learn what it means to be afraid.[47]

(laughing)

In times gone by, you pretended to fear God and his random
acts of chance, but your god was an anarchist who tried to
do a little of this and a little of that. He thought he could be
both powerful and good at the same time, but that's both
disorganized and dishonest. Me? I chose power alone. I chose
domination—and you can see now it's heavier than hell itself.

For thousands of years, I've covered your cities and fields
with mass graves. My dead have fertilized the sands of Libya
and black Ethiopia. Persia's soil is still slicked with the sweat
of my corpses. I've filled Athens with cleansing fires, lit

thousands of funeral pyres on its beaches, covered the Greek
sea with so much human ash it turned gray. The gods, the poor
gods themselves, were sickened to their very core. And when
the cathedrals succeeded the temples, my black horsemen
filled them with screaming corpses. For centuries, and on all
five continents, I've relentlessly killed without a moment's
hesitation.[48]

Not so bad, of course—it was the right idea, just not
the whole idea. A single death is, if you want my opinion,
refreshing, but the return on investment is small. At the end of
the day, it's not worth losing a slave over. The ideal investment
would return a majority of slaves with a minority of well-
chosen dead. Today, we've practically perfected the technique.
That's why, after having killed or debased the necessary
number of people, we bring the rest of the population to their
knees, too. No beauty, no greatness will resist us. We will
triumph over everything.

THE SECRETARY

We'll triumph over everything except pride.

THE PLAGUE

Maybe they'll tire of pride . . .
Man is smarter than we think.

Off in the distance, commotion and trumpets.

THE PLAGUE

Listen! My opportunity's coming around. Your former masters
are on their way back, and you'll find they're just as blind
as ever to the injuries plaguing other people, just as drunk

on inaction and forgetfulness. You'll tire of seeing stupidity triumph without a fight. Cruelty is revolting, but idiocy is discouraging. Credit the stupid for preparing my way. They are my strength and my hope. Perhaps a day will come when all sacrifice will seem to you in vain, when the interminable shouting of your filthy rebellions will finally die out. That day, I will truly reign in servitude's definitive silence.

(*laughing*)

It's a question of persistence, isn't it? Well, you can rest assured, I have the low brow of the stubborn.

He walks toward the back.

THE SECRETARY
I'm older than you are, and I know their love can be persistent, too.

THE PLAGUE
Love? What's that?

He exits.

THE SECRETARY
Get up, woman! I'm tired. It's time to get this over with.

VICTORIA *gets up, and at the same time,* DIEGO *falls to the ground. The* SECRETARY *backs into the shadows.* VICTORIA *rushes over to* DIEGO.

VICTORIA

Oh, Diego, what've you done to our happiness?

DIEGO

Goodbye, Victoria. I'm happy.

VICTORIA

Don't say that, my love. That's a man's word, a horrible man's word.

(*starting to cry*)

No one has the right to be happy about dying.

DIEGO

I'm happy, Victoria.[49] I did what I had to do. I did the right thing.

VICTORIA

No. The right thing to do was to choose me over heaven itself. To put me ahead of the entire planet.

DIEGO

I've accepted death. That's my strength. But it's a strength that devours everything. It leaves no place for happiness.

VICTORIA

What good's your strength to me? It's a man I loved.

DIEGO

The fight's dried me up. I'm no longer a man, and it's only right that I should die.

VICTORIA

(*throwing herself on him*)

Then take me with you!

DIEGO

No, this world needs you. It needs our women to teach it how to live. We . . . we've never been capable of anything but dying.

VICTORIA

Oh, it was too easy, wasn't it, to love each other in silence, to suffer what had to be suffered. I preferred your fear.

DIEGO
(*looking at* VICTORIA)

I loved you with all my soul.

VICTORIA
(*crying out*)

It wasn't enough. No! It isn't enough! What am I going to do with just your soul?

> *The* SECRETARY's *hand reaches out toward* DIEGO. *In pantomime, the death throes begin. The women rush over to* VICTORIA *and surround her.*

THE WOMEN

Woe unto him! Woe unto all those who desert our bodies! Mercy unto us, especially us, we who are the deserted and who will carry this world through all our years, the world their pride pretends to transform. Ah! If everything can't be saved, let us at least learn to preserve the house of love. Come plague, come war, and all the doors closed tight, with you next to us, we'll fight it out until the end, and then, instead of this solitary death, peopled with ideas, nourished on words, you would know death beside us, we and you entangled in the terrible embrace of love. But men prefer ideas. They flee their mother, hold their lover at arm's length, and then there they go, off on adventures, wounded without cuts, dead without daggers, shadow chasers, solitary singers, calling out beneath a wordless sky, asking for an impossible reunion, and walking from solitude to solitude, toward the final isolation, death in the open desert.

DIEGO *dies.*

The women mourn while the wind blows in a little stronger.

THE SECRETARY

Don't cry, women. The earth is sweet for those who've loved it well.

She exits.

VICTORIA *and the women go over to* DIEGO *and take him away.*

The background noises grow clearer.

A new type of music bursts forth, and NADA *is heard screaming from atop the fortifications.*

NADA

There they are! The old fellows are arriving, the ones from before, the ones from forever, the petrified, the reassuring, the comfortable, the dead-end cul-de-sacs, the well-bred, the status quo, tradition finally taking its seat again, prosperous and freshly shaven. A sigh of relief all around. Now we can start all over, and from scratch, of course. Here they are, the small-time tailors of nothingness, ready to give you a custom fit. Don't worry about a thing—their technique is impeccable. Rather than shutting up the ones who protest, they shut their own ears instead. Once we were dumb, now we'll be deaf.

Fanfare.

NADA

Heads up! The ones who write history are returning. They'll fill us in on all the details. Tell us who the heroes are. Store them away somewhere nice and cold. Down beneath the paving stones. But don't complain—up above the stones, society really is far too confused.

Official ceremonies are pantomimed in the background.

NADA

Just look at that. What do you think they're doing over there? Not a minute to lose. Why, they're adorning themselves with decorations, of course. Feasts of hatred are always being set out, the exhausted earth covered in the gallows' dead wood. The blood of the ones you call the just still brightens the world's walls, and what are they doing? They're adorning themselves with decorations, of course! Rejoice!

The prizewinning speeches are about to be delivered, crafted especially for you. But before they build their platform, I'd like to summarize my own. That guy, the one I quite liked despite myself, was robbed by death.

> The FISHERMAN *takes a run at* NADA. *The guards stop him.*

NADA

You see, Fisherman, governments come and governments go, but the police always stay the same. That's justice for you.

THE CHORUS

No, there is no justice, there are only limits. And those who pretend nothing is regulated, just like those who intend to regulate everything, both equally surpass the limits. Open the doors, let the wind and salt come and scour this city.

> *The doors are opened, the wind blows stronger and stronger.*

NADA

There is a justice—it's the kind done to my disgust. Yes, you'll start all over, but that's none of my business now. Don't count on me to provide you with the perfect fall guy—I don't have the virtue of melancholy. O old world, it's time to go. Your executioners are tired and their hatred has grown much too cold. I know too many things now. Even contempt has had its day. Farewell, good people. One day you'll learn we can't live well while knowing man is nothing and God's true face is terrible.

NADA runs through the stormy wind blowing in, out onto the jetty, and jettisons himself into the sea. The FISHERMAN *runs after him.*

THE FISHERMAN

He went over the edge. The swells are sweeping him away, knocking him around, smothering him in their frothy manes. That lying mouth of his is filling with salt, and at last it'll speak no more. Look, the raging sea's turning the color of anemones. It's avenging us. Its anger is our anger. The sea's putting out the rallying cry, a call to all its men,[50] a meeting of the solitary. O wave, O sea, homeland of insurgents, behold your people, who will never give in and never give up. A great tidal wave fed on bitter waters is coming to wash away your terrible cities.

CURTAINS

The Just

A PLAY IN FIVE ACTS

O love! O life! Not life but love in death.

Romeo and Juliet (act IV, scene V)[1]

Foreword

In February 1905, in Moscow, a group of terrorists belonging to the Socialist Revolutionary Party organized a bomb attack against the Grand Duke Sergei Alexandrovich, the tsar's uncle. This attack, and the unique circumstances that preceded and followed it, are the subject of *The Just*. As hard to believe as some of the situations in the play may be, they are nevertheless based in history. This is not to say, as you'll see, that *The Just* is a historical play. But all my characters really existed and behaved as I've shown them. I've only tried to make believable what was already true.

I've even kept the real name, Kalyayev, for *The Just*'s hero. I didn't do so out of a lack of imagination but out of respect for the men and women who, in the midst of the most unforgiving of tasks, were unable to shake off their own hearts. It's true that we've made progress since then, and that the hatred that weighed as an intolerable suffering on these exceptional souls has now become a comfortable system. All the more reason to evoke these great shades, their just rebellion, their difficult fraternity, and the boundless effort they made to come to terms with murder—and in doing so, to say where our fidelity lies.

The Just was staged for the first time on December 15, 1949, at the Théâtre Hébertot, under the direction of Paul Œttly, with set design and costumes by De Rosnay.[2]

CHARACTERS

Dora Doulebov[3]   Ivan Kalyayev[4]

The Grand Duchess[5]   Stepan Fedorov

Boris Annenkov[6]   Alexis Voinov[7]

Skuratov   Foka

The Guard

ACT I

The terrorists' apartment. Morning.
The curtain silently rises. DORA *and* ANNENKOV
*are onstage, motionless. A single chime is heard from
the front door.* ANNENKOV *waves his hand to stop*
DORA, *who seems about to say something. The chime
sounds twice in a row, in rapid succession.*

ANNENKOV

It's him.

> *He exits.* DORA *waits, still not moving.*
> ANNENKOV *returns with* STEPAN *and takes
> him by the shoulders.*

ANNENKOV

It's him! It's Stepan.

DORA
(*going to* STEPAN *and taking his hand*)

I'm so happy to see you, Stepan.

STEPAN

Hello, Dora.

DORA
(*looking at him*)

Three years, already.

STEPAN

Yes, three years. I was on my way to join you the day they arrested me.

DORA

We were waiting for you. The more time passed, the deeper my heart sank. We couldn't even look at each other anymore.

ANNENKOV

Then we had to change apartments again, like before.

STEPAN

I know.

DORA

And out there, Stepan?

STEPAN

Out there?

DORA

The labor camp?

STEPAN

You escape.

ANNENKOV

We were happy when we heard you'd made it to Switzerland.

STEPAN

Switzerland's only another camp, Boria.[8]

ANNENKOV

What are you saying? At least they're free there.

STEPAN

As long as there's a single man on earth enslaved, freedom is a camp. I was free, and yet I couldn't stop thinking of Russia and her slaves.

Silence.

ANNENKOV

I'm glad the party sent you here, Stepan.

STEPAN

They had to. I was suffocating. Oh, to act, to act at last.

(*looking at Annenkov*)

We are going to kill him, aren't we?

ANNENKOV

I'm sure of it.

STEPAN

We are going to kill that executioner. But you're the leader, Boria, and I'll do as you say.

ANNENKOV

You don't need to promise me anything, Stepan. We're all brothers here.

STEPAN

A person needs discipline. I began to realize that in the camp. The Socialist Revolutionary Party⁹ needs discipline. It's with discipline we'll kill the Grand Duke and topple the rule of tyranny.

DORA
(*going to him*)

Sit, Stepan. You must be tired after such a long trip.

STEPAN

I'm never tired.

Silence. DORA *goes to sit down.*

STEPAN

Is everything ready, Boria?

ANNENKOV
(*changing his tone*)

We've had two of our people studying the Grand Duke's movements over the past month. Dora's put together all the necessary information.

STEPAN

Has the proclamation been drafted?[10]

ANNENKOV

Yes. All of Russia will know that Grand Duke Sergei was executed by a bomb belonging to the paramilitary wing of the Socialist Revolutionary Party in order to hasten the liberation of the Russian people. The imperial court will also be informed that we're determined to employ terror until the land is returned to the people. Yes, Stepan, yes. Everything is ready. The time is close at hand.

STEPAN

What should I be doing?[11]

ANNENKOV

You'll start out by helping Dora. The man you're replacing, Schweitzer,[12] he was the one working with her before.

STEPAN

He was killed?

ANNENKOV

Yes.

STEPAN

How?

DORA

An accident.

> STEPAN *looks at* DORA. DORA *turns her eyes away.*

STEPAN

And after that?

ANNENKOV

After that, we'll see. You have to be ready to take our place, if it comes to that, and to maintain communication with the Central Committee.

STEPAN

Who are our comrades in all this?

ANNENKOV

You met Voinov in Switzerland. I have confidence in him, despite his youth. You don't know Yanek.[13]

STEPAN

Yanek?

ANNENKOV

Kalyayev. We also call him the Poet.

STEPAN

That's no kind of name for a terrorist.

ANNENKOV
(*laughing*)
Yanek thinks otherwise. He says that poetry is revolutionary.[14]

STEPAN
The bomb's the only thing that's revolutionary.

Silence.

STEPAN
Do you think I'll be able to help you, Dora?

DORA
Yes. Just be careful not to break the tube.

STEPAN
And if it breaks?

DORA
That's how Schweitzer died.

A moment passes.

DORA
Why're you smiling, Stepan?

STEPAN
I'm smiling?

DORA
Yes.

STEPAN
It happens sometimes.

A moment passes. STEPAN *seems to be contemplating something.*

STEPAN

Would a single bomb be enough to blow up this house, Dora?

DORA

A single one, no. But it would do some damage.

STEPAN

How many would it take to blow up Moscow?

DORA

Have you lost your mind! What are you talking about?

STEPAN

Nothing.

> *Someone rings once at the door. They listen and wait. Two more rings.* ANNENKOV *goes into the anteroom and then returns with* VOINOV.

VOINOV

Stepan!

STEPAN

Hello.

> *They shake hands.* VOINOV *goes over to* DORA *and hugs her.*

ANNENKOV

Everything went okay, Alexis?

VOINOV

Yes.

ANNENKOV

You studied the route from the palace to the theater?

VOIONOV

I can even draw it for you now. Look.

(*drawing*)

Here are the turns, the narrow lanes, the congestion. The
carriage will pass right under our windows.

ANNENKOV

What do these two crosses stand for?

VOINOV

A small square where the horses will slow down and the
theater where they'll stop. The best spots, in my opinion.

ANNENKOV

Give it here.

STEPAN

Informants?

VOINOV
(*hesitant*)

There are a lot of them.

STEPAN

They worry you?

VOINOV

They don't put me at ease.

ANNENKOV

Nobody's at ease with them around. Don't let it bother you.

VOINOV

I fear nothing. It's just I'm not used to lying, that's all.

STEPAN

Everybody lies. You just have to lie well.

VOINOV

It's not so easy. When I was a student, my friends used to make fun of me because I didn't know how to fake it. I said what was on my mind. Eventually, they kicked me out of the university.

STEPAN

For what?

VOINOV

In history class, the professor asked me how Peter the Great managed to build Saint Petersburg.

STEPAN

Good question.

VOINOV

With blood and whips, I said. I was chased out.

STEPAN

And then . . . ?

VOINOV

Then I realized it wasn't enough simply to denounce injustice. You have to give your life for the struggle, too. Now, I'm happy.

STEPAN

And yet, now you lie?

VOINOV

I lie. But the day I throw the bomb, I will no longer be lying.

> *Someone rings at the door, two chimes, then one.* DORA *takes off.*

ANNENKOV

It's Yanek.

STEPAN

It's not the same pattern.

ANNENKOV

Yanek likes to have fun with these things. He's got his own
personal pattern.

> STEPAN *shrugs his shoulders.* DORA *can
> be heard talking in the antechamber.* DORA
> *and* KALYAYEV *enter, arm in arm,* KALYAYEV
> *laughing.*

DORA

Yanek, this is Stepan. He's taking Schweitzer's place.

KALYAYEV

Welcome to our home, brother.

STEPAN

Thank you.

> DORA *and* KALYAYEV *go and sit down, fac-
> ing the others.*

ANNENKOV

Are you sure you'll recognize the carriage, Yanek?

KALYAYEV

Yes, I got two good long looks at it. Just let it appear out there
on the horizon, and I'll be able to pick it out among thousands
of others. I've noted every detail. For example, one of the glass
panes on the left-side lantern is chipped.

VOINOV

And the informants?

KALYAYEV

Swarms of them. But we're old friends. They buy me cigarettes.

He laughs.

ANNENKOV

Has Pavel confirmed our information?

KALYAYEV

The Grand Duke will be at the theater this week. Pavel will know the exact day soon and then have a message given to the doorman.

He turns to DORA *and smiles.*

KALYAYEV

We're lucky, Dora.

DORA
(*looking at him*)

So, you're no longer a door-to-door salesman, then? Look at you, a true gentleman now. How handsome you are. You don't miss your old sheepskin coat?

KALYAYEV
(*laughing*)

I was very proud of it, it's true.

(*to* STEPAN *and* ANNENKOV)

I spent two months watching the door-to-door salesmen hawk their wares, and then another month rehearsing in my small room. My colleagues never suspected a thing. "A first-rate hustler," they said. "He could even sell the tsar's horses." Then they'd try to imitate me when they went out.

DORA

You got a kick out of that, I'm sure.

KALYAYEV

You know I can't help myself. The disguises, the new life . . . It was all so much fun.

DORA

Me? I don't like disguises.

(*pointing at her dress*)

Just look at this luxurious rag. Boria could have found me something else to wear. An actress! No, my heart's too simple for that.

KALYAYEV
(*with a laugh*)

But you look so pretty in that dress.

DORA

Pretty! I'd be happy to be so, but let's not think about that.

KALYAYEV

Why not? Your eyes are always so sad, Dora. You have to be joyous, you have to be proud. Beauty exists. Joy exists. "In those quiet places my heart yearned for you—"

DORA
(*smiling*)

"I breathed an eternal summer."

KALYAYEV

Oh, Dora, you do remember those lines. Are you smiling? That makes me so happy.[15]

STEPAN
(*cutting in*)

We're wasting our time. Boria, shouldn't we be letting the doorman know to expect a message?

KALYAYEV *looks at him, surprised.*

ANNENKOV

Yes. You want to go down, Dora? And don't forget the tip. After that, Voinov can help you get things together in the other room.

They exit at opposite sides. STEPAN *takes a purposeful step toward* ANNENKOV.

STEPAN

I want to throw the bomb.

ANNENKOV

No, Stepan. The decision's already been made.

STEPAN

I beg you. You know what it means to me.

ANNENKOV

No. The rules are the rules.

A moment passes in silence.

ANNENKOV

I don't get to throw one, either. Me! I'll be waiting here. The rules apply to everyone.

STEPAN

Who will throw the first bomb?

KALYAYEV

Me. Voinov will throw the second.

STEPAN

You?

KALYAYEV

You're surprised by that? So then, you don't trust me?

STEPAN

It requires experience.

KALYAYEV

Experience? You know very well a person only ever throws a bomb once, and after that . . . Nobody ever throws twice.

STEPAN

It requires a steady hand.

KALYAYEV
(*holding out his hand*)

Look. Do you think mine's going to shake?

STEPAN *turns away*.

KALYAYEV

It won't shake. What? Am I going to hesitate when the tyrant's right there in front of me? How can you think that? And even if it did shake, still, I know a sure enough way to kill the Grand Duke.

ANNENKOV

How's that?

KALYAYEV

Throw myself under the horses' feet.[16]

> STEPAN *shrugs his shoulders and goes to sit down in the back.*

ANNENKOV

No, that's not what the situation calls for. You'd have to try to escape. The Organization needs you. You have to preserve yourself.

KALYAYEV

I'll do as you say, Boria. What an honor, what an honor for me! Oh, how I'll live up to the moment.

ANNENKOV

Stepan, you'll be positioned out on the street while Yanek and Alexis are keeping an eye on the carriage. You'll walk past our window from time to time, and we'll have a signal. Dora and I will be waiting here. When the moment comes, we'll issue the proclamation. With a little luck, the Grand Duke will be struck down.

KALYAYEV
(*with great excitement*)

Oh yes, I'll strike him down! And how joyous it will be if we succeed! The Grand Duke, he's nothing. We have to strike even higher!

ANNENKOV

First, the Grand Duke.

KALYAYEV

And if we fail, Boria? Well then, we do like the Japanese did.

ANNENKOV

What're you talking about?

KALYAYEV

The Japanese, during the war, they didn't surrender. They committed suicide.

ANNENKOV

No. No thinking about suicide.

KALYAYEV

About what then?

ANNENKOV

About terror, resurgent.

STEPAN
(*speaking from the back*)

In order to kill yourself, you have to love yourself, and a true revolutionary can't love himself.

KALYAYEV
(*swinging around to face him*)

A true revolutionary? Why are you treating me like this? What have I done to you?

STEPAN

I don't like people who join a revolution because they're bored.

ANNENKOV

Stepan!

STEPAN
(*standing and walking toward them*)

Yes, I can be blunt, but it's because hatred isn't a game for me. We're not here to pat each other on the back. We're here to succeed.

KALYAYEV
(*gently*)

Why do you insult me so? Who says I'm bored?

STEPAN

Oh, I don't know. You change the pattern for the door, you
have fun playing the role of a huckster, you speak in verse, you
want to throw yourself under the horses' feet, and now, suicide.

(*looking at him*)

I don't trust you.

KALYAYEV
(*controlling himself*)

You don't know me, brother. I love life. I'm not bored. I joined
the revolution because I love life.

STEPAN

I don't love life, I love justice, which is a higher cause than life.

KALYAYEV
(*with visible effort*)

Each serves justice in their own way. We have to accept that
we're different. We have to love each other, if we can.

STEPAN

We can't.

KALYAYEV
(*exploding*)

Then why are you here with us?

STEPAN

I'm here to kill a man, not to love or applaud differences.

KALYAYEV
(*violently*)

You're not going to get it done alone, and you're not going to get it done in the name of nothing. You'll do it with us and in the name of the Russian people. There, that's your justification.

STEPAN
(*same manner*)

I don't need your justification. I got mine in the camp three years ago, a justification that came in a single night and that will last forever. I'm not going to put up with—

ANNENKOV

Enough! Have the two of you lost your mind? Do you remember who we are? Brothers! Linked one to the other, turned toward the execution of tyrants, aimed at the liberation of the country. We kill together and nothing can separate us.

Silence. He looks at them.

ANNENKOV

Come, Stepan. We have to figure out what the signal will be.

STEPAN *exits.*

ANNENKOV
(*to* KALYAYEV)

It's nothing. Stepan's suffered a great deal. I'll talk to him.

KALYAYEV
(*very pale*)

He insulted me, Boria.

> DORA *enters. She notices* KALYAYEV'S *demeanor.*

DORA

What's wrong?

ANNENKOV

Nothing.

> *He exits.*

DORA
(*to* KALYAYEV)

What's wrong?

KALYAYEV

We're already butting heads. He doesn't like me.

> *Without saying anything,* DORA *goes over and sits down. A moment passes.*

DORA

I don't think he likes anyone. He'll be happier when it's all over. Don't be sad.

KALYAYEV

I am sad. I need you all to love me. I've given everything up for the Organization. How can I bear my brothers turning away from me? Sometimes, it feels like they don't understand me. Is it my fault? I can be clumsy, I know that.

DORA

They love you, and they understand you. Stepan's different.

KALYAYEV

No, I know what he thinks. Schweitzer already said it. "Too *special* to be a revolutionary." I'd like to tell them I'm not special. They think I'm a little crazy, too impulsive. But I believe in the same cause they do. I want to sacrifice myself, like they do. I can be clever, too, you know. Taciturn, covert, efficient. Life's the only thing that still seems wondrous to me. I love beauty, love bliss. That's why I hate despotism. But how am I to explain that to them? The revolution—of course—but revolution for the sake of life, to give life a chance, you know?

DORA
(*eagerly*)

Yes.

(*pausing a moment, then in a lower voice*)

And yet, we bring death.

KALYAYEV

We who?

Oh, you mean . . .

That's not the same thing. Oh, no. Not the same thing at all. We would kill to build a world where no one ever kills again. We accept being criminals so the world may finally be filled with innocents.

DORA

And if that weren't to be?

KALYAYEV

Don't say that! You know very well that's impossible. It would mean Stepan was right, and we'd have to spit in the face of beauty.

DORA

I've been with the Organization much longer than you. I know nothing's so simple. But you . . . you have faith. We all need faith.

KALYAYEV

Faith? No. Only one person has ever had that.

DORA

But your soul is strong, you have fortitude, and you'd throw it all away just to see things through. Why'd you ask to throw the first bomb?

KALYAYEV

Can a person really talk of terrorist action without taking part in it?[17]

DORA

No.

KALYAYEV

You have to be out on the front line.

DORA
(*seeming to consider his words*)

Yes. There's the front line and the final moment. We have to think about that. That's when we'll need courage, excitement . . . that's when you'll need it.

KALYAYEV

For a year now, I've thought of nothing else. I've lived my whole life for this moment. And I know now that what I'd like is to perish right there next to the Grand Duke, my blood slowly dripping out to the last drop or burning up all at once in an explosion of flames, leaving nothing behind. Do you understand why I asked to throw the bomb? To die for the cause is the only way to live up to the cause. That's the justification.

DORA

Yes! That's the sort of death I desire, too.

KALYAYEV

Yes, it's the sort of happiness a person can envy. Sometimes, at night, I toss and turn on my straw mattress, the one from when I used to sell door to door, a single thought tormenting me—they've made murderers out of us. But then, at the same time, I think how I'm going to die, and that sets my heart at ease. I smile, you know, and then calmly drift off to sleep like a child.

DORA

That's a good way to do things, Yanek. To kill and die. But, in my opinion, there's an even greater happiness.

> *A moment passes.* KALYAYEV *looks at her. She lowers her eyes.*

DORA

The gallows.

KALYAYEV
(*feverish*)

I've thought about that. Dying during the bombing leaves something unfinished. Whereas between the bombing and the gallows, there lies the whole of eternity, maybe the only one that exists for man.[18]

DORA
(*insistent, taking his hands*)

You have to take comfort in that thought. We pay more than our share.

KALYAYEV

What're you talking about?

DORA

We're obligated to kill, aren't we? We deliberately sacrifice one, and only one, life.

KALYAYEV

Yes.

DORA

But to go to the bombing first and then to the gallows, that would be to give your life twice. We pay more than our share.

KALYAYEV

Yes, that would be to die twice. Thank you, Dora. Nobody can hold anything against us. Now, I'm sure of myself.

Silence.

KALYAYEV

What is it, Dora? You're not saying anything.

DORA

I still want to help you. Only . . .

KALYAYEV

Only?

DORA

No, it's crazy. I'm crazy.

KALYAYEV

Do you not trust me?

DORA

No, no, my darling, I don't trust me. Ever since Schweitzer died, I've been having these strange ideas from time to time.

And then, it's not really for me to tell you what's going to be difficult or not.

KALYAYEV

I like difficult. If you truly respect me, then speak.

DORA
(*looking at him*)

I know. You're brave, and that's what worries me. You laugh, you get yourself all worked up, and you head straight for the sacrifice, full of passion. But in a couple of hours, you're going to have to step out of this dream state and act. Maybe it would be better if we discuss things ahead of time—to avoid a surprise . . . a slipup.

KALYAYEV

I won't slip up. Say what you're thinking.

DORA

It's just, the bombing, the gallows, dying twice over, all of that's the easy part. Your heart's strong enough for that. But the front line . . .

(*falling silent, looking at him,
and seeming to hesitate*)

Out on the front line, you'll see him.

KALYAYEV

Who?

DORA

The Grand Duke.

KALYAYEV

For barely a second.

DORA

A second during which you'll look at him. Oh, Yanek, you
have to know, you have to be forewarned. A man is a man. The
Grand Duke, maybe he has sympathetic eyes. You'll see him
scratch his ear or give a delighted smile. Who knows? Maybe
he'll have a small cut from his razor, and if he looks at you,
then—

KALYAYEV

It's not him I'm killing. It's despotism.

DORA

Of course, of course. Despotism must be killed. I'll go and
get the bomb ready, and when the time comes to seal up the
tube—you know, that's the most difficult part, when your
nerves are all frayed—at that moment I'll have a strange
happiness in my heart. But I don't know the Grand Duke, and
it wouldn't be quite so easy if while I was doing all of this, he
was sitting there right in front of me. You . . . you're going to
see him up close. Very close.

KALYAYEV
(*fiercely*)

I won't see him.

DORA

Why not? Are you going to close your eyes?

KALYAYEV

No, but God willing, hatred will arrive at just the right
moment and blind me.

> *Someone rings at the door. A single chime. They*
> *don't move a muscle.* STEPAN *and* VOINOV *enter.*

Voices in the antechamber. ANNENKOV *enters.*

ANNENKOV

It was the doorman. The Grand Duke will be at the theater tomorrow.

(*looking them over*)

Everything has to be ready, Dora.

DORA
(*in a dull and quiet voice*)

Yes.

She slowly exits.

KALYAYEV

I will kill him. With pleasure!

CURTAINS

ACT II

The next evening, same place.[19]

ANNENKOV *is by the window,* DORA *next to the table.*

ANNENKOV

They're in position. Stepan just lit his cigarette.

DORA

What time is the Grand Duke supposed to be here?

ANNENKOV

Any minute now. Listen. Is that a carriage? No.

DORA

Sit. Be patient.

ANNENKOV

And the bombs?

DORA

Sit. There's nothing more we can do.

ANNENKOV

There is—we can envy them.

DORA

Your place is here. You're the leader.

ANNENKOV

I'm the leader, but Yanek's better than I am, and maybe he's the one who—

DORA

The risk's the same for all of us—those of us who are throwing bombs and those of us who aren't.

ANNENKOV

In the end, the risk's the same, but in the moment, it's Yanek and Alexis who're in the line of fire, and I know I'm not supposed to be with them, but still, I worry, sometimes, that I've accepted my role a little too easily. After all, it's mighty convenient to be forced not to throw a bomb.

DORA

And so what if it's true? The important thing is that you do what *you* have to do, and that you see it through to the end.

ANNENKOV

You certainly are calm about all this.

DORA

I'm not calm, I'm afraid. I've been with you for three years now, and for two of those I've been making bombs. I've done everything I was supposed to do, and I don't think I've forgotten a thing.

ANNENKOV

Of course, Dora.

DORA

For three years I've been afraid, and it's the type of fear that barely lets up when you sleep, that waits for you all fresh and ready in the morning. So you see, I've had to get used to it. I've had to learn how to be calm at the very moment I'm most afraid. That's not something to be proud of.

ANNENKOV

But you should be proud. Me? I've learned to control nothing. Do you know, I miss the old days, the high life, the women . . .

oh, yes, I loved the women, the wine, those nights that seemed as if they'd never end.

DORA

I figured as much, Boria. That's why I like you so much. Your heart hasn't died. And even if it still longs for pleasure, well, that's still so much better than that horrid silence that sometimes settles in in place of a scream.

ANNENKOV

What're you saying? You? It's not possible.

DORA

Listen.

DORA *quickly gets to her feet. The sound of a carriage, then silence.*

DORA

It's not him. My heart's racing. You see, I still haven't learned a thing.

ANNENKOV *goes over to the window.*

ANNENKOV

Wait a second. Stepan just gave the signal. It's him.

Indeed, the rolling of a carriage can be heard in the distance, getting closer and closer, passing beneath the windows, and beginning to move away. A long silence.

ANNENKOV

In a few seconds . . .

They listen.

ANNENKOV

It feels like it's taking forever.

DORA *gestures. A long silence. The sound of bells in the distance.*

ANNENKOV

Something's not right. Yanek should've thrown the bomb by now. The carriage must already be at the theater. And what about Alexis? Look! Stepan's turning around. He's running back to the theater.

DORA
(*throwing herself against him*)

Yanek's been arrested. He's definitely been arrested. We have to do something.

ANNENKOV

Wait a second.

He listens.

ANNENKOV

No. It's over.

DORA

How could this have happened? How could Yanek have been arrested before even doing anything when I know he was ready to do everything. He wanted prison, a trial. But after having killed the Grand Duke! Not like this—no, not like this!

ANNENKOV
(*looking out the window*)

It's Voinov! Quick!

DORA *goes to open the door.*

VOINOV *enters, a distraught look on his face.*

ANNENKOV

Speak, Alexis, quickly.

VOINOV

I know nothing. I was waiting for the first bomb to go off, I saw the carriage take the turn, and then nothing happened. I panicked. I thought you must have changed the plan at the last minute, and I hesitated, and then I ran all the way back here.

ANNENKOV

And Yanek?

VOINOV

I haven't seen him.

DORA

They've arrested him.

ANNENKOV
(*still looking outside*)

There he is!

Same process as when VOINOV *arrived.* KALY-
AYEV *enters, face covered in tears.*

KALYAYEV
(*beside himself*)

Forgive me, brothers. I couldn't do it.

DORA *goes to him and takes his hand.*

DORA

It's okay, it's nothing.

ANNENKOV

What happened?

DORA
(*to* KALYAYEV)

It's nothing. Sometimes, at the last second, everything falls apart.

ANNENKOV

But that's impossible.

DORA

Leave him alone. You're not the only one, Yanek. Schweitzer, the first time, he wasn't able to do it, either.

ANNENKOV

Did you get scared, Yanek?

KALYAYEV
(*startled*)

Scared, no. You have no right—

A knock at the door in the agreed-upon pattern. ANNENKOV *signals for* VOINOV *to go check it out.* KALYAYEV *hunches forward, overwhelmed. Silence.* STEPAN *enters.*

ANNENKOV

So?

STEPAN

There were children in the carriage with the Grand Duke.

ANNENKOV

Children?

STEPAN

Yes. The Grand Duke's niece and nephew.[20]

ANNENKOV

Orlov said the Grand Duke would be alone.

STEPAN

The Grand Duchess was also in the carriage. Too many
people for our poet, I guess. Luckily, the informants didn't see
anything.

> ANNENKOV *speaks to* STEPAN *in a low voice.*
> *Everyone is looking at* KALYAYEV, *who then lifts*
> *his gaze to* STEPAN.

KALYAYEV
(*beside himself*)

I couldn't have known there'd be children. Of all things,
children. Have you ever looked at a child? That serious look
they sometimes give you. I've never been able to bear that
look. Only a second before, I'd been standing there in the
shadows at the corner of the square, and I was happy. When
the carriage lanterns began to glow in the distance, my heart
began to beat with joy, I swear to you. It beat faster and faster
the closer the carriage got. It was making so much noise, I

could hardly contain myself. I think I was laughing and I was chanting, "Yes, yes." Do you understand what I'm saying?

> *He turns his gaze from* STEPAN *and returns to his hunched posture.*

KALYAYEV

I ran toward it. And that's when I saw them. They weren't laughing, no, not them. They were sitting there perfectly straight, staring out into space. How sad they seemed! Lost in those fancy clothes, hands in their laps, bodies held rigid, each of them on their own side of the vehicle. I didn't see the Grand Duchess. I saw only them. If they'd looked at me, I think I would have thrown the bomb, if only to blow away those sad little looks. But they just sat there staring straight ahead.

> *He lifts his eyes to the others. Silence.*

KALYAYEV
(*in an even lower voice*)

After that, I don't know what happened. My arm grew weak. My legs began to shake. A second more, and it was too late.

> *Silence. He looks at the ground.*

KALYAYEV

Was I dreaming, Dora, or were the bells ringing right at that moment?

DORA

No, Yanek, you weren't dreaming.

She places her hand on his arm. KALYAYEV
raises his head and sees them all looking at him.
He stands up.

KALYAYEV

Look at me, brothers. Look at me, Boria. I am not a coward. I
didn't lose my nerve. I just didn't expect them. It all happened
so fast. Those two serious little faces and that terrible weight in
my hand. It was at them I'd have to throw the thing. Just like
that. Right at them. Oh, no, I couldn't do it.

He looks at each of them in turn.

KALYAYEV

Back in the day, back in Ukraine, when I'd take our carriage
out for a drive, I drove like the wind, afraid of nothing.
Nothing in the whole wide world, except for hitting a child. I
always imagined the shock, that fragile head hitting the road,
the body in midair . . .

He falls silent.

KALYAYEV

Help me . . .

Silence.

KALYAYEV

I wanted to kill myself, you know. I only came back because I
thought I owed you an explanation, because you're the only

ones who can judge me, who can tell me if I was right or wrong. Because your judgment can't be wrong. But now you're not saying anything.

> DORA *moves closer to him, touching him. He looks at them and speaks in a sad and gloomy voice.*

KALYAYEV

Here's what I suggest. If you decide it's necessary to kill the children, I'll wait for them as the theater lets out, and then I'll throw a bomb at their carriage, just me, all on my own. I know I won't miss my target. Just make a decision, and I'll do what the Organization tells me to do.

STEPAN

The Organization ordered you to kill the Grand Duke.

KALYAYEV

That's true—but it didn't ask me to murder children.

ANNENKOV

Yanek's right. We hadn't planned on this.

STEPAN

He should have obeyed.

ANNENKOV

I'm responsible for what's happened. Everything should have been planned out so that none of us could have been unsure about what to do. All we can do now is decide if we should let this opportunity slip away completely or if we should order Yanek to go and wait for the theater to let out. Alexis?

VOINOV

I don't know. I think I would've done what Yanek did. But I'm not even sure.

(*voice lower*)

My hands are shaking.

ANNENKOV

Dora?

DORA
(*emphatically*)

I would have lost my nerve, like Yanek did. How can I tell other people to do what I couldn't do myself?

STEPAN

Do all of you really understand what this decision means? Two months of tailing and shadowing, of terrible dangers encountered and avoided. Two months lost forever. Igor arrested for nothing. Rykov hanged for nothing.[21] And what, now we start all over again? Again with those long weeks spent staking things out, plotting things out, the constant, endless stress, on and on until the next opportune moment presents itself. Have you gone mad?

ANNENKOV

The Grand Duke will be back at the theater in two days, you know that.

STEPAN

Two days during which we risk being caught. You said it yourself.

KALYAYEV

I'm going.

DORA

Wait!

(*to* STEPAN)

Could you really—you, Stepan—with your eyes wide open, fire at a child point-blank?

STEPAN

I could do it if the Organization ordered me to do it.

DORA

Why'd you just close your eyes, then?

STEPAN

Me? I closed my eyes?

DORA

Yes.

STEPAN

Then it must have been to better imagine the scene and respond with full knowledge of the facts.

DORA

Open your eyes. Can't you see the Organization would lose its power and influence if it tolerated, even for a single second, children being blown to bits by our bombs.

STEPAN

My heart doesn't bleed enough for such nonsense. When we decide to stop worrying about children, that's the day we'll be masters of the universe. That's the day the revolution will triumph.[22]

DORA

That's the day the whole of humanity will hate the revolution.

STEPAN

What does it matter, as long as we love the revolution with enough strength to impose it on the whole of humanity and save them from themselves and their servitude?

DORA

And if the whole of humanity rejects the revolution? If all the people you're fighting for refuse to let their children be killed? Won't we have to kill them, too?

STEPAN

Yes, if that's what has to be done, then we'll do it until they understand. I love the people, too, you know.

DORA

That's not what love looks like.

STEPAN

Says who?

DORA

Me, Dora.

STEPAN

You're a woman, and you have a misguided idea of love.[23]

DORA
(*emphatically*)

But I have a pretty good idea of what shame is.

STEPAN

I've only ever been ashamed of myself once, one single time, and it wasn't because of anything I did, it was because of what they did. It was when they gave me the whip. And I was given the whip. Do you know what that is, the whip? Vera was right there next to me—she committed suicide in protest.[24] But me? I've gone on living. What could I possibly be ashamed of now?

ANNENKOV

Everyone here loves and respects you, Stepan, and no matter what reasons you may have, I cannot allow you to go on saying

that everything is permitted, that anything goes.[25] Hundreds
of our brothers have died so that the rest of us would know
that not everything is permitted.

STEPAN

Nothing that can serve our cause is forbidden.

ANNENKOV
(*angry*)

Is joining the police and playing both sides, as Evno suggested,
is that permitted?[26] Would you do that?

STEPAN

If necessary, yes.

ANNENKOV
(*standing up*)

We'll pretend we didn't hear what you just said, Stepan, in
consideration of all that you've done for and with us. Only
remember this—the question at hand right now, at this
moment, is are we going to throw bombs at those two children?

STEPAN

Children! That's the only word you know how to say. Do you
understand nothing, then? Because Yanek didn't kill those
two, thousands of Russian children will die of hunger in
the years to come. Have you ever seen a child die of hunger?
Me? I have. And let me tell you, to die by a bomb is a delight
compared to that. But Yanek, he's never seen it. All he saw
were the Grand Duke's two well-trained little pups. Are you
not men? Do you live only in the present moment? Go on,
then. Give your charity. Cure nothing but the day's sickness
and forget the revolution that wants to cure the entire disease,
present and future.

DORA

Yanek is willing to kill the Grand Duke, because the Grand Duke's death will bring us closer to a time when Russian children won't die of hunger anymore. That's no easy thing in itself. But the death of the Grand Duke's niece and nephew, that won't prevent a single child from dying of hunger. Even in destruction, there's order, there are limits.

STEPAN

(*emphatically*)

There are no limits. The truth is you don't believe in the revolution.

Everyone stands, except YANEK.

STEPAN

You don't believe in it. If you fully and completely believed in it, if you were certain that, through our sacrifices and our victories, we would be able to build a Russia free of despotism, a land of freedom that would one day stretch across the globe, if you had no doubt that man, freed of his masters and prejudices, would then lift the true face of god to the heavens, what would the death of two children weigh? You'd be justified in doing anything—anything, do you hear me? If the deaths of these two are stopping you, it's because you're not sure you can justify it. You don't believe in the revolution.

Silence. KALYAYEV *stands up.*

KALYAYEV[27]

I'm ashamed of myself, Stepan, but even so, I can't let you keep
going on like this. I'm willing to kill to overthrow despotism,
but behind what you're saying I see the coming of a despotism
that, if it were ever to be put in place, would make me a
murderer even though I'm trying to do justice and right what's
wrong.

STEPAN

Whether you're a doer of justice doesn't matter, so long
as justice is done—even if by murderers. You and I, we're
nothing.

KALYAYEV

We're something and you clearly know it. After all, it's your
pride talking now.

STEPAN

My pride's no one's business but my own. But the people's
pride, their rebellion, the injustice in which they live—that,
that is all of our business.

KALYAYEV

People don't live on justice alone.

STEPAN

When their bread's being stolen from them, what else should
they live on, if not justice?

KALYAYEV

Justice and innocence.

STEPAN

Innocence? I think I may have heard of that. But I've chosen to
ignore it and to have thousands of other people ignore it, too,
so that one day it can take on a deeper meaning.

KALYAYEV[28]
But to deny a person everything that keeps them going, you'd
have to be absolutely certain that day is going to come.

STEPAN
I'm certain.

KALYAYEV
You can't be. To know which one of us is right, you or I, we'd
have to sacrifice maybe three generations, wage a couple of
wars, a few terrifying revolutions, and then, by the time all
that blood's dried on the land, you and I, we'll have long since
returned to dust.

STEPAN
Others will come after us, and I recognize and welcome them
as my brothers.

KALYAYEV
(*crying out*)
Others, yes, of course! But me, I love the people who are
alive today, living on the same earth as I am, and it's them I
recognize and welcome, and it's for them that I struggle. It's
for them that I'm willing to die. I refuse to strike my brother's
face for some far-distant city I'm not even sure will ever exist. I
refuse to add to living injustice for a justice of the dead.

(*in a lower but firm voice*)

Brothers, let me be frank with you and say, at the very least,
what even the humblest of our peasants would say—killing
children is incompatible with honor. And if a day comes,
while I'm alive, that the revolution feels the need to rid itself
of honor, then I will walk away from it. If it should be your

decision, then in a few minutes I'll go to that theater, but it's myself I'll throw beneath the horses' hooves.

STEPAN

Honor is a luxury reserved for those who have carriages.

KALYAYEV

No. It's the last bit of wealth still owned by the poor. You know it very well and you also know there's honor in revolution. Honor is the thing for which we're willing to die. It's the thing that allowed you to stand tall beneath the whip that day, Stepan, and it's the thing that makes you say what you're still saying now.

STEPAN
(*yelling*)

Shut up. Don't you dare talk about that.

KALYAYEV
(*getting carried away*)

Why should I shut up? I let you say that I don't believe in the revolution, which is like saying I'd kill the Grand Duke for nothing, that I'd be a murderer. I let you say it and I didn't lash out at you.

ANNENKOV

Yanek!

STEPAN

Sometimes not killing enough is killing for nothing.

ANNENKOV

No one here agrees with you, Stepan. The decision's been made.

STEPAN

Then I'll yield. But let me repeat that terror is not for the faint of heart. We are killers, and we chose to be so.

KALYAYEV
(*beside himself*)

No, I've chosen to die so that killing won't win. I've chosen to
be innocent.[29]

ANNENKOV

Yanek, Stepan, enough! The Organization's decided that the
killing of these children would be pointless. We have to set up
a new stakeout. We'll have to be ready in two days.

STEPAN

And if the children are there again?

ANNENKOV

We'll wait for another opportunity.

STEPAN

And if the Grand Duchess is accompanying the Grand Duke?

KALYAYEV

I won't spare her.

ANNENKOV

Listen.

> *The sound of a carriage.* KALYAYEV *is irresist-
> ibly drawn to the window. The others wait. The
> carriage gets closer, passes beneath the window,
> and disappears into the distance.*

> VOINOV *looks at* DORA, *who then comes over
> to him.*

VOINOV

Let's get back to it, Dora.

STEPAN
(*disgusted*)

Yes, Alexis, let's get back to it. We really must do
something—for honor!

CURTAINS

ACT III

Same time, same place, two days later.

STEPAN

What's Voinov doing? He's supposed to be here.

ANNENKOV

He needed some sleep. And we still have a half hour ahead of us.

STEPAN

I can go find out the latest.

ANNENKOV

No. We have to limit our risks.

Silence.

ANNENKOV

Why aren't you saying anything, Yanek?

KALYAYEV

I don't have anything to say. You don't need to worry.

The doorbell rings.

KALYAYEV

That's him.

VOINOV *enters.*

ANNENKOV

Did you sleep?

VOINOV

A little, yes.

ANNENKOV

Did you sleep through the night?

VOINOV

No.

ANNENKOV

You needed to. There are ways, you know.

VOINOV

I tried. I was too tired.

ANNENKOV

Your hands are shaking.

VOINOV

No.

Everybody looks at him.

VOINOV

Why are you all looking at me? Can't a person be tired?

ANNENKOV

A person can be tired. We have only your best interests in mind.

VOINOV
(*suddenly exploding*)

You should have had our best interests in mind the other
day. If we'd thrown the bomb two days ago, we wouldn't be
so tired now.

KALYAYEV

Forgive me, Alexis. I've made things harder for us.

VOINOV
(*voice lower*)

Says who? Harder how? I'm tired, that's all.

DORA

It won't be much longer now. It'll all be over in an hour.

VOINOV

Yes, it'll all be over. In an hour . . .

> *He looks around.* DORA *goes over to him and takes his hand. He lets her do so, but then wrenches it away.*

VOINOV

I'd like to talk to you, Boria.

ANNENKOV

In private?

VOINOV

In private.

> *They look at each other.* KALYAYEV, DORA, *and* STEPAN *exit.*

ANNENKOV

What's wrong?

> VOINOV *remains silent.*

ANNENKOV

Please, just tell me.

VOINOV

I'm ashamed, Boria.

Silence.

VOINOV

I'm ashamed. I have to be honest with you.

ANNENKOV

You don't want to throw the bomb?

VOINOV

I won't be *able* to throw it.

ANNENKOV

Are you afraid? Is that what this is about? There's no shame in that.

VOINOV

I'm afraid, and I'm ashamed of being afraid.

ANNENKOV

Just the other day, you were so upbeat, so strong. Your eyes were gleaming as you left.

VOINOV

I've always been afraid. The other day, I'd gathered up my courage, that's all. When I heard the carriage wheels rolling in the distance, I said to myself, "Here we go! Only another minute now." I clenched my teeth. All my muscles were tense. I was going to throw the bomb as hard as I possibly could, as if the impact alone had to be enough to kill the Grand Duke. I was waiting for the first explosion to sound, to set off all the energy that had built up inside me—but nothing. The carriage was there in front of me—how quickly it moved—and then it had passed, and I understood then that Yanek hadn't thrown the bomb. At that moment, a terrible chill gripped me, and I suddenly felt as weak as a child.

ANNENKOV

It's nothing, Alexis. You'll be full of life again soon.

VOINOV

It's been two days now, and life hasn't returned. I lied to you a minute ago. I didn't sleep at all last night. My heart was beating so fast. Oh, Boria, I'm hopeless.

ANNENKOV

You shouldn't feel that way. We've all been where you are. You won't throw the bomb. A month's rest in Finland and you'll come back to us good as new.

VOINOV

No. It's not like that. If I don't throw the bomb now, I never will.

ANNENKOV

Well then?

VOINOV

I'm not cut out for terrorism. I can see that now. It'd be best for me to leave you all. I'll fight for us through committees, work on propaganda.

ANNENKOV

The risks are the same.

VOINOV

Yes, but with that kind of work, a person can take action with their eyes shut, knowing nothing.

ANNENKOV

What're you trying to say?

VOINOV

(*feverishly*)

When you know nothing, it's easy to hold meetings, to discuss
the situation, and then to send off orders for someone to be
executed. You're still risking your life, of course, but you're
doing so in the dark, without seeing a thing. To stand out in
the streets as night falls over the city, though, to stand amid
the crowds hurrying to get back to a bowl of warm soup, to
children, to the warmth of a wife, to stand there tall and silent,
with the bomb weighing heavy in your hand, and to know that
in three minutes, two minutes, a couple more seconds, you'll
throw yourself in front of that glittering carriage—now that
is terror. And I understand now that there's no way I'd ever be
able to go back to it without feeling as if the blood had been
drained from my body. Yes, I'm ashamed. I aimed too high. I
have to work at my own level. A very low level. The only level
for which I'm fit.

ANNENKOV

There is no low level. Prison and the gallows are always waiting
at the end.

VOINOV

But you don't see them like you see the person you're going to
kill. They're left to the imagination. Luckily, I don't have an
imagination.

(*a nervous laugh*)

You know, I've never really been able to believe in the secret
police. Kind of odd for a terrorist, isn't it? First time I get a
good kick in the gut, then I'll believe in them. Not before.

ANNENKOV

And when you're in prison? In prison, you know and you see.
There is no more forgetting.

VOINOV

In prison, there are no decisions to be made. Yes, that's it!
No more making decisions. No more having to tell yourself,
"Let's go, it's up to you. You're the one who has to decide the
exact second you'll wind up and throw." I'm sure now that if
I'm arrested, I won't try to escape. To escape, you need to be
inventive, you need to take initiative. If you don't escape, the
initiative is left for others to take. They have all the work
to do.

ANNENKOV

And sometimes their work is to hang you.

VOINOV
(*hopeless*)

Sometimes. But it'll be easier to die than to hold my life and
the life of another right there in the palm of my hand and to
decide at which moment I should hurl both those lives into
the flames. No, Boria. The only way to free myself is to accept
what I am.

ANNENKOV *remains silent.*

VOINOV

Even cowards can serve the revolution. They just need to find
their place.

ANNENKOV

Then we're all cowards, only we haven't had the chance to
prove it yet. You'll do what you need to do.

VOINOV

I'd prefer to leave right away. I don't think I could look them in the face. But you'll tell them?

ANNENKOV

I'll tell them.

He steps toward him.

VOINOV

Tell Yanek it's not his fault, and that I love him, as I love all of you.

Silence. ANNENKOV *hugs him.*

ANNENKOV

Goodbye, brother. It'll all work out. Russia will be happy.

VOINOV
(*running off*)

Oh, yes. How happy she will be! How happy she will be!

ANNENKOV *goes to the door.*

ANNENKOV

Come in.

They all enter with DORA.

STEPAN

What's wrong?

ANNENKOV

Voinov isn't going to throw the bomb. He's exhausted. It wouldn't be safe.

KALYAYEV

It's my fault, isn't it, Boria?

ANNENKOV

He made me promise to tell you that he loves you.

KALYAYEV

Will we see him again?

ANNENKOV

Maybe. But for the time being, he's leaving us.

STEPAN

Why?

ANNENKOV

He'll be more useful serving on committees.

STEPAN

Did he ask to do that? Is it because he's scared?

ANNENKOV

No. The decision was entirely my own.

STEPAN

You would take a man from us an hour before the bombing?

ANNENKOV

An hour before the bombing, I had to make my own decision. It's too late to discuss it now. I'll be taking Voinov's place.

STEPAN

His place belongs to me.

KALYAYEV
(*to* ANNENKOV)

You're the leader. Your job is to stay here.

ANNENKOV

It's true that a leader's job is to be a coward sometimes—but
only if he's willing to test his own courage every now and
again. I've made my decision. You'll take my place, Stepan. For
as long as necessary. Let's get to it. You'll need to familiarize
yourself with the instructions.

> *They exit.* KALYAYEV *goes to sit down.* DORA
> *goes to him, hand outstretched, then changes her
> mind.*

DORA

It's not your fault.

KALYAYEV

I hurt him. Hurt him bad. Do you know what he said to me
the other day?

DORA

He kept saying over and over how happy he was.

KALYAYEV

Yes, but he told me there was no happiness for him outside
our group. "There's us," he said. "The Organization. And then
there's nothing. We're like a brotherhood of knights." Oh,
what a pity, Dora.

DORA

He'll come back.

KALYAYEV

No. I can imagine how I'd feel if I were in his place. I'd be
hopeless.

DORA

And you don't feel that way now?

KALYAYEV
(*with sadness*)

Now? I'm with you and I'm as happy as he was.

DORA
(*slowly*)

What great happiness.

KALYAYEV

What truly great happiness. Don't you agree?

DORA

I agree. But then why are you so sad? Two days ago, your face was glowing. It was as if you were headed off to a wonderful celebration. Today—

KALYAYEV
(*standing up, greatly agitated*)

Today, I know what I didn't know then. You were right. It's not so simple. I believed it was easy to kill, thought a cause and courage were enough. But I'm not so big as all that. I know now there's no happiness in hate. All this evil, all this evil, in me and in others. Murder, cowardice, injustice. Oh, I have to, I have to kill him . . . I'll do whatever it takes. Go beyond even hatred!

DORA

Beyond? There is nothing beyond.

KALYAYEV

There's love.

DORA

Love? No, that's not what we need.

KALYAYEV

Oh, Dora, how can you say that? You, whose heart I know.

DORA

There's too much blood. Too much barbarity. Those who truly love justice have no right to love. They stand tall, as I do, head held high, eyes fixed and staring. What role could love play in hearts so proud? Love gently bows heads, Yanek, but we—we have stiff necks.

KALYAYEV

But we love our people.

DORA

We love them, it's true. We love them with a vast and restless love, an unassisted love, an unhappy love. We live apart from them, closed up in our rooms, lost in our thoughts. And the people themselves—do they love us? Do they know that we love them? The people, they remain silent. And what a silence, what a silence it is . . .

KALYAYEV

But that's just it—that's love, to give everything, to sacrifice everything, without the hope of getting anything in return.

DORA

Maybe that is love—an unconditional, pure, and solitary joy. That's certainly the kind that burns inside me. But I do wonder, sometimes, if love isn't really something else, if maybe it doesn't have to be a monologue, if there isn't, sometimes, a response. I can imagine it, you know. The sun shining, heads gently bowing, the heart letting go of its pride, arms opening up. Oh, Yanek, if we could only, even for just one hour, forget the world's atrocious misery and finally let ourselves go.[30] Just one little hour of selfishness, can you imagine that?

KALYAYEV

Yes, Dora. It's called tenderness.

DORA

You always know these things, my darling. It's called tenderness. But do you really understand it? Do you love justice with tenderness?

KALYAYEV *remains silent.*

DORA

Do you love our people with that same sense of abandon and gentleness, or is it just the opposite, a love of the fiery flames of vengeance and rebellion?

KALYAYEV *still remains silent.*

DORA

You see.

(*walking over to him, speaking in a very weak voice*)

And me? Do you love me with tenderness?

KALYAYEV *looks at her. A moment passes in silence.*

KALYAYEV

Nobody will ever love you as I love you.

DORA

I know. But isn't it better to love like everyone else loves?

KALYAYEV

I'm not just anyone. I love you as I am.

DORA

You love me more than justice, more than the Organization?

KALYAYEV

I don't separate things out like that—you, the Organization, justice.

DORA

Okay, but answer me, please, just answer me. Do you love me, just me, tenderly, selfishly? Would you love me if I were unjust?

KALYAYEV

If you were unjust and if I were able to love you, then it wouldn't be you that I loved.

DORA

You didn't answer. Just tell me—would you love me if I wasn't in the Organization?

KALYAYEV

Well, where would you be, then?

DORA

I remember a time when I was doing my studies. I used to laugh. I was beautiful back then. I would spend hours just walking around and dreaming. Would you love me if I was lighthearted and carefree?

KALYAYEV
(*hesitating, then very low*)

I'm dying to say yes.

DORA
(*crying out*)

Then say yes, my darling. If you really mean it and if it's true. Yes, before justice, ahead of misery and all those people in chains. Yes, yes, please, despite children living in agony, despite people being hanged and whipped to death—

KALYAYEV

Stop talking, Dora.

DORA

No. We have to let our heart speak at least once. I'm waiting for you to call out to me—me, Dora. For you to call out above this world poisoned with injustice—

KALYAYEV
(*harshly*)

Stop talking! My heart speaks of nothing but you. But now is not the time for me to waver.

DORA
(*beside herself*)

Now? Yes, I forgot . . .

(*laughing as if she were crying*)

No, no, it's all right, my darling. Don't be angry, I was being unreasonable. It's just the fatigue talking. I couldn't have said it, either, I couldn't have. I love you with that same single-minded love, alongside justice and prisons. The summer, Yanek, do you remember it? No, never mind. Winter is eternal. We're not of this world. We're the just. There's a warmth that's not for us.[31]

(turning away)

Oh, have pity on the just!

KALYAYEV
(looking at her, hope drained away)
Yes, that's our role, a role that makes love impossible. But I will kill the Grand Duke, and when I do, then there'll be a sort of peace, for you and for me.

DORA
Peace! When will we find that?

KALYAYEV
(forcefully)
In another day.

ANNENKOV *and* STEPAN *enter.* DORA *and* KALYAYEV *step away from each other.*

ANNENKOV
Yanek!

KALYAYEV
Right away.

He takes a deep breath.

KALYAYEV
At last, at last . . .

STEPAN
(coming over to him)
Goodbye, brother. I'm with you.

KALYAYEV

Goodbye, Stepan.

He turns to DORA.

KALYAYEV

Goodbye, Dora.

DORA *goes to him. They stand very close to each other but don't touch.*

DORA

No, not goodbye. Until next time. Until next time, my darling. We'll meet again.

He looks at her. Silence.

KALYAYEV

Until next time. I . . . Russia will be beautiful.[32]

DORA
(*in tears*)

Russia will be beautiful.

KALYAYEV *crosses himself in front of the icon.*[33]

He leaves with ANNENKOV.

STEPAN *goes to the window.* DORA *doesn't move, her gaze glued to the door.*

STEPAN

Look how tall he walks. I was wrong, you know, not to trust
Yanek. I didn't like that enthusiasm of his. He crossed himself,
did you see that? Is he a believer?

DORA

He doesn't practice.

STEPAN

He's got a religious soul, though. That's the difference between
us. I'm harsher than he is, I know that. For those of us who
don't believe in God, it's absolute justice, or it's all hopeless.

DORA

For him, justice itself is hopeless.

STEPAN

Yes, a weak soul, but a strong hand. He's better than his soul,
though, and he will kill him, of that I am certain. And that's
good. Very good indeed. To destroy—well, that's how it has to
be. But why aren't you saying anything?

He examines her.

STEPAN

You love him?

DORA

People need time for love. We hardly have enough time for
justice.

STEPAN

You're right. There's too much to be done. The world has to be
torn down and rebuilt from top to bottom . . . and then . . .

(*looking out the window*)

I can't see them anymore. They must be in position.

DORA

And then . . .

STEPAN

Then we'll love each other.

DORA

If we're still around.

STEPAN

Other people will love each other. It's all the same.

DORA

Can you say "hatred," Stepan?

STEPAN

What?

DORA

That one word, "hatred." Say it out loud.

STEPAN

Hatred.

DORA

That's good. Yanek said it very poorly.

A moment passes. STEPAN *walks over to her.*

STEPAN

I know you look down on me, but are you really so sure you're
right?

(*pausing a moment, then with increasing force*)

You're all out here haggling about what you'll do in the name
of your despicable love, but me, I love nothing, and I hate,

yes, I hate my fellow man. What do I want with their love? I learned all about it three years ago in the prison camp, and for three years I've been carrying it on my back. You want me to feel moved and to carry the bomb like a cross? No! No! I've gone too far, I've seen too many things. Look.

> *He tears his shirt open.* DORA *makes a move toward him, then steps back at the sight of the scars from the whip.*

STEPAN

These are the scars. The scars of their love. Are you still looking down on me now?

> *She goes over and abruptly embraces him.*

DORA

Who could look down on suffering? I love you, too.

STEPAN
(looking at her and speaking softly)
Forgive me, Dora.

> *A moment passes. He turns away.*

STEPAN

Maybe it's the fatigue talking. The years of struggle, of anxiety, the informants, the prison camp . . . and to top it all off, this.

(gesturing at his scars)

Where would I find the strength to love? Well, at least I still have the strength to hate, and that's better than feeling nothing at all.

DORA

Yes, that is better.

He looks at her. The clock strikes seven.

STEPAN
(*spinning around*)
The Grand Duke will be here any second.

DORA *goes to the window and presses herself against the panes. A long silence. And then, in the distance, the carriage. It approaches the apartment, then passes by.*

STEPAN

If he's alone . . .

The carriage moves off in the distance. An immense explosion. DORA *jumps back, startled, and hides her head in her hands. A long silence.*

STEPAN

Boria didn't throw his bomb. It was Yanek! Yanek did it! For the people! For happiness!

DORA
(*weeping against him*)

We're the ones who killed him. We're the ones who killed him.
I did.

STEPAN
(*crying out*)

Who did we kill? Yanek?

DORA

The Grand Duke.

CURTAINS

ACT IV[34]

A cell in the Pugachev Tower at Butyrka Prison.
Morning.
As the curtains rise, KALYAYEV *is in his cell, gazing*
at the door. A GUARD *enters, followed by a prisoner*
carrying a bucket.

THE GUARD

Clean it up. And do it quickly.

The GUARD *walks over to the window and*
stands there. FOKA *begins to clean without look-*
ing at KALYAYEV. *Silence.*

KALYAYEV

What's your name, brother?

FOKA

Foka.

KALYAYEV

You're a prisoner?

FOKA

Looks like it.

KALYAYEV

What are you in for?

FOKA

Murder.

KALYAYEV

You were hungry?

THE GUARD

Lower.

KALYAYEV

What's that?

THE GUARD

Lower. I'm letting you talk despite the rules, so speak a little
lower. Like the old man's doing.

KALYAYEV

You were hungry?

FOKA

No, I was thirsty.

KALYAYEV

And?

FOKA

And there was an ax. I chopped it all down. Seems I killed
three people.

KALYAYEV *looks at him.*

FOKA

Not going to call me brother anymore, are you, boyar?[35] Cold
shoulder now, I suppose?

KALYAYEV

No. I killed someone, too.

FOKA

How many?

KALYAYEV

I'll tell you if you really want me to, brother, but first, tell
me—you regret what happened, don't you?

FOKA

Of course. Twenty years is a steep price to pay. It leaves you a
few regrets.

KALYAYEV

Twenty years. I'm arriving at twenty-three, and I'll be going
with gray hair.

FOKA

Oh, who knows? Maybe it'll go better for you. A judge, he
has his ups and downs, highs and lows. Lots of factors. Is he
married? Who's he married to? Anyway, you're a boyar. Price
isn't the same as for us poor devils. You'll get away with it.

KALYAYEV

I don't think so. And I don't want it to be so. I couldn't bear
twenty years of shame.

FOKA

Shame? What shame? But then, of course that's the sort of
thing boyars worry about. How many did you kill?

KALYAYEV

Only one.

FOKA

What's that? That's nothing.

KALYAYEV

I killed Grand Duke Sergei.

FOKA

The Grand Duke? Ha! Isn't that going a little far? You boyars
really are something! That's pretty serious, isn't it?

KALYAYEV

It's pretty serious. But it had to be done.

FOKA

Why? You lived at court? It was over a woman, no? Good-looking guy like you.

KALYAYEV

I'm a socialist.

THE GUARD

Lower.

KALYAYEV
(*louder*)

I am a revolutionary socialist.

FOKA

That's some story you got there. Why'd you have to go and be that thing you just said? All you had to do was go with the flow, and everything would have been just fine. The world's made for boyars like you.

KALYAYEV

No, it's made for you. There's too much poverty, too many crimes. When there's less poverty, there'll be fewer crimes. If the world were a free place, you wouldn't be here.

FOKA

Yes and no. At the end of the day, free or not, it's never good to drink one too many.

KALYAYEV

It's never good, that's true. But a person drinks because he feels humiliated. There'll come a time when drinking will no longer serve any purpose, when no one will feel such shame, neither boyars nor poor devils. We'll all be brothers then and justice will render our hearts transparent. You know what I'm talking about?

FOKA
Yes. You're talking about the Kingdom of God.

THE GUARD
Lower.

KALYAYEV
Don't call it that, brother. God can do nothing for us. Justice is in our hands.

A moment passes in silence.

KALYAYEV
You don't know what I mean? Do you know the legend of Saint Dimitri?[36]

FOKA
No.

KALYAYEV
Well, he had a meeting scheduled with God out on the steppe, and as he's rushing over there, he comes across a peasant whose cart is stuck in the mud. So Saint Dimitri stops to help him. The mud is thick, the pothole's wide and deep. It takes an hour of struggling to break the thing free, and once they do, Saint Dimitri runs off to his appointment—but God's no longer there.

FOKA
So?

KALYAYEV
So, there are people who always arrive late to appointments, because there are too many carts stuck in the mud and too many brothers in need of help.

Foka backs away.

KALYAYEV

What's wrong?

THE GUARD

Lower. And you, old man, hurry it up.

FOKA

It's just a little suspicious. It's not normal. Who goes and gets themselves thrown in prison for stories about saints and carts? And then there's also the—

The GUARD *laughs.*

KALYAYEV
(*looking at him*)

What's that about?

FOKA

What do they do to people who kill Grand Dukes?

KALYAYEV

They hang them.

FOKA

Ah!

He gathers himself to leave, while the GUARD *laughs even harder.*

KALYAYEV

Don't go. What did I do?

FOKA

You didn't do anything. Even being the boyar you are, still, I'm not trying to play tricks on you. We're sitting here chatting, passing the time like this, but if you're going to be hanged, it's just not right.

KALYAYEV

Why not?

THE GUARD
(laughing)

Go on, old man, speak up.

FOKA

Because you can't be talking to me like a brother when I'm the one who hangs the condemned.

KALYAYEV

But aren't you a convict, too?

FOKA

Well, that's just it. They offered me the job and said that, in exchange for each person I hang, they'd take a year off my sentence. That's a bargain.

KALYAYEV

To be forgiven for your crimes, they make you commit new ones?

FOKA

Oh, they're not crimes if I'm ordered to do them. And anyway, they don't care. If you want my opinion, they're not Christians.

KALYAYEV

And how many so far?

FOKA

Two so far.

KALYAYEV backs away. FOKA and the GUARD
head for the door. The GUARD gives FOKA a shove.

KALYAYEV

So then, you're an executioner?

FOKA
(*reaching the door*)

And you, boyar?

> *He exits. Footsteps can be heard, as well as orders being given.* SKURATOV, *very elegant, enters with the* GUARD.

SKURATOV

Leave us. Good morning. You don't know who I am? Well, I know who you are.

(*laughing*)

Already famous, huh?

(*looking him over*)

May I introduce myself?

KALYAYEV *doesn't respond.*

SKURATOV

You have nothing to say? Well, I understand. It's the solitary, isn't it? A week in solitary confinement, that's pretty rough. In any case, we're taking you out of solitary today, and now you'll be allowed visitors. That's why I'm here, really. I already sent Foka in to see you. Remarkable, isn't he? I thought he might

interest you. Are you happy? It's good to see a few faces after a
week without any, no?

KALYAYEV

That all depends on the face.

SKURATOV

Well said, you were right on top of that one. A man who
knows what he wants.

A moment passes.

SKURATOV

What you're really saying, if I catch your drift, is that you don't
like my face.

KALYAYEV

That's right.

SKURATOV

I'm disappointed to hear that. But it's just a misunderstanding.
The lighting's bad in here, for one thing, and for another, when
you're in a basement, nobody looks friendly. Not to mention,
you don't know me yet, and sometimes, an off-putting face can
change when you get to know a person's heart.

KALYAYEV

Enough. Who are you?

SKURATOV

Skuratov, chief of police.

KALYAYEV

A lackey, then. A servant.

SKURATOV

At your service. But if I were in your place, I'd be showing a
little less pride. Perhaps you'll come around. A person starts

out wanting justice and ends up putting a police force in place.
Anyway, I'm not afraid of the truth. I'll be frank with you.
You interest me, and I'm here to offer you the possibility of a
pardon.[37]

KALYAYEV

What pardon?

SKURATOV

What do you mean, what pardon? I'm offering to save your
life.

KALYAYEV

Who asked you to do that?

SKURATOV

A person doesn't ask for life, my dear boy. They're given it.
Have you never pardoned anyone?

A moment passes.

SKURATOV

Think carefully.

KALYAYEV

I refuse your pardon, now and forever.

SKURATOV

Hear me out, at least. I'm not your enemy, despite what it
might look like.[38] I'm even willing to admit that you're right to
think as you do. Aside from the part about murder—

KALYAYEV

I forbid you to use that word.

SKURATOV
(*looking at him*)

Ah, so I touched a nerve, did I?

A moment passes.

SKURATOV

Really, I'd like to help you.

KALYAYEV

To help me? I'm prepared to pay the necessary price, but what I can't stand is the familiar tone you're taking with me, as if we're friends. Leave me alone.

SKURATOV

The charges against you—

KALYAYEV

Correct that.

SKURATOV

Did you say something?

KALYAYEV

Correct that. I'm a prisoner of war, not a charged man.

SKURATOV

As you wish. Either way, there's been damage done, hasn't there? Let's set aside the Grand Duke and politics for a moment. At the very least, we can say that a man has died—and what a death it was!

KALYAYEV

I didn't throw the bomb at a man, I threw it at your tyranny.

SKURATOV

No doubt. But it's a man it hit—and it didn't go well for him. You see, my dear boy, when we found the body, the head was nowhere to be seen. Gone, that head was! As for the rest, we could just make out an arm and a little stump of a leg.

KALYAYEV

I executed a sentence.

SKURATOV

Perhaps, perhaps. But we're not accusing you of a sentence.
What is a sentence, after all, but some words to be argued
about for nights on end. What we're accusing you of . . . no,
you wouldn't like that word . . . hmm . . . let's just call it an
amateurish, slightly messy bit of work, the results of which,
well, they're indisputable. Everyone could see the results. Just
ask the Grand Duchess. There was blood, you know, so much
blood everywhere.

KALYAYEV

Stop talking.

SKURATOV

Very well. I simply wanted to say that if you insist on speaking
of sentences, saying that the Party, and only the Party, acted
as judge and executioner, that the Grand Duke was killed not
by a bomb but by a cause, by an idea, well then, you'll have no
need of a pardon. Suppose, however, we return to the evidence
at hand. Suppose you were the one who blew the Grand
Duke's head off. That would change everything then, wouldn't
it? Then, you would need a pardon—and I want to help you
with that. Purely out of compassion, believe me.

(*smiling*)

What can I say? I'm just not interested in ideas and causes.
Me? I'm interested in people.

KALYAYEV
(*exploding*)

My character is far beyond you and your masters. You can kill
me, but you cannot judge me. I know where you're going with

all this. You're looking for a weak spot, waiting for me to feel
ashamed, to cry, to repent. You will get nothing. Who I am is
of no concern to you. What concerns you is our hatred, my
hatred and that of my brothers. It is at your service.

SKURATOV

Hatred? Again with the ideas. What's not an idea, however, is
murder. And its consequences, of course. By which I mean to
say, repentance and punishment. There. Now that's the heart
of the matter. The reason I became a policeman, by the way. To
be at the heart of things. But you don't like such personal talk.

> *A moment passes. He slowly makes his way
> over to* KALYAYEV.

SKURATOV

All I wanted to say is that you mustn't pretend to forget the
Grand Duke's head. If you were to bear it in mind, ideas would
no longer be of any use to you. You'd feel shame, for example,
rather than being proud of what you've done. And as soon as
you feel shame, you'll wish to go on living so you can make
amends. The most important thing is that you decide to live.

KALYAYEV

And if I decide to do that?

SKURATOV

A pardon for you and your friends.

KALYAYEV

You've arrested them?

SKURATOV

No, actually, we haven't. But if you decide to live, we will arrest
them.

KALYAYEV

Are you saying what I think you're saying?

SKURATOV

Surely, I am. Don't go getting all angry again, though. Think about it. Seen from the point of view of the idea, the cause, you can't deliver them to us. Seen from the point of view of the evidence, on the other hand, you'd be doing them a favor. You'd be saving them from further trouble while, at the same time, wrenching them free from the gallows. Above all else, though, you'd find your own peace of mind. From any point of view, it's a golden opportunity.

KALYAYEV *remains silent.*

SKURATOV

Well?

KALYAYEV[39]

My brothers will give you a response soon enough.

SKURATOV

Another crime! Clearly, that's your calling. Well then, my mission has come to an end. My heart is heavy, but I can see that you're holding fast to your ideas and that I can't separate you from them.

KALYAYEV

You can't separate me from my brothers.

SKURATOV

Until next time, then.

He feigns as if to leave, then turns back.

SKURATOV

Tell me, why did you spare the Grand Duchess and her niece and nephew?

KALYAYEV

Who told you that?

SKURATOV

Your informant informed us, too. At least about some things. But why'd you spare them?

KALYAYEV

That doesn't concern you.

SKURATOV
(*laughing*)

You don't think so? I'm going to tell you why it does. An idea can kill a Grand Duke, but it's much harder for an idea to kill children. That right there is what you discovered. So then, that begs the question—if an idea isn't enough to kill children, is it really enough reason to kill a Grand Duke?

KALYAYEV *makes a move as if to respond.*

SKURATOV

Oh no, no. Don't answer me, you don't have to answer to me. You're going to answer to the Grand Duchess.

KALYAYEV

The Grand Duchess?

SKURATOV

Yes, she wants to see you. The main reason I came here was to make sure such a conversation would be possible. It is. It might even make you change your mind. The Grand Duchess is a Christian. The soul, you see, is her specialty.

He laughs.

KALYAYEV

I don't want to see her.

SKURATOV

I'm sorry, but she insists. And after all, you owe her a little
consideration. They say that since her husband's death, she hasn't
been quite right in the head. We didn't want to upset her.

(*at the door*)

If you do change your mind, don't forget my offer. I'll be
back.

A moment passes. He stands listening.

SKURATOV

Here she comes now. First the police, then religion. You sure
are being spoiled. But it all makes sense. The pieces fit. Just
imagine God without prisons. What solitude!

He exits. Voices can be heard, some giving orders.

The GRAND DUCHESS *enters. She stands still
and silent.*

The door is open.

KALYAYEV

What do you want?

THE GRAND DUCHESS
(uncovering her face)

Look.

KALYAYEV *remains silent.*

THE GRAND DUCHESS

So many things die with a man.

KALYAYEV

I'm aware of that.

THE GRAND DUCHESS
(in a natural voice, though small and worn down)

Murderers can't be aware of that. If they were aware of it, how
could they murder?

Silence.

KALYAYEV

Okay, I've seen you. Now I'd like to be left alone.

THE GRAND DUCHESS

No, I get to look at you, too.

He backs away. She sits down, as if out of energy.

THE GRAND DUCHESS

I can't be alone anymore. It used to be that if I was suffering, he
could see my suffering, and that made the suffering okay. But
now . . . No, I just couldn't bear to be alone anymore, sitting

there silently, not saying a word. But whom to talk to? Other people don't know what it's like. They pretend to be sad. They put it on for an hour or two. Then they go off to eat—and to sleep. Most of all, to sleep . . . I imagined you must be like me. You don't sleep, I'm sure of it. And to whom can one speak of the crime if not to the murderer?

KALYAYEV

What crime? All I remember is an act of justice.

THE GRAND DUCHESS

The same voice! You sound just like him. All men use that same tone of voice when speaking of justice. He'd say, "This is just," and we weren't allowed to say a word. He was wrong, perhaps. You are wrong—

KALYAYEV

He was the incarnation of supreme injustice, the kind that's pressed down over the Russian people for centuries, and for being that, he received his privileged isolation. If I should be wrong, prison and death is the payment I'll receive.

THE GRAND DUCHESS

Yes, you are suffering. But he—he is dead, and you are the one who killed him.

KALYAYEV

He died unexpectedly. That sort of death, it's nothing.

THE GRAND DUCHESS

Nothing?

(*in a lower voice*)

Oh, right—they took you away immediately. I heard you were giving your speech right there amid the police. I understand.

That must have made it easier. Me? I arrived a few seconds
later. I saw. I dragged everything I could onto the stretcher. So
much blood everywhere.

A moment passes.

THE GRAND DUCHESS

I had a white dress on—

KALYAYEV

Stop talking.

THE GRAND DUCHESS

Why? I speak the truth. Do you know what he did two hours
before dying? He slept. In an armchair, feet up on a stool . . . as
always. He slept, and you, you waited for him, waited there in
that cruel night.

(*crying*)

Help me now.

He backs away, stiff.

THE GRAND DUCHESS

You're young. You can't be evil.

KALYAYEV

I haven't had time to be young.

THE GRAND DUCHESS

Why are you so inflexible? Have you never felt sorry for yourself?

KALYAYEV

No.

THE GRAND DUCHESS

You're wrong about that. You take comfort in it. Me? I no
longer feel sorry for anyone but myself.

A moment passes.

THE GRAND DUCHESS

I'm in such pain. You should have killed me with him rather
than sparing me.

KALYAYEV

It wasn't you I spared. It was the children who were with you.

THE GRAND DUCHESS

I know. I didn't really love them all that much.

A moment passes.

THE GRAND DUCHESS

They're the Grand Duke's niece and nephew. Weren't they
guilty, like their uncle?

KALYAYEV

No.

THE GRAND DUCHESS

Are you familiar with them? My niece, she has a wicked heart.
She refuses to bring alms to the poor, to carry them in her own
two hands, because she's afraid to touch them. Isn't she unjust?
She is unjust. He at least loved the peasants. He drank with
them. And you killed him. Surely, you're unjust, too. The earth
is forsaken.

KALYAYEV

It's pointless, what you're doing. Trying to weaken my resolve and render me hopeless. It won't work. Leave me alone.

THE GRAND DUCHESS

Don't you want to pray with me? To repent? Then we wouldn't be alone anymore.

KALYAYEV

Leave me alone so I can prepare to die. If I don't die, then that's when I'll become a murderer.

She stands up.

THE GRAND DUCHESS

Die? You want to die? No.

She rushes over to him, greatly agitated.

THE GRAND DUCHESS

You have to live and accept that you're a murderer. Did you not kill him? God will justify you.

KALYAYEV

Whose God? Mine or yours?

THE GRAND DUCHESS

The one of the Holy Church.

KALYAYEV

The church has no business here.

THE GRAND DUCHESS

The church serves a master who, like you, knows what prison's like.

KALYAYEV

Times have changed. The Holy Church picks and chooses
from its master's legacy.

THE GRAND DUCHESS

Picks and chooses? What are you trying to say?

KALYAYEV

The Holy Church has kept forgiveness all for itself and left the
rest of us to take care of charity.

THE GRAND DUCHESS

Us, who?

KALYAYEV
(*crying out*)

All the people you hang.

Silence.

THE GRAND DUCHESS
(*gently*)

I'm not your enemy.

KALYAYEV
(*hopeless*)

You are, as are all people of your kind and class. You know
what's even more despicable than being a criminal? Forcing a
life of crime on someone who isn't cut out for it. Look at me. I
swear to you, I am not cut out for killing.

THE GRAND DUCHESS

Don't speak to me as if I were your enemy. Look.

She goes over and closes the door.

THE GRAND DUCHESS

I'm putting my life in your hands.

She begins to cry.

THE GRAND DUCHESS

We may be separated by blood, but you can join with me in God, here where our reasons for hardship meet. Pray with me, at least.

KALYAYEV

I must refuse.

(*going over to her*)

You touched my heart just now, and I feel nothing but compassion for you. Now you'll be able to understand where I'm coming from, because now I have nothing left to hide from you. I no longer count on meeting God, but in dying, I'll be precisely on time for the meeting I'd planned with those I love, my brothers, who are thinking of me right now. To pray would be to betray them.

THE GRAND DUCHESS

What are you trying to say?

KALYAYEV
(*elated*)

Nothing, except that I'll be happy. I have a long struggle to bear and I will bear it. But when the verdict is delivered, and the execution set, then, standing at the foot of the scaffold, I'll turn away from you, from this hideous world, and I'll let myself go, go to that love that will fulfill me. Now do you understand where I'm coming from?

THE GRAND DUCHESS
There is no love beyond the love of God.

KALYAYEV
Yes, there is—love for the creatures of the earth.

THE GRAND DUCHESS
The creatures of the earth are despicable. What's to be done but to forgive or destroy them?

KALYAYEV
Die alongside them.

THE GRAND DUCHESS
We die alone. He died alone.[40]

KALYAYEV
(*hopeless*)
Die alongside them! Today, those who love each other have to die together if they wish to be reunited. Injustice separates us. Shame, sorrow, the harm we do to others separates. Crime separates us. Living is a torture, because living separates us.

THE GRAND DUCHESS
God reunites us.

KALYAYEV
Not here on earth—and my engagements are here on earth.[41]

THE GRAND DUCHESS
The same engagements as a dog, nose to the ground, sniffing, sniffing, always sniffing, always disappointed.

KALYAYEV
(*turning toward the window*)
I'll know soon enough.

A moment passes.

KALYAYEV

But even now, can't we imagine two people who have renounced all joy, who love each other in sorrow, and who are unable to arrange any engagement outside that sorrow?

(*turning to look at her*)

Can't we imagine these two people tied together by the same noose?

THE GRAND DUCHESS

What kind of awful love is that?

KALYAYEV

The only kind you and yours have ever allowed us.

THE GRAND DUCHESS

I loved, too, you know. The person you killed.

KALYAYEV

I understand that now. That's why I forgive you for the harm you and yours have done to me.

A moment passes.

KALYAYEV

Now, leave me alone.

A long silence.

THE GRAND DUCHESS
(*standing up*)

I'll leave you alone, but now I know the reason I came here was
to lead you to God. You want to judge and save yourself all on
your own. You can't. But God can, if you live. I'll ask that you
receive grace.[42]

KALYAYEV

I beg you, please don't. Leave me alone to die or I'll hate you as
long as I live.

THE GRAND DUCHESS
(*arriving at the door*)

I'll ask that you receive grace, from man and from God.

KALYAYEV

No, no, I forbid you.

> He runs to the door where SKURATOV sud-
> denly appears. KALYAYEV backs away, closing
> his eyes. Silence. He opens his eyes and looks at
> SKURATOV.

KALYAYEV

I needed to see you.

SKURATOV

I'm delighted to hear it. Why?

KALYAYEV

I needed to be able to look down on someone again.

SKURATOV

That's a shame. I've come for my response.

KALYAYEV

Now you have it.

SKURATOV
(*changing his tone*)

No, I don't have it yet. Listen to me very carefully. I arranged this meeting with the Grand Duchess today so that tomorrow I'd be able to publish news of it in the papers. The report will be perfectly accurate, except on one point. It will include your confession, your statement of repentance. Your comrades will think you've betrayed them.

KALYAYEV
(*calmly*)

They won't believe it.

SKURATOV

I'll only stop the story from being printed if you confess. You have the night to decide.

He heads for the door.

KALYAYEV
(*speaking louder*)

They won't believe it.

SKURATOV
(*turning back*)

Why not? Have they never sinned?[43]

KALYAYEV

You don't understand their love.

SKURATOV

No, but I know a person can't believe in brotherhood all night long without having a single second of weakness. I await that weakness.

He shuts the door behind him.

SKURATOV

No rush. I'm a patient man.

They remain there, face-to-face.

CURTAINS

ACT V

A different apartment, but in the same style as the previous one.
One week later. Nighttime.
Silence. DORA *paces back and forth.*

ANNENKOV

Rest, Dora.

DORA

I'm cold.

ANNENKOV

Come over here and lie down. Get under the covers.

DORA
(*continuing to pace*)

The night is so long. And how cold I am, Boria.

A knock at the door. One rap, then two.

ANNENKOV *goes to open it.* STEPAN *and* VOINOV *enter.* VOINOV *goes over to* DORA *and hugs her. She holds him tight against her.*

DORA

Alexis!

STEPAN

Orlov said tonight may be the night. All the off-duty NCOs are being summoned. That will allow him to be there, too.

ANNENKOV

Where are you meeting him?

STEPAN

He'll be waiting for us, for Voinov and me, at the restaurant on Sofiyskaya Street.

DORA
(*sitting down, out of energy*)

It's tonight, Boria.

ANNENKOV

All's not lost. It's still up to the tsar.

STEPAN

It'll be up to the tsar—if Yanek asked for his pardon.

DORA

He didn't ask.

STEPAN

Why would he have seen the Grand Duchess if not to ask for her pardon? She's telling everyone he repented. How can we know what's true?

DORA

We know what he said in court and what he wrote to us. Didn't Yanek say he regretted having only a single life to throw in defiance of autocracy? The man who said that, could he really beg for a pardon? Could he really repent? No. He wanted—he wants—to die. He wouldn't abandon his convictions.[44]

STEPAN

He was wrong to see the Grand Duchess.

DORA

Only he can be the judge of that.

STEPAN

He shouldn't have seen her. Not according to our rules.

DORA

Our rule is to kill, nothing more. Now, he's free, free at last.

STEPAN

Not yet.

DORA

He is free. He has the right to do what he wants, as close to death as he is—and he is going to die. So be happy!

ANNENKOV

Dora!

DORA

Of course, if he were forgiven, what a victory that would be! But it would be proof, wouldn't it, that what the Grand Duchess said is true—that he repented, that he betrayed himself. Betrayed us. If, on the other hand, he is to die, then you'll believe in him and that will allow you to go on loving him.

(*looking at them*)

Your love comes at a steep price.

VOINOV
(*going toward her*)

No, Dora. We never doubted him.

DORA
(*pacing back and forth*)

Yes . . . Maybe . . . Forgive me. But what does it matter, after
all? We'll find out tonight. Oh, poor Alexis! Why did you
come back here?

VOINOV

To replace him. When I read the speech he gave at the trial, I
was so proud I cried. When I read, "Death will be my ultimate
protest against a world of blood and tears," I started shaking.

DORA

A world of blood and tears . . . It's true, he did say that.

VOINOV

He did say it. Oh, Dora, what courage! And then, when he
concluded with that great cry of his, "If I've lived up to that
human protest against violence, may death crown my work by
the purity of the cause," that's when I decided to come back.

DORA
(*hiding her head in her hands*)

He wanted purity, it's true. But what an awful crowning
achievement.[45]

VOINOV

Don't cry, Dora. He asked that nobody cry over his death. Oh,
I understand him so well now. I can't doubt him. I suffered
because I was a coward. Then, in Tiflis, I threw a bomb.
Now, I'm no different than Yanek. When I heard he'd been
sentenced to death, I had only one thought—to take his place,
since I couldn't be by his side.

DORA

Who could take his place tonight? He's going to be all alone,
Alexis.

VOINOV

Our pride will support him, as his example supports us.
Don't cry.

DORA

Look at me. My eyes are dry. But proud? Oh no, never again
will I be able to be proud.

STEPAN

Don't get me wrong, Dora, but I hope Yanek lives. We need
men like him.

DORA

He doesn't hope to live. So we have to want him to die.

ANNENKOV

You've gone mad.

DORA

We have to want it. I know his heart. It's the only way he'll be
at peace. Oh yes, let him die!

(*in a lower voice*)

But let it be quick.

STEPAN

I'm going, Boria. Come on, Alexis. Orlov's waiting for us.

ANNENKOV

Yes, but hurry back.

STEPAN *and* VOINOV *head for the door.* STE-
PAN *looks back in* DORA's *direction.*

STEPAN

We'll know soon. Look after her.

DORA *is at the window.* ANNENKOV *is watching her.*

DORA

Death! The gallows! And death again! Oh, Boria.

ANNENKOV

Yes, sister, but there's no other way.

DORA

Don't say that. If death's the only possible way, then we're on the wrong track. The track that leads to life, to sunlight, that's the right one. A person can't always be cold.[46]

ANNENKOV

This track leads to life, too. To the lives of others. Russia will live. Our grandchildren will live. Remember what Yanek said. "Russia will be beautiful."

DORA

Others . . . our grandchildren . . . Yes, but Yanek's in prison, and the noose is cold. He's going to die. Maybe he's already dead, dead so that others may live. Oh, Boria, and if the others don't live? If he died for nothing?

ANNENKOV

Don't say that.

Silence.

DORA

How cold it is. And yet it's spring. There are trees out in the prison yard, I know there are. He must see them.

ANNENKOV

Wait until we know. Try not to shiver so much.

DORA

I'm so cold it feels as if I were already dead.

A moment passes.

DORA

All of this, it ages you so quickly. We'll never be children again, Boria. Childhood escapes us with the first murder. I throw a bomb, and in a single second, an entire life elapses, you see. Yes, after that happens, we can die. We've come full circle.

ANNENKOV

Then we'll die fighting, like men do.

DORA

You moved too quickly. You're not men anymore.

ANNENKOV

Suffering and misery move quickly, too. This world of ours no longer has a place for patience and maturation. Russia is pressed for time.

DORA

I know. We've taken the world's suffering on our shoulders. He took it on, too. What courage! But I sometimes wonder if it's pride that'll be punished.

ANNENKOV

We'll pay for that pride with our life. No one can take it any further than that. We have a right to our pride.

DORA

Are we sure no one will ever take it any further than that? Sometimes, when I listen to Stepan speak, I get so afraid. Others may come after us and see what we've done as giving

them permission to kill, and maybe they won't feel it necessary
to pay with their life.[47]

ANNENKOV

That would be cowardly, Dora.

DORA

Who's to say? Maybe that's what justice looks like—and then
no one will ever dare look it in the face again.

ANNENKOV

Dora!

She doesn't say anything.

ANNENKOV

Are you having doubts? This isn't like you.

DORA

I'm cold. I'm thinking of him out there, refusing to let himself
shiver so that he doesn't look afraid.

ANNENKOV

Are you no longer with us?

DORA
(*throwing herself against him*)

Oh, Boria, I'm with you. I'll do whatever it takes. I despise
tyranny, and I know there's no other way for us. But my heart
was filled with joy when I first set out on this path, and now,
as I continue on, it's filled with sadness. That's the difference.
We're prisoners now.

ANNENKOV

All of Russia is imprisoned. We're going to blow the walls
to bits.

DORA

Just give me a bomb to throw, and you'll see. I'll walk straight
into the inferno, and I'll be up to the challenge. It's easy, it's so
much easier to die from your contradictions than to live with
them.[48] Have you ever loved, Boria? Just love, all on its own?

ANNENKOV

I have, but it was so long ago I can't even remember.

DORA

How long ago?

ANNENKOV

Four years ago.

DORA

And you've been leading the Organization for how long?

ANNENKOV

Four years.

A moment passes.

ANNENKOV

Now it's the Organization I love.

DORA
(*walking toward the window*)

To love, yes, but to be loved! No, we have to keep moving
onward. A person might like to stop. Onward! Onward! A
person might like to reach out her arms and let herself go. But
no, that dirty injustice sticks to us like glue. Onward! Here
we stand, doomed to be greater than ourselves. People, faces,
those are the things we'd like to love. To love in place of justice.
No, we have to move onward. Onward, Dora! Onward, Yanek!

(*crying*)

But for him, the end is coming.

> ANNENKOV
> (*taking her in his arms*)

He'll be pardoned.

> DORA
> (*looking at him*)

You know very well he won't. You know very well he won't
allow it.

He looks away from her.

> DORA

He may already be out in the yard. All those people suddenly
falling silent the moment he appears. Please don't let him be
cold. Do you know how a person is hanged, Boria?

> ANNENKOV

From the end of a rope, Dora. Enough!

> DORA
> (*blindly*)

The executioner jumps onto the person's shoulders. The neck
snaps. Awful, isn't it?

> ANNENKOV

Yes. In a way. But in another way, it's a sort of happiness.

> DORA

Happiness?

> ANNENKOV

To feel a person's hand on your shoulder before dying.

DORA *throws herself onto an armchair.*

Silence.

ANNENKOV

After all this, you'll have to go away. We'll have a little rest.

DORA
(*beside herself*)

Go away? With whom?

ANNENKOV

With me, Dora.

DORA
(*looking at him*)

Go away!

She turns to the window.

DORA

The sun is rising. Yanek's already dead, I'm sure of it.

ANNENKOV

I'm your brother.

DORA

Yes, you're my brother, you're all my brothers, and I love you all.

We hear rain begin to fall. The day is breaking. DORA *speaks in a hushed voice.*

DORA

But what an awful taste brotherhood sometimes has.

A knock at the door. VOINOV *and* STEPAN
enter. Nobody moves a muscle. DORA *sways but*
steadies herself with visible effort.

STEPAN
(*in a hushed voice*)
Yanek didn't betray anyone.

ANNENKOV
Orlov could see?

STEPAN
Yes.

DORA
(*taking a firm step forward*)
Sit. Tell us about it.

STEPAN
What's the use?

DORA
Tell us everything. I have a right to know. I demand that you
tell me. In detail.

STEPAN
I wouldn't even know how. And anyway, we have to go now.

DORA
No. You're going to talk. When was he told?

STEPAN
At ten P.M.

DORA
When was he hanged?

STEPAN
At two A.M.

DORA

So, he waited four hours, then?[49]

STEPAN

Yes, without a word. And then it all happened very quickly.
Now, it's over.

DORA

Four hours without speaking? Wait. How was he dressed? Did
he have his sheepskin coat?

STEPAN

No. He was all in black, no overcoat. He did have a black
fedora, though.

DORA

What was the weather like?

STEPAN

It was pitch-black. The snow was dirty. And then the rain came
and turned it into a sticky sludge.

DORA

Did he shake?

STEPAN

No.

DORA

Did Orlov catch his eye?

STEPAN

No.

DORA

What was he looking at?

STEPAN

Everyone, Orlov said, without seeing anything.

DORA

And then? And then?

STEPAN

Leave it alone, Dora.

DORA

No, I want to know. His death, if nothing else, belongs to me.

STEPAN

They read him the verdict.

DORA

What was he doing at that very moment?

STEPAN

Nothing. He shook his leg, only once, to get rid of a little spot of sludge that had stained his shoe.[50]

DORA
(*head in hands*)

A spot of sludge!

ANNENKOV
(*suddenly breaking in*)

How do you know that?

STEPAN *doesn't say anything.*

ANNENKOV

You asked Orlov to tell you all of this? Why?

STEPAN
(*turning his eyes away*)

There was something between Yanek and me.

ANNENKOV

What was it?

STEPAN

I envied him.

DORA

And then, Stepan? And then?

STEPAN

Father Florensky came and presented the crucifix to him. He refused to kiss it. He said, "I've already told you that I'm done with life and that I'm prepared for death."

DORA

How'd his voice sound?

STEPAN

Exactly the same. Minus that feverish restlessness you knew in him.

DORA

Did he seem happy?

ANNENKOV

Have you gone mad?

DORA

Yes, yes, I'm sure he did, he seemed happy. He refused to let himself be happy in this life so he'd be better prepared to sacrifice himself, and it would be too unjust if he didn't experience happiness at that last moment of death. He was happy and he calmly walked to the gallows, didn't he?[51]

STEPAN

He walked. There was singing and an accordion down on the river below. And then some dogs barked.

DORA

That's when he climbed up ...

STEPAN

He climbed up. He sunk into the night. You could only vaguely make out the shroud the executioner put over him.

DORA

What then, what then?

STEPAN

A few muffled sounds.

DORA

A few muffled sounds. Yanek! What happened next?

STEPAN *remains silent.*

DORA
(*forcefully*)

Next, tell me.

STEPAN *remains silent.*

DORA

Speak, Alexis. Next?

VOINOV

An awful sound.

DORA

Aah.

She throws herself against the wall.

STEPAN *looks away.* ANNENKOV, *expression-less, cries.* DORA *turns, back pressed against the wall, and looks at them.*

DORA
(*voice changed, disoriented*)

Don't cry. No, no, don't cry. We can all clearly see this is
the day of justification. Something is rising up at this very
moment, a testimony, our testimony, for all who rebel—Yanek
is a murderer no more. An awful sound! All it took was an
awful sound, and just like that, he's returned to childhood joys.
You remember his laugh? Sometimes he laughed for no reason
at all. How young he was then! He must be laughing now. He
must be laughing, face pressed against the earth.

She goes over to ANNENKOV.

DORA
You're my brother, Boria? You said you'd help me?

ANNENKOV
Yes.

DORA
Then do this for me. Give me the bomb.

ANNENKOV *looks at her.*

DORA
Yes, next time. I want to throw it. I want to be the first one to
throw.

ANNENKOV
You know very well we don't want women out on the front
lines.

DORA
(*crying out*)

Am I a woman, now?

They look at her. Silence.

VOINOV
(*gently*)

Allow it, Boria.

STEPAN

Yes, allow it.

ANNENKOV

It would have been your turn, Stepan.

STEPAN
(*looking at* DORA)

Allow it.[52] She's just like me now.

DORA

You'll give it to me, won't you? I'll throw it, and then, later, on
a cold night . . .

ANNENKOV

Yes, Dora.

DORA
(*crying*)

Yanek! A cold night, and that same noose. It'll all be so much
easier now.

CURTAINS

Appendix I

———

ORIGINAL PROLOGUE TO
The Misunderstanding[1]

PROLOGUE

In a small monastery in Budějovice.
MARIA is on a bench. JAN enters. Both are wearing their traveling clothes. In the background, a monk, motionless.

MARIA
(*far away*)

Yes?

JAN
(*the same manner*)

No.

He quickly moves toward her.

MARIA

You didn't find them?

JAN

I saw them.

MARIA

Were they surprised? Happy?

JAN

No.

(*hesitating*)

They didn't recognize me.

MARIA

But that's not possible. A mother always recognizes her son.
It's the least she can do.

JAN

Yes. But I guess twenty years of separation and silence changes
things a little. I was a teenager when I left for Africa, and my
sister was a little girl. Now, I'm a man, and my mother has
gotten old, and her eyesight isn't so good anymore. I barely
recognized her myself.

MARIA

All the same, I imagine you must have spoken to them.

JAN

Barely. I didn't remember the inn very well. When I entered,
they were there in the waiting area, and I could tell by the
way they were looking at me that they didn't recognize me.
I hesitated. I said, "Hello," took a couple of steps, and sat
down. In my memory, the room was very different. But my
memory was off. I kept waiting for the moment, for that cry
of surprise [to come from them]. I asked for a drink, my sister
got up without a word, [while] an old man with a distracted
look about him came to serve me. My mother stared at me the
whole time, but I could swear she never saw me. In the end, no
one cried out.

(*pausing*)

I drank my beer.

MARIA
(*shaking her head*)

Oh, Jan! How's one to know with you. You do everything by halves. You're even half-dressed.

(*mechanically ties the belt of his coat, which has come undone*)

Hair barely combed.

(*arranges the strands of hair that have fallen onto his forehead*)

Only one foot in this world of ours. Is it really worth it, damming up so much and never knowing how to express yourself? What were you doing the whole time you were there?

JAN

I don't know. I guess I was thinking about the teenager I once was. Basically, everything was more difficult than I thought it would be.

MARIA

Just a minute. Let's try to speak clearly. They didn't recognize you, okay, very well. But in that case, you speak out, you say, "It's me," and then everything falls into place.

JAN

Yes, that's what's you do in such cases. But really, Maria, what happened to me is quite simple. I hadn't prepared anything. In my mind, a son's return goes without saying. Everything seemed settled in advance, so there were no questions to be considered. I was going to say, "It's me," and we'd hug and cry. The only thing I was planning on was the surprise I'd give them. I had all these

fantasies in my head. But that's not how it went. Me? I'd
half expected the prodigal's feast, and they gave me a beer, paid
for in cash. In the moment, it took the words right out of my
mouth.

(*pausing*)

Then I told myself that everything doesn't always work out on
the first try and that sometimes you have to keep at it a little.

MARIA

Oh, Jan. This just isn't healthy. There was nothing to keep at.
That's just another one of your ideas. I'm sure a single word
would have been enough.

JAN

It wasn't an idea, Maria, it was circumstance. Once you've
started something, you have to keep at it. Yes, a single word
would have surely been enough. But really, I'm not like you,
you who always knows the right thing to do without even
thinking about it. Everything was so strange. I just wanted to
go a little further, take a few more steps . . . I asked my mother
if there was a room available. She looked at me, and I thought
she recognized me. But all she said, with no expression, was
"Yes." And when you think about it, what's so surprising about
that? The only thing I was thinking then was that going home
again isn't as easy as they say and that it takes a little time to
make a son out of a stranger.

MARIA
(*agitated*)

No, this isn't healthy, and this story of yours doesn't make any
sense. Why didn't you let them know you were coming? There

are times you have to do what any other person would do.
When you want to be recognized, you give your name—that's
obvious. You end up getting everything all confused by
pretending to be something you're not. How could you not be
treated as a stranger in a house where you present yourself as a
stranger?

(hanging on to him)

Try to understand me, Jan. You were still a child when you
left, and now you've come back after twenty years. That
your mother doesn't recognize her child in the man you've
become—okay, that makes sense. But that you're patiently
waiting around to be recognized—no, that makes no sense at
all. No one's ever had such an idea before, to carry things
so far.

JAN

Come on, Maria, it's not so serious as all that. It's only a little
hiccup, and I'll figure out a way to be recognized. It's only a
matter of finding the right words.

MARIA

There's only one way, which is to do the first thing anyone else
would do, to say, "It's me," and let your heart speak.

JAN

The heart isn't so simple.

MARIA

But it uses only simple words. It really wouldn't have been
so difficult to say: "I'm your son, this is my wife. We've been
living together in a country we love. But it wasn't enough to
make me happy, and now I need to be with you."

JAN
(*after a silence*)

That's not fair, Maria. Sooner or later, I was going to have to
come back. My father was the only obstacle, and when I heard
that he'd died, I thought it would all be very easy. I still think
so. Things simply got off to a bad start. Even when I was a
child, my mother's indifference, her distance, it confused me.
But it will all sort itself out in time.

(*looks away from her and undoes his coat belt*)

I know I didn't do my best thinking, but until now you've
always tried to understand my clumsiness, and you've never
had a mind to be upset about it.

MARIA
(*turning to face the monastery garden*)

Maybe you're right. Forgive me. It's just I've been feeling so
suspicious about everything since we arrived in this country. I
search in vain here for a single happy face. Everything's so sad
in this Europe of yours. I haven't heard you laugh once since
we arrived; and me, I've become this suspicious person. A little
while ago, I was waiting in the chapel.
Even those baroque angels didn't look happy being what they
are. Let's get out of here, Jan. I'm not of their kind. We're not
going to find happiness here.

JAN

It's not happiness we came to find. We already have happiness.

MARIA
(*emphatically*)

So then why not be satisfied with it?

JAN

I have my reasons, Maria. And anyway, it would be quite
something to bring everyone I love together—my mother, my
sister, and you. It seems I'd finally have nothing left to desire.
Even in the midst of our happiness, I wasn't comfortable
whenever I thought of my mother. That's why I have to go
back home now. I'll probably be able to take you over there
tomorrow.

MARIA
(*crying out*)

You want to leave me here alone?

JAN

Yes, but just until tomorrow. I have to sort this thing out
myself. By tomorrow, my mother will have recognized me and
everything will be as it should be.

(*looking at her*)

What's so terrible about that? A single night goes by quickly,
and it's an experiment worth trying. Tomorrow, we'll be
laughing about these fears of yours.

*Previously facing away, she now comes back
over to him and looks him in the face.*

MARIA

We've been married for five years, Jan?

JAN

Almost five years.

MARIA
(*lowering her head*)

And this is the first night we'll have been apart.

> *He doesn't say anything, and she looks back up at him.*

MARIA

I've always loved everything about you, even the things I didn't understand, and I really believe that, deep down, I wouldn't want you to be any other way. I'm not a very difficult wife. But here, this is the last place I'd want to go back to an empty bed. And for me, your departure is like being abandoned.

JAN
(*enthusiastically*)

You mustn't doubt my love, Maria.

MARIA

Oh, I don't doubt it. But there's your love, and then there are your dreams. You run away from me so often it's almost as if you need a break from me, but I—I can't take a break from you, and tonight—

> (*in tears, she throws herself against him*)

—tonight I won't be able to bear it.

JAN
(*caressing her*)

This is a little childish, isn't it?

MARIA

Of course it's a little childish, but we were so happy back there and it's not my fault if the nights in this country scare me. I don't want you to leave me alone here.

JAN

But that makes no sense.

She steps away from him.

MARIA

People who really love each other always see the sense in not being apart.

JAN
(*gently*)

Oh, you know I really love you, you animal.

MARIA
(*shaking her head*)

No, men never know how to really love. Nothing satisfies them. All they know how to do is dream, how to come up with new dams,[2] how to look for new lands and new homes. While we . . . we know you have to dive headfirst into love, share the same bed, join hands, fear absence. When we love, we dream of nothing else.

JAN

Now you're the one seeing things in an unhealthy light. There's nothing more to this than getting to know my mother again, to be done with all these memories I've been dragging around for the past twenty years. As for my dreams, you have to take them as they are. I'd be nothing without them, and you'd love me less if I didn't have them.

MARIA
(*having suddenly turned her back to him*)

I know you're always able to come up with good reasons,
convincing reasons, but I'm not going to listen to you anymore.
I'm going to cover my ears whenever you use that voice, the one
I know so well. It's the voice of your solitude, not of your love.

JAN
(*coming up behind her*)

Let's not go there, Maria. Let's have a serious talk. I have to go
back there. I've been smiling at all these warning bells of yours
because what I'm going off to do isn't such a terrible thing.
It's not such a big deal to sleep under the same roof as one's
mother. God will take care of the rest. Though God also knows
I'm not forgetting you in all this. I just want you to understand
that eventually a man has to go back to the country of his
youth. Until now, despite our happiness, I've lived in exile. A
person can't spend his whole life as a stranger, living far from
his homeland. It's true a man needs happiness, but he also
needs to find out who he really is. I imagine my mother and
my country will be able to help. I'm not looking any further
than that. You're not saying anything, Maria?

MARIA

I'm listening to you.

JAN

That's all I had to say. Don't judge my doubts and concerns too
harshly. It all makes sense. Maybe it's pride that makes a person
want to be recognized without making himself recognized.
But it means a lot to me. And in any case, it would already be
quite something to know, yes or no, if these dreams of mine
make sense.

MARIA
(*back still turned*)

I hope it'll be a "Yes," that they do make sense. But me, I dream only of that country where we were happy.

JAN
(*even sadder*)

To be able to speak the same language, loving each other isn't enough. And maybe that's why I'm here. But let me go do this. With a little goodwill, I'll end up finding the words that'll make it all right.

MARIA
(*quickly turning around*)

Don't leave me! I don't know any other word but love.

JAN
(*taking her against him*)

There must be others: memory, knowledge. But for the moment, it's only a matter of recovering a house, my parents, the language of my childhood. After that, everything will be just fine.

MARIA
(*defeated*)

Oh, go on dreaming then. If I can feel your shoulder beneath my hand, if I have your love, what does it matter anyway? It's usually impossible to be unhappy when I'm pressed against you. I hold on tight and wait for you to come down from the clouds, and then my time comes around. What makes me unhappy today is that I'm so sure of your love, and yet so certain you're still going to leave me. That's why a man's love is heartbreaking. He can't keep himself from leaving what he loves best.

JAN
(*taking her face in his hands and smiling*)

That's true, Maria, but really, look at me, I'm in no great danger. On the contrary, I'm full of hope, and I'm so close to happiness. Sleep in peace this evening. All you have to do is entrust me to my mother and sister for one night. For the rest, trust in those baroque angels all the same.

She pulls away from him a little.

MARIA

Go, then, and may my love protect you.

He takes a couple of steps.

MARIA
(*showing her hands to him*)

But see how bereft I am.

He stops to look at her; she gives a sad smile.

MARIA

You go off to make discoveries, and you leave me behind to wait.

He hesitates, then goes.

CURTAINS

Appendix II

ORIGINAL ENDING TO
State of Emergency[1]

NADA

Oh, dear! Here come our old alcaldes now. We were wrong to underestimate them.

THE FISHERMAN

Shut up, drunkard. Try to forget all that.

NADA

A mistake, salmon slayer, a big mistake! Those who are coming now, they don't like changes. Anything that stirs disturbs them—and you've stirred up far too much. You're the one who has to be forgotten. Once a rebel, always a rebel, and even enemy governments think alike when it comes to distrusting people like you. Tread carefully, Fisherman, the smell of herring follows you.

THE FISHERMAN

The smell of entrails is certainly going to be following me after I've split you open and hung you by the gullet on the biggest hook I own.

All the while, the PLAGUE*'s guards have been changing their uniforms on stage, putting back on the ones from the first part. Now, they're the* GOVERNOR*'s guards.*

NADA

You have no manners, Fisherman. And that'll do you no good.
Me? I know the ways of this world. That's why I'm happy to
see the old chickens come home to roost. My opinion, given
my interest in nothingness, is that I've never been better served
than by our once-great men. Experience has proven their
method so much the better. Rather than shutting up the ones
who protest, they shut their own ears instead. Let's be deaf,
too, live nothing, and praise be to our governor.

> *The* GOVERNOR *and the* ALCALDES *make
> their entrance in a sort of grotesque ballet. The*
> GOVERNOR *is passing out medals.*

THE GOVERNOR

A happy, happy city is the one that recovers its once and
future masters. Every one of you gets a medal. You've driven
out the usurper and returned our city to its quiet liberties.
How proud I shall be to have been your governor, to have
directed the destiny of this city right through this difficult
moment it's now faced, and to have finally negotiated a deft
armistice with the invader, one without which your courage
would have been in vain. I give thanks, thanks to the heavens
to be able to see so many of you alive today and to recover
your affection while also recovering leadership of my
government.

> *The old people do a little ballet dance.*

CHORUS OF OLD PEOPLE

I give you a medal, you give me a medal, he gives himself a medal. We give ourselves medals . . .

THE GOVERNOR
(*handing them out*)

You . . .

(*looking at the* FIRST ALCALDE)

We appoint you officer of civil collaboration. You . . .

His words can't be heard, but we see him giving NADA *a medal.*

THE OLD PEOPLE

All for one, all for happiness, all with medals! And now, let's start where we left off.

THE PEOPLE

Yes, let's start where we left off. Those who could have started fresh are dead. So, we have to start where we left off. Who will speak for the dead? Who will say that this isn't what they wanted? Nobody will speak. He who hopes to earn the right to speak gives his life. Death, then, gets the right, but death can't speak. So, others will do the talking, and they don't have the right. But now no one has the right to tell them so. So, let's start where we left off.

The CHORUS *gathers around* DIEGO.

THE CHORUS

But he remains the example, of the arm's strength, of
friendship, of hope finally and at last. We are still there in that
night, having nothing but our own will to help us. But we draw
on the world's splendor, and we draw on our own grief. Beauty
will one day rise up.

THE GOVERNOR

For Diego, killed in action, we reserve the highest honors.
We'll bury him in an unmarked grave, for what use
would his name serve? Twice a year, a domestic cult will
pay its respects to him, the anonymous hero who will
symbolize a humanity that's likely ill-defined, but one about
which I certainly agree something must be done from time
to time.

VICTORIA

What remains for us is this terrible love, this sheaf of cries, the
strength of misfortune. We will never give up!

The wind grows stronger. Trumpets. Silence.

FIRST ALCALDE

Where were you during the plague?

SECOND ALCALDE

What plague?

Trumpets. NADA *steps up and to the left, the*
GOVERNOR *and the* ALCALDES *behind him.*

NADA

Such was the terrible plague. It killed what deserved to live and spared what should die. It suppressed thousands of men, and yet left me alive. That's why I say justice exists!

>*But the wind suddenly blows into a storm and the* FISHERMAN, *at the head of the* CHORUS, *leaps to the center of the stage, sweeping everything up with his net. The* WOMEN *join back up with the* MEN, *and they gather behind the* FISHERMAN, *while everything bows beneath the furious winds and rumbles coming from the sea.*

THE CHORUS

Step back! There is no justice, there are only limits. And you who want nothing regulated, like those who make regulations for everything, oh, how you both surpass the limits. The time has come to say it loud and clear. Open the doors, let the wind and salt come and scour this city!

>*One by one, the doors are opened.*

THE CHORUS

Look! The raging sea's turning the color of anemones. Its anger is our anger, its cry the rallying cry put out to all its men.

>*Sailors and fishermen begin to appear in the doorways, gradually joining the* PEOPLE *and filling the stage.*

THE CHORUS

Here they come on the wind, gathering from all horizons,[2] brought together at the tip of this continent, here where the water shoulders up to the fixed earth. The wind is blowing, the night's full of signs, the time has come to cast off.

> *Men hoist flags resembling sails, winches turn, sailors run all over the stage, which seems to rock on its keel like a sailboat tossed by a storm.*

THE CHORUS

Brothers, chase out those rats! Diego was right!

> NADA *and the old leaders are thrown overboard. The sea can be seen rising in the last of the doors.*

THE CHORUS

O wave, O sea, homeland of insurgents, behold your people whose victory I announce. A great tidal wave, nourished on bitter waters, is coming to wash away your terrible cities.

> *A gigantic wave sweeps over the ship's deck.*

CURTAINS

Appendix III

ORIGINAL OPENING TO *The Just*[1]

The Noose[2]

(1948/1949)

Ivan Kalyayev—23 years old

Boris Annenkov—26 years old

Stepan Fedorov—25 years old

Alexis Voinarov—22 years old[3]

Dora—24 years old

Examining Magistrate[4]

The Doorman

The Grand Duchess—30 years old

ACT I

SCENE I

The terrorists' apartment, Quai de la Fonderie. Morning.

VOINAROV

Well, I had a job here at one point. Don't have it anymore. Nothing lasts.

THE DOORMAN

What happened?

V

I broke a glass.

THE D

A glass? But that's no big deal. In my day, a person didn't lose their job over so little.

V

Everything changes, Brother. I broke that glass while making up the bedroom. Madame heard. ~~And I heard it, too. What a voice!~~[5] And when she heard, she yelled. And boy, can she yell! [. . .][6] "A glass! You broke a glass! You good-for-nothing son of a bitch."

THE D

Son of a bitch? She really went for it. These actresses are all the same. And what'd you do?

V

Me? I said, "Son of a bitch? I guess we come from the same litter."

THE D

No, you didn't dare say that. Well, that's telling them good. And then?

V

And then? Madame cried. And boy, can she cry! And the monsieur heard her, and he came over, and without asking what happened, he grabs me by the ~~collar~~ neck and throws me out the door.

THE D

Without even asking what happened?

V

Without even asking what happened.

THE D

Raw deal. Go ask for forgiveness.

V

Pointless. They won't forgive me. Madame holds a grudge, you know.

THE D

Well, it's not by singing at the Bouffes[7] that a person learns good manners. Still, she [. . .] coin in hand. You should go back and give it a try.

V

Ah, it's impossible. Monsieur [. . .] of rage. Bad luck it was such a nice glass.

THE D

He's a decent guy, though. Always has his nose in a book. He'll forgive you. People who read a lot always forgive. ~~I've seen that myself.~~ I've seen it myself.

V

Monsieur never reads. Where'd you get such an idea, Doorman?

THE D

It's just that he receives so many pamphlets.

V

They're catalogues. Monsieur sells machinery.

THE D

Oh, that's a tough one. If he's in machinery, he won't forgive.

V

Machines have nothing to do with anything, you fool.

THE D

Believe what you want. I've been a doorman for thirty-seven years, and I've seen just about everything. I know there's no smoke without fire. Forgiveness—

V

Shh! The monsieur.

ANNENKOV *enters.*

A

Well, funny guy. You got your bags packed?

V

I [. . .], Your Honor. But I'd just like to say first that I'm devoted to monsieur and madame—

A

Enough! The [. . .]. Your bags!

VOINAROV *exits.*

A
(*to the* DOORMAN)
And you? What are you doing here?

THE D
Your Honor, I came up to . . . well, there's a door-to-door
salesman out front asking to see madame. I chased him off, but
he came back. He's insistent, this guy. He says madame ordered
some lace from him and that she'll be very angry if we don't
let him in. I tried my best to tell him that this isn't the sort of
place, thank God, for door-to-door salesmen, but he said that
madame told him—

> *A great cry from behind the door.* DORA
> *enters, wearing a feathered hat and a [. . .].*

D
No, ~~you will not~~ don't go and throw the salesman out, my dearest.
He's quite right. I ran into him yesterday on the canal. He showed
me some enchanting lace, truly enchanting, and as I didn't have
the time to carry it home, ~~I asked him~~ I begged the salesman to
bring it over this morning. Let him up, won't you? For my sake.

A
But, my darling, you know it's forbidden to let people in. The
doorman is right in this case.

D
Of course, the doorman is right, my dearest. But he'll make an
exception for me.

(slipping him some money)

Won't he?

THE D

Certainly, madame, certainly. Nothing could be easier, Your Honor, I assure you.

> *He exits.* ANNENKOV *looks to* DORA *and puts a finger over his lips. Silence. A noise at the door. The* DOORMAN *and the* SALESMAN *enter.*

A

Now hold on just a minute, you.

THE SALESMAN

I'll hold on, Your Honor. I'll hold on as long as you please. And I thank you, madame, for having been so kind as to tell the doorman you were expecting me. And I thank you, too, monsieur. And I ~~say to you~~ beg you not to rush. I'll hold on, all right.

A

So you said. Another man! Has the other one left?

THE D

Pardon me, Your Honor. I'll be out front.

> *He exits. Enter* IVAN, *with two suitcases.* DORA *and* ANNENKOV *hurry over to him. They hear voices out front. They wait. Footsteps on the staircase. And the* DOORMAN *once again.*

THE D

It's me again, Your Honor. The coachman's brought madame's hats.

A

Great, now it's hats.

D

Here I am, having forgotten all about them. But you're going to like them a lot, too, really.

A

I don't understand. Tell the girl to bring them up. Why isn't she bringing them up?

THE D

It's just that there are a lot of them.

A

How many?

D

Very few, my dearest, I promise. Barely a dozen. I just ordered them from—

A

Yes [. . .] go help the coachman before you leave.

(*to the* SALESMAN)

You, too, would you?

THE SALESMAN

With pleasure, Your Honor. With devotion.

A

You, too [. . .].

THE D

But two men will be enough.

A

Yes—enough to mangle them completely. ~~Don't forget~~ I don't want to have to pay for them twice.

> *They exit one after the other. Silence.* ANNEN-
> KOV *and* DORA *step away from each other.*

D

(voice changed)

Oh, Boris, provided—

> ANNENKOV. *A nervous, mechanical gesture.*
> *Silence. The* SALESMAN *enters, then* STEPAN,
> *carrying large hatboxes he sets down as if they*
> *have some weight to them. Enter the* DOORMAN,
> *who sets one down, then fumbles with another.*
> DORA, *close by, takes it from his hands. [. . .]*

THE D

Oh, pardon me, madame, I didn't know.

> *Enter* VOINAROV.

THE D

These are the last of them, madame.

A
(*to the* DOORMAN)

All right. Now don't let anyone else up.

> *The* DOORMAN *exits, his footsteps growing fainter.* DORA *throws herself on the* SALESMAN, *whom she squeezes tight, crying and laughing.* ANNENKOV, VOINAROV, *and* STEPAN *surround them, [. . .], hugging each other at random. We hear:* "Yanek, Yanek, Dora, Dora."

STEPAN

Careful!

KALYAYEV

What?

STEPAN

The dynamite.

> ANNENKOV *and* VOINAROV *carefully carry the boxes to the other room.*

D
(*taking off her hat*)

Look at you, all decked out! Like a real door-to-door salesman.

YANEK
(*laughing*)

Yes . . .

D

That's great, Yanek. You seem to be having a lot of fun.

YANEK

It's true that it all seemed like a game at first. I was excited by it. But now I'm done with all that, Dora.

D

A person never gets accustomed to lying. Me? I'd had enough of this luxurious rag right from the start. You may as well find me something else to wear, Boris. An actress! No, my heart's too simple for that.

KALYAYEV
(*with a laugh*)

But you look so pretty in that dress.

D

Pretty! I'd be happy to be so, but let's not think about it.

Notes

Author's Preface to the American Edition

1. Camus has rounded off the dates. *Caligula* premiered September 26, 1945, not in 1946 as indicated here, and *The Just,* the last of the plays in this collection, premiered December 15, 1949.

2. The reference is to the inscription on Jacques de La Palice's gravestone, which reads: "Here lies Lord de La Palice. If he weren't dead, he'd still be envied." Initially, the last word "envie" was misread as "en vie," rendering the sentence: "If he weren't dead, he'd still be alive." From this, the term "lapalissade" was coined, referring to a painfully obvious truism. In effect, then, Camus is saying that Caligula's ideology is just a basic fact of life.

3. Camus recycled a good bit of his preface from pieces he had previously written. This line, for example, comes from an article he wrote in October 1944 in *Le Figaro,* where, among other things, he defends *The Misunderstanding*'s dialogue: "In a sense, perhaps the play is lacking. Some awkward descriptions, some monotonous passages, a certain uncertainty in the son's character. All these things may rightly bother the viewer. But in another sense, I have the feeling, why not admit it, that something about my dialogue wasn't quite understood and that the audience alone is responsible for this. [. . .] The language was a shock. I knew it would be. But if I'd dressed my characters in peploses, maybe then everyone would have applauded. Still, having contemporary characters speak the language of tragedy was the point, and my thought was that the viewer should get

used to it. As willing as I may be to make concessions with the play, when it comes to this particular issue, I will never give up on my original intention."

This despite having been told by both critics and friends, such as his philosophy teacher, Jean Grenier, that *The Misunderstanding*'s dialogue was "perhaps too oratorical," with "symbolism better suited to a book than the stage." Nevertheless, Camus said he was committed to a tone that did "neither too much nor too little, that created distance without being ridiculous," though he admitted that he "wasn't sure he'd succeeded." Perhaps it was the director of the play, Marcel Herrand, who best summarized Camus's intentions: "The author has attempted to resolve the problem by (1) choosing a rather lofty tone, one that is 'written' enough to remain tragic while also being natural enough to be accepted (2) creating distance not through the action but through the personality of each character (3) gradually heightening the effects and the language so that the tone and characters start out rather natural and then reach higher and higher from one act to the next, until they arrive at the heights of myth."

Caligula

1.   In January 1937, when twenty-three years old, Camus jotted an initial outline for *Caligula* in his notebooks, with the first extant pages appearing the next year. The first full version of the play, titled *Caligula, or The Player,* was completed in September 1939 and was followed by a second version in February 1941. These first two drafts, which share much in common, are significantly different from the version that would go on to be published in 1944. Camus would continue to revise the play throughout the rest of his life. His final revision, completed in 1958, serves as the source text for this translation. A small selection of variants from the earlier drafts will appear in the notes that follow.

2.   The 1941 typescript bears an epigraph from Suetonius's *The Twelve Caesars*: "A man should either be frugal or be Caesar." In addition to the epigraph, two major changes were made between the 1939 and 1941 drafts, the first being the addition of act III (moving what was act III in 1939 to act IV in 1941), and the second being the addition of Helicon, who was not yet present in the 1939 draft.

3.   On the first handwritten version of the play, the title "Caligula's Despair" appears here. On the typescript from 1941, at the bottom of the

page, Camus added: "The opening of the play, up until Caligula's entrance, is performed very quickly."

4.   Because the play was revised over such a long period of time, a few small inconsistencies appear in the text. In several earlier versions of the play, for example, the patricians were referred to as senators, a term that, though mostly eliminated in later revisions, still appears in several places in the final draft. To give just one more example, in a line of stage direction in the final revision, we are told that Caesonia is "pulling away" from Caligula, but the earlier indication that Caligula "puts his arms around her waist" no longer appears.

5.   1941: "He looked like a wounded animal."

6.   In the initial version of the play, much of the dialogue is simpler and more direct. This line, for example, reads: "He'll get over it."

7.   The three replies that follow appear only in the final version of the play.

8.   In 1941, instead of the final sentence now in place, we find: "But especially when I think of how she left me alone."

9.   In the 1939 draft, Helicon was yet to be added to the scene, and in 1941, he was given only two lines. In place of his response here, Cherea says: "Yeah, yeah. We're not at the Senate. And we all know that if your sister wasn't so ugly, Patricius, you wouldn't have so many insightful ideas about matters of state."

10.   In the 1939 and 1941 drafts, the stage direction and the rest of the scene continue as follows, with only minor differences between the two early versions: "*He gives a little laugh, then speaks to himself gently.* / CALIGULA: Monster, Caligula. A monster for having loved too much. (*his tone changes, becomes graver*) I ran, you know. It's a long time, three days. I had no clue, before. But it's my fault. (*his voice suddenly filled with sorrow*) It's ridiculous to believe that love is met with love. Human beings die in your hands, there, that's the truth of it. (*gasping and holding his sides*) And when they're dead, it's no longer them. (*sitting and explaining to his image*) It wasn't her anymore. I ran, you know. I returned from far away! I carried her on my back. She, alive, far from that corpse with a stranger's face, she was heavy. She was heavy and warm. It was her body, her hot and supple truth. She still belonged to me. She still loved me here on this earth. (*standing up and suddenly busying himself*) But I have a lot to do now. I still have to take her far away from here, out to that countryside she loved—out

where she walked so precisely that, in my eyes, the swaying of her shoulders was in perfect harmony with that line of hills on the horizon. / *He stops, increasingly lost. He turns his back to the mirror and leans against it. He closes his eyes for a moment. We hear his raspy breathing. He grumbles a few words that can't be made out.* / CALIGULA (*in a voice that seems barely conscious*): Monster, Caligula, monster. We have to go now. Who can live with these empty hands that once held all the world's hope in them? How can you escape that? (*laughing a forced laugh*) Sign a contract with your solitude, eh? Make do with the life you have. Give yourself reasons, make yourself a nice little life of consolation. So little for Caligula. (*smacking his open hand against the mirror*) So little for you, isn't it? / *Voices can be heard. Caligula stands up and looks to both sides. He speaks the name Drusilla, looks in the mirror, and runs from the laughing face he sees there.*"

11.   The line "I'm too smart for that" doesn't appear until the final version.

12.   1939 and 1941: "And all Caligula sees is Drusilla's shadow."

13.   In 1944, this reads just "freedom," rather than "my freedom."

14.   Aside from the addition of the third act and the introduction of Helicon as a character, one of the main differences between the initial 1939 and 1941 drafts and the later published version of the play is that the earlier drafts placed a much greater emphasis on Drusilla as a driving force of Caligula's actions. The excerpt that follows, perhaps the most powerful of these early scenes, picks up after Caesonia has suggested that Caligula get some rest. It runs through the bottom of page 31, after which the rest of the scene plays out in a similar fashion in both the earlier and later drafts.

> CALIGULA: Don't talk to me about all that. It disgusts me. / *He goes and sits by the mirror and puts his head in his hands.* / CALIGULA: I'd like to get better but I can't. When I didn't know a person could die, everything seemed believable. Even their gods, even their hopes and their speeches. Not now, though. Now I have nothing but this ludicrous power. The more excessive it is, the more ridiculous. Because it's worthless compared to some of those nights when Drusilla turned toward me. It wasn't her then, it was the world laughing through her teeth. / CAESONIA: Don't think about all that, you— / CALIGULA (*violently*): Oh, yes, we have to think about it. On the contrary,

we have to think about it. (*twitching and becoming nervous again*)
One night while I was next to her, I realized that all my riches
were of this earth. And it's that night I can't escape now. (*voice
dull*) With her, it's the whole world I've just lost. / CAESONIA:
Caligula! / CALIGULA (*as if lost in a dream, emphatically*):
Me? I'm not an idealist. I'm not a poet. I can't be satisfied with
memories. I wouldn't know how to be. That's a vice I don't know.
I've never masturbated. Same thing. At twelve years old, already
I knew love. I didn't have time to start imagining things. What I
need is a body, a woman with arms and the scent of love on her.
All that other stuff is for bureaucrats or actors, for the impotent.
And yet, that's the saddest part: since that night, that's all I've
had left—the memory and its decay. Is it time, then, to become a
bureaucrat? / *He gets up and goes to the mirror. Caesonia reaches
her arms out to him, but he doesn't see her.* / CALIGULA: She
had a gentle voice, and she spoke so smoothly. But today her
body is no more real to me than the reflection in this mirror. The
conversation between this mirror and me, between her shadow
and me, if you only knew, Caesonia, the awful desire I have to
play it out. / CAESONIA (*crying out*): No, please, stop talking. / CALIGULA: She's the one who spoke first. / CAESONIA
(*throwing herself on him and clutching at his arms*): You're going to
stop talking. You're not going to do that. / *Caligula gently removes
her hands from him and approaches the mirror with an unspeak-
able smile.* / CALIGULA: What she said didn't really matter at
first. It was just to set the tone. The "A" of a language of music and
blood—the heart's music and the blood's desire. / *He reaches out
toward the mirror. Caesonia sits down and hides her head in her
hands.* / *The scene that follows, grotesque in effect, should never be
so in tone.* / SCENE XI / CALIGULA (*still the same distraught
demeanor*): I was the one who started it. (*acting it out*) Wouldn't
you like to come over here next to me, Drusilla? (*confidentially,
as an aside*) That's what I said to her. Closer. Closer still. So that
there . . . No, don't be afraid. It's not desire speaking—not yet
or not anymore, I don't know. When I lay my hand on another
woman's body, it's your flesh I regret not touching my lips. And
when someone other than you leans against my shoulder, I'd cut

them down without cracking a smile just to see them attempt those gestures of tenderness that belong only to you. / *He stops and spins around, then begins speaking in Drusilla's voice, slower and more painfully than before.* / CALIGULA: Be quiet, Caius, (*confidentially, as an aside*) She often begged me to be quiet. Don't arouse my regrets. It's so awful to have to love in shame. O my brother! When I see my companions get all quiet and pensive, when I read in their eyes those tender and secret images they so fiercely caress, oh, how I envy them that love they could confess but choose to keep quiet. Because they keep it sealed in to better preserve it. Whereas I, I keep quiet due to the misery into which my love plunges me. (*voice weakening*) And yet, on evenings like this evening, before this canvas filled with soft and shining stars, how can I not falter before this pure and all-consuming love of mine? / *Caesonia, crying, waves a hand. She's choked up.* / CAESONIA: Enough. / CALIGULA: Pure, Drusilla. Pure as the purest stars. I loved you, Drusilla. As one loves the sea or the night, with that sinking feeling, slow and hopeless as a shipwreck. And every time I sank into that love, I sealed myself away from the world's noises, from that infernal torment of hate. Don't leave me, Drusilla. I'm afraid. I'm afraid of the enormous solitude these monsters bring. Don't step away from me. Oh, that softness, this transcendence. / *He stops abruptly, choking with tears, then does an about-face, turning toward Caesonia and taking her by the shoulders. His voice is shattered and emphatic.* / CALIGULA: That's what won't stop stalking me. That transcendence . . . you see, and the stinking decay that became of it in a matter of hours. You heard what the man said: the treasury! Oh, at last, now I'm really going to live. To live, Caesonia, to live is the opposite of to love. I can promise you that. What a fine spectacle, Caesonia. We must have crowds, an audience, victims, and the guilty.

15.   In the 1939 and 1941 drafts, Caligula's dialogue reads: "No more Drusilla, you see. No more Drusilla. And you know what's left? Come even closer. Look. Closer. Look."

16.   On the first handwritten version of the play, the title "Caligula's Game" appears here. On the version used for the Angers Festival in 1957,

Camus wrote here "musical intermission," followed by "Cherea is very tired and doesn't move throughout the first part of the Act."

17. In 1947, Helicon replies, "Mucius is right. You really have to love your wife. Otherwise, how could you put up with her?"

18. The reference is to Matthew 10:34: "Do not suppose that I have come to bring peace to the earth. I did not come to bring peace, but a sword." In other words, all Caligula retains from Christ's message is the unrest and division.

19. In 1944, the line reads: "It's absurd, but that's how it is."

20. In 1947, the direction reads: "Scipio suddenly pushes away, as if bitten by a snake, and looks at Caligula in horror."

21. On the second handwritten version of the play, the title "Caligula's Divinity" appears here.

22. The reference is to Job 10:4, where the phrase is often translated into English as "eyes of flesh." Of this line, Bible scholar Robert Alter writes: "Job's complaint against God for persecuting him has two complementary sides. On the one hand, since God enjoys the perspective of divinity, it makes no sense for Him to treat Job as though He were an ignorant and angry human being. On the other hand (verses 20–23), since Job is a mere mortal whose days are few, it is unreasonable that this brief life span should be loaded with misery."

23. In 1941, instead of this reply, Scipio says, "A coward."

24. This scene is absent from the 1941 and 1944 versions of the play. It introduces a discrepancy, whereby scenes V and VI in the 1958 version are scenes IV and V in the 1944 version.

25. Literally "vague ideas." Throughout the plays, and especially in *The Just*, Camus's characters place abstract "ideas" in opposition to concrete "actions."

26. The first two scenes of act IV do not appear in either the 1941 or the 1944 versions of the play.

27. According to Roger Quilliot, on the version of the play used for the Angers Festival in 1957, Camus wrote that the following scene takes place at Cherea's home. In notes Camus made on the 1947 version, he added "Helicon watches the scene from above," and then, more specifically, "Helicon watches from the landing of the stairs."

28. The term Camus uses here, "honnête homme," has a long history in France. In his *French Literature: A Very Short Introduction,* John D.

Lyons writes that the "polite and decorous 17th-century French" placed "great emphasis on avoiding highly visible partisanship and zealotry, and on being a reasonable person, an amusing, sensitive, and accommodating companion—in short, an *honnête homme*. This term is not easily translated, and it is important to note right away that it does not mean 'honest man.' [...] The *honnête homme* is someone who 'fits in,' who is not notably eccentric."

29.	In 1944, an additional line here reads: "The healthy detest the sick. The happy can't see the unfortunate."

30.	This bit of dialogue brings the play full circle: Caligula has now come to understand what the patricians understood in the very first scene.

31.	In the 1941 draft alone, this line reads: "She was just an alibi."

32.	This last sentence doesn't appear in earlier versions of the play. It was added during the war.

33.	The two sentences preceding this one were added during the war.

34.	According to Roger Quilliot, on the version of the play used for the Angers Festival in 1957, Camus wrote the following stage direction: "A man rises up at the top of the stairs and strikes Helicon down. Helicon falls and slides down the stairs, his hand reaching out to Caius."

35.	In January 1937, Camus recorded a basic outline for *Caligula* in his notebook. The entry concludes with the following:

> End: Caligula appears, opening the curtain:
> "No, Caligula's not dead. He's there, and there. He's inside each one of you. If you were given the power, if you had the heart, if you loved life, you'd see it run wild, that monster or angel you carry inside you. Our day is dying for having believed in values, for believing things could be beautiful and cease to be absurd. Farewell, I'm headed back to history, where I've been locked away for so long by those who're afraid to love too intensely."

Later in the notebooks, Camus writes:

> Add to proofs for Caligula: "Come then, the tragedy is over, the failure truly complete. I'll turn and go now. I've played my part in this fight for the impossible. Now we wait for death, already knowing death delivers from nothing."

The Misunderstanding

1.   There exist at least five or six versions of this opening note. The version given here is the one that appeared in the original playbill in June 1944. Two shorter versions of the note are housed at the Camus archive, and a longer version was published in *Figaro Littéraire* in October 1944.

2.   *The Misunderstanding* went through several drafts and type-scripts before its theatrical premiere on June 24, 1944. Sketches of the play, originally titled *Budějovice,* begin to appear in Camus's notebooks in 1939, with the first complete draft having been finished in July 1943. The text underwent heavy revisions for a 1955 TV adaptation and was revised once more for the play's 1958 reprinting. This final 1958 revision serves as the source text for this translation.

3.   In earlier versions, Camus lists the characters, along with their ages, as follows: THE SISTER, 30; THE WIFE, 30; THE MOTHER, 60; THE SON, 38; THE OLD SERVANT, 70. An additional note mentions that the play takes place: "In Budějovice, a small city in Czechoslovakia." In later drafts, proper names replaced these archetypal terms, and the Old Servant's age was removed.

4.   In an earlier version, the line reads: "It's easier to kill shadows." The change from "shadows" to "what you don't recognize" is a good example of how Camus, an inveterate editor of his own work, began to thread the play's theme throughout as he revised.

5.   Worth noting, given the play's emphasis on saying things clearly, is that the French word "barrage" ("dam"), which appears throughout the play, also forms part of the phrase "barrage de la langue" ("language barrier").

6.   In most of the preceding drafts, this line reads: "Soon you'll have your rest and I'll finally get to see what I've never before seen."

7.   In an earlier version: "Maybe that's why I find it hard to feel culpable and feel only capable. I'm barely able to feel much more than tired."

8.   In an earlier version, it's at the end of scene I that the Old Servant sees Jan and Maria approaching and goes to hide. Scene II takes place outside the inn, with Maria and Jan arriving together, rather than with Maria secretly following him. Before they reach the door, Jan asks Maria to leave him. After that, the dialogue, with a few grammatical variations, picks up as in this final version.

9.   The reference is to Luke 15:11–32, the parable of the prodigal son.

10.   In an October 13, 1955, letter addressed to his old friend Charles Poncet, Camus makes a related observation: "We need to speak the same language as everyone for the good of everyone."

11.   A bit of thematic language is perhaps lost here. A literal translation would be: "He doesn't resemble everyone else, that's all."

12.   In an earlier version, Jan gives his age as thirty-five and says that he was born January 8, 1909.

13.   In an earlier draft, Jan says that he's from Prague and Martha immediately responds, "Then you're Czech, of course."

14.   In an early draft, Jan says, "No, I came from Morocco," which Camus later amended to just "Morocco." When Martha then looks confused, Jan says, "Yes, from Morocco. From abroad." In one of the later drafts, Jan says, "No, I came from the South."

15.   In several of the earlier versions, Jan is insistent, not hesitant, when presenting his passport, and rather than the Old Servant coming in to distract Martha from looking at the passport, the stage directions are as follows: "She takes it in her hands, but is clearly thinking of other things. She seems as if she's weighing it, then returns it to him." In returning it, Martha says, "No, you hold on to it. When you're down there in Morocco, do you live close to the sea?"

16.   In previous versions, Martha's dialogue read: "I didn't see it. I'm not here to look at your hands, I'm here to fill out your form. Can you give me your wife's address?"

17.   In previous versions, Camus played with slight variations of an additional line here, one of which reads: "She's followed me all through the years, and no doubt, that's why I know she's my daughter. If not for that, I would've perhaps forgotten her, too."

18.   In a typed draft, Jan has an additional line here: "I'm still too young to believe it."

19.   In the original manuscript, the Mother added: "And I'd need no help to hold him up all on my own." In a later draft, this addition is replaced by: "They could support the weight of a man."

20.   The French word "familiarité," given here in a transparent translation for its thematic meaning, might more naturally appear here as "intimacy."

21.   In an earlier version, Martha adds: "What's the point of not looking at the man if you're just going to think about him? You said it

yourself—it's easier to kill shadows. But don't make that unknown shadow into your own personal ghost."

22.   In an earlier draft, at the top of the page, Camus wrote: "G wants to know if you're mine. Stranger!" The rest of scene II, and those that follow, went through several different variations and arrangements before this final version.

23.   In the first published version, Jan continues: "I owe them something. I'm responsible for them. And if that's how it is, then it's not enough to make them recognize you, to say, 'It's me.' You still have to earn their love."

24.   In earlier versions, Jan adds: "This is how it is in all hotel rooms, where all the hours of night are difficult for the lonely man."

25.   In French, "mal entendu" (misheard) recalls the title of the play, *Le Malentendu* (*The Misunderstanding*).

26.   In the first published version, Martha continues: "But since it's here now, I suppose you'll have it." After the stage direction, she adds: "It won't go on your bill. / JAN: Oh, it's not that. I'm glad you brought it. / MARTHA: I assure you, it's nothing. What we do is in our interest. / JAN: You certainly don't want me to have any illusions. But I can't see how all this is in your interest. / MARTHA: And yet it is. Sometimes it takes only a cup of tea to retain a client."

27.   In earlier versions, the Mother says, "It was only a misunderstanding."

28.   In a typed version of the play, Camus wrote "mother's love" in the margins of this dialogue.

29.   In the original manuscript, after this line, Martha says, "Never has a murder cost me less."

30.   In earlier versions, the Mother says, "This morning, it seems you are. Certain actions seem to suit you."

31.   In most preceding drafts, after this line and before the next, the Mother says, "That's not how it's supposed to go."

32.   In the first draft, the Mother adds: "But if it's of any consolation to you, I've just learned that my son's love was stronger than mine, and that it's for not having known how to respond to such love that I'll die."

33.   A call back to Caligula and forward to Dora in *The Just* (cf. note 31, *The Just*).

34.   In *The Rebel*, Camus links this idea with Dostoyevsky, writing: "Ivan [Karamazov] rejects the deep dependence between suffering and

truth that was introduced by Christianity. Ivan's innermost cry, the one that opens the most earth-shattering abyss beneath the rebel's steps, is *even if*: 'My indignation would persist even if I were wrong.'"

35.   In an early draft, this clause reads: "the sky is like a lid."

36.   In earlier versions, "this country's" is specified as "Moravia's."

37.   In the first handwritten draft, a clause is added here: "exiled from happiness."

38.   In earlier versions, the focus is on the sister rather than the wife: "My brother isn't here because he's dead."

39.   In the first handwritten draft, this sentence continues: "and you come from a country I now detest."

40.   In the first, handwritten draft, the word "God" is absent from the sentence. In the second handwritten draft, Camus wrote and crossed out: "Oh, the pain of this wound that's opened as suddenly as a severed limb."

41.   Around the time Camus was working on the play, he recorded the following entry in his notebook: "Shakyamuni remained in the desert for many years, motionless, eyes lifted to the heavens. The gods themselves envied such wisdom, such a fate of stone. In his steady, outstretched hands, swallows made their nest. But one day they flew off, never to return, and he who'd killed off all the will and desire, all the glory and pain, inside himself, began to cry. This is how flowers are born from stones." Camus would later expand on this idea in the final section of his essay "The Minotaur, or A Stop in Oran."

State of Emergency

1.   *State of Emergency* has its origins in sketches for a play begun in May 1942 by French actor and director Jean-Louis Barrault, who went through several possible titles—*The Purifying Evil, The Plague, The Tragedy of the Plague, The Purifying Tragedy of the Plague, The Evil*—before settling on *Le Mal des ardents,* a reference to a series of French epidemics of ergot poisoning in which victims described feeling as if they were on fire. (In English, ergotism is commonly referred to as Saint Anthony's fire, though the term "mal des ardents" is often used to refer to the French epidemics in particular.) Barrault's early work on the play was based in part on Daniel Defoe's *A Journal of the Plague Year,* and by the time Barrault handed the script off to Camus, he had already written the first act

in its entirety, as well as an outline for the rest of the play, much of which Camus would rewrite after deciding to scrap Defoe's text as source material. Camus himself went through several possible titles, beginning with *Love of Life,* then *The Inquisition at Cadiz,* then just *The Inquisition, The Grand Inquisitors, The Scourge, The Rising Wind,* and *Us and Them.* In his memoirs, Barrault recalled that in order to finally settle on something, he and Camus played a game whereby one would say, "Get dressed, darling, we're going to see …" and then the other would fill in a title, hoping to hear it click. Camus himself told a journalist that the play went through at least seven different versions before finally premiering as *State of Emergency* (or, more academically, *State of Exception*).

2.   Fundamental differences exist between Barrault's early version of the play and Camus's rewrites. Many of the characters either hadn't been written yet or had been written in different form. The character known as Diego in Camus's version was known as Daniel [Defoe] in Barrault's version and played a role more like the one eventually played by Nada, who was initially named Rien (that is, he went from being named Nothing in French to being named Nothing in Spanish). The differences and variants noted below all follow Camus's initial rewrite and do not include changes strictly from Barrault's original.

3.   Up through the final typescript, there was another bit of stage direction here that read: "For a second, we catch sight of a hand, finger pointing toward the city."

4.   This set of stage directions is taken almost verbatim from Barrault's initial draft.

5.   The refrain, repeated throughout the play, is a holdover from Defoe's *A Journal of the Plague Year,* where it appears as follows:

> Nay, some were so Enthusiastically bold, as to run about the Streets, with their Oral Predictions, pretending they were sent to preach to the City. [. . .] So this poor naked Creature cry'd, *O! the Great, and the Dreadful God!* and said no more, but repeated those Words continually, with a Voice and Countenance full of horror, a swift Pace, and no Body cou'd ever find him to stop, or rest, or take any Sustenance, at least, that ever I cou'd hear of. I met this poor Creature several Times in the Streets, and would have spoke to him, but he would not enter into Speech with me, or any one else; but held on his dismal Cries continually.

6.   In earlier typescripts, Diego says instead: "I'm young and not as learned as Nada."

7.   The concluding words in the Mass of the Roman Rite and the Lutheran Divine Service. The exact translation of the Latin phrase is contested but means something along the lines of: "Go forth, mass is finished." Here, Nada deliberately profanes the sacred phrase in order to mock Judge Casado's self-righteous statements.

8.   The copla Diego recites here comes from a book Camus ushered to print in 1946 when he directed a series for the Algeria-based publisher Edmond Charlot. That book, *333 Coplas populaires andalouses,* is the inspiration for several of the exchanges between Diego and Victoria, and perhaps accounts in part for the mannered nature of their dialogue.

9.   In French, the reference is specifically to "poule au pot," which many consider a national dish and which dates to King Henry IV's seventeenth-century declaration: "I want every laborer in my kingdom to be able to put a chicken in the pot on Sundays." (Several variations of the quote exist.)

10.   In earlier drafts, an extra sentence appears here: "Bread is rare, but with a little money we can have brioche, and that's a great consolation."

11.   In an earlier draft, this read: ". . . and all us unemployed folks would suddenly find work, and thanks to you . . ."

12.   The term "alcalde" refers to a Spanish municipal magistrate or mayor who holds both judicial and administrative duties.

13.   The earlier typescripts add: "A huge scorpion clings to his throat." Originally, scorpions served as a sign of the plague, and one or two references to these scorpions remain in the final text even though they no longer fit the final scenario. See, for example, the first unattributed voice to speak shortly after this passage.

14.   This comes directly from Defoe's *A Journal of the Plague Year.*

15.   The idea of alternating scenes is a holdover from Barrault's original script.

16.   This reference to Psalm 91:3 originates in Defoe and is a holdover from Barrault's script.

17.   This exchange between Diego and Victoria finds some resonance in 1 Corinthians 13:3.

18.   From the previously cited *333 Coplas populaires andalouses.*

19. The reference here is to Leibniz's *Théodicée* (*Theodicy*), in which the author attempts to rebut Pierre Bayle's argument that there can be no logical resolution to the problem of evil. The way Leibniz seeks to resolve the problem is, in short, by stating that the current world in which we live is the best of all possible worlds that could exist. In his book *Various Thoughts on the Occasion of a Comet,* Bayle argues that celestial occurrences, such as comets, have a natural basis and are not signs from God. Furthermore, Bayle, who fled his homeland due to religious persecution, implies that atheists may in fact be more virtuous than the religious. Camus quotes from Bayle in his notebooks, and Bayle seems to have been an influence on the writing of this play, though it's not clear if Camus read Bayle's book itself or only read about it in Georges Palante's *The Individualist Sensibility*.

20. The language used here originates in Defoe and is a holdover from Barrault's script. The word "sovereign" has slipped through, even though there is no longer any king in the play, as there was in Barrault's draft. In Camus's earlier rewrite, this bit of dialogue was delivered by the Mayor, not the Secretary. The First Alcalde's question was also added by Camus.

21. In an earlier version: "... this exile."

22. On the penultimate draft, Camus crossed out an additional line here that reads: "Until now, you've lived on songs; from now on, you'll dance to the tune of true progress."

23. In *The Plague*, Tarrou says that he likes lines and waiting rooms because they make him feel as if he's "not wasting his time," as they allow him to "experience it in all its length."

24. In an earlier draft, the Plague's dialogue ends: "You, my dear friend, start drawing up our lists. The guards are going to mark our stars on the houses I plan to take good care of." This is followed by a reply from the Secretary that was ultimately cut: "Come, my children, there's no need to panic. It seems everything's quite clear, isn't that so? We're going to line ourselves up, nice and easy, and get the census operations under way. Nobody here wants to hurt you, and to prove it, as soon as you get on the list, from my own hand we'll draw up a nice little certificate of existence for each of you."

25. A coryphaeus is the leader of a Greek chorus.

26. This incident comes from an anecdote recounted in Defoe's *A Journal of the Plague Year*.

27. Throughout the play, the character's name is given in Spanish, as Nada, but here, when he responds to the Secretary asking him what his name is, he responds with the French, Rien. (cf. note 2, *State of Emergency*).

28. This stage direction, and the one below indicating the Fisherman's entrance, are absent from earlier drafts.

29. In an earlier draft, the dialogue continues: "This one wants to be heard. She wants to talk about the only thing that matters. We don't understand what's going on, and we don't want to understand. It's not our business. But we know what matters and we know that the sole evil is being separated from what we love. Our business is heartbreak." In French, there's a somewhat stronger connection between being "separated" ("séparer") and "heartbreak" ("déchirement"), the latter word also meaning division, tearing apart, or ripping.

30. In earlier drafts, the exchange that follows appears later in the play, and in its place here a spotlight shines on the Plague at center stage: "Start the interrogations! Deport what's important! Suppress private life. ~~The very word private should no longer be used except in the sense of privation.~~ Deprivation, now that's a word we have in our vocabulary. But private life, conversation, residence, consultant, those expressions are forbidden. All for one and each for none—that's what's written on the front of our monuments!"

In an earlier handwritten draft, instead of the above, the following exchange appears: "A general tax is being instituted, one that will hit all social classes equally and that will replace the previously levied flat-rate contribution, whether direct or indirect. / THE BANKER: That's a big undertaking. / —Needless to say, the flat-rate contributions will continue to be levied until the smooth functioning of the general tax proves to be completely satisfactory. / —Will the previous taxes then be revoked? / —If the new tax is satisfactory, it'll mean everyone is happy, and if everyone is happy there'll be no need to revoke the previous taxes. / Even as a banker, I would have never thought of that approach."

31. In French, the word "piétner," in its various forms, can mean both the literal "to advance with small steps" as well as the figurative "to get nowhere, to mark time." The word is used in both senses, here and in *The Plague*, where, for example, the citizens of Oran experience their exile as "an endless, suffocating stagnation."

32. The effect of separation plays a central role in *The Plague,* so much so that Camus once thought of titling the novel *The Separated.*

33. In earlier drafts, this first statement was followed by: "Laws change, judges remain. We serve the law because it's the law."

34. In earlier drafts, the dialogue continues: "But covetous violence committed with a cool head, oh, Judge, that's what deserves condemnation." The reply that follows is then spoken by the Judge, not the Judge's Daughter.

35. Previously: "The order's been given for all business owners to have their workers vote in favor of the new government."

36. The dialogue begins with a line that was eventually crossed out: "It's not madness, Diego, it's the wisdom of those who love each other."

37. This scene is inspired by a passage in Defoe's *A Journal of the Plague Year.*

38. This is in opposition to *Caligula* and *The Just,* where the protagonists are not on the right path/track (cf. note 46, *The Just*).

39. In the typescript, Diego continues: "Are you going to lie to Spain? Here in this land of courage, rebellion rules. Lift your head and hold your chin up high. We know well, we do, that there's pride in being human. Throw off your gags and shout out with me that you're no longer afraid, that only on paper does this sovereign reign. We're the ones who know the truth, we here on this red earth, lovers of women, warmed by that bitter cry. O Saint Rebellion, living refusal, honor of the people. Give them the strength of your cry, give them your silent anger, your steady hand, and your steadfast heart. Tear away their fear, tear it off and hand it to them so that they can see that it's nothing. Throw it to the ground so they can finally shuffle over it. Come on, all of you, happiness isn't going to return all on its own."

40. In earlier drafts, the Plague continues by calling for the garrote, a device used to execute a person via strangulation: "THE PLAGUE: Set up the garrotes. / THE SECRETARY: Probably for nothing, as usual. / THE PLAGUE: Is your spirit flagging, my dear friend? / THE SECRETARY: No, just a little migraine. / THE PLAGUE: Well then, let's get to work. Guards!"

41. In an earlier draft, Nada continues: "Is it within regulations to remove your gag and shout out sentences that don't come from any official guidelines? No, case closed! Let's suppress the shouting and the shouters!"

42.   In earlier drafts, there is an exchange that precedes this: "NADA: But they suppress everything that's not within regulations. That is to say, they end up suppressing everything that should be penalized. And what becomes of regulations when they're deprived of penalties? Nothing. That's how suppression becomes all-encompassing, and that's what had to be proven. / THE PLAGUE: Are you ready?"

43.   On the final typescript, Camus crossed out a line here that reads: "What these people need is the garrote."

44.   Literally, "Eternity, it is I." The reference is to the French "L'état, c'est moi," often attributed to Louis XIV. Its use here calls backs to Nada's claim earlier in the play that the governor "is the state."

45.   In the handwritten draft, the first sentence is followed by: "Until now, things weren't serious. It was all talk of ~~revolution~~ rebelling."

46.   In *333 Coplas populaires andalouses,* there's a note that reads: "La Rambla, not far from Córdoba. Famous pottery." While we know that Camus used *333 Coplas populaires andalouses* as a reference in the writing of this play, and while La Rambla is indeed a municipality in Córdoba, Spain, the various spellings of the Spanish word that appear in the different drafts ("ramblais," "remblais"), as well as other indications, make it likely that the reference here is to the more general "Rambla," or "Main Street" (perhaps the most well-known one being La Rambla in Barcelona).

47.   The French word used here is "souverain," but "sovereign" is a holdover from earlier drafts and no longer applies to the given scenario (cf. note 20, *State of Emergency*). Several versions of the Plague's tirade exist, but one of the more striking differences between them is that the Plague was originally to turn into "a huge and hideous scorpion" at this point in the dialogue.

48.   In a handwritten draft, the Plague continues here with the following: "I've killed off entire populations forever. I've triumphed over everything but the human heart. So, yes, really, why go on? Here, I'm giving your city back to you—to you, not to the governor who betrayed all of you. But don't be too triumphant. You'll see, they'll come back (*a commotion in the background, trumpets, etc.*), and with them my hope. Thanks to them, I may come back, too. And I expect that eventually even human beings will tire of all this, that all forms of rebellion will appear to be in vain. That day, the day the relentless cry of heroic rebellion finally falls silent, the day

silence spreads over the ~~entire~~ earth, that's the day I'll truly reign. It's only a question of persistence."

49.   In previous typescripts, the rest of Diego's dialogue, as well as Victoria's current response, are replaced by the following: "A good death is one you can choose. / VICTORIA: Why didn't you choose to be happy?"

50.   The final typescript produced before publication ends here.

The Just

1.   The epigraph, which Camus added as the play was being sent off to the printer, appears in English in the original French publication. The quote tells readers that, like Romeo and Juliet, Kalyayev and Dora are fated to be together only in death. Or, as Kalyayev puts it in act IV: "Today, those who love each other have to die together if they wish to be reunited."

2.   The play went through several titles before Camus settled on *The Just* (cf. note 2, appendix 3). When the theater putting on the play first advertised it as *The Innocents,* Jean Grenier, who had been one of Camus's schoolteachers, wrote to him to say: "Antigone is innocent; Saint-Just is just. Innocence is a negative state; a just person acts, more or less acting as a 'justicer.' Justice has the right to be harmful. The Grand Duke's children are innocent. —Your characters aren't trying to prove that they're innocent, they're proclaiming that they're just." Grenier's use of the word "justicer," an archaic term in English, gets at the idea that the characters are both "righters of wrongs" as well as "vigilantes." That is to say, they are *self-proclaimed* "dispensers of justice," righting what *they* believe to be wrong, despite whether others agree or not.

Later in the play, Stepan will put it like this: "Whether you're a doer of justice [justicer] doesn't matter, so long as justice is done—even if by murderers." And yet, in rejecting Stepan's position, Kalyayev also seems to rebut the one advanced by Grenier: "I've chosen to die," Kalyayev says, "so that killing won't win. I've chosen to be innocent."

3.   Dora Vladimirovna Brilliant served as Camus's model. She was born into a family of Jewish merchants in 1879 in Kherson, Ukraine, and she joined the Socialist Revolutionary Party in 1902, taking an active role in the assassination attempts on Vyacheslav von Plehve, the minister of the

interior, as well as on Grand Duke Sergei Alexandrovich. She was arrested and imprisoned in the Peter and Paul Fortress. She died in October 1907.

4.   Ivan Platonovich Kalyayev (1877–1905) was born in Warsaw and attended Saint Petersburg University until 1899, when he was arrested for taking part in student protests and, as a result, was exiled to Ekaterinoslav. Not long after, he joined Lenin's Union of Struggle for the Liberation of the Working Class but became disillusioned with their lack of action. It was at this time that he joined the Socialist Revolutionary Party's Combat Organization, where he served as backup bomb thrower during the July 28, 1904, assassination of Vyacheslav von Plehve before going on to assassinate Grand Duke Sergei. He was arrested at the scene, sentenced to death April 18, 1905, and hanged on May 23.

5.   Grand Duchess Elizabeth Feodorovna (1864–1918) was born Princess Elisabeth of Hesse and by Rhine. She was eight years older than her sister, Alexandra, the future Russian empress. In 1884, she married Grand Duke Sergei Alexandrovich of Russia, brother of Alexander III. After the events depicted in this play, she went on to become a nun and she founded the Marfo-Mariinsky Convent, which was dedicated to caring for those in need. In 1918, Lenin had her arrested and exiled, and on July 17, she was beaten and thrown into a mine shaft, where, despite the fall, and despite two grenades being thrown in after her, she survived and, according to one of her killers, could be heard singing hymns. She eventually died in the mine shaft from her wounds and was later canonized.

6.   Boris Savinkov (1879–1925), one of the leaders of the Combat Organization, served as the model for Annenkov. He organized the attacks on Vyacheslav von Plehve and on Grand Duke Sergei. He was arrested and sentenced to death after being betrayed by his superior, double agent Yevno Azef. Savinkov escaped from prison and went to France, where he served in the French army and wrote his *Memoirs of a Terrorist,* one of Camus's central references for this play.

7.   Piotr Kulikovsky (code name: Alexandrovitch), a young teacher who took part in preparations to assassinate Grand Duke Sergei, serves as the base for the character Voinov, though Camus reworked Savinkov's account of Alexandrovitch's participation in the assassination. The character name Voinov comes in part from Socialist Revolutionary Party member Boris Vnorovsky-Mishchenko, who along with his brother Vladimir carried out a failed assassination attempt on Admiral Fyodor Dubasov, and

in part from Ivan Avksentievich Voinov, a Bolshevik journalist and poet who was killed in Petrograd in 1917 during the July Days.

8.   Boria is a nickname for Boris.

9.   The Socialist Revolutionary Party grew out of the Narodnik movement and went on to play a direct role in the Russian Revolution of 1905.

10.   Camus referenced the actual proclamation the Central Committee issued the day after the attack but uses his own summary of it here.

11.   The phrase "Que faire?" a version of which Camus uses here, is as common in French as it is in English, which makes it hard to know if Camus is winking at Nikolai Chernyshevsky's novel, *What Is to Be Done?*, which was written in 1863, and which would go on to inspire both Tolstoy, in 1886, and Lenin, in 1902, to write pamphlets with the same title. Of Chernyshevsky's novel, Lenin said: "It completely reshaped me. This is a book that changes one for a whole lifetime." Joseph Frank, author of a five-volume biography of Dostoyevsky and his times, has said: "Chernyshevsky's novel, far more than Marx's *Capital,* supplied the emotional dynamic that eventually went to make the Russian Revolution." The phrase also appears a couple of times in Camus's notebooks, where it often follows an entry about Communism or the Soviet Union.

12.   Maximilian Illitch Schweitzer (1881–1905), code name Pavel, took part in the attack on Plehve alongside Kalyayev and Sazonov. He died, as Camus indicates, by setting off a bomb intended for an attack on Grand Duke Vladimir Alexandrovich.

13.   The members of the Combat Organization affectionately referred to Kalyayev as "Jan," the Polish equivalent of Ivan, on account of his slight Polish accent. Yanek is Camus's phonetic rendering of the name.

14.   Kalyayev was an admirer of Maurice Maeterlinck, as well as the Russian Symbolists, whom, according to Igor Sazonov, he called "artistic revolutionaries."

15.   In an early typescript, the exchange that follows is replaced with this one: "STEPAN: Get to work, Dora. Beauty is a luxury, and we have to spit in its face. / *Dora sets a small package on the table.* / YANEK: That's not true. Beauty is also revolutionary. / STEPAN (*pointing at the package*): The bomb is revolutionary, nothing else. And anyway, I don't want to talk about all this. You're too young, Yanek. Just tell me, did you pack the sulfuric acid separately? / YANEK: Yes, it's in the crate we marked Mademoiselle instead of Madame. There's no confusing it. / STEPAN:

I have to help you prepare them, Dora. Do you think I'll learn quickly? / DORA: No doubt. The system is simple. The hard part is sealing the tube of sulfuric acid without breaking the gelatin, because otherwise . . . / STEPAN: Otherwise? / DORA: We blow up. / YANEK: Why are you smiling, Stepan? / STEPAN: I'm smiling? / YANEK: Yes. Like a kid who just got a new toy. / STEPAN: It's something like that. Dora, would a single bomb be enough to blow up the whole house? / DORA: What's wrong with you? / STEPAN: Nothing. / *Annenkov and Voinov enter.* / ANNENKOV: Come on, we've got only another minute. We have to act now."

16. Kalyayev's comportment with regard to suicide comes from Savinkov's *Memoirs of a Terrorist.*

17. A true-to-life quote from Kalyayev that Camus also includes in "The Delicate Murderers," originally published in *La Table ronde* in 1948 and later incorporated into *The Rebel.*

18. This is almost a direct quote from Kalyayev's testimony as recorded by Sazonov in his *Memoirs of I. P. Kalyayev.*

19. In an early draft, this is followed by an extra line of stage direction: "When Annenkov and Dora, the terrorists, reappear onstage, they look completely different from Act I. They're no longer commoners but aristocrats wearing suits and dresses, and a beard and mustache."

20. In "The Delicate Murderers," Camus states that the children in the carriage, Maria and Dimitri, were those of Grand Duke Paul Alexandrovich and Princess Alexandra of Greece. Alexandra had died after giving birth to Dimitri, and when Paul's second marriage ran afoul of the tsar's rules, he was banished from Russia and the children were placed with Grand Duke Sergei, one of Paul's brothers. On the day of the attack, Maria was fifteen and Dimitri fourteen.

21. The references are to Igor Sazonov and Alexei Rykov. The latter was put to death during the Great Purge.

22. With this, Camus pits Stepan against Ivan of *The Brothers Karamazov*:

While there is still time, I hasten to protect myself, and so I renounce the higher harmony altogether. It's not worth the tears of that one tortured child who beat itself on the breast with its little fist and prayed in its stinking outhouse, with its unexpiated tears to "dear, kind God"! It's not worth it, because those tears are unatoned for. They must be atoned for, or there can be no harmony. But how? How are you going to atone for them? Is it possible? By their being avenged? But what do I care for avenging them? What do I care for a hell for oppressors? What good can hell do, since those children have already been tortured? And what becomes of harmony, if there is hell? I want to forgive. I want to embrace. I don't want more suffering. And if the sufferings of children go to swell the sum of sufferings which was necessary to pay for truth, then I protest that the truth is not worth such a price. [trans. Constance Garnett]

23.   On an early typescript, Stepan continues: "That terrible explosion that will annihilate all of us, that's the very explosion of love. / ANNENKOV: We're not gods here to brand all of humanity with our fiery truth. / STEPAN: We'll be gods or we'll be nothing. / ~~VOINOV~~ ANNENKOV: So then, you'll be nothing, ~~or worse yet, a man who's ashamed of himself.~~ To be nothing is easy. It's a break. But what awaits you has a name. / STEPAN: What name? / ANNENKOV: Shame."

24.   Vera Figner (1852–1942) was a Russian revolutionary who, as a leader of People's Will, helped plan the assassination of Alexander II, for which she was eventually arrested and sentenced to death. The sentence was commuted to twenty years in prison, after which Figner was released in exile, and she wrote her immensely popular *Memoirs of a Revolutionist.*

In his notebooks, Camus records an entry about Vera Figner alongside one about the Kara Katorga Tragedy, in which Nadezhda Sigida was given twenty lashes with a birch rod, an incident that led her, as well as more than twenty others, to protest by taking poison.

25.   Camus discusses Dostoyevsky's "everything is permitted" in several of his works, notably, for example, in *The Myth of Sisyphus,* as well as in *The Rebel,* where the idea is linked to Sergey Nechayev's *Catechism of a Revolutionary.* In his notebooks, Camus sums up Nechayev's position as "*Everything that serves the revolution is moral.*"

26.   Yevno Fishelevich Azef (1869–1918), a double agent who served both the Russian secret police and the Socialist Revolutionary Party. In 1904, he took over as leader of the Combat Organization, where he organized many successful attacks—notably the assassination described in this play—while simultaneously handing names over to the secret police.

27.   In an early typescript, Kalyayev replies: "I let you talk, Stepan,

because I wanted to hear you out. But I can't let you go on. Every word you say is an insult to us and to the revolution. ~~But maybe you're right.~~ You're right—I don't believe in a revolution carried out by gods. I believe in one carried out by men."

28.   In an early typescript, Kalyayev replies: "I'm not sure of anything, but I know that as we blindly advance in this awful struggle, we have to hold two or three things tight, so that one day the struggle will make sense."

29.   Similarly, in *The Plague,* Jean Tarrou says, "I try to be an innocent murderer."

30.   In several of the typescripts, this line is followed by: "Let ourselves feel a heartbeat that's not our own."

31.   In the second typescript, this is followed by: "For us, it's blood and a cold noose."

32.   This exchange between Kalyayev and Dora recalls the end of *The Brothers Karamazov,* which Camus discusses in *The Myth of Sisyphus,* where Alyosha says, "Certainly we shall all rise again, certainly we shall see each other and shall tell each other with joy and gladness all that has happened!" To which Kolya replies, "Oh, how splendid it will be!" (trans. Constance Garnett).

33.   This detail comes from Savinkov's *Memoirs of a Terrorist.* Camus comments on it in "The Delicate Murderers" in *The Rebel.*

34.   Camus reworked act IV multiple times, but in such a way that it's hard to put together a single coherent earlier or original version. The whole scene with the Grand Duchess was rewritten several times, as was the final scene with Skuratov. Only one or two exemplary variants will be given here.

35.   The term "boyar" originally referred to a high-ranking member of the Russian nobility, but in the period in which the play takes place, the power the boyars once had was gone.

36.   The tale that follows is Camus's own reworking of the Russian legend of Saint Nicolas and Saint Cassian as told by Vladimir Soloviev in *Russia and the Universal Church.* In Camus's telling, Kalyayev follows the path set out by Ivan Karamazov, who, in order to make himself understood, recounted the legend of the Grand Inquisitor to Alyosha.

37.   The term used here, and throughout this exchange, is "grâce." As

Skuratov seems to use the word in the sense of "pardon," the Grand Duchess in the sense of "divine grace," and Kalyayev in the sense of "forgiveness," it will appear in each of these ways in English according to who is speaking, though it's worth keeping in mind that it is always "grâce" in French. For more on this, see the introduction.

38.   In the second typescript, this is followed by: "I have liberal sentiments and I'm willing to admit that you're right to think as you do. / (*a pause*) / ~~This is all an awful tragedy.~~ All I have to say is that a little more justice certainly wouldn't do the world any harm." This then led directly to Skuratov's line: "Really, I'd like to help you."

39.   In the second typescript, the exchange appears as follows: "KALYAYEV: If I had a weapon, I'd cut you down like a dog. / SKURATOV: Yet another crime. Have you seen the face of a man struck point-blank? No? It simply goes gray. That's the ~~gray~~ face you have to come to terms with, with that look the body takes on afterward, all blown to bits, with these things rather than with ~~your beautiful ideas~~ an idea. ~~To stare death in the face~~ To call things by their name, that's true morality. / KALYAYEV: I know your sort of morality. / SKURATOV: It's not mine. It was someone else who said, 'Thou shalt not kill.' / KALYAYEV: No, it is indeed not yours, for you never followed it. You annexed it just like you annexed the human conscience in whose name you carry out the most savage reprisals. A great principle in one hand, an ax in the other. That's your government. One that has to be met with precisely the same tone. To the executioner the execution responds. To the gun, to the labor camp, to the whip the bomb responds. That's what my party has to say to you. The bomb will blow off your autocrats' heads one after the other, until the last one of you, frightened to the core, kneels before the now-armed people and begs forgiveness for the centuries of misery and servitude into which your ilk have plunged Russia. / SKURATOV: A lovely project, without a doubt. Well then, my job here is done."

40.   In French, as in the English, the "He" who died alone is ambiguous. He could be God or the Grand Duke.

41.   An idea that appears early in Camus's notebooks, where he writes: "I'm happy in this world, for my kingdom is of this world. A passing cloud and a fading moment." In his early essay, "L'Envers et l'endroit," Camus puts it: "At this hour, my whole kingdom is of this world."

42.   In Edvard Radzinsky's *The Last Tsar: The Life and Death of Nicholas II,* he writes that

> on the eve of the funeral [Princess Elisabeth] demanded to be taken to the prison where Kalyayev was being held. Brought into his cell, she asked, "Why did you kill my husband?"
>
> "I killed Sergei Alexandrovich because he was a weapon of tyranny. I was taking revenge for the people."
>
> "Do not listen to your pride. Repent . . . and I will beg the Sovereign to give you your life. I will ask him for you. I myself have already forgiven you."
>
> On the eve of revolution, she had already found a way out; forgiveness! Forgive through the impossible pain and blood—and thereby stop it then, at the beginning, this bloody wheel. By her example, poor Ella appealed to society, calling upon the people to live in Christian faith.
>
> "No!" replied Kalyayev. "I do not repent. I must die for my deed and I will. . . . My death will be more useful to my cause than Sergei Alexandrovich's death."

Nevertheless, Princess Elisabeth did write to the emperor to ask that Kalyayev be pardoned. Of note in this passage, too, is that Radzinsky's translator, Marian Schwartz, has opted for the English word "forgiveness," even with Princess Elisabeth.

43.   Informally, the word used here, "pécher," can mean to err or falter, in the sense of showing weakness, but given the thematic elements at play in the scene, as well as Kalyayev's conviction that to betray his comrades would be one of the worst things he could possibly do, the traditional meaning, "sinned," has been used.

44.   Some of what is said here, and in the replies that follow, comes directly from Kalyayev's real-life letters.

45.   This exchange between Voinov and Dora recalls a statement by Vera Figner that Camus recorded in his notebook: "I had to live, to live to be judged, for it's the trial that crowns the revolutionary's activity."

46.   A reference to Camus's Caligula, who says, "I'm full of hatred. I didn't take the right path. I've gotten nowhere, achieved nothing. My freedom isn't the right kind."

Taking Dora's words here as Camus's own, William Faulkner wrote of Camus:

> He said that if the only solution to the human dilemma is death, then we are on the wrong road. The right track is the one that leads to life, to the sunlight. One cannot unceasingly suffer from the cold.
>
> So he did revolt. He did refuse to suffer from the unceasing cold. He did refuse to follow a track which led only to death. . . . The track he followed was the only possible one which could not lead only to death. The track he followed led into the sunlight in being that one devoted to making, with our frail powers and our absurd material, something which had not existed in life until we made it.

47.   In one of his final letters, the real-life Kalyayev wrote: "Now that I've got one foot in the grave, everything in me is focused on one thing: my honor as a revolutionary. . . . Sometimes it seems to me some villain will insult my ashes with a factum."

48.   Dora's claim highlights one of Camus's core principles, as set out in *The Myth of Sisyphus* and *The Rebel,* as well as in some of his lyrical essays. Put simply, a contradiction arises when a person realizes that life has no inherent meaning and yet, while keeping that realization at the front of the mind, continues to live and act as if it did have a meaning. For Camus, to live with such knowledge is incredibly difficult but absolutely necessary. If, instead of living with this contradiction, a person chooses to commit suicide, whether physically or mentally (by escaping into a totalizing belief system), then the contradiction disappears. Here Dora is suggesting that suicide is the easy way out.

49.   This detail matches the historical record. In Camus's telling, it serves to recall Dora and Kalyayev's discussion in act I about the "eternity" that exists between the attack and the gallows. The details that follow about Kalyayev's attire also match the historical record.

50.   A detail added by Camus. In *The Myth of Sisyphus,* Camus argues that suicide is the opposite of absurd rebellion, and he illustrates the point in writing: "It [absurd rebellion] avoids suicide, given it's simultaneously an awareness of and refusal of death. In the condemned man's last thoughts,

as he's about to take that vertiginous fall, the absurd is that shoelace he catches sight of a couple of yards below, despite what's about to happen."

George Orwell makes a similar point in "A Hanging," where he writes:

> It was about forty yards to the gallows. I watched the bare brown back of the prisoner marching in front of me. [. . .] And once, in spite of the men who gripped him by each shoulder, he stepped slightly aside to avoid a puddle on the path.
>
> It is curious, but till that moment I had never realized what it means to destroy a healthy, conscious man. When I saw the prisoner step aside to avoid the puddle, I saw the mystery, the unspeakable wrongness, of cutting a life short when it is in full tide.

51.   After the attack, the real-life Kalyayev stated several times that he was happy. In a last letter to his mother, he writes: "So, I'm going to die. I'm happy, for I face my end in full possession of my faculties."

Like the detail about the stain on the boot, the detail that follows about the dog barking also resonates with Orwell's "A Hanging."

52.   In the second typescript, Stepan's response ends here, and the play concludes as follows: "ANNENKOV: It's your turn, Stepan, You're going to give it up? / STEPAN: For her. She's just like me now. She knows what I know. / DORA: You'll give it to me, won't you? I'll throw it. I'll walk toward the act. And then, later, on a cold night . . . Yanek! A cold night. A cold night."

Appendix I. Original Prologue to *The Misunderstanding*

1.   The first draft of *The Misunderstanding,* completed in July 1943, as well as a later draft completed that September, both contain a prologue. It was this second draft, now housed at the Harry Ransom Center at the University of Texas at Austin, that Camus had sent to his publisher with a cover page reading: "A Tragedy in a Prologue and Three Acts." By the time the play was published by Gallimard on June 23, 1944, the prologue had been removed, and the title page then read: "A Play in Three Acts." It is not known whether Camus decided on his own to remove the prologue or if the change was suggested by his publisher.

2.   The primary definition of "barrage" ("dam") has been maintained here for thematic reasons, though "how to put up new roadblocks" better captures the sense of Maria's statement. For more on "barrage," see *The Misunderstanding,* note 5.

Appendix II. Original Ending to *State of Emergency*

1.   This early version of the final scene comes from the first complete typescript, which was based on an edited handwritten draft of the play. The ending that follows picks up during Nada's speech on page 380, following the line: "Store them away somewhere nice and cold."

2.   The phrase used here can also mean "from all walks of life."

Appendix III. Original Opening to *The Just*

1.   The alternate opening given here appears only in the first handwritten draft of the play, composed of sixty-eight quickly scrawled pages of rushing text. The writing is often hard to make out, the characters often referred to only by initials. The body of the manuscript alternates between blue and black ink and bears Camus's handwritten edits. It's likely Camus cut this initial opening due to its comic tone, which remains at odds with the formality of the rest of the play, and also due to how closely drawn the scene is from Boris Savinkov's *Memoirs of a Terrorist*.

2.   *La Corde*—which translates as *The Noose* in the given context, but which also means *The Rope*—appears as the title on the first three drafts of the play that would become *The Just*. The title was changed in part because the actors refused to use it during rehearsals, seeing it as a bad omen, as well as, according to Camus's friend Roger Quilliot, because there was concern a mischievous critic might take advantage of it. Camus next thought of calling the play *The Guilty*, before switching to *The Innocent*, and finally settling on *Les Justes*, which carries the sense of just as well as righteous.

3.   In the published version, Voinarov, already a shortening of Voinarovski, would be further shortened to Voinov.

4.   Examining magistrates (investigating judges) play a central role in civil law systems such as the one in France. Common law systems, often found in English-speaking countries, do not have an equivalent position.

5.   Camus crossed things out and edited in whatever color ink was not being used in the main body of the text.

6.   Words and phrases that could not be made out in the original handwritten text are here marked with [. . .].

7.   The reference is to the Théâtre des Bouffes-Parisiens, which opened in 1855 as a venue for comic operettas, one form of which is the opéra bouffe, traditionally known for its farcical, satirical subject matter.